# The Bottom Five

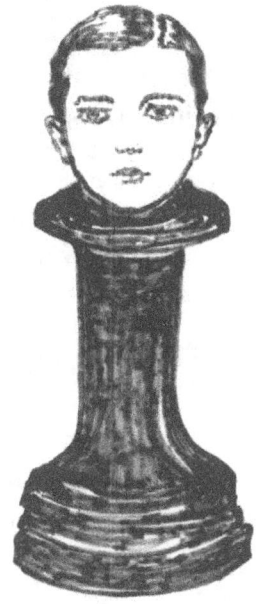

## A Novel

# BENSON S. FORBES

*Cover design and illustration by Shari S. Forbes*

ISBN-10: 0615754074
ISBN-13: 978-0615754079


Revised and Republished in 2013
By
Shari S. Forbes
PO Box 1424
Sherwood, Oregon 97140

*This book is dedicated to all those who so enthusiastically volunteered to fight for King and Country, only to find themselves used as sacrificial pawns in the game of war.*

# 11 a.m., Armistice Day, November 1936

THE TWO MEN and the boy stood in the square gazing in silence at the monument, their collars drawn up to ward off the cold mists of that November day in the south of England. The taller of the two men was expensively dressed in a black suit, top coat and bowler hat. He leaned heavily on an ebony walking stick topped with a gold lion. The other man, whose sandy-colored hair was streaked with white, wore a brown tweed cap and coat and stood with one hand on the boy's shoulder. The boy wore a dark blue and gray school uniform and was a replica of the sandy-haired man minus the bristling mustache.

When the minute of silence ended and the rest of the small crowd began to disperse, the two men turned to face each other with tears glistening in their eyes. "Well, Sam, it's been a long time," said the man with the stick. Then he looked down at the boy and smiled. "I believe this can be none other than your son. Looks just like you did when we were at King Charles."

"You've got that right," said the sandy-haired man. "Toby, say hello to Mr. Simpson. We were in the war together."

"Pleased to meet you, Mr. Simpson," said the boy, shyly clasping Simpson's proffered hand.

"I see by your uniform that you go to King Charles. How old are you, lad?" asked Simpson, smiling down at him.

"I'm fifteen and in my last year at King Charles."

"You don't say! Well, I hope you haven't had the canings that your dad and I got when we were in our last year at King Charles!" said Simpson, winking at the boy's father.

"Canings! Oh, no, Sir!" exclaimed the lad. His eyes widened in horror.

"Is Nicholson still the headmaster there?"

"No, Sir. He died just before I started at King Charles. Our headmaster's name is Mr. Bertram."

"Ah, that's the reason, then. Nicholson was very quick with the cane."

"And so was Alwood, God rest his soul," said Sam.

Toby looked up at his father. "Who was Alwood?"

"Our teacher during our last year at King Charles," replied Sam with a solemn expression. "He was killed in the war. His name is listed on that monument, along with the rest of the Bridgefield volunteers who died."

Sam led his son closer to the monument and pointed to the name of George Alwood. He turned to Simpson. "See that, Freddie?"

"Yes, I saw it," said Simpson sadly. "Along with all the others..." He put a hand up to his eyes to stanch the tears that had begun anew.

Toby looked up at his father again. "There are so many names," he said. "Looks like half the town. Did you know many of them?"

"Oh, yes. So many of our chums and mates," said Sam. He began pointing to names on the list. "That one and that one, and that..." Halfway down the list he paused. "And that one there," he said with a catch in his voice. "That one was a great hero. He was our mate and our leader. He saved our lives, didn't he, Freddie?"

"Yes, indeed he did...more than once," said Simpson as he gazed reverently at the name. "At Ypres and then again at the Somme." He looked at Toby. "Did you know your dad is a hero as well?"

Toby looked up at Sam. "Dad is a hero? I didn't know that."

Sam looked down at the ground modestly and shrugged his shoulders. "Oh, me. I ain't no hero," he muttered.

"Oh, yes you are," said Simpson. "At least to me. You saved my life and you know it."

"How was that, then?" asked Toby.

"He cut off my legs," said Simpson.

Toby looked at his father in wide-eyed surprise. "You cut off his legs? Why did you do that, Dad? You never told me that story."

"It's not something I like to talk about, Toby. Just as soon forget about it," said Sam. He looked off into the distance, avoiding the boy's eyes.

"Well, I'll never forget it, Sam," said Simpson. "You were the only one who could do it, and it had to be done. Otherwise, I'd have died." He turned to the boy. "You see, Toby, the reason I walk the way I do and lean on this stick is because I have wooden legs," he said, striking the stick against his right shin. It sounded like a wooden mallet striking a butcher block. "Just like a certain other war hero we knew, eh Sam?"

Sam grinned and nodded. "Yes, indeed."

Simpson reached into his waistcoat pocket and pulled something out. He held up a gold coin and smiled at Sam. "Remember this? Do you still have yours?"

Sam smiled broadly. "Yes, I do. I always have it with me."

Toby looked questioningly from one man to the other, but they said nothing more. They just stood there smiling at each other, remembering. "Our teacher told us that England lost a whole generation of men in that war," he said. "How did the two of you manage to survive?"

"We managed to survive because we were members of The Bottom Five," said Simpson, grinning at Sam.

Sam grinned back. "That's right," he said. "It all started on the first day of the autumn term at King Charles. We were the same age as you are now," he said to Toby. "In fact, it was because of The Bottom Five that I met your mum and have you now. Right, Freddie?"

The two men chuckled as if at a private joke.

"You met Mum when you were fifteen?" prompted the boy.

7

"Yes, I did, but we didn't get married until after the war."

"Well, I want to hear all about the Bottom Five and why that kept you alive during the war and what it had to do with Mum and why you're a war hero," demanded Toby in an exasperated tone of voice.

Sam looked at him for a moment with a frown. "I suppose it's time for you to know...," he said slowly. "But it's a long story and it's too cold to stand out here in the rain. I'm taking Mr. Simpson to the White Horse for a pint. Guess there's no harm in you coming along with us."

"The White Horse! Haven't been there for years. It will be great to have a pint or two and talk over the old times," said Simpson.

"Ben and Nan are still the proprietors, and they will like putting in a word or two," said Sam.

"Good. Let's go then!" cried Simpson. "Looking forward to it and getting out of this drizzle."

"But, Dad, Mum says I'm not old enough...," said Toby.

Simpson clapped him on the back. "Don't worry. You're with us. Your dad and I used to go there when we were your age."

"Mum will have a fit if she learns I've been in the pub," said Toby with a worried look.

"Ah, I think today she will understand," said Sam. "Leave your mum to me."

As they turned and walked across the road toward the White Horse pub, what had been a cold drizzle became a steady downpour. "Bloody weather!" said Simpson, shaking his head as he hobbled with some difficulty across the road. "Remember what a lovely autumn we had that last year at King Charles?"

Sam nodded, and then pointed at the display outside the newspaper shop on the corner next to the White Horse. "Look at that headine, Freddie. The bloody Germans are at it again," he said with disgust.

# Chapter 1
## *The Bottom Five*

THE SOFT GLOW of a September sunrise cast shadows on shop-lined roads in the small country town of Bridgefield in the south of England. Lamplighters were making their rounds, using long poles to turn off streetlights lit by gas from the sewers below.

On this first day of the autumn school term in 1911, the sunrise promised another glorious day. All was silent, save for the tentative chirping of birds. As the sun rose just above the horizon, the muffled clopping of horse's hooves, creaking harness, and squeaking wagon wheels broke the silence.

Shopkeepers and their assistants rushed to open their doors and lift shutters in anticipation of receiving the supply of goods that the wagon drivers were delivering.

On the High Street, Sam Baldwin emerged from his butcher shop just as a wagon laden with sides of beef and pork and trussed poultry pulled up. He finished tying the strings of his white canvas apron, adjusted the garters on his sleeves, and twisted the right side of his handlebar mustache.

"Nice morning, no sign of rain," he remarked as the wagon driver jumped down and prepared to carry the inventory into the shop.

"You're right there," said the driver as he hoisted a side of pork onto his shoulder and carried it into the shop where he would hang it on a meat hook suspended from a ceiling beam.

"Nice autumn bodes a hard winter," said Percy Summers, the greengrocer whose shop was next door to Sam's. Percy was unpacking an array of fruits and vegetables and arranging them neatly in open boxes under the awning in front of his shop.

"Could be right. The robins have red breasts," chuckled Sam.

"And the badgers have retired to bed early," laughed George Norton, proprietor of the bookshop, who had just stepped outside in time to overhear the conversation. "All in all, we've had a fine summer and now an even better autumn, from the looks of things. Suppose young Sam is not happy about returning to school on a day like this, eh?"

"Oh, well, I think he's looking forward to it, being it's his last year at King Charles, which means he can go on to the Commerce School and then carry on in my footsteps," said Sam.

The wagon driver came out of the butcher shop, leaving a display of chickens, ducks and pheasants, still with their feathers intact, hanging upside down beside the sides of beef and pork. "See you Wednesday, Mr. Baldwin," he said. He climbed up on the wagon seat, took up the reins, clucked to his horse, and drove off.

"Would you look at that?" said Sam, pointing to a pile of horse dung in the road. "Beau Nash would have a fit!"

"Who is Beau Nash?" asked Percy as Sam picked up a shovel and prepared to dispense with the eye sore.

"He's the one who put Bridgefield on the map," said George. "Of course, you wouldn't know that since you just moved here, would you?"

"No, but I guess it's time for a history lesson," said Percy, grinning and winking at Sam. "Understand you're the unofficial town historian. What's the story, then?"

"Back in the Eighteenth Century, this dandy, Beau Nash, set the fashion trends for the royalty and the wealthy upper crust in London. The story is he was passing through here and stopped to water himself and his horse and discovered the mineral water spring."

"You mean Euphoria Springs, where they charge you a farthing a cup to drink the water," said Sam as he shoveled horse dung into a burlap bag.

"That's it all right. Old Beau had a tremendous hangover from the night before, and after he drank the mineral water, he claimed it cured it," said George.

"Did you hear that?" roared Sam. "A cure for a hangover right here in our own back yard!"

"I'll drink to that!" yelled the baker from the other side of the road. "We're in the wrong business, lads. Should be selling that mineral water."

"Anyway, Nash quickly spread the word amongst his society friends," continued George. "First came the large mansions and inns to accommodate the wealthy society types who wanted to entertain their friends and escape the filth and squalor of London town. Then, many of them actually moved here on a permanent basis, maintaining their townhouses in London for business and pleasure trips."

"So, Bridgefield grew into what it is because of a hangover?" asked Percy, grinning.

"That's right. It's probably the reason Bridgefield has more pubs than any other town of its size in the south of England," said George.

"Wish I had known about that water last night. Stayed longer than I should at the White Horse," said Percy, rubbing his forehead. "Must lay in a supply of that mineral water."

"You'd best be quick about it, Percy. I see your wife coming down the street, and she has a wild look in her eye," said Sam, as he returned the shovel to its post.

"Oh, bloody hell! I'm in for a tongue lashing now," cried Percy. He quickly ducked into his shop.

George and Sam were still chuckling over Percy's plight, when a sandy-haired boy in a blue and gray school uniform appeared in the doorway of the butcher shop.

"I see you are ready for school," said Sam. "Better be off. Don't want to be late on the first day. Remember what I said. Study hard and you can work here with me."

The boy did not utter a word. He just looked at his father, put on his cap, stuffed two sandwiches into his book satchel, and walked off up High Street in the direction of King Charles School. He turned right on Vale Road, and left on Station Road. He walked down the long steep hill and arrived at the school playground a few minutes before eight o'clock. A crowd of boys were already on the playground, many of them playing football.

He walked up to a tall lanky boy who was standing under a chestnut tree watching the other students. "Hello, Spindle," he said. "See most of the lads are already here. Is that Bouncer out there on the football field?"

"Hi, Sam," said Spindle. "That's Bouncer, all right. Haven't seen Pete yet. Oh, here he comes now." Sam turned to look in the direction Spindle indicated, and saw a tall blond boy walking across the playground with a leather book satchel slung over his shoulder.

"What's up, Pete?" asked Spindle when the boy strolled up to them.

"Looking for Ginger," replied Pete, surveying the crowd of students gathered on the school playground.

"He's not back from hop picking yet, staying another week. His mum told my mum. Picking is good, paying a penny a bushel," said Spindle. "I wish I could earn money like that."

"Wish I could be picking. It beats being here and having to work in the butcher shop after school," said Sam.

"Me, too," said Pete. "How I hate school. I hope we don't get Alwood. He's the meanest teacher here."

"Alwood is a new teacher. How do you know that?" asked Spindle.

"Charlie Stevens said he comes from London and uses the cane if you don't get the right answer."

"He'd better not use it on me. If he does, I'll tell my big brother and he'll punch him in the eye," laughed Spindle.

"But your brother's in the Navy, how could he do that?"

"I'll tell him about Alwood when he is on leave."

"Who's that gangly chap over there? He must be new. I know most of the other fellows," said Sam pointing to a boy standing by himself on the edge of the playground. He had dark brown hair sleeked down under his school cap and dark brown eyes that seemed too large for his rather small face.

"Oh, I think that is Freddie Simpson, son of the barrister who lives in Queen Anne's Gardens. He's been going to some hoity-toity boarding school up near London, but his mum missed him and wants him to stay at home, so he's finishing up at King Charles with us. I overheard my dad telling my mum about it. My dad is on the town council with Mr. Simpson," said Spindle.

"Freddie Simpson, eh? He looks like a bit of a wanker," said Pete derisively.

A ball landed at Pete's feet.

"Kick the ball! Kick the ball!" yelled Bouncer, emerging from the crowd of students.

Spindle ran for the ball, but Pete kicked it instead. It glanced off his shoe and went high into the air. Suddenly there was the sound of shattering glass, and the boys went silent. After a heartbeat, raucous cheers and laughter filled the air.

"Good kick, Pete," laughed Bouncer putting his arm around Pete's shoulder. "With a kick like that, you'll make the football team."

"You're in big trouble now. It's a bad omen to break a window on the first day of school," said Spindle.

"Don't worry. We won't say you did it," said Bouncer, punching Pete playfully on the arm.

The ringing of a bell cut through the playground clamor, and the boys grew silent as they saw the teachers emerging from the main entrance of the school with clipboards in hand. Mr. Nicholson, the headmaster, strode angrily toward them waving a bamboo cane with every step he took.

"Everyone stay where you are!" screamed Nicholson coming to a halt in front of the students.

Pete's face turned white and he began to tremble.

"Who broke the window?" yelled Nicholson. "I want to know who is responsible for this atrocious act!"

Only the cawing of a flock of rooks calling to each other in the nearby oak trees could be heard.

"I said, who broke the window?" yelled Nicholson again, punctuating his remark with a sharp crack of the cane against his brown leather boot.

Again, there was no response.

"I will count to ten. If the guilty one does not own up, everyone will have one hour detention."

Silence.

"One, two, three, four, five..."

Pete's face turned an even paler shade, and he feared Nicholson would notice that his legs were trembling.

"Six, seven, eight... two more to go gentleman – no more chances after that."

"Please, Sir, that fellow over there kicked the ball! I saw him do it!" called out Freddie Simpson, pointing to Pete.

"No he didn't, it was you, you bloody liar!" shouted Spindle, pointing at Simpson.

"What is your name young man?" asked Nicholson, looking at Pete.

"Peter Court, Sir," said Pete with a tremor in his voice.

Nicholson turned back to the crowd of students. "Who else saw Mr. Court kick the ball?" he asked.

The students did not respond.

He pointed the cane at Pete. "Very well. I have my witness. Peter Court is responsible, and he will get ten strokes of the cane."

"He didn't do it. I did," yelled Bouncer, stepping in front of Pete and blocking Nicholson's view with his large, muscular frame.

"All right, then. Step forward the guilty party and the two that lied. You will each get ten strokes of the cane," ordered Nicholson. He cracked the cane against the side of his boot again, splitting the end for more effective punishment.

Bouncer strode confidently up to the headmaster, as Spindle and Freddie followed hesitantly in his wake.

"Bend over and touch your toes," said Nicholson, grabbing Spindle by the shoulder and forcing him over, his backside facing the students so they could witness the severity of the punishment.

The thwack of the cane when it struck Spindle's bottom sent a shudder through the playground. At each stroke of the cane, Spindle uttered a small moan. After the fifth stroke, the headmaster paused. "You take your punishment well. It appears the cane is not doing its proper job," he sneered.

He lifted the cane higher over his shoulder and brought it down with greater force. The watching students groaned collectively upon hearing the louder crack of the cane as it connected with Spindle's bottom. The impact of the blow caused Spindle to lose his balance and forced him to his hands and knees.

"Stay where you are!" Nicholson ordered as he prepared to strike again.

Spindle could no longer feel the cane. His bottom was numb and his brain was spinning. After the tenth stroke, he got to his feet, turned and faced the students with a smirk. A loud cheer went up from the audience.

Nicholson's face went purple. "There'll be none of that!" he roared. "This is not a football game, and there are no heroes here!"

The cheering died instantly.

"And now for the guilty party!" He pointed the cane menacingly at Bouncer.

Bouncer didn't hesitate. He strode up to Nicholson, bent over and touched his toes.

"Take that for breaking the window!" shouted Nicholson as he brought the cane down on Bouncer's backside.

Bouncer did not flinch. The whacking of the cane resounded loudly throughout the playground. After the tenth stroke Bouncer jumped to his feet and smiled broadly. An even louder cheer went up from the onlookers.

"This is the last warning!" yelled Nicholson. "Any more of that and all of you will get two hours of detention!"

The playground went silent. Not even the cawing of the rooks remained.

"And now for the second liar," said Nicholson, turning towards a trembling Freddie Simpson. He grabbed Freddie roughly by the shoulder and pushed him over so that he was touching his toes with his fingers.

Simpson collapsed onto the ground, whimpering, after the first stroke.

"Get up, you wimp, and take your punishment like a man," said the headmaster.

Simpson got to his feet and bent over again. After five consecutive whacks of the cane, he lay down on the ground sobbing and wouldn't get up.

"Get up, you wimp, and take your punishment," said Nicholson, his face flushed with anger.

Simpson didn't move. He just lay there.

The headmaster pulled a pocket watch from his waistcoat and looked at it. Then he looked at Freddie. "Because it is time for classes to begin, the remaining strokes will be converted to eight hours of detention," he announced.

"Can I have my ball back, Sir?" queried a voice from the crowd.

The playground erupted in laughter again.

Nicholson just glared.

The students moved closer together as the teachers walked up behind Nicholson for the opening of school announcements and class assignments. When everyone had settled down, Nicholson began.

"Good morning, gentlemen. Welcome to King Charles School. For those of you who are attending for the first time, we have a tradition here. We must all do our best and act as diplomats for the school." Nicholson paused and looked sternly around at the students' solemn faces.

"To wear the school uniform is an honor. When you are wearing it, whether here at school or away from school, you must be on your best behavior. King Charles is renowned as one of the best schools in the land. You will be watched closely and any reported misbehavior will be acted upon immediately." He paused, letting his warning sink in. The boys squirmed and glanced at Spindle and Bouncer.

"Many noble and famous people have attended our school – amongst them, Prime Ministers, war heroes and diplomats. There is no doubt in my mind that all of you, with hard study, will be well prepared to gain success in whatever careers you may choose."

"What about shopkeepers?" queried an anonymous voice from the back of the crowd.

Nicholson looked sternly at the students, attempting to identify the questioner. Then, a slow smile crept onto his face. "Oh, yes, indeed, shopkeepers," he said. "And butchers, greengrocers and bakers, too."

17

This brought cheers and laughter from the students. Nicholson turned and nodded at the teachers who stepped forward and in turn called out the names of students listed on their rosters. As their names were called, the students formed lines in front of their teachers. After the last name had been called, the students quietly made their way to their assigned classrooms.

"Did it hurt much, Spindle?" whispered Pete as the two boys walked together to their classroom.

"Only when I was on my hands and knees," Spindle grinned as he rubbed his bottom. "Must have hit a bone."

"Thanks for taking the caning for me," mumbled Pete, hanging his head.

"Not to worry. We'll get our own back. That bloody Freddie Simpson shouldn't have opened his mouth. If it wasn't for him, none of us would have been caned."

"Bouncer took it well. He didn't show any pain at all."

"I know. He's as strong as a horse. Must be all that muscle."

"Are you going to tell your big brother what happened?"

"No, not this time," laughed Spindle.

Upon entering their classroom, Spindle and Bouncer were surrounded by the other students. All wanted to know if the caning hurt.

"Nah," said Bouncer, thrusting out his chest.

"Yeah, if it hadn't been for that rat Simpson, none of us would have been thrashed," said Spindle, pointing at Freddie Simpson who was standing alone on the fringe of the crowd.

"But if it weren't for me, we'd all be doing detention," said Freddie, the color rising in his cheeks. "As it is, I'm the only one who has to do detention, and instead of one hour, I have to do eight."

The students jeered at Simpson, holding their noses.

Pete hung back, hanging his head.

The jeering abruptly ceased when the teacher entered and slapped his roster and bamboo cane down on the lectern at the front of the room.

"Welcome to the senior class. Please find a desk and sit down," he said.

Students hustled to find desks at the back of the classroom. None wanted to sit in the front row, because they knew that once seated, they would be there for the rest of the school year, and teachers had a tendency to pick on students in the front. Spindle, Pete and Bouncer found seats together at the back of the classroom.

"My name is Mr. Alwood and I will be your teacher for this year."

Spindle and Pete glanced at each other in dismay.

"Bloody hell! We're in for it now!" muttered Pete.

"I will prepare you for the real world – the world you will face when you leave school next year," Alwood continued. "It is my intention that all of you will be good enough to pass the examination and receive the General Certificate at the end of this school year. This will qualify you to gain entrance to either the polytechnic college or commerce school."

He looked around the classroom sternly. The boys fidgeted in their seats, each thinking of the promise he had made to his parents. In each boy's case, his parents had agreed to allow him to continue one more year of schooling, provided that he worked hard and attained the General Certificate, which opened the door for a professional career.

Alwood paused, took off his wire-rimmed glasses and wiped them with a white handkerchief before he continued.

"I see no reason why each and every one of you cannot continue your education. After all, you have already passed the Eleven Plus Exam; otherwise, you wouldn't be here."

"Can't remember taking that," whispered Spindle. "If I did, it wasn't called the 'Eleven Plus.'"

"Nor do I," whispered Bouncer. "Should have left school when I was fourteen."

"My goal is to make you learn. I want discipline. Any misconduct will be dealt with swiftly. You are here to learn, and learn you shall.

There will be no excuses. You have only one year left to learn what is needed. It is my task to prepare you for the final exam, and I expect you to give everything you have toward that end."

"Please, Sir, I need to go to the bathroom," interrupted a student in the front row.

Alwood stared. "How dare you interrupt me, young man. We have no bathrooms here, just toilets."

The students giggled.

Alwood grinned briefly, then checked himself. "Stop this childish giggling immediately! Quiet in the classroom."

"Please, Sir, I need to go to the toilet," said the student again

Alwood frowned at him over his glasses. "What is your name, young man?"

"James Taylor, Sir," said the student squirming in his seat.

Alwood opened the attendance book, made a check mark by Taylor's name and began calling the other students' names. As each student responded with the familiar "Here, Sir!" Alwood studied him for a moment before entering the check mark beside his name.

"Patrick Murphy," called out Alwood looking around the class.

"Please, Sir, Ginger..., no, I mean, Patrick..., is still on holiday and he won't be back for another week," responded Spindle.

"I see no notation here," said Alwood looking at the attendance book.

"It's true, Sir. Ginger's mum told my mum. He is staying with his aunt in Great Yarmouth."

"And what is your name young man?" asked Alwood, peering at Spindle over his glasses.

"Everyone calls me Spindle, but my real name is Brian Adams."

"Well, Mr. Adams, your mother's words have no meaning here. In the future do not interrupt me. You only speak when you are asked to do so. And why on earth are you called Spindle?"

"Can't be sure, Sir. I think it's because I am tall and lanky."

Alwood smiled and shook his head.

"Please, Sir, I really need to go to the toilet," said Taylor putting his hand up again.

Alwood glared at him. "Going to the toilet will mean three strokes of the cane," he warned.

Taylor nodded, quickly got up from his desk and left the classroom holding his crotch. When he returned, Alwood had finished calling attendance. He closed the attendance book with a snap, picked up the cane, and looked at Taylor.

"Mr. Taylor, step forward for your punishment," he ordered.

Taylor went to the front of the classroom.

"Assume the position," Alwood ordered. Taylor bent over and touched his toes. After Alwood had administered the three strokes, Taylor returned to his seat, rubbing his bottom.

"Let that be a lesson to each of you. You go to the toilet before class, and you only speak when you are asked to do so," said Alwood returning the cane to its position on his lectern.

The classroom door opened and Nicholson's angry face appeared in the doorway.

"Mr. Alwood, I wish to speak with you," he demanded.

Alwood joined Nicholson outside the classroom, closing the door behind him.

"What have you done now, Bouncer?" called out Sam Baldwin.

The sound of Bouncer's name elicited another cheer from the students.

"Broken another window," joked Spindle.

The classroom filled with laughter.

"James Taylor, come here!" said Alwood as he entered the classroom with the headmaster close upon his heels.

"Why, Sir? I haven't done anything wrong," replied James walking down to the front.

"Empty your pockets," ordered Alwood.

Taylor froze.

"I said, empty your pockets, Mr. Taylor," Alwood repeated.

When Taylor still didn't respond, Alwood pointed at Spindle and Bouncer. "Mr. Adams and Mr. Russell, I need your assistance," he said. "Hold Taylor's arms, so I can search his pockets."

"What are you looking for?" asked James, his face bright red. "Those are my things."

As Spindle and Bouncer held Taylor's arms, Alwood emptied his pockets.

"Here it is," shouted Alwood holding up a tobacco tin, a pipe and a box of Swan matches. "Here's what we are looking for! Smoking in the toilet!"

James lowered his head.

"Come with me," ordered Nicholson.

Alwood handed the headmaster the smoking kit, and Taylor followed Nicholson out of the room with fear written on his face.

"He's in for a thrashing now," whispered Pete as Spindle and Bouncer returned to their desks and sat down.

"A thrashing, you say. It will be worse than that," said Alwood, overhearing Pete's comment. He opened a wooden cabinet and retrieved writing paper, ink and steel-nib pens.

"Mr. Simpson will be responsible for filling the ink pots, and Mr. Baldwin will hand out the paper and pens," Alwood announced.

They went from desk to desk – Baldwin handing out paper and pens, and Simpson filling the inkwells.

"Teacher's pet," whispered Bouncer as Simpson filled his ink well.

"It's better than being fat and ugly," Simpson muttered.

"You'll be ugly when I blacken your eye!" Bouncer kicked Simpson on the leg. He winced and moved on to fill Spindle's ink well.

"This morning we will discuss careers. Then, you will write two hundred and fifty words about the career that you have chosen to pursue. If you don't know what you are going to do, put up your hand."

Andrew Hopkins put up his hand.

"Don't you know what you want to do?" asked Alwood.

"I don't want a job, I want to go to University and become a politician," replied Andrew.

"Politicians are elected. You need a professional job," scowled Alwood.

Spindle was next to put up his hand.

"You don't know what you want to do, either, Mr. Adams?" asked Alwood.

"No, Sir," said Spindle.

"What does your father do?" Alwood wanted to know.

"He works for the gas company," replied Spindle.

"What does he do there?"

"I don't know for sure. All that I know is that he smells of gas and is covered with coal dust when he comes home."

The students snorted. "What do you mean, Spindle?" said Sam. "We all know your father runs the accounting department at the gas company. Or has he been demoted to shoveling coal?"

"That's enough of that, Mr. Baldwin," said Alwood. He turned his attention back to Spindle. "Hmmm. All right, Mr. Adams, you will write about being a bank manager."

Bouncer put up his hand.

"And what does your father do, Mr. Russell?" inquired Alwood.

"I don't have a father. He was killed in the Boer War."

Alwood hesitated. "Sorry to hear that. I fought in the Boer War also." He cleared his throat. "Well, then, what does your mother do?"

"I don't have a mother, either. She died while having me. I live with my aunt now, and she is too old to work," Bouncer replied.

Alwood thought for a moment. "You will be a solicitor. Write about that, Mr. Russell."

"I don't know about solicitors, Sir. What do they do?"

"They do legal work, write wills and prepare documents, that type of thing."

Bouncer looked glum scratching his head.

Pete was next to put up his hand.

"And, what do you have to say, Mr. Court?" asked Alwood, becoming impatient.

"My father is a steward on *The Lusitania*, Sir," said Pete.

Alwood thought for a moment, studying Pete. "Well, write about becoming a ship's captain then, Mr. Court."

"What about working on automobiles?"

"Too expensive. People cannot afford them. Besides, they are always breaking down. There will always be a need for ships," snapped Alwood.

With no more hands showing, Alwood randomly picked students to tell what careers they had chosen.

"What about you, Mr. Simpson. What sort of job do you want?"

Simpson stood up blushing. "I want to be a Scotland Yard detective, Sir."

"Why that?"

"To catch Jack the Ripper, Sir."

"Good idea, Simpson," smiled Alwood.

Simpson looked over his shoulder and smirked at Bouncer before sitting down.

"What a wanker," Bouncer muttered out of the side of his mouth.

"Bloody right!" returned Spindle.

Alwood looked around the classroom for another candidate for his questioning. The pupils kept their heads bowed not wishing to be selected.

"And you, Mr. Baldwin, what is your ambition?"

Sam Baldwin stood up hesitantly, a flush spreading across his face. "To be a butcher, Sir."

"Why a butcher, Mr. Baldwin?"

"That's what my father does. He wants me to work for him after I leave Commerce School."

Alwood looked at Baldwin and smiled. "Ah! Baldwin the butcher. I know your father's shop. I often buy meat there. You are lucky to have that opportunity."

Alwood once again looked around the classroom, then at his pocket watch. "You will begin writing now. You have 20 minutes to work on your essays before the mid-morning break. Be sure to use correct spelling, do not print, and use your best handwriting," he instructed.

The boys picked up their pens and dipped them in their inkwells. Soon the scratching sound of pens on paper was all that could be heard until the morning break bell interrupted them.

"Leave your pen and papers on your desk, and be sure to use the toilet before you return to class," said Alwood.

Once outside on the playground, Bouncer produced a string holding a horse chestnut. "Let's play conkers," he said.

"I go first," said Spindle producing his own conker.

Bouncer held the string, the weight of the chestnut pulling it tight.

"Do you want to be a bank manager?" Bouncer asked Spindle.

"No, I want to be an accountant like my dad," he replied as he struck Bouncer's conker with his own.

"What about you, Bouncer? Do you want to be a solicitor?" asked Pete.

"No, I want to be a millionaire," laughed Bouncer hitting Spindle's conker in return. "What about you, Pete? What do you really want to be?"

"Not a ship's captain, that's for sure. Automobiles will be the thing to get into."

"Only if you can afford them," said Spindle. His next strike split Bouncer's conker, and the two halves of the chestnut fell to the ground.

"It's my turn now," said Pete. "Watch out, Spindle. I'm going to break your conker."

"Only if you can strike better than you can kick," joked Spindle, as Pete lined up his conker and prepared to strike.

"Can I play conkers with you?" interrupted Freddie, who had walked up to the group.

"Well, if it isn't Inky, the teacher's pet," sneered Bouncer.

"I didn't want the job of filling and cleaning ink pots. Alwood only chose me because he knew it was a dirty job," replied Freddie.

"Shall we let him play conkers with us?" asked Pete.

Bouncer thought for a moment. "Only if he pays us a farthing each," he decreed.

"I'll pay you tomorrow," said Freddie grinning.

"Before you can join us you have to swear that you will not get us into trouble again," said Spindle.

"I promise I won't do it again," Freddie solemnly swore, making an imaginary X mark over his heart with the index finger of his right hand.

"And stop being clever," said Bouncer.

"All right, I won't be clever anymore."

"And you will share your sandwiches," pronounced Spindle.

Freddie nodded in agreement.

"All right, you can play conkers with us this time and we'll see if you keep your word," said Bouncer.

"I wonder what happened to James," said Pete as he sliced his conker against Spindle's.

"Nicholson must have given him a hiding and then sent him home," speculated Bouncer.

"His father will be mad when he finds out," said Freddie. "It was only last Sunday that he gave a sermon on the evils of pipe smoking."

"How do you know that?" asked Bouncer.

"His father is the vicar at St. Barnabas where we go to church," replied Freddie.

"Is that right? Didn't know Jimmy's father was a vicar," said Spindle. "By the way, Freddie, what's this about wanting to be a detective and catch Jack the Ripper? Is that what you really want to do?"

"Sure. My father says the one who catches him would be famous and I want to be famous."

"My aunt says it was a Harley Street Surgeon that did it because he wanted the body parts to practice on," said Bouncer.

"Ugh!" said Spindle, as the two halves of Pete's conker fell to the ground.

"You have a two-timer now, Spindle," observed Bouncer.

"Ok, Inky, you're up," said Spindle, twiddling the string attached to his conker.

Freddie held his conker tight taking aim at Spindle's chestnut. When Freddie let go, Spindle moved his string. Instead of hitting Spindle's conker, Freddie hit himself in the leg.

"That's not fair. I want another throw," said Freddie wincing and rubbing his leg.

"Serves you right. You shouldn't have squealed on Pete this morning," said Spindle. "You don't deserve another throw. I win."

Before they could resolve the dispute, the bell rang signaling the end of the mid-morning break, and the boys rushed to use the toilet before returning to class.

When the students were settled at their desks, Alwood again looked at his pocket watch and announced, "You have until lunch time to finish the assignment. Those who do not finish at that time will complete the essays after school today."

The class was silent as students wrote rapidly to meet the deadline. After half an hour, Freddie raised his hand.

"What is it?" asked Alwood.

"I've finished, Sir," replied Freddie with a huge grin on his face.

"Splendid, Mr. Simpson. Anyone else?" he asked.

No other hands went up.

At about five minutes before noon, other students' hands began going up except those belonging to Spindle, Bouncer and Pete who were still busily scratching away in an effort to complete the required number of words before the bell rang.

Alwood held his watch in front of him. Just before the noon bell sounded, he snapped his cane on the lectern. "That's it, Gentlemen. Time's up. Pens down. Mr. Baldwin, collect the papers and bring them to me," said Alwood impatiently.

Sam walked quickly from desk to desk, collecting the papers. "Did you finish?" he whispered to Bouncer.

"Just barely," said Bouncer.

"Me, too," said Spindle, as he handed Sam his essay. "Pete finished just before us. At least we won't have to stay after school."

Sam took the boys' essays to the front of the room and handed them to Alwood.

"Thank you, Mr. Baldwin. Now, Gentlemen, after lunch we will have a history lesson. Don't be late," said Alwood just as the noon bell sounded.

The boys retrieved parcels containing sandwiches from their desks, jumped up and jostled each other as they crowded out the door and ran for the playground.

Spindle, Bouncer, Pete and Sam headed for the far side of the playground with Freddie trailing along at a distance.

"You're lucky, Sam," said Spindle, as the boys unwrapped their lunches. "You have a job already, and you know what you are going to do. Not like us."

"Not what you think," said Sam. "I'm stuck. I really want to be a veterinarian, not a butcher, but my dad is set on me carrying on in the family business."

"Well, at least you have good lunches," said Pete as he observed Sam unwrap his lunch of sausages and bread.

"Oh, it's bangers every day. I get tired of them. Would like to have something else," said Sam with a grimace.

"Well, 'Banger' Baldwin, how would you like to trade? I have bread and cheese here," said Spindle, wrinkling his nose.

"I've an idea. Let's sneak over to the girls' school when we're finished eating," said Bouncer.

"Can I come too?" asked Freddie, who had sidled up to them.

"You broke your promise," said Spindle.

"What do you mean?"

"You're being clever again. You know, telling Alwood you were finished," said Spindle.

"Didn't mean to be clever. Got carried away I suppose," said Freddie, hanging his head.

"You can come only if you share your sandwiches," said Bouncer.

Freddie opened his parcel and produced two egg and cucumber sandwiches, which he passed around to the other boys.

"Nice sandwich. I wish my aunt could make sandwiches like these," said Bouncer after he had taken a bite.

The boys took turns taking bites of Freddie's sandwiches until they were consumed. Then they stole quickly and quietly through the small wood that separated King Charles from Rosemead Finishing School for Girls.

"Get on your hands and knees and be quiet," whispered Spindle when the muffled sound of girls' voices could be heard coming from the other side of a boxwood hedge that separated Rosemead's playground from the wood.

The boys crawled on their hands and knees and crouched next to the hedge. They took turns peeking through a small hole in the hedge where they could see five girls sitting in a circle on the ground eating their lunches.

"Who are they? Does anyone know?" whispered Bouncer.

Freddie peeked through the hole. "The short one is my cousin Martha," he whispered. "The blond one is Phoebe Smith, and the red-haired girl sitting next to Martha is Susan Davenville. The girl with the dark hair is Elizabeth Manson, and the plump one is Rose Blackmun. They all live in Queen Anne's Gardens where I live," he added.

"What was that noise?" asked Martha suddenly. "I thought I heard a voice."

Freddie quickly withdrew from the opening in the hedge and put his finger to his lips. The boys froze.

"Must have been a bird or a field mouse," said Susan after a moment. "Are all of you coming to my birthday party?"

"When is it?" asked Phoebe.

"Saturday. I want all of you to come," Susan said.

"What do you want for your sixteenth birthday?" asked Phoebe.

Susan thought for a moment. "A boyfriend," she said.

"Why do you want a boyfriend?" asked Elizabeth.

"I want to do the same things as my older sister Paulina."

"And what is that?" asked Martha.

"She lets her boyfriend put his hand into her blouse. They do other things as well," said Susan with a knowing smile.

The girls moved closer together and lowered their voices. The boys moved closer to the hedge.

"What other things do they do?" asked Rose in a low voice.

"It gives me goose bumps when I think about it. I get this tingling feeling down here," she said, blushing and pointing to her lap.

"I feel like that, too, sometimes when I think about boys," giggled Elizabeth.

"I was in the lower gardens by the lake when I heard my sister and her fiancée George Edmundson talking in the summerhouse. I hid behind the rhododendrons to watch, and I saw Paulina undo George's trousers and take out his ... John Henry," Susan said in a conspiratorial tone.

"His what?" interrupted Phoebe, her eyes wide.

"You know. The thing boys have down here between their legs," said Susan pointing to her lap again.

"What happened then?" inquired Rose.

"She held it in her hand and pulled back and forth on it, and it kept getting bigger and bigger."

"What did George do?" asked Elizabeth.

"He was breathing hard like he had been running, and then he put one hand up under her skirt and the other into her blouse."

"How long did that go on?" asked Elizabeth blushing.

"Can't be sure. She kept pulling on his John Henry, and then George whispered something in her ear, and she hiked up her skirts and sat on his lap facing him. He bounced her up and down for a while, and then his eyes sort of rolled up in his head and they both moaned as if they were in pain. And that's all I saw because I didn't want them to catch me watching, so I sneaked away."

"Now, I feel that tingling sensation," said Phoebe, hugging herself.

"Why would you want a boyfriend to make you moan in pain? That doesn't sound as if it would be very pleasant," remarked Rose.

"I don't think it's really painful if the boy is someone you really like," said Susan, with a knowing air.

"Is there a boy you like?" asked Rose.

"Maybe, but I think he has a girlfriend already."

"Who is it? Is it someone we know?" asked Martha.

"I'm not saying, other than I think he goes to King Charles," replied Susan, blushing again.

The boys looked at each other with raised eyebrows.

"What time is your party?" asked Elizabeth.

"Mother said for you to be there at four."

"Are any boys invited?"

"Haven't asked any yet, but I would like to. Mother said I could invite five more friends in addition to ourselves."

"My cousin Freddie goes to King Charles," said Martha. "I could ask him for names of some boys to invite."

Spindle jabbed Freddie in the ribs and pointed at himself and the other boys.

31

"All right, Martha. Have Freddie give you a list of names and what they look like and I will decide who to invite," said Susan.

"What are you young ladies talking about all huddled together?" interrupted the headmistress as she walked up to where the girls were sitting.

"Talking about cooking, Miss Desmond," answered Rose.

"What sort of cooking? Must be a secret recipe, the way you are all sitting so close together and whispering," said the headmistress, peering at them through her lorgnette.

"We were wondering how to cook leeks, Ma'am," said Susan with a straight face.

"Leeks? That's easy. You just boil them in water," said Miss Desmond.

"Oh, we thought you had to pull them first," said Martha, grinning

The girls burst out in giggles.

"You young ladies are quite silly," said Miss Desmond. "You'd better get to your class now and learn how to cook properly."

The girls rose from their seats on the ground, brushed off their skirts and followed the headmistress, nudging each other and giggling as they disappeared into the school building.

The boys collapsed on the ground behind the hedge holding their sides and roaring with laughter.

"Did you know what they were talking about?" asked Freddie.

"Yes. It made me excited just listening," said Spindle, tears of laughter rolling down his cheeks.

"Has a girl ever pulled on your John Henry, Spindle?" asked Pete who was choking back laughter and struggling to get up off the ground.

"Yes. Just once. I was on holiday last summer when I met this girl on the beach. We got very friendly and started kissing. Then, we ended up doing the same things Susan described."

"Well, did you moan in pain?" asked Pete.

"I moaned all right, but it wasn't in pain," said Spindle with a broad grin.

"What do you mean?" asked Freddie in a serious voice. "I don't understand what those girls were talking about."

"Soaking willies," laughed Spindle.

"Willies? I know what my willie is, but I've never soaked it, and don't know why I would want to," said Freddie with a puzzled look.

"Have any of the rest of you soaked your willie?" asked Spindle.

Pete, Sam and Bouncer all shook their heads.

"Well, I've pulled on mine," said Sam.

"I still don't know what you are talking about," said Freddie.

"Who is George Edmundson?" interjected Bouncer.

"He's the younger son of Lord Edmundson, who has an estate in Queen Anne's Gardens," said Freddie. "He went to Eton and then Oxford, but I don't think he finished. A couple of years ago, he went on the Grand Tour and when he returned he met Paulina at her coming-out party, and they got engaged this summer. I don't think he has a career. Spends a lot of time going to the races and his club, that sort of thing."

"I heard about him from my brother," said Spindle. "He got a girl pregnant when he was home from Oxford, and she had a baby. Her father kicked her out, and she had to live with an aunt in Cornwall somewhere."

"You mean the girl had a baby? How did George make her do that?" asked Freddie looking bewildered.

"Soaking his willie," said Spindle, laughing.

"Spindle, have you seen a girl naked?" asked Pete.

"No, not a real girl. I saw my sister once without any clothes, but that doesn't count."

"What about the girl who pulled your willie? Was she wearing clothes?" asked Bouncer.

"Yes. She just hiked up her skirts and pulled down her knickers, so I didn't see anything," said Spindle.

"Would it be different if girls didn't wear any clothes?" asked Sam.

"No, I don't think so," replied Spindle smiling.

"Do you want to go to Susan's birthday party?" asked Freddie trying to change the subject.

"We will all go together or not at all," said Bouncer.

"I'll ask my cousin to put our names on the list for Susan."

"Must not say how you knew about the party. Must be a secret," cautioned Spindle.

"I promise," said Freddie smiling and puffing out his chest.

"You promised not to be clever before, and look what happened," Spindle reminded him, clipping his ear.

"I won't do it again," gasped Freddie, rubbing his ear.

Suddenly, the bell rang.

"Bloody hell! We're in for it now. We're going to be late for class!" cried Bouncer.

The five boys sprinted through the wood and across the playground as fast as they could run. When they burst through the classroom door gasping for breath, the other students were all seated at their desks, and Alwood was waiting for them with the cane.

"Three strokes each for being late," he said, raising the cane over his head.

After receiving their punishment, the boys sat down at their desks.

"Not as bad as Nicholson's," whispered Spindle.

Bouncer nodded in agreement.

Alwood went to the blackboard, picked up a piece of chalk and wrote the words "British Empire."

"Name in alphabetical order the colonies and territories which make up our Empire, beginning with Mr. Baldwin in the front row."

"Africa," called out Sam smiling.

"No, try again," said Alwood.

"Argentina," said Sam, the smile fading from his face.

"Wrong again," said Alwood holding the cane over Sam's head.

Sam hesitated looking at the cane. "Australia," he said.

Alwood lowered the cane and wrote "Australia" on the board.

"Next," said Alwood pointing the cane at the boy seated next to Sam.

"Britain," called out the boy.

Alwood shook his head.

"Bethlehem," called out the boy again.

Alwood raised the cane.

"Bermuda!" shouted the boy.

Alwood added "Bermuda" to the list.

After the twenty-sixth letter, Alwood started the alphabet over again. When he reached Pete, he asked for a colony beginning with the letter "H." Pete gulped as Alwood pointed the cane at him.

"Say Hong Kong," whispered Bouncer.

"Hong Kong," called out Pete.

Alwood smiled.

"Where is Hong Kong, Mr. Court?"

Pete's face turned red.

"Mr. Court, where is Hong Kong?" Alwood repeated, pointing the cane at him.

Pete hesitated.

"I will count to three for an answer," said Alwood angrily.

Pete felt the tension building in the classroom.

"One," said Alwood striking his lectern with the cane. The sound of the cane striking oak sent shivers through the class.

"Two," screamed Alwood striking the lectern again.

Pete's legs shook.

"In the British Empire, Sir!" Pete shouted before Alwood struck again.

"Next," said Alwood, pointing the cane at Bouncer.

The boys gave a muffled cheer, and Pete breathed an audible sigh of relief.

"India," smiled Bouncer.

Alwood pointed to the blackboard. Bouncer could see India was already written down.

"Isle of Wight," said Bouncer frowning.

Laughter filled the classroom.

Alwood struck the lectern with the cane.

"Don't know," said Bouncer with a shrug of his shoulders.

"Next," said Alwood.

Spindle looked at the blackboard.

"There are no others beginning with 'I', Sir," he said.

"That's correct," said Alwood, turning his attention to the class as a whole. "All right, Gentlemen, are there any others not already listed?"

"Zululand!" yelled Freddie.

"Zululand?" repeated Alwood.

"Yes, Sir, it's in Africa," replied Freddie.

"Must be a new colony," mumbled Alwood, adding it to the list. Then he instructed Sam to hand out paper and looked at his pocket watch. "Now, Gentlemen, you have ten minutes before school is out for the day. Copy this list carefully and study it. If you don't know the colonies the next time you are asked, you will get one of these." He whacked the cane on the lectern again.

The boys peered at the blackboard and feverishly copied the list.

"All right, that's it for today, Gentlemen," announced Alwood when the ten minutes had expired. "I will see you back here tomorrow morning in your seats promptly at nine o'clock. Don't be late and be sure to use the toilet before you come to class." He snapped his attendance book shut and marched out of the room.

"Not a bad day at school," said Spindle as Bouncer, Sam and Pete joined him outside the school entryway. They began walking home together.

"Wait for me!" yelled Freddie, rushing to catch up with them.

"Thought you had detention," said Bouncer.

"No. Nicholson let me off being it's the first day of school," said Freddie, shifting his book bag to his other shoulder and falling into step with the others.

"Well, we certainly started out the year with a wallop," laughed Bouncer. "We all had canings. We should start a club."

"If it wasn't for those girls, neither Sam nor I would have had a caning," said Pete.

"My bottom still hurts," said Freddie importantly. "I had two canings."

"I know! Let's call ourselves The Bottom Five, seeing as how we have the sorest bottoms in school today," said Spindle.

* * *

# Chapter 2
## *The Bristol Bomber*

THE BOYS WERE howling with laughter and clapping Spindle on the back as they continued up the hill on Station Road.

"The Bottom Five, it is," said Pete. "I nominate Bouncer for club president because he took the canings better than all of us."

"I should get to be president. I had two canings *and* detention," sniffed Freddie.

Spindle took a swipe at Freddie's ear. "Take that for 'Zululand'!" he said.

"Is Zululand really a colony?" asked Sam.

"Don't know," laughed Freddie as he dodged Spindle's blow. "I made it up because one of my uncles was killed by a Zulu spear."

They all laughed.

"I hope we get to go to Susan Davenville's birthday party," said Pete.

"I know what you mean. My willie has been twitching ever since we heard her talk about her sister and George Edmundson," said Spindle.

"I've been thinking about what she said, too, and I've got the same feeling," said Sam, pointing between his legs.

"Have you had it before?" asked Spindle smiling.

"Not like this."

"What does it feel like?" asked Freddie curiously.

"It's my willie. It..."

"It what?" asked Freddie.

"My willie was swollen in class, and it swells up every time I think of Susan," said Sam with a grin.

"Join the club," laughed Spindle.

"Swollen? How do you get it to go away?" asked Freddie.

"There are two ways to handle it," laughed Spindle, winking at the other boys.

"What ways?" asked Freddie.

"Girls for one and...," Spindle hesitated, looking at Freddie's serious expression.

"And?" he prompted.

"You will find out soon enough," said Spindle with a grin.

"I want to know now," said Freddie.

"It will happen on its own. You will know what to do when the time comes," said Bouncer.

"Why don't you tell me? What's the big secret?"

"It's not our job to explain," said Bouncer. "Ask your father."

Freddie started to ask another question, but Pete interrupted. "What are you doing tonight, Freddie?" he asked.

"I'm going over to my cousin's house to see about getting us on the list for Susan's party."

"Good," said Sam. "I know. Freddie can be our club's social director."

The boys were still laughing about Sam's suggestion when they arrived at the top of the hill on Station Road and sat down on a low wall beside a horse trough to watch the traffic and passersby. Horses struggled to pull an assortment of wagons and carriages up the hill.

"Look! Here comes a horseless carriage!" shouted Sam, pointing down the hill.

"Well, I never! It's a Bristol Bomber!" cried Pete, as the boys all stared at the black open automobile chugging noisily up the hill towards them.

Horses began snorting and rolling their eyes as the contraption approached them.

"Better get ready to run," said Pete, pointing at a closed carriage whose horse was shrieking and beginning to rear directly in front of them.

The Bristol stopped behind the carriage, its engine clanking loudly. The coachman's face had turned beet red as he stood up in the box and attempted to restrain the horse. By now, the horse was foaming at the mouth and standing on its hind legs, trying to shake the harness free. The coachman was shouting at the horse over the racket of the Bristol Bomber, making the horse even more frantic. To add to the uproar, pedestrians and shoppers scattered, and shopkeepers ran out to see what was happening. A small crowd gathered where the boys were sitting. "My God! Someone's going to be killed!" shouted a voice from the crowd.

"Come on! Let's help the coachman," said Bouncer, jumping up. The other boys followed and grabbed the horse's bridle on either side. Bouncer stroked the horse and spoke calmly in its ear. After a few moments the horse settled down and stood still, hanging its head and blowing heavily.

"It's a good thing you had the brake on," called out Pete to the coachman. "Otherwise the horse would have bolted!"

"Aye, right you are," the coachman replied, nodding and wiping his brow as he sat back down.

"Thank you for helping, lads," said a middle-aged gentleman who climbed out of the carriage door. He was wearing a dark suit and a bowler hat.

"Move on, I can't wait all day!" yelled the Bristol driver.

"I'll move when I am quite ready!" roared the passenger, turning to glare at the Bristol driver. "If it wasn't for that contraption, my horse wouldn't have reared and caused the delay in the first place!"

He turned and hobbled toward the boys, leaning heavily on a walking stick.

"You were very brave, young men. I certainly appreciate what you did. Here is my card. If I can ever do anything for you, please let me know." He handed each boy a small white calling card.

"Thank you, Sir. Only pleased to help," said Spindle, looking at the name on the card.

"Please accept these as a token for my gratitude," the passenger continued as he handed each boy a half sovereign.

"Thank you, Sir, thank you very much," said Bouncer, admiring the glint of the gold coin in his palm.

"Hurry up there! Are you drunk? I'm late for an appointment!" shouted the Bristol driver, revving his engine and creating an even greater racket.

"Get that contraption off the road! Nothing but a nuisance!" roared the passenger. He shook his fist at the Bristol driver as he hobbled back to his carriage.

The boys stuck out their tongues and shook their fists at the driver as well.

"You little bastards! What are your names? I'm going to report you!" yelled the enraged driver.

"None of your damn business!" retorted the passenger as he climbed back into the carriage.

The carriage driver tipped his hat to the boys. "Thank you lads. Very brave of you," he said as he released the brake and took up the reins. "Giddyap, Ben," he called, and the passenger waved out the window at the boys as the carriage moved on.

The Bristol driver revved the engine again as he prepared to drive on. He shook his fist at the boys. "I know those uniforms. You go to King Charles School, and I know the headmaster well. He will hear of your insolence, and he won't be pleased, I can tell you. Gives the school a bad name, it does."

With that, he drove on, raising a great cloud of dust and creating bedlam in the road ahead of him.

A shopkeeper emerged from the crowd and patted Bouncer on the back. "Don't worry, lads. When the headmaster finds out who was in the carriage, he'll go easy on you. You saved the day here."

With a thumbs-up motion, the shopkeeper turned on his heels and returned to his business and the rest of the crowd dispersed.

"Fancy getting a half sovereign. That's more than my dad earns in a week," laughed Spindle.

"I have a full sovereign at home that my uncle gave me for Christmas," announced Freddie.

Spindle cuffed his ear. "You're being clever again, Inky," he warned.

"Well, I've never had one of these before," said Sam.

"Nor have I," said Pete.

"Must get home now. My aunt gets upset if I'm not there in time for tea," said Bouncer. "See you tomorrow."

"Right," said Spindle as he and Pete headed off in the same direction as Bouncer. "Do your best to get us on Susan's birthday party list, Freddie," he said over his shoulder.

"I promise," said Freddie as he went on up the hill toward Queen Anne's Gardens. Sam strode off down the hill toward the High Street where he lived with his family over the butcher shop.

At 8:30 the next morning, the boys were playing conkers again on the school playground when Freddie appeared.

"Any luck on the party?" asked Spindle.

"I spoke to Martha, and she is going to give our names to Susan," Freddie replied.

"Let's go to the girls' school at lunch time and see what she says," said Spindle.

Bouncer, Pete and Sam nodded their agreement.

"Not me, I don't want another caning," said Freddie.

At lunch break, Spindle, Bouncer, Pete and Sam crouched behind the boxwood hedge again, waiting for Susan and her friends to appear.

"Here they come," whispered Spindle seeing Susan and three others walk in their direction.

The girls sat down in a circle close to the hedge.

"We'd better get closer to hear what they are saying," whispered Bouncer.

The boys crept on their hands and knees along the hedgerow.

"Miss Desmond is a cow," said Phoebe.

"I know, she shouldn't have embarrassed Elizabeth by sending her home," replied Rose.

"Elizabeth didn't know she had blood on her frock. It must have got there when she was sitting down," said Susan.

"When I have my monthly, my mother makes me bring extra clothes to school. Just in case." said Martha.

"The older I get, the worse it is," said Rose.

"Poor Elizabeth. So embarrassing," said Phoebe.

The girls were quiet for a moment. Then Martha broke the silence. "I know some nice boys for your party, Susan," she said.

"You do?" asked Susan excitedly.

"They are friends of my cousin Freddie."

"How old are they? Do they have girlfriends?" asked Rose.

"They're in the last year at King Charles. I don't think they have any girlfriends," said Martha. She handed Susan a piece of paper. Rose and Phoebe peered over Susan's shoulder as she read the names on the list.

"I don't recognize any of those names, except Freddie's," said Phoebe. "They don't live in Queen Anne's Gardens, except Freddie, of course."

"Doesn't matter," said Susan. "It makes no difference to me or to my father so long as they are decent."

"Well, are they nice looking?" Rose wanted to know.

"I don't know them myself," said Martha, "but Freddie described them to me. Brian Adams is called Spindle because he is lean and tall, and John Russell is called Bouncer because he is strong and muscular and a good football player. Then, there is Peter Court who is also tall and has blond hair. Sam Baldwin is somewhat short, and has sandy-colored hair and freckles."

Behind the hedge, the boys were jabbing each other and suppressing outbursts of laughter as they heard the descriptions.

"What about Freddie? What does he look like?" asked Rose.

"Like a cocker spaniel, but he is pleasant enough looking and he is clever like his father," answered Martha.

"Oh, I know his father. He's a barrister and has been to our house for dinner," said Phoebe.

Rose turned to Susan. "Well, then, are you going to invite them?" she asked.

Susan sat smiling for a few moments twiddling a piece of grass. "Do they shave, Martha?"

"I can't be sure," replied Martha.

"What's shaving got to do with it?" asked Phoebe.

"My mother says to keep away from boys who shave," replied Susan.

"Why?" asked Rose.

"If they shave, it means they can do the same things George Edmundson does to my sister," said Susan with a mischievous gleam in her green eyes.

"Would that make a difference as to whether you invite them or not?" asked Martha.

"I most certainly would invite them if I knew they shaved," said Susan. This brought a hailstorm of laughter from the girls. The boys were rolling on the ground behind the hedge, rubbing their faces for signs of whiskers, and trying to keep howls of laughter from escaping and giving them away.

"If they are in the final year at King Charles, they are probably only fifteen," speculated Rose. "On the other hand, my brother began shaving when he was fourteen."

The girls looked at Susan, waiting for her decision. Susan twirled the blade of grass thoughtfully between her fingers. "All right. I'll take the chance and invite them on one condition," she decided.

"What is that?" asked Phoebe.

"There are five of us and five of them. I get to choose the one I want first. After all, it's my birthday."

"Are you going to do what you talked about yesterday?" asked Rose blushing.

"I don't know. It will depend on how I feel Saturday," said Susan. She turned to Martha. "I will bring the invitations tomorrow so you can give them to Freddie to give to the rest of the boys," she said.

"Better get back. We don't want another caning," whispered Pete.

A twig snapped under Sam's knee as the boys crawled away.

"Did you hear something?" asked Martha.

"Must be foxes in the woods," replied Rose.

When the boys reached the school playground, it was still crowded with students.

"Oh, good. Won't be late this time," said Sam.

"I wonder which one of us Susan will choose," said Spindle.

"What about Freddie? She might choose him," said Bouncer.

"Well, you're the only one who shaves, Bouncer," said Pete.

Bouncer rubbed his hand over his strong, chiseled face. His smoky blue eyes sparkled with merriment in the bright autumn sunlight. "Oh, I've been shaving for a few years now. Have lots of thick hair, you know. Got it from my dad." He ran his hand through his thick curly black hair.

"Well, I started shaving last week," said Spindle. "I was starting to get a mustache." He drew a finger across his upper lip and then slicked back his straight reddish-brown hair, emulating Bouncer.

"Hah! You call that fuzz a mustache?" said Pete, peering closely at Spindle's upper lip.

"Soon will be." Spindle drew himself up to his full height. "I have to shave it once a week, or it's noticeable," he added in a defensive tone.

"What's noticeable?" asked Freddie, who had just walked up to join them.

"Talking about shaving," explained Sam.

"Oh," said Freddie. "Well, did you find out anything interesting at the girls' school?"

"Your cousin Martha is working on it. She should tell you tonight, but it looks as if we're in," said Spindle. "Susan said she'd give Martha the invitations to give to you."

"We'd better be invited. Otherwise, Martha will have to give me back my two shillings," said Freddie smugly. "Were all the girls there today?"

"All but Elizabeth who got sent home. She is having her monthly, whatever that means," said Sam.

"What's that?" asked Freddie with a puzzled frown.

"It's something girls have when they're not pregnant," said Spindle.

"Susan said Elizabeth had blood on her dress," said Sam.

"Blood? Where does that come from?" asked Freddie, concern showing in his eyes.

Spindle thought for a moment before attempting to answer. "The same place willie goes and where babies come out."

"Don't start talking about willies again. I asked my father about willies last night, and he boxed my ears. He said my mother would tell me when the time comes," said Freddie.

The other boys looked at each other knowingly.

The school bell rang, and the boys went to their classroom where Alwood was waiting. He looked closely at each boy as they filed into the room.

"Mr. Adams, Mr. Russell, Mr. Court, and Mr. Baldwin, stand here," he ordered, pointing his cane at the front of his lectern.

After the other pupils had taken their seats, Alwood looked sternly at the class. "Mr. Nicholson received a complaint during lunchtime from a local businessman who reported that five boys wearing King Charles uniforms acted rudely towards him after school yesterday. In fact, they stuck out their tongues and made indecent gestures toward him. His description of the culprits matches the four of you," he said, gesturing toward the four boys standing in front of the lectern. "Now, who is the fifth one?" he demanded.

The four boys looked uneasily at each other.

"Sir, the gentleman is only telling you half the story," said Bouncer.

"I don't care about half the story. Who was with you? Who was the fifth boy?" demanded Alwood.

"There was no fifth boy, Sir. It was just ... the four of us." Out of the corner of his eye, Bouncer could see Freddie busily arranging pen and papers on his desk in the front row.

Alwood turned to Spindle and poked his arm with the cane. "The name of the fifth boy, Mr. Adams!" he shouted. Spindle didn't respond. "Mr. Court? Mr. Baldwin?" No response. Alwood turned his attention to the other students. "All right then. Let the fifth boy step forward."

The class was silent. Suddenly, Freddie jumped up from his desk. "I'm the one, I'm the fifth boy," he said in a trembling voice. He walked on unsteady feet to join the others at the front of the classroom.

"The five of you are to report immediately to the headmaster's office. Now!" directed Alwood, pointing the cane at the door. The boys filed out, heads down.

"Brave of you to own up, Freddie. We wouldn't have told," said Pete, as they walked down the hallway toward the headmaster's office.

"Well, I'm part of the club, you know, and we all stand together," said Freddie.

"Good job, Inky," said Spindle. "The Bottom Five will stick together."

"Right now, looks as if The Bottom Five are in for another caning," muttered Sam. "And it's only the second day of school."

"Are you the five boys whom Mr. Nicholson received a complaint about?" inquired Mr. Finch, the headmaster's secretary.

"That we are," said Bouncer, who led the way into the headmaster's outer office.

"The gentleman who lodged the complaint reported that your behavior was quite upsetting, and that you were quite rude to him. You have soiled King Charles's reputation. It doesn't set well to be rude in public when you are wearing the school's uniforms, you know, especially toward such an influential businessman as Mr. Squires," the secretary admonished.

"Begging your pardon, Sir, but it appears that Mr. Squires has not told Mr. Nicholson the whole story," said Spindle. "He nearly caused a horse to bolt, and someone could have been killed."

"How is that?" asked Finch.

"Well, you see, he raced his horseless carriage up the hill on Station Road and spooked a horse pulling a carriage with a crippled gentleman in it."

"That's no reason to be rude," said Finch.

"Well, Mr. Squires was quite rude to Major ..." Spindle pulled the calling card from his back pocket and looked at it. "Major General Wallis. He was the passenger in the carriage."

Finch looked at the card and then at the boys. "Is that true?"

"Yes, Sir," the boys said in unison.

"Wait here," said Finch. He knocked on the door to the headmaster's office, went in and closed the door behind him.

The boys waited nervously. "Another caning, for sure," whispered Pete.

"The headmaster will see you now," said Finch with a smile as he opened the door to Nicholson's office.

48

Nicholson looked up from some papers as the boys filed in silently and stood at attention in front of his desk. "Sit down, Gentlemen," he said, waving them toward some chairs. "Finch has spoken to me about the incident. Can you prove your side of the story?"

"The passenger in the carriage gave each of us his calling card and a half sovereign for helping to calm his horse and prevent an accident. Also, there was a crowd of passersby and several shopkeepers who saw what happened, Sir," said Spindle.

"A half sovereign?" exclaimed Nicholson.

"Yes, Sir, a half sovereign each," replied Bouncer.

"Is that true, Mr. Court?

"Yes, Sir, I have my half sovereign here," said Pete, drawing the coin from his pocket and handing it to Nicholson.

Nicholson sat back in his chair, examining the coin. After a bit, he smiled broadly. "You say you stopped his horse from bolting because of Mr. Squires's horseless contraption?"

"Yes, Sir. Mr. Squires was very rude toward the passenger. He accused the Major of being drunk because he had trouble walking," said Bouncer.

Nicholson leaned forward and returned the coin to Pete. Then he sat back in his chair again, resting his elbows on the armrests and steepling his fingers together under his chin. "Well, lads, this is quite a story. Do you know who you rescued?"

The boys looked at each other and shrugged their shoulders. "No, Sir, other than the name on the card," said Spindle.

"Major General Wallis is one of our country's heroes. He fought with Kitchener in the Sudan. Lost both his legs in relieving Khartoum. That is why he has difficulty walking. Has wooden legs." Nicholson leaned forward, clasped his hands on the desk in front of him, and looked from boy to boy with a smile as he waited for them to absorb this information.

Then, Nicholson stood up and picked up the ever-present cane that was leaning against the wall behind his desk. "However, rudeness must be punished, and we must appease Mr. Squires to save King Charles's reputation," he said as he came around to the front of the desk. "You will each receive three strokes of the cane. Bend over and touch your toes," he ordered.

The boys did as instructed, bending over with their bottoms facing the desk. The headmaster called out each boy's name and counted out the three strokes in a loud voice as he struck the desk with the cane.

"Now, let that be a lesson to you!" Nicholson pronounced in a loud voice as he flung open the door of his office. "Don't be rude when you are wearing a school uniform, especially to someone who is driving a Bristol Bomber! Return to your classroom now and tell your chums about the severity of the punishment for being rude in public and tarnishing King Charles's name. If I hear you downplayed the punishment in order to make yourselves heroes in front of the other boys, you will get a worse thrashing."

"Yes, Sir, worst caning I ever had," said Bouncer rubbing his bottom as the boys filed past Finch's desk and walked meekly down the hall toward their classroom.

\* \* \*

# Chapter 3
## *The Davenville Party*

O N SATURDAY AFTERNOON
The Bottom Five met at the horse
trough on Station Road.

"What do you have in the parcels?" asked Freddie.

"A birthday present for Susan," replied Pete holding up a brown
paper package tied with string.

"What did you buy, Pete?" asked Spindle.

Pete only smiled.

"What did you buy, Bouncer?" asked Spindle again.

"It's a surprise," answered Bouncer, chuckling. "What did you
buy?"

Spindle laughed shaking his head. "Mine's a surprise, too."

"My mother had my father buy Susan a music box from a
jeweler's on Regent Street when he was in London," said Freddie
proudly, holding up an elegantly wrapped package done up with a green
silk bow.

The other boys rolled their eyes. "Regent Street – that's bloody expensive. Trying to outshine us again, Freddie?" said Spindle.

"Nah," said Freddie blushing. "It was my mother's idea."

"Well, all I have is a pound of pork sausages from our shop," said Sam. "That was my dad's idea. He won't let me spend the half sovereign."

The boys laughed and Pete clapped him on the back. "Think of it this way, Banger! Maybe the music box is big enough to keep the sausages in it."

Sam looked dejected. Bouncer patted him on the shoulder. "It's all right, Sam," he said. "If Susan's worth her salt, she'll appreciate everyone's gift, no matter what it is."

Freddie led the way as the boys walked up Vale Road past the White Horse Pub where Ben Ashley, the landlord, was ringing the 3 o'clock closing bell.

The boys paused and looked in the open door of the pub.

"Where are you lads off to dressed up in all your finery?" asked Ben when he saw them at the door.

"Going to Susan Davenville's birthday party, Mr. Ashley," said Spindle.

"Oh, mixing with the upper crust now, are we? Better act like gentlemen. That's Lord Davenville's daughter. Lord Alfred is a personal friend of the King, you know."

"Won't be long before we'll be buying a pint in your pub," said Spindle with a twinkle in his eye.

"Only when you are sixteen." Ben winked at the boys. All of them but Freddie had visited the pub in the past year. "But you'll only get beer and cider at the White Horse, not champagne like you'll get at Lord Alfred's."

The boys continued on up Vale Road passing rows of attached houses where domestic servants and shopkeeper's assistants lived. At the end of Vale Road they turned right and proceeded through a massive sandstone arch that marked the entrance into Queen Anne's Gardens where the wealthy lived in large estates behind high stone walls.

The boys looked about in awe. "What mansions!" exclaimed Sam. "That one over there is bigger than King Charles School. Which one do you live in, Freddie?"

"That one up ahead with the wrought-iron gates," he answered. "I think Susan's house is bigger than ours, though."

After walking another half mile, Freddie stopped in front of a large gate protected on each side by two great stone lions mounted on pedestals. A massive arch over the gate displayed the family crest and the name of the estate, Davenville House.

A uniformed servant emerged from the gatehouse on the other side, and Freddie passed his invitation through the gate to him. "Ah, Master Simpson, you are here for Miss Susan's party, and these must be the other four guests," said the servant as he swung the gates open.

"That's correct," said Freddie.

"The birthday party is being held on the terrace that overlooks the rose gardens at the back of the house," said the gateman.

"Thank you," said Freddie. He motioned to the boys to follow him. "Martha said she would meet us and help with the introductions," he told them as they walked up the long driveway lined with ancient oak trees whose branches touched overhead as if they were shaking hands.

As they rounded a bend in the driveway, a massive three-story Georgian sandstone house came into view. A butler appeared at the columned entryway and peered up at the bright autumn sky. He noticed the boys walking up the driveway as it formed a circle in front of the house.

"Good afternoon, Gentlemen. Welcome to Davenville House. Pleased to see the weather will hold for Miss Susan's party on the terrace. Just follow the path through the hydrangea garden, and it will lead you directly there. The young ladies are already here."

Freddie nodded and led the boys along the path. The rest of the boys had gone silent, looking about them in awe. At the back of the house, a series of French doors opened onto a huge flagstone terrace. The terrace looked down on rose gardens laid out in six hexagonal shapes defined by meticulously pruned low boxwood hedges. Manicured grass paths divided the rose beds and converged in a center circle where a huge stone fountain held court. Beyond the rose gardens, the boys could see stone steps leading down to a lower lawn where girls in white dresses were playing croquet. Beyond the lower lawn was a lake with a summerhouse on its far side.

As the boys came up onto the terrace, Martha approached them from where she had been standing by the dining table. "Oh, here you are at last, Freddie. Been waiting for you. Introduce me to your friends," she said with a smile.

After the introductions, a maid took the boys' packages and added them to the other gifts displayed on a side table draped in purple moiré. Another maid stepped forward and offered them glasses of lemonade from a silver tray.

"Would you look at that," said Spindle, staring at the huge dining table covered with fine white linen and all laid out with gold-rimmed china bearing the family crest, heavily engraved silverware, and gold-rimmed crystal glasses. A massive bouquet of purple and gold asters, deep pink freesia, and white roses dominated the center of the table.

"Follow me," said Martha. "We're playing croquet on the lower lawn. I'll introduce you and then you can join us. We'll start a new set."

The boys glanced at each other as they followed Martha and Freddie through the rose gardens. "Never played croquet, have you?" whispered Pete, nudging Sam.

Sam shook his head.

"What about you, Spindle? Bouncer?"

"No, never been to an upper crust party before," said Spindle.

"I've never played croquet either, but it can't be that much different from rugby," said Bouncer with the confidant air of an athlete.

As they walked down the stone steps to the lower level, they could see the girls on the far side of the lawn. Clad in white lawn dresses and sporting large straw hats with gaily-colored ribbons, the four girls were concentrating their attention on two balls lying side by side near a wicket.

"I've brought the rest of your guests, Susan," said Martha, raising her voice enough to be heard across the distance.

Susan paused, dropped her mallet, whipped off her hat and looked toward them, shading her eyes with her hand. Her red hair flamed in the bright autumn sunlight. "Won't be a moment. We're just finishing this game, and I am about to win!" she called back.

Martha and the boys watched as Susan put her hat back on, picked up her mallet, and placed her left foot on one of the balls. She smacked the ball under her foot with the mallet, sending the other ball careening off away from the wicket.

"Looks as if Susan is indeed on the verge of winning," said Martha. "All she has to do now is drive her ball through the last set of wickets and hit the stake before anyone else. Why don't we sit down and drink our lemonade? Shouldn't be long before they join us." Martha pointed toward white wicker chairs and tables arranged on a stone-surfaced area just to the left of the steps.

The boys took seats and watched as the game progressed. "Have any of you ever played croquet? I mean with the exception of Freddie. I know he has played croquet," asked Martha.

The boys shook their heads. "No," said Bouncer, "but it doesn't look as if it's terribly difficult. Just knocking balls about with a wooden mallet, somewhat like polo."

"But where are the ponies?" asked Spindle, jabbing him in the ribs.

"It's more difficult than you imagine," said Freddie, puffing up importantly. "Lots of strategy involved, you see. The object is to get through all nine wickets and hit the last stake before anyone else. You must attempt to cripple your opposition by stroking the ball just hard enough to tap their ball and then you can send their ball awry making it more difficult for them to line up for the wicket."

Freddie rose from his seat and began demonstrating croquet moves. "Now, there are two ways you can send their ball astray," he began.

"Right. I think we have the idea," Spindle interrupted. "Being clever again, aren't you, Freddie?"

Freddie blushed and sat back down. At this point, a shriek from the far end of the lawn drew their attention back to the girls. Susan had thrown her mallet down on the ground and was tossing her hat in the air.

"Well, that's it," said Martha. "Susan has won. Only appropriate, I suppose, since it's her birthday."

The boys stood up as the girls began walking toward them, Susan in the lead. Susan took off her hat and placed it on one of the tables. As she smoothed back her hair, her face still flushed with the excitement of her croquet victory, she smiled at the boys. "Welcome to my birthday party," she said. "So pleased you could come."

"Shall I introduce everyone?" asked Martha.

Susan put a finger to her mouth, her green eyes crinkling with mischief. "No, let me guess. I believe I know who each of these gentlemen is by your description. We'll make a game of it. If I am wrong in identifying one of you, then that person can have an extra slice of my birthday cake later."

The boys smiled back at her nodding their agreement. "Now, let me see," said Susan, walking up to Freddie and extending her hand. "You are Freddie Simpson, Martha's cousin. You have the very same eyes. Am I correct?"

"Indeed you are," said Freddie, clasping her hand. "Quite pleased to meet you, Miss Davenville, and to be invited to your party."

"Oh, please call me Susan. I don't stand on formalities." Susan moved on to Sam and extended her hand. "And I see by your sandy hair and freckles that you are Sam Baldwin," she said.

Sam turned red and looked down at the ground as he shook Susan's hand. "That's right, Miss," he mumbled. "Guess I will always have these freckles. They come from me mum."

"Nothing to be ashamed of, Sam. I find them charming. Welcome to my party."

Sam turned even redder and continued staring at the ground as Susan moved on to Spindle. She stood back, looked up at Spindle's face and put a finger alongside her mouth in thought. Spindle looked directly into her eyes with a mischievous grin. Susan smiled back at him. "Well, you can only be Brian Adams who is called Spindle because you are tall and lanky," she said.

"You've got that right – the one and only," said Spindle.

"Pleased to meet you, Spindle," said Susan, shaking his hand.

"Very pleased to meet you, Miss ... Susan," said Spindle, with a flirtatious glint in his eyes.

"Too bad you won't get that extra slice of cake, Spindle. Looks as if you could use it," said Susan mischievously.

She moved on to Bouncer and gazed into his eyes. Bouncer gazed back with a solemn, steady expression. "And you can be none other than John Russell who is called Bouncer," said Susan. "Your nickname serves you well. You are indeed quite muscular, and I see that you shave as well." She glanced over her shoulder and smiled at the other girls who began to giggle.

Bouncer, who could sense his chums' reactions to her shaving comment, held his ground, refusing to let it rattle him. "That's right, Miss Davenville. Been shaving since I was fourteen. Runs in the family, you know. Come from a long line of he-men military types."

"I see," said Susan, extending her hand. "Quite pleased to meet you, Bouncer, and please call me Susan."

Bouncer took Susan's hand and bowed over it briefly. "I'm quite pleased to meet you, too, Susan, and most happy to be invited to your birthday party."

Susan smiled at him and then turned her attention to Pete. "And, of course, you have to be Peter Court."

Pete smiled at her shyly. "Not fair. You recognized me by process of elimination," he said.

"Oh, I would have recognized you because you're the only one with blond hair," said Susan, holding out her hand. "However, to make you feel better about it, I'll let you have that extra slice of cake. Welcome to my party, Peter."

"Please, Miss, call me Pete as all my friends do," he said, shaking her hand.

"Right. Pete it is, then, and I am Susan."

Susan turned and motioned to the other girls to join her. "Now, then, you must meet my other guests. Freddie, Sam, Spindle, Bouncer and Pete, please meet my friends Rose Blackmun, Phoebe Smith and Elizabeth Manson. You have already been introduced to Martha Simpson."

After her guests had shaken hands all around, Susan announced, "All right. Here is the plan. My parents have invited some other guests who will arrive for dinner on the terrace at 5:30. I propose we all have a game of croquet until dinner is announced. We'll play as partners – boy teams and girl teams, except for Martha and Freddie who can be a team to even things out. I pick Phoebe as my partner, so that means Rose and Elizabeth are partners. You boys can decide whom you will team up with. Come on girls, let's show them how to play croquet!"

The girls and Freddie walked off across the lawn to where the croquet wickets were laid out. The other boys followed at a distance.

"Now, we're in for it," said Sam. "Don't know the first thing about croquet."

"Come on, Sam, you play cricket. It can't be more difficult than that," said Bouncer, clapping him on the shoulder. "You can be my partner, and we'll show them a thing or two."

"No, you won't," said Spindle. "Pete's my partner, and if he can hit a ball with a croquet mallet the same way he kicks one, we're sure to win!"

Pete punched him on the arm.

After the girls' teams had played, Bouncer and Sam were the first boys' team to play. "You go first, Bouncer," said Sam, hanging back. Bouncer strode confidently up to their ball and gave it a whack with the mallet. The ball shot wildly across the closely clipped lawn, surpassing two wickets.

"My, what strength! No wonder they call you Bouncer," laughed Susan, who was standing near her ball that was neatly lined up to go through the first wicket. Bouncer's face turned red.

"It'll be up to you to get our ball back in position for the first wicket on our next turn, Sam," he muttered. "Guess you only have to tap the thing to make it go. Sorry."

"Watch out, Susan. Your ball is in jeopardy now," said Spindle, who was next up. He sent his ball driving straight at Susan and Phoebe's ball. It connected with a smart click, sending their ball straight through the wicket. Spindle and Pete's ball glanced off the side and shot off past the wicket in the same direction as Bouncer's.

Susan and Phoebe gave a little cheer. "Thanks, Spindle. You've just put us through the wicket and given us an extra turn!" said Phoebe.

Pete gave Spindle a little jab with his elbow. "Guess I'm not the only one who knows how to knock a ball, eh?"

"Well, at least I hit what I was aiming for," said Spindle.

The two boys' teams had to waste a couple of turns just getting their balls back in line for the first wicket.

And so it went. Bouncer and Sam had just gotten through the fifth wicket, and Spindle and Pete had just wasted yet another turn trying to line up for the fourth, when it was Susan and Phoebe's turn. Freddie and Martha's ball lay just ahead of theirs, directly in line to go through the final set of wickets to the winner's stake. Susan marched up to the ball and tapped it. It rolled up and touched Freddie and Martha's ball.

"Ok, Phoebe, this is it," said Susan. "Knock their ball out of the way, and I'll drive ours home."

Phoebe walked up to the two balls and neatly croqueted Freddie and Martha's ball out of range. Susan then sent their ball through the wickets to the winner's stake.

"We win!" said Susan, grabbing Phoebe's hand and raising their arms in a victory salute.

The girls and Freddie walked back to where Bouncer, Sam, Spindle and Pete were arguing and pointing at each other with their mallets.

"Don't feel bad," said Susan. "I have to win. It's my birthday. We'd better go up to the terrace now. I think I see Janet coming to announce dinner."

She and the other girls turned and began walking toward the steps to the rose garden.

"Just a girls' game, eh? Couldn't be that difficult, eh?" jibed Freddie under his breath as he walked past the other boys.

Spindle took a swipe at him as he walked by. "Just wait till we get you on the rugby field, Inky!" he warned.

As they came up the steps to the rose garden, they could see a number of adults gathered on the terrace.

"Would you look at those clothes," said Spindle. "Looks like the way they dress at the Opera House."

"They'd never let the likes of us into the Opera House dressed as we are, even if we had the money," said Sam.

"Buck up, lads. Just be polite and be yourselves. After all, Susan knew we wasn't upper crust when she invited us," said Bouncer with an assured air he didn't really feel.

"Just hope I can keep my knees from knockin'," breathed Pete as they followed the girls and Freddie up the steps to the terrace.

"Ah, there's my Susan, my birthday girl!" cried out a tall, distinguished gentleman, breaking away from the covey of adults and coming toward them. He was elegantly dressed in black tails, diamond cufflinks sparkling at his wrists. "Have you been having a good time, my pet?" he asked as he walked up to Susan and embraced her.

"Oh, yes, Papa! I won both sets of croquet!" Susan smiled up at her father, her face flushed with pleasure.

"Well, then, that's a good omen for a sixteenth birthday, isn't it? Means you are destined to be a winner for the rest of your life."

"Oh, Papa, I was destined to be a winner when fate chose you for my father," said Susan coquettishly.

"What flattery. I see that finishing school has taught you a thing or two about getting your way!" he laughed. "Now, mind your manners, and introduce me to your guests. What a charming group of young people you have here."

"Oh, yes, I am truly blessed to have such fine friends," said Susan, turning to face the group of young people. "Ladies and gentlemen, may I present my father, Lord Alfred Davenville. Father, you have already met my friends Phoebe Smith, Rose Blackmun, Elizabeth Manson and Martha Simpson."

"Yes, of course, so pleased to see all of you again," said Lord Alfred. He took each girl's hand in turn, bowing slightly over it, as he looked into her eyes and pronounced her name. Each girl gave a slight curtsey and murmured "Lord Davenville" in response. Then, he turned his attention to the boys. "And whom might these fine young gentlemen be?"

"Father, may I present Mr. Freddie Simpson, Martha's cousin," said Susan.

"Ah, Mr. Simpson. You are the son of Stanford Simpson, the barrister, are you not? I know him well."

"That is correct," said Freddie, stepping up and shaking his hand. "It is an honor to meet you, Sir."

"And this is Mr. Brian Adams," announced Susan, as she and her father turned to the next boy in line.

"Mr. Adams," said Lord Alfred, extending his hand.

"Lord Davenville," murmured Spindle, bowing slightly over Lord Alfred's hand as he shook it.

"Adams. Are you by chance related to Mr. Thomas Adams of the Bridgefield Gas Works?"

"Yes, Sir. He is my father," said Spindle, somewhat astonished.

"A good man, your father," said Lord Alfred. "He's a valuable member of the town council, helps keep Bridgefield up to snuff in terms of progress."

Spindle smiled with pride as Lord Davenville turned to the next boy.

"May I present Mr. Samuel Baldwin," said Susan.

"Mr. Baldwin - of Baldwin the Butcher's?" inquired Lord Alfred as he clasped Sam's hand.

"Yes, sir, Lord Davenville, Sir," said Sam, blushing to the roots of his hair and looking down.

"Well, well, Mr. Baldwin, it's a pleasure to meet you. Your family runs a fine business - much better cuts of meat than can be bought in any London butcher shop, I assure you. These family businesses are the mainstay of our society, you know. Do you intend to carry on in the shop?"

"Yes, sir, I guess so ... at least that is what my da ... er, father wants," said Sam. He squirmed and glanced at Spindle as Lord Alfred turned his attention to Pete. Spindle grinned at Sam and gave him a thumbs-up.

"Father, this is Mr. Peter Court," said Susan.

"Ah, Mr. Court. So pleased you could come to Susan's party."

Pete fumbled slightly as he clasped Lord Alfred's hand. "Very pleased to be invited. It's an honor to meet you, Sir."

Lord Alfred turned to Bouncer. "And this is Mr. John Russell," said Susan.

"Mr. Russell," said Lord Alfred offering his hand.

Bouncer gripped his hand firmly. Lord Alfred paused and contemplated Bouncer's face as he was shaking his hand. "Russell? Not the son of Captain Henry Russell?"

Bouncer nodded. "Yes, Sir. He was my father, but I never knew him. He was killed before I was born."

"Well, this is truly remarkable. Captain Russell was a great military man and a hero."

"Yes, Sir, he was killed in the Boer War," said Bouncer.

"Mr. Russell, you can take pride in your heritage. Your father, Captain Henry Russell, and his men broke through the lines and began a rear attack on the Boers at Cherieberg. This action relieved the pressure on the rest of our troops and enabled us to win the battle, forcing the Boers to retreat to the Transvaal. Although he was killed, it was your father who saved the day for us through his courage and leadership."

"Thank you, Sir. Didn't know that. This is the first time I heard my father was a hero. Only knew he was killed in the war and that he came from a long line of military men."

"I also come from a long line of military men. My grandfather fought with Wellington at Waterloo, and my father distinguished himself in action in the Crimea. What about you, Mr. Russell? Do you plan to pursue a military career as well?"

"Haven't thought much about it, Sir. But if we go to war, I know I would volunteer," said Bouncer.

"The way things are developing in Europe, you may soon well have the opportunity to do just that," said Lord Alfred, frowning. Then, he smiled. "Well, enough of that. This is an occasion for celebration, not talk of war." He turned to Susan. "Why don't we join the rest of the guests and you can introduce your friends, my dear? Everyone is here except Uncle Frederick and Aunt Daisy, and they should join us shortly. You know Uncle Frederick and that damnable contraption of his."

Susan smiled, and turned to her friends. "Uncle Frederick has one of those horseless carriages," she explained. "It's called a Bristol something or other."

The boys glanced at each other in alarm as Susan and the girls followed Lord Alfred to the far side of the terrace where the adults were gathered in lounge chairs brought out for the occasion.

"Bloody hell, you don't suppose Uncle Frederick is the bloke in the Bristol Bomber, do you?" whispered Spindle. The other boys shrugged and looked concerned as they walked across to the other side of the terrace.

A tall, dark-haired gentleman was embracing Susan as the boys caught up with the rest of the group. "Happy birthday, my sweet Susan," he was saying. "Sixteen. Now, you are a proper young lady."

Susan smiled up at him happily. "Oh, Uncle Dickie, so pleased you could come. Papa said you were awfully busy." She turned to her friends. "Everyone, this is Uncle Dickie, my father's brother, Richard Davenville. He works in the colonial office."

After introductions had been made all around, Dickie turned to Susan. "Is Tommy coming, then?"

"Oh, no. Papa said he is much too busy with his patients." She turned back to her guests. "Uncle Tommy – Thomas Davenville – is my father's youngest brother. He just got married in August and is a surgeon in Harley Street. We all went up to London for the wedding. It was splendid. His bride, Ann, is just a few months older than I am," she explained. "Oh, dear. I see mother giving me a frown. Had better introduce you to the ladies now."

The group followed Susan to the lounge chairs where four ladies were seated, sipping lemonade. They were resplendently arrayed in elegant evening gowns. After Susan introduced her grandmother, Lady Victoria Davenville, her mother, Lady Mary Davenville, and her sister Paulina, she introduced Paulina's fiancé George Edmundson and then Edward Dumfries, the Vicar of St. John the Apostle, and his wife Helen.

These introductions had just been completed when the loud racket of an approaching vehicle cut into the conversation.

"Well, I hear Frederick and Daisy have arrived at last," remarked Lord Alfred. "That blasted contraption of his makes the most infernal noise!"

The boys glanced at each other apprehensively. In short order, the butler appeared at the doorway to the terrace followed by a flustered-looking dark-haired lady and a rather corpulent, ruddy-faced gentleman.

"Mr. and Mrs. Squires," announced the butler.

"Squires? Oh, bugger. It *is* him," muttered Spindle under his breath. The boys tried to shrink back behind the other guests as Squires and his wife walked out onto the terrace. Susan went up to greet them. Daisy embraced her, and then stepped back holding her at arm's length, looking at her appraisingly.

"My dear, just look at you," she said. "Our sweet little Susan all grown up into the proper young lady, now, aren't you?"

"So pleased you and Uncle Frederick are here for my party," said Susan. "But where is Rupert?"

"Oh, he's off up in London this weekend on a school assignment," said Squires. "That boy of ours is really going places when he graduates from the Poly. Smart as a whip, you know."

"Yes, well ... he really wanted to attend your party and sends you his birthday greetings and love," said Daisy somewhat hastily, giving Squires a look.

"We'll miss him," said Susan. "But come say hello to everyone and meet my friends."

As they followed Susan toward the other group of guests, Squires stopped short and pointed to the boys who were trying to make themselves inconspicuous by standing behind the girls. "What are those scoundrels doing here?" he roared rudely.

"What do you mean?" asked Susan. "They are my guests – friends of Martha's cousin Freddie Simpson. They attend King Charles School."

"I bloody well know where they go to school. I reported them to the headmaster. William Nicholson assured me that they received a severe caning for what they did," said Squires, shaking his fist at the boys. The other guests were now looking at the boys who were blushing and looking at the ground.

"Here, here, Squires," said Lord Alfred, stepping forward. "What could these boys have possibly done to upset you in this manner?"

"They were very rude to me on Station Road last Monday. Made obscene gestures at me. They were wearing King Charles uniforms, so I knew exactly where to report them. William Nicholson is a friend of mine, you know," he added importantly.

Lord Alfred turned to the boys. "Is this true, boys?" he asked.

Lady Mary turned to Paulina, who was seated next to her, and murmured, "Just what one could expect from the working class. I told Susan it was a mistake to invite them."

"Right you are," said George who was standing behind Paulina and sneering at the boys.

"Oh, mother, please," said Paulina. "You know how Uncle Frederick exaggerates." Lady Mary glared at her daughter, but said no more.

Bouncer stepped forward to respond to Lord Alfred's question. "Yes, Lord Davenville, Sir, it is true that we were rude to Mr. Squires and we received a caning for it, but that is not the whole story." The rest of the boys nodded their heads in agreement.

"Oh, posh!" blustered Squires. "You see, they admit it. They were extremely rude and they were punished for it. That's the end of the story!"

Lord Alfred turned and glared at Squires. "That's enough. The boys deserve a chance to tell their side of the story, and I want to hear it."

Squires started to say something, but Daisy put her hand on his arm. "That's right, Frederick. You've made an accusation in front of everyone, and in all fairness, the boys have a right to tell their side."

Squires mumbled something under his breath and turned even redder, but he acceded to his wife's request.

"Please continue, Mr. Russell," said Lord Alfred, turning his attention back to Bouncer.

Bouncer took a deep breath, looked directly at Lord Alfred, and told the story about the five of them calming the rearing carriage horse on Station Road.

"When the horse was finally calmed down, a gentleman got out of the carriage – "

"The man was drunk!" interrupted Squires, who could no longer contain himself.

"Oh, no, begging your pardon, Sir. The gentleman was not drunk; he was crippled, leaning on a walking stick. He gave each of us a half sovereign for helping prevent an accident," said Bouncer.

"Doddering old fool, he was. Holding up traffic, making me late for an appointment," shouted Squires. "When I asked him to get on with it, he was very rude to me."

"And, again, begging your pardon, Sir, but you were quite rude to him also," said Bouncer. Squires started to spout off again, but Lord Alfred held up his hand and nodded for Bouncer to continue.

"The gentleman gave us each his card and told us to call on him if we ever needed anything," Bouncer continued. He produced the gentleman's card from his pocket. "You see, I have mine here – Major General Phillip Wallis."

"My word! Major General Wallis, the hero of Khartoum?" exclaimed Vicar Dumfries.

"Yes, Sir," said Bouncer. "That is what Mr. Nicholson told us when he saw the card and the half sovereigns."

"Well, of course, that explains the walking stick," said the Vicar. "Major General Wallis lost both his legs in bringing water to Kitchener's relief column. He has wooden legs and has been decorated many times over for his heroism."

"Oh, Frederick, and you accused him of being drunk? Major General Wallis? You should be ashamed," said Daisy, frowning up at Squires and shaking her head.

"Well, how was I to know who he was?" muttered Squires sheepishly. "At any rate, it still is no excuse for these boys to be rude to me," he said in a louder, more defiant tone.

"Right. Now that we know the story, let's drop it," said Lord Alfred. "After all, it is Susan's birthday – a time for celebration and gaiety, not bickering." He turned to his daughter. "Susan, lead us to table and show us where we are to sit," he said.

Susan smiled at him in relief. "Please, everyone, come to the dining table. You'll find place cards with your names in front of your table setting."

"How nice, Susan. Demonstrating what you've learned in finishing school, I see," remarked Lady Victoria as Richard helped her to her feet.

As the guests walked toward the table, Lord Alfred took Squires aside. "Just a bit of advice. Best not to go on about that incident any further. I saw Wallis at a meeting in London on Thursday, and he told me all about how these boys had performed a heroic deed in preventing an accident with his horse. He was most impressed with them and quite upset with the rudeness of the Bristol driver. Wallis doesn't know the name of the driver of that contraption and will probably forget about it unless you continue to carry on. I urge you to drop the whole matter and not bring it up again. 'Twould be most embarrassing to me if Wallis were to discover that the driver is my brother-in-law," he warned. "You understand my meaning?"

Squires shrugged his shoulders. "All right, Lord Alfred. I'll not say anything further, but I don't care if it was Major General Wallis - those boys deserved to be punished for their rudeness ... "

Lord Alfred raised a finger and waggled it back and forth in Squires's face, and Squires, heeding the warning, fell silent.

After the guests were all seated, Lord Alfred presiding at one end of the table, Susan at the other, the butler supervised the maids who served the first course of oysters baked in the half shell. A wine steward poured champagne all the way around. When the servants had gone back into the house, Lord Alfred raised his glass. "A toast to Susan, our birthday girl," he said. "Rather, a toast to our young lady, now that she is sixteen."

"Hear, hear!" exclaimed Uncle Dickie as the rest of the guests raised their glasses in salute and drank.

"Thank you, Papa," said Susan. "And now, I would like to propose a toast to Paulina and George, who just became engaged a couple of weeks ago. May you have a long and happy marriage."

"Congratulations, Paulina. Have you set the wedding date yet?" asked Helen Dumfries, the vicar's wife.

"Yes," said Paulina, happily smiling at George and squeezing his hand under the table. "We're to be married on Easter Sunday in April."

"Taking our wedding trip on the White Star Line, the maiden voyage of *The Titanic*. She sails later that week," said George pompously.

"*The Titanic!*" exclaimed Pete. "Supposed to be the fastest ship, yet. My father is a steward on *The Lusitania* that set all the speed records so far."

"A steward, you say? Well, he wouldn't get to enjoy the luxuries, as we will. We have a suite with our own private promenade on the upper class deck," said George.

"Thanks to Papa," said Paulina hastily. "The trip is a wedding present from my parents," she explained for the benefit of the other guests.

"Oh, it will be grand," exclaimed Lady Victoria. "Dickie and I sailed to New York last year on *The Lusitania*, you know. Superb accommodations. Dickie had business in America for the colonial office, and I just went along for the pleasure of it."

"That's right," said Richard, patting her hand. "And a great deal of pleasure she had. There was a certain Italian count on board who made it his duty to see that mother was never lacking for entertainment."

"Oh, Dickie, you know he was just being friendly because we were seated at the Captain's table. He was quite charming, though," she said with a twinkle in her eye.

"Charming, indeed. A bit of a rogue, I'd say," said Richard with a chuckle. Then he turned his attention to Susan. "And what of Miss Susan? Now that you're a lady and will soon be out of finishing school, what do you plan to do? Break a lot of young hearts, I'd wager."

Before Susan could respond, Lady Mary, who was sitting on Lord Alfred's left, said, "She will do what other young ladies of our class do. We will present her in the spring. She will meet all the *proper* eligible young gentlemen of our class and make a suitable marriage, just as Paulina has done."

An embarrassed hush fell over the table as the guests noticed her looking meaningfully at the boys as she emphasized the word "proper."

Lord Alfred put his hand over hers and squeezed it. "I believe our Susan has other ideas, Mary," he said.

"Yes," said Susan. "I don't fancy getting married right away. I'd like to have some adventure first. Possibly a career."

"A career? How fascinating!" said Aunt Daisy. "Young ladies these days have ever so many more choices than we had at your age. What sort of career do you have in mind?"

"I believe I would like to study medicine and become a nurse," said Susan. "Uncle Tommy could help me. Perhaps I could go to London to live with him while I am studying," she said.

"Unthinkable!" whispered Mary, abruptly removing her hand from under Lord Alfred's and glaring at him.

"We'll talk about it later," he whispered back.

The servants returned to serve the second course, ladling vichyssoise into the guests' soup bowls from a silver tureen.

"What is this?" mumbled Sam. "Can't be soup. It's cold."

"It's vichyssoise," said Rose, who was sitting between Sam and Freddie. "It's just a fancy French name for cold potato and leek soup. You eat it just like regular soup."

Sam followed Rose's lead and tasted the soup. "Mmmmm. It's good. Never had cold soup before."

"Tell us, Richard, what's new at the Colonial Office? From what I've been reading in *The Times*, you must be quite busy," said Vicar Dumfries.

"Yes, you're right there. The empire is not like it used to be. New dominions to administer. Famine here, famine there. Uprisings on our colony borders."

"What of South Africa? Has it settled down? Are the Boers behaving themselves?" asked Squires, who up to this point had remained silent.

"Creating the new dominion has caused less tension, in my opinion. Now that Kitchener's been named consul general of Egypt, things are improving there as well."

"Gold and diamonds – the cause of all that trouble," said the vicar, shaking his head sadly. "Greed can make man forget his true destiny. The Chinese are at it, too, I understand. How does that affect Hong Kong?"

Richard took a sip of champagne before responding. "Everything is safe in Hong Kong because the Chinese are not looking for land expansion. Rather, they are engaged in an internal revolution – another of many in that part of the world. Hong Kong is ours under treaty, so the Chinese may do what they may." Not wanting to dominate the conversation, Richard turned to Lord Alfred.

"How is the world from the viewpoint of higher levels?" he asked. "It appears the Germans and the Austro-Hungarians are arming to the teeth."

Lord Alfred put down his soup spoon and sat back in his chair with a concerned frown on his face. "A spark could set them off, I'm afraid. Unlike the Chinese, the Germans and the Hungarians want land and commercial expansion."

"Commercial expansion?" asked the vicar.

Before Lord Alfred could respond, Squires interjected. "Means they want more money, of course."

Lord Alfred frowned at him. "It's not as simple as that, Squires. Has to do more with trade and markets. You see, industrialized countries such as our own can produce more goods than they can consume. Thus, they must find external markets."

"So what does that have to do with the Germans being upset?" queried Squires.

Richard, sensing the tension between his brother and Squires, jumped in. "Jealousy of our Empire," he said. "You see, our colonies and dominions provide a vast market for our production. The colonies provide us with inexpensive raw materials to produce the goods that we in turn ship back to them. What we charge is purely up to us as there is no competition. The Germans have industrialized well, and they have a huge production potential, but their market is limited because they have few colonies. They have colonized only those areas we British thought were not worthwhile."

"Quite right," said Squires. "If it wasn't for us, most of the people in our colonies would still be wearing loin cloths and eating wild plants." He looked around the table for appreciation at his attempted humor, but received none. The other guests were staring at their plates, and Lord Alfred was glowering at him.

"Tut, tut," murmured the vicar. "All men are equal in the sight of God."

The conversation was suspended, as the servants appeared to serve the main course, roasted saddle of lamb with root vegetables. When the servants had departed and the wine steward had poured claret, Lord Alfred spoke again.

"Despite the royal connection to the Kaiser, there is a great deal of tension between the Germans and ourselves. The Kaiser has ambitions for a Navy and an empire like our own. King George has tried to mediate and to temper the situation, but, unfortunately, the Kaiser will not listen. Family jealousy, I suppose."

"King George is such a dear man," interjected Lady Mary. "We had special invitations to his coronation last year. Alfred is on the Privy Council, you know, and is a personal friend of the King. They were at Eton together."

Lord Alfred laid his hand over hers and gave her a small, meaningful smile. "The King has many friends, my dear," he said quietly.

"Our Navy is the biggest and best in the world. The Kaiser cannot hope to match that," remarked George. Paulina smiled at him and squeezed his hand under the table.

"Quite right, our Navy is the best, but it would be a mistake to underestimate the Germans," said Lord Alfred. "They have been building battleships."

"That's quite true, Lord Davenville, Sir," Spindle suddenly blurted out. The adults looked at him as if he were some sort of strange insect that had just invaded their picnic. Lord Alfred, however, smiled and nodded for him to continue.

"My brother is in the Navy, Sir," he said somewhat nervously, "and he says the Germans have built many submarines and there is no defense against them."

"Submarines? Sounds like some sort of American slang word," said George. Paulina glared at him and removed her hand.

"Don't be silly, George," she said in a low voice.

"I've read about these submarines," said the vicar. "Some sort of underwater boat. But how are they a threat to our battleships?"

Spindle looked at Lord Alfred who nodded for him to continue.

"Well, Sir, my brother says they fire a kind of self-propelled underwater bomb called a torpedo. They can do this and not be detected until it is too late. They can rip a hole in a ship and sink it or cause it to explode."

"An underwater bomb! Sounds like something we British would invent," said George, trying to regain his credibility with Paulina. "Surely, our Navy has these underwater boats?"

"My brother says he has seen only one during the entire time he's been in the Navy," said Spindle.

"Well, from what I understand, the French have more to fear from the Germans than we do," remarked the vicar.

"Ho! If the French and the Germans go at it, well be it," spouted Squires. "Bloody French have always been a thorn in England's side – always out for themselves and their own benefit. I say let them have at it, and we won't have to get involved."

"Again, it is not that simple, Squires. We could very well get involved, and I do wish you would keep your remarks about other nationalities to yourself. They are not welcome in my house," said Lord Alfred, glaring at him again.

Another embarrassed hush fell over the table as Squires reddened at the rebuke.

Richard broke the silence. "Oh, yes, we could certainly be involved if Germany attacks France because of the agree – ." He broke off and glanced at his brother.

"It's all right," said Lord Alfred. "It's no longer a secret. Came out in *The Times*."

"Yes, well, as I was saying, we could easily become involved in a war because of our agreement with France and Russia," continued Richard.

"Ah, yes," said the vicar. "I do recall reading something about it in *The Times*. Seems France and Russia made a secret pact back in 1890 to come to one another's aid if either was attacked. Seems Britain has joined the pact – something they're calling a Triple Entente."

"That's correct, Vicar Dumfries," said Lord Alfred. "We actually entered into such an agreement with France in 1904, and then in 1907, we formally joined with France in their Dual Alliance with Russia, making it a Triple Alliance. This was all top secret until just recently. So, you see, we have little choice. If France is attacked, we must go to war as well." He picked up his glass of claret and contemplated it somberly for a moment before taking a sip.

"My, my, all this talk of war. So depressing," commented Lady Victoria, shaking her head.

Lord Alfred smiled at her. "You're quite right, Mother. Let's talk of other more pleasant things."

"Has anyone read Mr. Kipling's latest book? I believe it's called *Rewards and Fairies* and has to do with England's history, particularly in our area. Since his return to England, Mr. Kipling has very nearly been our neighbor. Has a house in Sussex Downs, you know," commented Daisy.

Susan smiled at her aunt. "Haven't read his latest, but we read *Puck of Pook's Hill* in school last year."

"We read *Kim* at King Charles," said Bouncer. "Our teacher told us Mr. Kipling's son John is just about our age. Wonder what it would be like to be the son of a Nobel Prize winner?"

"You'd have to know how to spell and mind your grammar," said Spindle. The girls giggled at his comment.

"I would be in deep trouble all the time," said Pete.

"Perhaps, but the son of a Nobel Prize winner would probably not know how to play croquet," retorted Elizabeth as she took another sip of claret.

"Or kick a ball," said Freddie. Pete blushed as the boys laughed at his expense.

More small talk among the adults and banter amongst the boys and girls ensued as the guests finished the main course. Soon, the butler appeared at Susan's side. She looked up at him. "Yes, Hendricks?"

He cleared his throat. "Miss Susan, I am to inform you that everything has been prepared in the music room as you instructed."

"Thank you, Hendricks," she said, then announced to the guests, "Ladies and Gentlemen, shall we adjourn to the music room for dessert and best of all opening of presents."

Lord Alfred looked at his pocket watch. "Splendid. Plenty of time before we must leave for the opera. To the music room it is, then."

"The music room. How nice," said Lady Victoria as Richard assisted her to her feet. "I feel a bit of chill in the air now, although it has been lovely to be able to dine on the terrace. Quite a lovely autumn this year."

The guests reconvened in the music room where they gathered around the piano and sang "Happy Birthday" to Susan as Paulina played. Then, Susan cut and served the cake while the wine steward served more champagne. As the guests sipped champagne and ate cake, Susan opened presents from the adults. When the last of the adults' presents had been opened, exclaimed over and set on display on a side table, Lord Alfred signaled the butler. "Are the carriages ready?" he asked.

"Yes, Sir. They are at the door."

"Good. Right on time." He turned to the rest of the guests and announced, "Ladies and gentlemen, it is time for us to be off to the opera. The carriages are waiting at the door."

He turned to Susan. "My dear, you and your young guests have a good time. We are seeing Mr. Mozart's "The Marriage of Figaro," which is rather lengthy, so we shan't be back until after midnight. Hendricks will see that the black carriage is available at 10:30 to take your guests home."

"Thank you, Papa, and thank you for the wonderful party," said Susan.

"Quite enjoyed it," said Lord Alfred. He turned to the boys. "Quite pleased to meet you, young gentlemen, and honored to have Wallis's saviors at my house."

"Thank you, Lord Davenville. We're very honored to have been invited," said Bouncer, speaking for the group.

Lord and Lady Davenville and their entourage departed for the opera with the exception of the vicar and his wife who left in their own carriage. Vicar Dumfries had to prepare for an early morning sermon.

When the adults had gone, Susan turned to her friends. "Let's go to the blue sitting room," she said. "It's much more cozy. I've had Hendricks light the fire in the fireplace. I'll open your presents there, and we'll have more champagne and cake and perhaps play a parlour game."

After they had gone to the sitting room and gathered in chairs around the fireplace, maids poured more champagne and departed, leaving birthday cake, champagne and cider on a side table.

"Now, we can relax," said Susan.

"That champagne has made me plenty relaxed," giggled Rose. "Is anyone else feeling giddy?"

"I've never drunk champagne before," said Spindle. "It's not as heavy as cider or beer. Must not pack as much of a wallop." Suddenly, he hiccupped loudly, and the room erupted in gales of laughter.

"The trick ish in knowing when to shtop drinking it," said Phoebe not realizing she was slurring.

"Right," said Pete. "Let's have some more."

"Yes, let's have some more while Susan opens her presents," said Martha. "Can't wait to see what everyone got for her."

"I'll pour," said Freddie, jumping up from his seat, and immediately sitting back down. "Phew! I got up too fast," he said. He got up more slowly, stood for a moment to get his bearings, and walked unsteadily to the side table to get two champagne bottles. "Looks as if there's just enough left to fill everyone's glasses one more time," he said.

"When the champagne's gone, we have cider," said Susan, with a giggle. She began opening presents, saving the boys' till last.

After she had displayed a cameo brooch from Martha, she picked up Freddie's package and unwrapped it. "Oh, how lovely!" she exclaimed. "A music box. Thank you, Freddie."

She wound it up, and a tiny ballerina began twirling to the tinkly strains of "Swan Lake." Then she picked up Sam's package wrapped in butcher paper. "Hmmmmm. This is from Sam," she said. "Wonder what it can be?"

Sam blushed and looked down at his feet. "Not much, I'm afraid," he mumbled.

Susan opened the package revealing the pound of sausages nestled inside. "Oh, Sam, how nice. I love these pork sausages. Are they from your father's butcher shop?"

Sam nodded, still refusing to look up.

"Never without sausages when Sam's around," said Spindle with a chuckle. "That's why we call him Banger."

"Well, I think it's a lovely gift. I'll ask cook to prepare them for breakfast tomorrow morning," said Susan.

She picked up Pete's package. "And this is from Pete," she announced. "Let's see what this is." She held up a mauve-colored fringed silk shawl. "Oh, how beautiful!" she exclaimed. "This will go very nicely with my new ivory silk dress from Grandmother. Thank you, Pete."

Pete held up his champagne glass. "Something elegant for an elegant girl," he said. "I'd love to see you in that outfit."

He didn't see Spindle and Bouncer glancing at him with a strange expression on their faces.

"Next we have a package from Spindle," said Susan, tearing it open and revealing an identical silk shawl in emerald green. "Oh, my!" she exclaimed. "Now, I have two shawls! This one will go perfectly with my green satin!"

"How did you end up with the same thing, Spindle?" asked Pete. "Were you following me around?"

"No, not at all," said Spindle, laughing at the irony of it. "I saw it in the shop and bought it because it matches Susan's eyes."

Susan's eyes narrowed as she looked at Spindle. "But we've never met before tonight," she said. "How did you know the color of my eyes?"

"Oh, ah... I, er, that is, Freddie told me," said Spindle.

"And how did Freddie know?" asked Susan.

"How did I know ...how did I know what?" blustered Freddie, shaking his head to clear the champagne haze.

"The color of my eyes," said Susan.

Freddie opened his mouth and paused when he saw Spindle staring intently at him.

"I told him," Martha interjected quickly, and Freddie's mouth snapped shut. "He asked what colors you wear so the boys would have an idea what to get for you."

"Oh, I see. How thoughtful," said Susan. "Well, Spindle, I love the green shawl and the reason you chose that color."

Spindle smiled at Susan and raised his glass to her in a silent salute. She smiled at him for a moment, and then picked up the last package.

"And this is from John – Bouncer," she said. She opened it, and everyone gasped as she pulled out another silk shawl, this one in midnight blue.

"Another shawl!" she exclaimed. "It's little wonder that you are chums. You apparently all think alike!"

Bouncer laughed good-naturedly. "Had a difficult time keeping mum when you opened Pete's and Spindle's," he said. "Had no idea we all bought the same thing. At least they're in different colors."

"They're wonderful," said Susan. "The blue is perfect for my blue taffeta. Thank you, Bouncer. Now, I have a complete wardrobe of shawls."

As her guests continued to make jokes and exclaim over the presents, Susan moved about the room turning off lights until there was only a warm glow provided by the fireplace and one corner lamp. When she returned to the group, she noticed that most of them had finished the champagne. Martha looked up at her. "Have you chosen, yet?" she asked in a soft voice.

Susan gave her a slight nod, then announced to the group. "We need to have a small break. All that champagne, you know. Girls come with me upstairs to my bedroom and we can freshen up a bit. Gentlemen, there is a water closet down the hallway next to the library. Feel free to help yourselves to the cider and more cake while we are gone."

After the girls had departed, Sam and Pete both jumped up and raced to the door. "Bloody hell!" exclaimed Sam. "I didn't think I could hold it any longer, and I didn't want to ask where the toilet was!"

"Me neither," said Pete. "Me first!" he told Sam as he elbowed past him in the doorway.

The boys took turns visiting the water closet and helping themselves to the hard cider on the side table. "Now cider is something I know about," said Spindle. "You can get this in the White Horse."

"Not till you're sixteen," joked Bouncer, taking a big gulp of cider.

"Let me try that shider," said Freddie, wobbling toward them with his glass held out in front of him. "Never had champagne or shider before. Mother won't allow it."

Bouncer filled Freddie's glass, and he took a sip. "Hey, thash good!" he said with a foolish grin. His knees buckled and he promptly sat down on the floor with a thump.

"Get up, Freddie. You're drunk," laughed Spindle, as he and Bouncer attempted to haul Freddie to his feet.

"But I didn't shpill any... " said Freddie, proudly holding up his glass of cider.

"Wonder what Susan and those girls are up to," said Pete. "Remember, Susan said she got first pick of which one of us she wants to be with. Hope it's me."

"Hope all you want. She's going to choose me," said Spindle. "I have this feeling..."

"In your willie?" giggled Freddie. Spindle cuffed his ear.

"No, you rotter. I can just tell by the way she looks at me that I'm the one," he said.

"I hope no one chooses me," said Sam. "I wouldn't know what to do with a girl."

"Don't worry, Sam. Girls find your freckles adorable," said Bouncer playfully. He turned to Spindle. "Don't be so bloody sure Susan will pick you. After all, she noticed that I shave," he reminded him.

"Nah. That won't get you anywhere. Remember, I picked out the shawl that matches her eyes," retorted Spindle.

"Yeah, and you bloody well nearly gave us away," said Pete. "How did you know that Susan had green eyes, anyway?" he jibed.

Upstairs, Susan gathered the girls around her in her bedroom. "He's here," she announced.

"Who's here?" asked Elizabeth.

"The boy I said I was interested in, but didn't know if he had a girlfriend. I saw him from a distance at the festival last summer, but I didn't know what his name was. He's the one I choose."

"Oh, how exciting," breathed Rose. "Which one is it? Is it Spindle?"

"I'm not telling yet," said Susan.

"Then, how are you going to choose him?"

"I have a plan," said Susan with a mysterious air. The girls gathered closer around. "I have devised a game for us to play. It's a variation on Blind Man's Bluff. The boys will be blindfolded. Then, I will stand in front of the boy I have chosen. The rest of you can choose the one you want. The rule of the game is that the boys must not know who they're with. We won't talk and give ourselves away by the sound of our voices. The boys can talk and touch, and we can touch them. We will lead them out into the gardens where we can be alone. And, just so it becomes more difficult for the boys to guess, after they are blindfolded, each one of us can put on one of my birthday presents. There are the three shawls, the cameo brooch from Martha, and the opal ring Papa gave me."

"But I don't understand. What is the point of the game? How does one know if you've won?" asked Phoebe.

"It's not that kind of game," said Susan. "None of the boys will know for certain who they're with. Only we will know, and we must make a pact to never tell who we are with. Remember, you cannot talk or whisper to your partner, only touch!"

"Mmmmm. This sounds exciting," said Elizabeth. "Maybe kissing."

"That's the idea," said Susan. "We can find out what it's like without feeling threatened. The boys not knowing who they're with adds to the excitement, don't you think?"

"I see what you mean!" cried Rose. "I like the idea – makes me tingly to think about it, but how will we end the game without them finding out?"

"I've thought of that," said Susan. "The carriage will be at the door at 10:30 to drive everyone home, so when you hear St. John's bell chime 10:00, you must lead your partner back to the sitting room and leave before they are allowed to take off their blindfolds. Meet me back here in my bedroom, and we'll take off the shawls and cameo, and I'll put the ring back on. Then we'll join them in the sitting room again as if nothing happened."

"This is going to be fun!" said Martha, with a sparkle in her eye. "Trying to think where I'll take my partner."

"Anywhere but the summerhouse. I get that," said Susan, with a sly smile.

"Mmmmm. The summerhouse! Are you going to do what Paulina did?" asked Rose, arching her eyebrows and rolling her eyes.

"I'm not saying," said Susan. "And none of you must say who I have chosen or who you are with. You must swear that you'll never tell. It will be our secret. Do you swear?"

"I swear!" cried the girls in unison, crossing their hearts.

"Now, what about the boys?" asked Martha. "Do you think they'll go along with this?"

"Oh, I think they'll be most happy to go along with it," said Susan. "Especially after they've had a glass or two of that cider."

"I think I could use a glass of cider myself," said Phoebe. "I think they're all rather attractive, even if they aren't in our class – except Freddie, of course," she added for Martha's benefit.

"Oh, I don't care about class," said Susan. "These boys are much more exciting than the ones Mother would deem proper. Boys in our social set are so ... so stodgy, or pompous, like George."

"Well, Paulina apparently finds George exciting," said Rose. The girls all giggled, remembering Susan's story.

Freddie was slouched in his chair, laughing and ducking as Spindle took another swipe at him when the girls walked back into the sitting room.

"Is everyone ready for more cider?" inquired Martha with a devilish grin.

"I'm ready for anything!" laughed Spindle as the boys all held out their glasses for a refill.

* * *

# Chapter 4
## *Too Much Ginger*

O N MONDAY MORNING Pete, Bouncer and Spindle were gathered under the conker tree on the playground at King Charles School.

Pete rubbed his head. "I still feel terrible. I drank too much champagne Saturday night."

"I know what you mean. I still have a headache, too," said Bouncer, rolling his eyes. "Shouldn't have drunk all that cider on top of the champagne. Hope I didn't make a fool of myself."

"Speaking of making a fool of oneself, poor Freddie was so drunk, I had to carry him into his house," laughed Spindle. "The butler opened the door, and his mum stood there scolding us the whole time I helped put him to bed. It was a good thing his dad was up in London."

"Do you remember what happened when the girls blindfolded us?" asked Pete. "All I remember is someone taking me by the hand and leading me outside. I think I sort of blanked out after that. The next thing I remember is stumbling into my house, trying not to wake up my mum."

"I don't remember much, either, but I do remember kissing a girl," said Bouncer. "I can't be sure who she was, except that I think she was wearing a shawl. What about you Spindle? What do you remember?"

"I'm not telling," said Spindle, with a sly grin. "Except that my girl was wearing a shawl. Felt like the one I gave Susan."

Pete scratched his head. "Now that you mention it, I remember that the girl I was with was wearing a shawl, too," he said with a frown.

Spindle burst out laughing. "I think I smell a rat," he said. "Those girls must have each worn something of Susan's so we wouldn't be able to tell who we were with. I was sure I was with Susan, but now I can't be sure. I wonder what Freddie and Sam remember?"

"They were both drunker than us, especially Freddie. I doubt they remember much of anything at all," said Bouncer.

"What are you blokes up to?" called out a voice, interrupting their speculation.

The boys turned and saw a tall skinny redheaded fellow striding jauntily towards them with a book bag slung haphazardly across his bony shoulders.

"Well, if it isn't Ginger, at last!" exclaimed Pete.

"What's new?" asked Ginger, as he joined them under the conker tree.

"Welcome back. How was your holiday in Great Yarmouth?" asked Spindle.

"Great Yarmouth, you say," said Ginger, raising his eyebrows. "I was hop picking in Lamberhurst. Made five shillings."

"Alwood, our teacher, thinks you were staying with your aunt in Great Yarmouth," cautioned Pete. "Watch out for Alwood. He uses the cane."

"Aunt? I don't have an aunt. Who told him that?"

The boys shook their heads. "We don't know, but it could have been Freddie Simpson," said Spindle, winking at Bouncer and Pete.

"Well, who's this Freddie Simpson, then? Never heard of him before," said Ginger. "What right does he have saying I'm visiting my aunt in Great Yarmouth? When I see him, I'll black his eye!"

"He's new at King Charles this year. Dad's a barrister, and they live in Queen Anne's Gardens," said Bouncer.

"What's he doing at King Charles then? Why isn't he up at Eton or the like?"

"He was until this year, but he's an only child, and his mum wanted him to be at home," said Spindle.

"Hmmmph!" snorted Ginger derisively. "Sounds a bit of a mum's boy to me."

"Oh, we all thought he was a bit of a wanker at first, too. We started calling him Inky because he was being clever in class, and Alwood chose him to fill the ink wells. But, we straightened him out, and he took some canings along with the rest of us," explained Bouncer.

"That's right," said Spindle. "He's part of our club now. We call ourselves The Bottom Five because we all got caned twice on the first day of school. Inky is our social director because he got us invited to Lord Davenville's daughter's birthday party last Saturday. And he was with us when we rescued Major General Wallis."

"Lord Davenville! That's about as upper crust as you can get, next to the Royal Family! And what's this about rescuing a Major General?" exclaimed Ginger.

"It's a long story. Lots to tell. But speaking of the devil, here comes Freddie now," said Pete nodding toward Freddie who was walking slowly toward them, along with Sam.

"Oh, there's Sam Baldwin. Haven't seen him since last term," said Ginger.

"He's a member of The Bottom Five, too," said Spindle. "We call him Banger, because of the sausages."

Ginger looked at him questioningly.

Spindle laughed. "We'll fill you in later," he said, as Freddie and Sam arrived.

"Freddie, meet Ginger – real name, Patrick Murphy. Ginger, meet Freddie Simpson," said Bouncer.

"Pleased to meet you, Ginger. I've heard about you," said Freddie, extending his hand.

"Pleased to meet you, too... Inky," said Ginger, shaking Freddie's hand. Freddie winced and reddened upon hearing his nickname. Ginger turned to Sam. "Good to see you, too, Sam. How are things at the butcher shop?"

Sam grinned at Ginger. "Pleased you're back, Ginger. We're all in the same class together. Things are fine at the butcher shop, except ..." Sam's face darkened. "Except my dad wants me to carry on there after I'm out of school, but I want to be a veterinarian."

"How are you feeling, Freddie?" asked Spindle.

"Bloody awful. I was sick all day yesterday and my mother really scolded me all day long, threatening to tell my father when he comes home this weekend. After I told her we weren't drunk before Lord Davenville left and promised I wouldn't drink champagne again, I finally got her to promise not to tell," said Freddie. "Thanks, Spindle, for helping me into the house."

"Well, that's what friends are for," said Spindle. "Remember, The Bottom Five stick together. What about you, Sam? Did you have a hangover?"

"Oh, yes. My dad kept trying to pour iron water down me all day yesterday. Said something about somebody named Beau Nash and that he'd discovered a cure for hangovers, but even the thought of water made me sick."

"Do you remember what happened at the party?" asked Bouncer.

"I remember Susan playing the piano, but everything's quite foggy after that," said Freddie, his face reddening.

"I remember the girls finally left the room so we could go to the toilet," said Sam. "I thought I was going to burst!"

"Don't you remember being blindfolded?" asked Pete.

"Vaguely," said Freddie. "Were we playing Blind Man's Bluff?"

"Yes," laughed Spindle, "but it was a whole different version than I'd ever played before. The girls invented the rules. Don't you remember?"

"I remember the blindfold and being led around outside," said Sam. "I think I got sick in a flower bed."

"Do you remember anything about the girl who was leading you around?" asked Bouncer.

Sam scratched his head and thought for a second. "Well, she was taller than me."

"Bloody hell, Sam! All those girls were taller than you!" roared Spindle.

Sam blushed. "Well, the only other thing I remember is that she put my hand on her chest and I could feel a brooch. It felt like a cameo brooch – like that one that Martha gave Susan."

"What's all this about girls and blindfolds?" asked Ginger.

"Another long story," said Spindle. "You see, we were at this birthday party for Susan Davenville, and ..." He was interrupted by the sound of the school bell.

"We'd better get to class before we're late! Don't want another caning to start off the second week!" said Freddie.

"We'll tell you all about it later, Ginger. Maybe at lunch time," said Spindle as he and the rest of the boys ran toward the school door.

When they entered the classroom, Alwood was standing at the lectern counting pupils as they took their seats. Ginger found a vacant seat in the front row.

"You must be Patrick Murphy. How's your aunt in Great Yarmouth?" asked Alwood, peering at Ginger over his wire-rimmed glasses.

"My friends call me Ginger," he answered.

"You are Patrick Murphy here, and you call me 'Sir,'" said Alwood, frowning.

"That's right, Sir, you call me Patrick Murphy. Only my friends call me Ginger." The classroom erupted in laughter.

"The class will come to order," called out Alwood, smacking his cane on the lectern and squelching the boys' laughter. "Stop your insolence, Mr. Murphy. There will be no comedians in my class."

"I'm just practicing, Sir. I want to be a comedian when I leave school," said Ginger.

"We will get to your career later, Mr. Murphy," said Alwood. He turned his gaze on James Taylor who was sitting next to Ginger. "I hope you haven't smoked that pipe lately, Mr. Taylor."

"No, Sir. The headmaster confiscated it. My dad said if I smoke again, he will make me confess in front of his congregation."

"It will be two weeks' suspension next time," said Alwood looking at the class. "Let that be a lesson to all of you."

"The King smokes cigars, and he's not dethroned for a week," said Ginger loudly.

Again, the class roared with laughter. Alwood picked up the blackboard eraser and threw it at Ginger intending to hit him on the head. Ginger ducked. The eraser hit the pupil sitting behind him.

"You hit me in the eye," called out the student holding his hand over his right eye.

"You have two, don't you?" said Alwood. "Besides you deserve it. You were laughing at Mr. Murphy's joke. The next time I will use the cane."

The class went silent. Alwood opened the attendance book and called their names.

"Patrick Murphy," said Alwood looking at Ginger when he got to the 'M's.

"Here, Sir," replied Ginger smiling.

"Where is your note?" asked Alwood. "The note from your aunt in Great Yarmouth saying you were on holiday there?"

"He's trapped now," whispered Bouncer.

"He'll find a way," murmured Spindle.

"Where is the note, Mr. Murphy?" asked Alwood again.

"I forgot the note, Sir, but I have a postcard," said Ginger.

"Postcard, what postcard? I need a note," said Alwood impatiently.

"Here it is, Sir," Ginger said producing a colored card from his jacket pocket and handing it to Alwood.

"It's from someone named Mabel saying she is having a wonderful time at the seaside," said Alwood, examining the card. "It doesn't say anything about you being there."

"Look at the front of the card, Sir."

Alwood turned the card over, looking closely at the cartoon picture. "What I see is a small man wearing a large woman's bathing costume and a large woman wearing only Wellington boots."

"Read the caption, Sir," said Ginger smiling. "It will answer your question."

Alwood read the print and smiled.

"Read it aloud, Sir, so the class can hear," suggested Ginger.

"'I wish I had gone hop picking instead of diving for oysters,' says the man's caption. ' I know. It's better than getting your feet wet,' says the woman's."

The classroom erupted with laughter.

"That's enough laughter," said Alwood scratching his head. "This will do until tomorrow when you bring me the note." He grinned and put the card on his lectern.

"I knew Ginger would come up with something," whispered Spindle.

"What did the postcard have to do with it?" asked Bouncer. "And who is Mabel anyway?"

"Didn't make sense to me," whispered Pete.

"I know, but it sounded funny," said Spindle smiling.

The rest of the morning passed without incident as Alwood led a discussion about careers based on the boys' essays. At lunchtime, the boys convened on the playground to share their sandwiches and bring Ginger up to date on the events of the previous week.

"So, none of you knows which girl you were with at the party?" asked Ginger after the boys told him about the blindfold game.

The boys shook their heads.

"Well, I want to see these girls," proclaimed Ginger. "Do you think they'll be at the same spot at the girls' school?"

"If they are, maybe they'll talk about who they were with at the party," said Spindle. "Let's sneak over there again."

"Not me," said Freddie. "I don't want to risk having another caning. I'm in enough trouble with my mother as it is."

"Me neither," said Sam. "I'm afraid that headmistress is going to spot us and then we'll really be in for it."

"Well, I'll take Ginger over to our spot behind the hedge," said Spindle. "How about you, Bouncer? Pete? Want to go along?"

"Sure," said Bouncer. "I'm curious to hear what they have to say about the party."

"Me, too," said Pete.

After taking a cautious look around the playground for any teachers prowling the vicinity, the four boys ran into the woods toward Rosemead School for Girls.

"There's the hedge that separates the girls' playground from the woods," whispered Spindle. "From here on, we have to crawl so we won't be spotted over the hedge."

Ginger nodded, and the four boys crept up to the hedge on their hands and knees. Spindle held up his hand and peeked through the hole in the hedge. "They're not there," he whispered. "Oh, wait. I see them now. They're on that seat up near the other corner of the hedge. Looks like Susan, Martha and Phoebe. I don't see Rose and Elizabeth."

He drew back from the hedge, and Bouncer crept up to look through the hole. "They're too far away for us to hear what they're saying," he said. "We'll have to get closer."

"The only way we can do that is to go over the barbed wire fence into Farmer Tindle's pasture, and crawl along the hedge to where they are sitting," said Spindle.

"I don't think we ought to do that," said Pete. "The headmistress might see us when we stand up to climb over the fence."

"Oh, come on," said Ginger. "I want to see what these girls are up to."

"Easy for you to say," said Bouncer. "You haven't gotten any canings yet. Besides, if the headmistress spotted us, then the girls would know we've been spying on them."

"Well, they don't know me, do they?" said Ginger. "I'll go and see what I can find out. You can stay here and wait for me."

"All right, but be careful, Ginger. If you get caught, we won't be able to do this anymore because they'll be wary," cautioned Spindle.

As Spindle, Bouncer and Pete crouched behind the hedge watching, Ginger rose slowly and quietly to his feet, keeping his head as low as possible in order not to be seen over the hedge. He placed one foot on the bottom wire and bent the top wire down as far as possible with his left hand being careful to avoid the sharp barbs. Then, he swung the other leg over the top wire.

"What are you doing young man?" called out a female voice suddenly from the other side of the hedge. Ginger started at the sound of the voice. He let go of the top wire and it snapped up viciously embedding the barbs in the crotch of his trousers where he straddled the fence.

"Looking for birds' nests," Ginger blurted out as he winced with pain.

"Bloody hell! It's the headmistress," whispered Bouncer. "Let's get out of here."

Spindle, Pete and Bouncer crawled off down the hedge and into the woods where they rose to their feet and ran back to the boys' school, leaving Ginger to fend for himself.

Miss Desmond, the headmistress, was peering angrily over the hedge at Ginger with her hands planted on her hips.

"What's wrong, Ma'am?" called out Phoebe. Susan, Phoebe and Martha, upon hearing the headmistress cry out, had walked up to see what was happening.

"There's a young man caught in the fence," replied Miss Desmond, pointing at Ginger, who was red-faced and struggling to extricate himself from the barbs.

"We'd better go around and help him, Miss Desmond," said Susan. "He looks as if he is in pain."

The girls followed Miss Desmond around the hedge to the barbed wire fence where Ginger was caught.

"What are you doing here?" asked Miss Desmond as she attempted to untangle Ginger's clothes from the wire.

"Looking for birds' nests," replied Ginger, attempting to keep the top wire of the fence down with one hand and holding his crotch with the other.

"Birds' nests? It's the wrong time of the year for egg hunting," responded the headmistress. "You were not spying on my girls were you?"

"No, Miss, just looking for nests."

"Are you bleeding?" asked Martha.

"The wire snapped up between my legs, and the barbs are in the crotch of my trousers. I might be bleeding. When I get loose, I'll have to take my trousers down and look," said Ginger with a straight face.

The girls put their hands up over their mouths and turned away so Ginger wouldn't see them giggling. The headmistress quickly removed her hands from Ginger's trousers. "Can you pull the rest of the barbs out?" she asked. "I've done as much as it's proper for me to do."

Ginger suppressed a grin. "I – I think so," he said. Grimacing, he pulled the last couple of barbs out and stepped back over the fence. He looked down at his crotch and cautiously felt around the area.

"You'd better go to a doctor for treatment," said the headmistress, averting her eyes in embarrassment.

Ginger started to walk away.

"Are you alone?" she asked, looking up at him again.

"It's just me."

"If it wasn't for your ... er, injury, I would get the police. You are trespassing on school grounds," she said.

"I didn't know I was, Miss. I thought I was in Farmer Tindle's pasture."

"Well, then, you are trespassing on his property, aren't you? In any event, Mr. Tindle rents this property from Rosemead School. Mind you, this would not go down well with your headmaster Mr. Nicholson. He is quite adamant about King Charles students not giving the school a bad reputation, especially when they are wearing the school uniform."

"Yes, Ma'am," said Ginger, hanging his head.

"Be off then, and tell any of your friends who may have come with you that I will have them arrested if they come here again."

"If you see any birds' nests, let me know," said Ginger as he limped away.

Pete, Spindle and Bouncer were anxiously waiting at the edge of the woods when Ginger returned.

"Are you all right, Ginger?" laughed Spindle.

"No thanks to the help I got from my chums," said Ginger. "I'm fine. Just scratched my legs, that's all."

"Sorry we deserted you, but we couldn't afford to be seen. The girls would have known we've been spying on them," said Bouncer. "At least they don't know who you are."

"We can't go there again. The headmistress said she would call the police next time," said Ginger. "She said to tell my friends that as well."

"Oh, no! Did she see us too?" asked Pete.

"No, I don't think so. I told her I was alone and that I was looking for birds' nests, but I don't think she really believed me," said Ginger.

"That's a pity. We wanted to find out what happened Saturday night," said Spindle.

"Do you really not know?" queried Ginger.

"Can't be sure," answered Bouncer. "We were drunk and blindfolded. Why didn't the headmistress call the police or report you to Nicholson?"

"I said I hurt my willie," chuckled Ginger, pointing at his crotch where the barbs had left snags in his trousers.

"Did you?"

"No."

The boys burst into laughter.

"Now, can I join The Bottom Five?" asked Ginger.

"Getting your bottom caught in barbed wire doesn't quite qualify you. But we'll take a vote after school, and maybe we can make you an honorary member," said Spindle.

Ginger's close encounter with the headmistress and the threat of being found out by the girls forced the boys to stay away from the girls' school. In the coming days, they occupied themselves with conker and football during free periods, but they could not stop reliving the Davenville party and continually speculating about who had been with whom during the blindfold game.

Finally, on Friday after school when the boys were sitting by the horse trough at the top of the hill on Station Road before going their separate ways, Spindle had had enough. "Bloody hell!" he spouted in exasperation. "We've been through this a thousand times. There must be some way of finding out!"

"Well, we can't very well walk up to Lord Davenville's, knock on the door and ask Susan to tell us, can't we?" groused Pete.

"Still ... there must be a way," said Spindle.

95

"Not sure I want to find out who I was with," said Sam. "I think I made a bloody fool of myself, getting sick in the flower bed and all."

"I suppose it doesn't matter," said Bouncer thoughtfully. "Not likely we'll ever see those girls again, anyway. The only reason we were invited to that party was because of a lark of Susan's and Freddie's connections. You remember how Lady Davenville looked down on us, as if we'd crawled up from the sewer."

"It did look as if it was all she could do to keep from holding her nose when she looked at us," laughed Pete.

"Except Inky, of course," noted Spindle. Suddenly, he sat up straight and snapped his fingers. "Inky ... , of course!" he exclaimed. "Freddie can find out for us," he said, pointing a finger at Freddie, who had been staring at the passing carriages lost in thought.

Freddie started. "Me? What do you mean?" he cried. "How can I find out?"

"You can find out from your cousin Martha, that's how!" said Spindle.

"Oh, I don't know ... ," said Freddie hesitantly.

"Are you going to see her anytime soon?" inquired Spindle.

Freddie studied his fingernails for a moment before replying. "Well, they are going to be at our house for dinner on Sunday," he said slowly.

"Well, can't you ask her then?" asked Spindle excitedly.

"Mmmm, I don't know. I'm afraid she'll say something in front of my parents about me being drunk. Don't want my mother all stirred up again or my father to find out. Best to let sleeping dogs lie."

"Oh, come on, Inky," prodded Spindle, poking Freddie on the arm. "You're the clever one in class. Find a way to pry it out of her. Besides, you owe it to me for carrying you into your house and putting you to bed."

Freddie hung his head in embarrassment. "I suppose you're right," he said reluctantly. "I'll give it a go, then, but I can't promise anything."

"That's the way of it," said Spindle, enthusiastically clapping Freddie on the shoulder. "See what you can find out and meet us under the conker tree at eight o'clock Monday morning."

"I'll do my best," said Freddie. "Must get on home now. My father will be back from London on the evening train. Don't want to rile my mother up again before he gets here."

"Hope he finds out and that's the end of it," said Ginger as the boys watched Freddie walk away. "I'm bloody well tired of hearing about it."

"Well, you're the one who mucked it up for us, aren't you?" said Spindle sarcastically. "You had to go over the barbed wire and get caught by the headmistress, didn't you?"

Ginger shrugged his shoulders. "Just trying to help, that's all. Besides, I was looking for birds' nests, remember?"

"That's right, and you stirred up a rat's nest instead," laughed Pete.

On Monday morning, the boys arrived nearly in unison at the conker tree in anticipation of Freddie's news.

"Well?" asked Spindle anxiously as Freddie joined them, a little out of breath.

Freddie looked glum. "She wouldn't tell me," he said.

"Not anything?" asked Bouncer.

"No, other than each of them wore one of Susan's gifts to confuse us, but we already figured that out, anyway," said Freddie.

"Why wouldn't she tell?" asked Pete.

"Said she and the other girls swore an oath never to tell. Said there was no use in asking because she would take it with her to the grave. Most dramatic, if you ask me," said Freddie, rolling his eyes.

"Didn't you try to be clever?" asked Spindle.

"Oh, yes. Tried everything I could think of - even tried to get her to tell me which of Susan's gifts she was wearing, but she saw through every trick. She got angry and threatened to tell her parents about how drunk I was if I didn't quit prying. I had to stop because her parents would be sure to tell my father," said Freddie sadly.

"Well, that's an end to it then," said Bouncer. "Guess we'll never find out, unless we can think of another way."

"Looks like it," said Freddie. "If I can think of another way to get it out of Martha, I'll let you know."

As the days and weeks passed, the boys gradually stopped talking amongst themselves about the Davenville party. Their days became caught up with Alwood's demanding assignments, playground activities and after-school jobs. As the autumn term drew to a close, the boys rarely spoke about the girls, but occasionally, in a quiet moment or during one of Alwood's boring classroom lectures, one of the boys would find himself examining his memory for a clue as to which girl he had been with.

The autumn term ended, and the Christmas holiday came and went. On the first day of the winter term, Freddie arrived at school early and impatiently paced up and down outside the door waiting for the other boys to arrive. When Spindle and Bouncer walked onto the playground together, Freddie beckoned to them excitedly.

"What's up?" asked Bouncer, as he and Spindle joined him.

"I have some news," said Freddie. "Where are Sam and Pete?"

The boys looked around the playground, and Spindle pointed toward the road. "Here they come now. Ginger's with them, as well. I'll go get them."

When the boys had gathered near the school door out of earshot of the other students and teachers, Spindle turned to Freddie. "We're all here. What's the news?"

"I saw Martha on Boxing Day," said Freddie. "We were over at her house. She told me that Susan Davenville is not coming back to Rosemead after the Christmas Holiday. She is not going to finish school. Moving up to London to live with her uncle and become a nurse."

"She said that's what she wanted to do when we were at her party, remember?" said Bouncer.

"Yes. I remember that," said Pete. "Bet Lady Davenville is having a fit."

"Lord Davenville didn't seem to be opposed to it, though. Imagine he helped Susan have her way," said Spindle. "Glad she's able to do what she wanted, but sorry she's so far away. I rather fancy Susan. Now, I doubt our paths will ever cross. What about the rest of the girls?"

"Oh, they're still here - finishing out the year at Rosemead," said Freddie.

A sly grin spread over Spindle's face. "Now that Susan's gone, maybe Martha will tell you who we were with at the party," he said.

Freddie held up his hands in protest. "I don't dare ask now," he said. "Martha and Susan are very close, you know. They'll write to each other, and Martha may be going up to London to visit her."

"I think we should just let it lie," said Bouncer. "As for you, Spindle, you probably fancy Susan because she's inaccessible."

"Yeah, you fancy every girl you meet," said Ginger.

"Not so!" said Spindle, punching Ginger on the arm. "Besides, I still think I'm the one Susan chose to be with at the party."

"Oh, you can't be sure, can you? I think it was me!" said Pete.

"The fact is, we can't be sure who we were with," said Bouncer. "Might as well forget it. If Susan had really fancied the one she was with, she would have found a way to make contact by now. She and those other girls were just on a lark, that's all."

"Bouncer's right. Lots of other fish in the sea," winked Ginger. "Besides, we're old enough to go to the pubs now, and who wants a girl telling you that you can't go?"

"That's right, Ginger. My mum nags at my dad all the time about being in the pub," said Sam. "She's always sending me over there to drag him home."

"Well, I want a girl and I want to go to the pubs, too," said Spindle grinning. "Guess I'll just have to find a girl who'll go to the pub with me."

"I'm not old enough to go to the pub," said Freddie with a sorrowful expression.

"Oh, never mind, Freddie, you can go with us. Besides, I've been going to The White Horse for a couple of years now. Ben looks the other way, but now that I'm 16, it don't matter," said Bouncer.

"Me, too," said Spindle. "Actually, I won't be 16 until March, but it's close enough."

"My father would really be upset if he found out I had gone to a pub before I'm old enough," said Freddie. "I'd better wait till after my birthday."

"When is your birthday, Freddie?" asked Pete.

"May 15," said Freddie.

"Well, then, we'll celebrate your birthday at The White Horse," said Bouncer jovially, clapping him on the back.

The boys forged their way through the winter term, forgetting about the Davenvilles until after the Easter Holiday. On the first week of the spring term, Freddie gathered them together for another announcement. His face was grim. "You remember hearing about *The Titanic* sinking?" he asked.

The boys nodded. They had talked about the tragedy in class earlier in the week when it had come out in the papers that the pride of the White Star Line had sunk after striking an iceberg.

"Well, I just found out last night that Susan Davenville's sister Paulina and George Edmundson were not among the survivors," said Freddie. "They had just been married on Easter Sunday, and were sailing to New York on *The Titanic* for their honeymoon."

The boys were silent for a moment, too shocked to speak.

Pete broke the silence. "Oh, that's bloody awful. I remember them talking about the trip at Susan's birthday party," he said with a quaver in his voice.

"My mother said Lady Davenville is hysterical with grief, and the doctor was called in to give her laudanum," said Freddie. "Vicar Dumfries has been sitting with the family trying to offer comfort."

"How is Lord Davenville taking it?" asked Bouncer.

"Father said he was the first to hear of it. He was in London attending a meeting of the King's Privy Council, and, of course, they had anxiously been waiting to hear who was on the list of those rescued when *The Carpathia* reached New York. Said he left the Council meeting and came directly home to be with his wife," said Freddie.

"Is there going to be a funeral?" asked Sam.

"Don't know for sure," said Freddie. "Just a private memorial for the immediate family only, I think. There are no bodies. They apparently went down with the ship. No one knows exactly what happened."

"What about Susan? Has she come home?" asked Spindle hopefully.

"Don't know," said Freddie. "My father didn't say anything about her. Imagine it's very difficult for her as well."

"I think we should send a sympathy letter to Lord Davenville," said Bouncer.

"Should we do that? Do you think he'll remember us?" asked Sam, somewhat timidly.

"Of course, he'll remember," said Bouncer. "He was very impressed with us for helping Major General Wallis, don't you remember?"

"I think he would appreciate getting a letter from us," said Freddie. "Let's write it during lunchtime, and I will see that it's delivered to him."

The boys sent their letter to Lord Davenville and read about George and Paulina in the paper later that week, along with the report of those who had survived and those who had perished in the tragedy. They heard no news of Susan. Freddie said Martha had not heard from her, even though she had sent her several letters.

The spring term seemed to fly as Alwood drove his students relentlessly in preparation for the General Certificate Exam that would dictate whether or not the boys qualified for further education. Alwood announced that the exam would be given on Wednesday, May 15, coincidentally on Freddie's birthday. Further pressure from their parents and their own ambitions caused the boys to grow more serious in class. They concentrated on stuffing their heads with the knowledge they would need to pass the exam - all but Ginger, who continued to entertain the class with his mischief, earning himself several of Alwood's canings.

"Don't you care about passing the exam?" asked Freddie one day at lunchtime after Alwood had caned Ginger for disrupting a history lesson. "I could help you study for it."

Ginger grinned. "Thanks for the offer, Inky, but I don't need it. I'm just waiting to get out of school so I can go to London and get a job. Don't care if I pass the exam. Don't want any further schooling."

"Suit yourself," said Freddie. "What kind of job do you want?"

"Want to be a comedian, like I told Alwood," said Ginger.

"Being a comedian should suit you, Ginger," commented Bouncer. "You always make us laugh."

"You can try out your jokes at The White Horse after the exam," said Spindle. "Remember, May 15 is Inky's birthday. What do you think Inky? Ginger can spice up your party."

Freddie grinned and punched Ginger on the arm. "Not too much spice, I hope. My mum told me too much ginger is bad for you."

* * *

# Chapter 5
## *Further Education*

O N THE SECOND Monday in August, Sam Baldwin stood outside his butcher shop waiting for the delivery wagon. It was a warm sunny morning, and he had risen earlier than usual. The other shopkeepers were just beginning to stir. He looked to the east and shaded his eyes against the sun as he heard the approaching wagon.

"Well, Bouncer, you're earlier than usual," he commented as the horse and wagon pulled up in front of his shop.

"Mornin' Mr. Baldwin," said Bouncer as he jumped down from the wagon seat. "It's a nice day. Thought I'd get an early start and be finished early."

"That hook over there," indicated Mr. Baldwin as Bouncer carried in a side of beef. "Suppose I'll only see you a few more times with school starting up in September, eh?"

Bouncer stretched his arms after hoisting the meat up onto the hook. "Haven't made up my mind about school yet. Would like to join the Army and go to India."

"The Army, you say? A good lot, that, but aren't you too young to join?"

"Have to be 18, but I could go now if I could get my aunt to sign the papers," said Bouncer wistfully. "Been working on her to sign, but she doesn't want to. Says too many men in my family have been killed in the military."

"Well, Bouncer, my advice to you is to sign up for the Poly and go to school till you're old enough. The Army will still be there. Would be a rotten shame for you not to go on to school after you passed the exam and all," said Mr. Baldwin.

"Suppose you're right," said Bouncer with a frown. "But I don't really fancy more schooling. Too bad I can't give my exam score to Sam. He really wanted to go on to school."

"Oh, that," said Mr. Baldwin with a wave of his hand. "Sam doesn't need the extra schooling to work here with me in the butcher shop. He'll end up taking over the business when I'm gone, you know."

"By the way, I want to thank you again for helping me get this job for the summer," said Bouncer.

"Oh, it was nothing, Bouncer. I thought of you right away when Harry broke his leg. He should be back on the job soon."

"Where is Sam this morning?" asked Bouncer looking around the shop for a sign of his friend.

"Still upstairs. I let him lay in a while this morning. He'll be down soon."

"Oh, well. Would you remind him that we're meeting at The White Horse around eight o'clock on Saturday night? Spindle and Freddie will be back from holiday."

"That I will," grinned Mr. Baldwin. "Having a class reunion, eh? What about Pete and Ginger?""

"Ginger has a job in London working at a cinema, and Pete joined the Merchant Navy – left for Liverpool last week. Don't expect we'll see them for a while. Neither of them cared whether or not they passed the exam. Didn't want to go on to school."

"What about Freddie and Spindle? Did they pass?"

"I'm sure Freddie passed and will be signing up to go to Commerce School. His dad wants him to be a solicitor. Don't know about Spindle. He left on holiday before we got the results. Must be off now or I won't finish early today."

Bouncer got as far as the door where he stopped abruptly and turned on his heel. "Nearly forgot. My aunt wants me to pick up some calf's liver and eggs," he announced.

"How is your aunt?" inquired Mr. Baldwin. "Haven't seen her for a while."

"Not well, I'm afraid. Been in bed most of the summer with some kind of ague. Also has trouble with her legs – rheumatism, I think."

"Sorry to hear that," said Mr. Baldwin, shaking his head. "Your aunt is such a nice lady."

Footsteps sounded on the staircase at the back of the shop. "Hello, Bouncer," said Sam as he walked into the shop tying on a white canvass apron.

"Well, if it isn't Banger at last," teased Bouncer. "Wish I could lay in on a Monday morning."

Sam grinned sheepishly and ran his hand through his rumpled hair.

Mr. Baldwin turned to his son. "Bouncer needs liver and eggs for his aunt. Would you get them? How much, Bouncer?"

"A pound of calf's liver and a dozen eggs."

Sam weighed the calf's liver, counted out 12 eggs and packaged them up, while Mr. Baldwin and Bouncer watched. Sam placed the parcels on the counter.

"How much?" asked Bouncer as he took some coins out of a small pouch he carried in his pocket.

Sam looked inquiringly at his father.

"Six pence and three farthings for the eggs, eight pence for the liver," said Mr. Baldwin. Bouncer handed him a two-shilling coin.

"Are you going to the Poly?" asked Sam as Mr. Baldwin counted out Bouncer's change.

"Don't know yet," replied Bouncer. "Want to join the Army, but my aunt won't sign the papers."

"Well, Sam is going to work in the shop with me. Going to be a butcher like me, and my father before me, aren't you, Sam?" smiled Mr. Baldwin.

"That's right, Dad," sighed Sam. "Don't really have a choice, since I didn't pass the exam," he said, looking wistfully at Bouncer.

"The Baldwins have been butchers in Bridgefield since 1856. It's something to be proud of, lad," said Mr. Baldwin, clapping his son on the shoulder.

"Well, I must be off," said Bouncer, feeling Sam's disappointment. "See you at The White Horse Saturday night, Banger. Don't forget."

Sam's face brightened. "I'll be there. Looking forward to seeing everyone," he said as Bouncer strode out of the shop with the parcels for his aunt.

Mr. Baldwin washed his hands and smiled at Sam. "So pleased to have you here, Son."

"You haven't told me how much you are going to pay," said Sam. "It's going to be more than five shillings a week, isn't it, Dad?"

"Let me think," said Mr. Baldwin drying his hands on a white towel. "If I pay you ten shillings and take out room and board, it would leave about five shillings."

"That's all, Dad?" asked Sam plaintively.

"Remember, Sam, one day this will all be yours, and besides, you will get Saturday afternoons off."

"But I wanted to be a veterinarian. I'll be an old man before I'm in charge here," commented Sam shaking his head.

Mr. Baldwin frowned at him and pointed at the back room. "Get back to work, Sam, and stop complaining," he directed.

Sam hung his head and marched off to the back room to cut a side of pork into roasts and chops.

The bell on the shop door rang as Sam's former teacher walked in.

"Good morning, Mr. Alwood. What can I get you today?" asked Mr. Baldwin.

Alwood looked at the meat display. "I would like two of those chops, please, Mr. Baldwin."

"Another school year starting soon," remarked Mr. Baldwin as he selected the chops.

"That's right. How is Sam doing? Is he enjoying the meat trade?"

"Nine and half pence, Mr. Alwood."

"I do hope my boys continue their education. It is so important in this changing world," commented Alwood as he counted out the money.

"How many passed the exam?"

"Out of thirty-six, twenty-eight passed," said Alwood proudly.

"Pretty good, Mr. Alwood."

"I hope those who didn't pass learn a trade, like Sam. He is lucky to have the opportunity to go directly to work in a well-established business such as yours."

"Thank you, Mr. Alwood. That's what I keep telling him." Mr. Baldwin handed Alwood a parcel containing the chops.

*  *  *

The sound of singing coming from inside The White Horse Pub on Saturday night could be heard several streets away. The landlord, Ben Ashley, had been serving customers for over twenty years. Customers entered, Ben recognized them right away and responded by pouring their regular drinks.

"How are you Spindle? Did you have a nice holiday?" called out Ben loudly as Spindle entered The White Horse.

"Too much tar on the beach. Got tarred up," called back Spindle.

"What about the weather? Did the sun shine?" asked Ben's wife, Nan, who emerged from a back room.

"Plenty of sunshine. It was too hot some days."

"Did your mum and dad have a nice time?" asked Nan.

"They did. I didn't," joked Spindle.

"Why was that, Spindle?" called out a customer who was sitting further down the bar.

"All they wanted to do was sit on the beach. I got bored."

"Wasn't there any young ladies about?" asked the customer.

"Several, but that was at night," said Spindle, turning red.

"Best time to meet them," said the customer.

"We're over here, Spindle," called out Bouncer from the corner table he and Sam had commandeered.

"There you are," said Spindle waving at his friends. "Bring us three half bitters, would you, Ben?" he said over his shoulder as he walked over to join them.

"Right. Coming right up," said Ben as he sat three half-pint glasses on the bar.

"Good to see you, lads," said Spindle as he sat down at the table. "Where's Inky?"

"Not here yet. Should be coming soon," said Bouncer glancing at the door.

"Did you bring any Hastings Rock back, Spindle?" asked Sam.

"Sure did. One for each of you," said Spindle. He drew two sticks of the peppermint sweets from his inside coat pocket and handed one to Sam and one to Bouncer.

Ben delivered the drinks, setting a half-pint glass of the dark, flat bitter ale before each of them. "That will be three pence, Spindle," he announced.

Spindle handed him a three-penny piece, with a quizzical look on his face. "Price has gone up, Ben?"

"You can blame the Germans for that," said Ben in a loud jovial voice that drew chuckles from the surrounding customers.

"What's the Germans got to do with the price of beer?" asked Sam.

"Higher taxes," announced a customer at the next table. "The King needs money to build more battleships to keep up with the Germans."

"Hope they stay afloat better than *The Titanic*," muttered Spindle just loud enough for Bouncer and Sam to hear.

Bouncer grimaced. "Well, Spindle, we're anxious to hear – did you pass the exam?" he asked, changing the subject.

"Sure did. How about you?"

"Oh, I passed all right, but it doesn't mean a bloody lot to me. Want to join the Army. Looks like I have to wait until I'm eighteen, as my aunt won't sign the papers to let me in earlier. Wish I could give my score to Sam, here."

"You didn't pass then, Sam?" inquired Spindle.

"No. Just two points short of passing, and now I'm stuck being a butcher," said Sam, looking dejectedly down into his glass. Suddenly, he raised his glass and drained it in two big gulps and slammed it down on the table in front of him.

Spindle raised his eyebrows and looked at Bouncer. Bouncer shook his head. "Ben!" called out Spindle, raising one finger in the air and pointing to Sam. Behind the bar, Ben nodded and placed another half-pint glass on the bar. Spindle turned to Sam. "Sorry to hear that, Sam. It's a shame. Know you wanted to go on to school and become a veterinarian. Maybe something will still turn up."

"Maybe," said Sam bitterly, still looking down at the table. Then, he brightened. "What about you, Spindle? Are you going on to school?"

"My dad's pressuring me to go to Commerce School and study accounting so I can follow in his footsteps at the gas works," said Spindle.

"Is that what you're going to do?" asked Bouncer.

Spindle grinned. "No. I'm signing up for the Poly on Monday. Think I'll study to be an engineer of some type. What about you, Bouncer?"

"Well, since my aunt won't let me join the Army, I guess I'll sign up for the Poly, too. We can go together on Monday. Ran across James Taylor the other day, and he's going to the Poly also."

"Anyone else?" asked Spindle.

"Don't know. Inky is going on to the Commerce School. His dad wants him to be a solicitor."

Suddenly, a hush fell over the pub as three young ladies appeared in the doorway.

"Sorry, young ladies, you can't come in without an escort," called out Ben from behind the bar.

"It's all right, Ben. They're with me," said Freddie who hastily walked in ahead of the girls. He looked about the pub.

"We're over here, Freddie," said Spindle. "Come on over. Plenty of chairs."

"Right!" said Freddie, waving at the boys. He turned back to the girls who had paused nervously in the doorway. "Right this way, ladies," he said and escorted the three girls to the table where Bouncer, Sam and Spindle had arisen to hold out chairs for them.

"You remember these fellows, don't you?" he asked.

"Of course!" laughed Martha. "The birthday party guests."

"Well, if it isn't Martha, Rose and Elizabeth," said Spindle. "Haven't seen you for nearly a year. What brings you to this part of town?"

"We were having a lawn party at my house and got bored," said Martha as the group settled into their seats. "Decided we wanted to have an adventure – find out what pubs are like. Freddie offered to escort us, and here we are."

"It's a nice surprise to see all of you again. I'll buy you ladies a drink. What will you have?" asked Bouncer with a happy grin on his face. "Afraid they don't have champagne at The White Horse, though," he added.

"Oh, that's quite all right," laughed Rose. "I had enough champagne at Susan's party to last me for several years!"

"So did I. Made me sick for a week," remarked Sam with a sheepish grin.

"You weren't the only one," said Freddie, rolling his eyes. Everyone laughed, remembering Freddie's inebriated state at the Davenville party.

"Do they have lemonade?" asked Elizabeth. "That's what I want."

"I believe they do," said Bouncer, raising his hand and motioning toward the bar.

Nan immediately appeared at their table. "What can I get for you, young ladies?" she inquired.

"We'd all like lemonade," responded Martha.

"And you, Freddie?" asked Nan, turning her gaze on him.

"I'll have a pint of Boddingtons, and bring another round of whatever they're drinking for my friends here," he said.

"Half bitters again?" Nan asked, looking inquiringly at the boys. They nodded and she scurried off to fill the orders.

"Can't believe it's been nearly a year since Susan's party," said Elizabeth. "You all look more grown up now, especially you, Spindle, with your mustache. Where is that tall blond boy? What was his name? Pete?"

"Pete left for Liverpool last week. Joined the Merchant Navy," explained Bouncer.

"What about the rest of you? What are you doing now that you're out of school?" asked Rose.

"Working in our butcher shop," said Sam, his face clouding over again. "My dad wants me to continue in the business after he's gone."

"Spindle and I are signing up for the Polytechnic School," said Bouncer, quickly before Sam had a chance to become depressed at his plight again. "I want to join the Army and go to India when I'm old enough. What about you, Freddie? Going to sign up for the Commerce School and be a solicitor like your dad wants?"

"Yes. I'm signing up next week. My father wasn't terribly keen on my idea of becoming a famous Scotland Yard detective, you know," he grinned.

"You are all looking very grown-up yourselves," said Spindle, smiling flirtatiously. "What are all of you going to do now that you're out of school?"

"I'm going back to school to learn to be a teacher," said Rose. "Then, I want to teach at Rosemead."

"I've always wanted to write," said Elizabeth. "I'm going to try my hand at writing a novel this year. I've always fancied those gothic novels, you know. Perhaps I'll be the next Charlotte Bronte, or Mrs. Shelley."

"All too tame for me," said Martha. "I want adventure. Been talking to my parents about letting me go to live with my aunt and uncle in Africa for a year. They have a plantation in Rhodesia."

"What about Phoebe? Where is she?" asked Bouncer.

"Oh, Phoebe is going to be the proper lady," sniffed Martha. "She's off on a tour of the continent with her parents this summer, and her aunt, who lives in Venice, is going to introduce her to society there. Expect Phoebe will soon be married to some Italian Count or other."

"What about Susan?" asked Spindle. "Freddie told us she left school at the end of the fall term to live with her uncle in London and study to become a nurse. Have you heard from her?"

Elizabeth and Rose glanced at Martha who looked somewhat uncomfortable as she responded slowly to the question. "I hadn't heard from her for quite a long while, and then I received a letter from her two weeks ago. Says she's been learning all about nursing in the hospital where her Uncle Tommy is a surgeon and that she's been assisting his wife Anne in caring for their little boy who was just born in June. She seems quite happy and enamoured with the baby. Her letter was full of descriptions of his antics."

"Does she ever come back to Bridgefield for visits?" asked Spindle.

"Hasn't been back that I know of," said Martha. "Lord and Lady Davenville spend a great deal of time in London, you know, especially after *The Titanic*. In fact, I believe Lady Davenville is not well at all. Never recovered from the shock."

"Such a pity, that," said Bouncer, shaking his head sadly. "We were all very sorry to hear about Paulina and George."

"Yes, a terrible tragedy," sighed Elizabeth. Tears glistened in her eyes.

A glum silence settled over the table as everyone remembered the tragic deaths of Susan's sister and her husband.

Spindle finally broke the silence. "Enough doom and gloom," he pronounced. "This is an occasion for gaiety. There's an orchestra and open dancing at the Bridgefield Hotel on Saturday nights. Why don't we all go?"

"I'm for that!" cried Freddie, nearly knocking over his half-full glass in his excitement. Everyone laughed at his clumsiness.

"Not drunk again, are you Freddie?" jibed Martha.

"Oh, no, not drunk, but feeling good," he said. "Feel like dancing. Feel like having some fun. What do you say? Shall we go to the Bridgefield Hotel?"

"Oh, yes, let's!" exclaimed Rose. Martha and Elizabeth nodded in agreement, their eyes shining with excitement.

"But are we properly dressed?" asked Elizabeth. "We aren't in evening attire."

"Not to worry. We're all dressed well enough. It's open to the public and not a formal event," explained Spindle.

"Let's go, then. What are we waiting for?" said Bouncer, pushing back his chair. "Come on, Sam."

Sam was smiling but somewhat hesitant. "Don't know how to dance ... ," he began, but Rose reached over and patted him on the arm.

"Don't worry, Sam. You can dance with me. I'll show you how."

Sam smiled and jumped to his feet. "All right, then. Let's go!"

"Good night! Have a good time and come back soon," called out Ben from behind the bar as the group walked out of the pub together.

When they entered the ballroom at the Bridgefield Hotel, the orchestra was already playing, and several couples were dancing. "Should we all sit together?" asked Elizabeth, noting that most of the women were seated on one side of the room, the men on the other.

"Of course," said Spindle. "We can take turns dancing with each other. There's a table and some chairs beside that potted palm by the terrace door."

The table he indicated was on the side of the room where most of the women were sitting in chairs lining the walls. Freddie took Martha's arm and led their small procession over to the table. When they were all seated, he announced, "Let's take turn choosing partners for dancing. Ladies should go first."

"All right, then," laughed Martha. "Come on, Freddie, let's lead the way. They're playing a waltz."

As Freddie and Martha walked onto the dance floor, Rose looked at Sam. "Come on, Sam. Might as well get your feet wet. The waltz is easy to learn."

Sam blushed. "All right. Guess I'm used to making a fool of meself."

"Don't worry," said Rose. "Just follow my lead and I'll show you what to do. We can dance over in that corner away from the others until you discover how." Sam followed Rose onto the floor.

"That leaves me," said Elizabeth. "Spindle, do you want to dance with me? Oh, dear, that leaves Bouncer sitting here by himself, though," she frowned.

"That's all right," Bouncer said good-naturedly. "I'll choose first on the next dance."

Spindle and Elizabeth stepped onto the floor and began to swirl around the room to the rhythms of the waltz.

Spindle smiled down at Elizabeth as they danced. "You dance well, Elizabeth," he remarked.

"Thank you, Spindle. We had a great deal of training at Rosemead," she said smiling up at him. "You dance well, too, and you look much better without a blindfold." Her eyes sparkled with mischief.

"Blindfold? Oh, you mean that game we played at Susan's party. That was a very unusual game that you girls devised," he said, looking closely at her.

Elizabeth laughed up at him. "Yes, it was an unusual game, wasn't it? It was all Susan's idea. Do you remember what happened?"

"I remember being blindfolded and led outside by a girl. She was wearing a shawl, and I remember other things as well, but I'd rather not say," he said, looking closely at her for a clue.

Elizabeth chuckled. "Susan said the blindfolds would allow us to experiment a bit without the fear of being discovered, and she was right."

"Who did you choose, Elizabeth? Was it me?" he asked, his eyes boring into hers.

Elizabeth did not flinch or look away. She continued to smile mischievously up at him. "I can't say," she said. "We swore an oath that we would never tell."

"Well, I wish I knew who I was with," said Spindle. "I found her very ... how shall I say? ... intriguing, and I would like to be with her again ... without the blindfold. Are you sure you won't tell?"

"No, Spindle, I won't tell. No use your trying to pry it out of me!"

"All right, then, but I intend to find out somehow, someday," said Spindle.

"Remember, curiosity killed the cat," chided Elizabeth, still smiling at him as the waltz ended and they walked back to the table to join the others.

As the orchestra struck up another tune, Bouncer announced, "It's my turn to choose a partner first. May I have this dance, Elizabeth?" He gave a little mock bow and Elizabeth laughed delightedly.

"Of course you may. Just be certain not to tread on my toes."

"Don't worry, I dance like a butterfly," said Bouncer, taking her arm and leading her onto the dance floor.

"More like a fly, I'd wager," teased Elizabeth, as they began to whirl exuberantly around the room.

"Rose, would you do me the honor?" asked Freddie. Rose nodded, and reached out to take Freddie's hand when she noticed that Sam suddenly looked a little downcast. She turned to him.

"Sam, why don't you dance with Martha? You are doing well, and Martha is very good at the waltz. I'll dance the next one with you and we can continue your instruction."

Sam brightened and smiled up at her, then turned to Martha. "Would you like to dance, Martha?"

"Of course, I'd be delighted," she said. "But what about Spindle?"

Spindle waved his hand in dismissal. "That's all right, I could do with a rest. I get first pick the next time around," he said.

As Spindle sat watching the others dance, a petite blond girl walked by his table. When she saw him, she stopped. "Hello, Spindle," she said.

Spindle looked up. "Well, I never! It's Daisy, isn't it? How are you? Haven't seen you since last summer," he exclaimed, rising to take her hand.

"Not since Hastings on the beach, eh, Spindle? Almost didn't recognize you with that mustache. My, you look all grown up now," said Daisy gazing up at him. Spindle seemed to tower over her. She ran her hand up his arm. "Would you like to dance with me, Spindle?"

Spindle felt a tingling in his spine at her touch. He smiled down at her, and took her arm. "It would be my pleasure," he said, as he led her onto the dance floor.

When the dance ended, Spindle and Daisy walked arm-in-arm back to the table where the others were gathered. "Everyone, this is Daisy Summers. She is joining us," he announced as he pulled a chair out for her next to his. Then he proceeded to make introductions around the table. When he introduced Freddie, Freddie looked intently at Daisy. "Daisy Summers? You look quite familiar although I don't recognize the name," he mused.

"I've seen you before, too, Mr. Simpson, at the chemist shop in the High Street. I work there," she added.

"You work?" asked Elizabeth with a raised eyebrow. "How long have you done that?"

"Three years, since I was fourteen," said Daisy, unruffled.

"You're seventeen, then?"

"That's right," said Daisy. "I'll be eighteen in December. How old are you?"

"All of us are sixteen. We just finished school in May," said Martha, with a broad sweep of her hand around the table indicating the boys as well as the girls.

"I'm older than sixteen," laughed Spindle.

"Bloody hell, Spindle. Who are you trying to fool? You're younger than me, and I haven't turned seventeen yet!" exploded Bouncer.

"I meant in spirit," said Spindle, looking at Daisy.

"You look older than sixteen with that mustache, Spindle. Do you shave the rest of your face every day?" asked Daisy.

"Certainly do. Want to feel?" joked Spindle.

Daisy put her hand up to his cheek. "Mmmmm, you certainly do shave," she said smiling at him as the others rolled their eyes and looked at each other in disgust.

Suddenly, a male voice crying "Ladies and Gentlemen, your attention please!" was heard above the din of voices in the ballroom. A hush fell over the room as everyone looked at the raised platform where the orchestra sat. The conductor was tapping his baton on his music stand. When he had everyone's attention, he announced, "Ladies and Gentleman, we will now play our final selection for the evening. Choose your partner for `The Merry Widow Waltz'."

"Now, we all have someone to dance with," smiled Freddie, as the conductor turned toward the orchestra and raised his baton.

"I'm choosing Daisy," said Spindle, winking at her.

Bouncer laughed as he drew a farthing from his pocket. "Heads I dance with Elizabeth, tails I dance with Martha."

"It doesn't work that way, Bouncer. I'm dancing with you," announced Martha. Bouncer grinned at her.

"What's the matter, Martha? You don't like bottoms?" joked Spindle getting up and extending his hand to Daisy.

"I like yours, Spindle," giggled Daisy, brushing her hand over his bottom as they walked to the dance floor.

"Hold me closer," she whispered, shortly after they had begun dancing. Spindle pulled her closer until their faces were touching. "You feel nice, Spindle, and your shaving cologne smells nice," whispered Daisy into his ear, sending shivers down his spine.

"Do you have a boyfriend, Daisy?" asked Spindle, squeezing her hand.

"I have one now," whispered Daisy, into his ear. Spindle turned his head slightly and grazed her cheek with his lips.

The orchestra stopped playing and the lights were brightened. Dancers gathered their belongings and went outside into the warm night air.

"Well, Freddie, you'd best escort us home," said Martha. "Our parents will be wondering where we are."

"Right," said Freddie. "I'll just pop up to the entry and hire a carriage."

Martha turned back to the rest of the group. "It's been a splendid evening. So nice to see all of you again."

"Too bad you have to leave. Enjoyed seeing all of you. What about next Saturday? There's open dancing here every Saturday evening. We could meet here again," said Bouncer.

"I'd like that," said Martha. "Perhaps I'd have the opportunity to dance with Spindle. Didn't have the chance to do that tonight," she said, looking at Spindle who had Daisy's arm tucked under his.

"Perhaps ... ," said Spindle, smiling down at Daisy who was looking up at him.

"What about you, Sam?" asked Rose. "Would you like to continue your dancing lessons next Saturday?"

Sam blushed and grinned at her. "Sure would," he said.

"What do you say, Elizabeth?" asked Bouncer.

"Of course. I'd love to. Never had the opportunity to dance with a butterfly before. I'd like to try it again," she said.

Bouncer laughed. "It's a date, then. We'll all meet here at nine o'clock."

A carriage pulled up, and Freddie climbed out. "Your carriage awaits, miladies," he announced with a mock bow.

"We've agreed to meet here again next Saturday. Will you escort us again, Freddie?" asked Martha.

"Oh, jolly good. Another round of dancing. I'd like that," he said jubilantly. As he assisted the girls into the carriage, he said, "See you chaps next Saturday night, then. Good luck signing up for the Poly, Bouncer and Spindle, and take care cutting those chops, Banger!"

"Right," said Bouncer. He and Sam waved as the carriage drove off.

"I'll see you Monday at the Poly, Bouncer. I'm going to walk Daisy home," said Spindle.

"Good night, then," said Bouncer.

"It looks as if Spindle has a new girlfriend," observed Sam, watching Daisy and Spindle walk off together in the direction of the park.

Bouncer frowned. "Daisy Summers. That name sounds familiar, but I can't think why," he mused.

He and Sam began walking down the street in silent contemplation. When they reached the corner where they would part, Bouncer snapped his fingers. "Now, I know who she is."

"Who?" asked Sam, starting out of his reverie.

"Daisy Summers. Works in the chemist's shop. She's Sidney Chapel's girlfriend."

"Sidney Chapel? The boxer?" asked Sam, raising his eyebrows.

"That's right. I saw him in The White Horse last week. He was telling me about Daisy. He's away for a couple of weeks. Fighting in London and Manchester, I think."

"Bloody hell, does Spindle know?"

"I doubt it. I'll tell him Monday. Wouldn't do for Sidney to find out Spindle's been with his girlfriend. He has a bad temper," said Bouncer with a worried expression.

"Well, must get home. See you next week, Bouncer," said Sam, as he turned and walked off toward the High Street. Bouncer walked the rest of the way home deep in thought.

On the first Monday in September, Bouncer and Spindle were seated in the assembly hall at Bridgefield Polytechnic School waiting to hear the headmaster's opening of school speech.

"How was the dance Saturday night? Did the girls show up?" inquired Spindle.

"Yes, they did, and we had a bloody good time," responded Bouncer with a grin. "Think Rose and Sam fancy each other. They danced together the whole evening. Freddie and I took turns dancing with Martha and Elizabeth. What about you? Were you out with Daisy again?"

Spindle smiled mysteriously. "Yes. I met her at the chemist's shop when she got off work and we went to the Wellington Head and had supper and several pints."

"The Wellington Head? That's over on Cromwell Road near the warehouses, isn't it? Why did you go there?"

"Daisy likes their steak and kidney pie. Said her brother used to go there before he moved to Blackpool."

"Remember what I told you about Sidney Chapel? Did you find out if he's Daisy's boyfriend?"

"Well, if he was, he's not anymore," said Spindle with a knowing grin. "I'm her boyfriend, now."

Bouncer started to say more, but at that moment, the headmaster appeared at the podium on the stage. "Good morning, Gentlemen. Welcome to Bridgefield Polytechnic," he said in a loud voice in order to be heard throughout the hall. "My name is Mr. James. I am pleased to see that all of you have made the right decision to continue your education. Classes will begin immediately following this assembly. If you are unsure of your classroom assignments, check the lists posted on the bulletin board outside my office."

Following the rest of the opening ceremonies and announcements, the students filed from the assembly room, some to their classes and others to the bulletin board.

"We have the same classrooms!" smiled Spindle looking at the list on the bulletin board.

"James Taylor, too," added Bouncer, laughing and pointing at Taylor's name on the list.

"I take it your aunt never agreed to sign the papers for you to join the Army?" asked Spindle as he and Bouncer walked off down the hallway toward their classroom.

"No, I'll join when I'm eighteen," replied Bouncer.

After they had taken seats next to each other in the classroom, a gray-haired man wearing wire-rimmed glasses and a black professor's gown over a dowdy dark suit entered the room and stood behind the lectern.

"Good morning, Gentlemen. I am Professor Brompton, and I will be your arithmetical teacher," he said.

"What is that?" asked Spindle in a low voice.

"He means numbers," whispered Bouncer.

"We will begin with square and cube roots of numbers," continued the teacher as he picked up a piece of chalk and stood next to the blackboard.

"Not my favorite subject," whispered Spindle.

"What is the cube root of forty-one?" asked Brompton.

The students dipped their pens into inkwells and began to work out the number on paper.

"Three point four four," called out James Taylor.

"The square root of ninety seven?"

"I'm baffled," whispered Spindle.

"Nine point eight four," again called out James Taylor.

"Mr. Taylor, why is it that you are so quick with the right answer?" asked Brompton.

"I'm using a root table," said James, holding it up.

"Put the table away and give me the cube root of one hundred and eleven."

The classroom went quiet as James tried to work out an answer.

"See, It's not easy without the table," laughed Brompton, and James looked dejected.

"It's ten point five," called out Bouncer smiling, holding up his computation.

Brompton smiled and wrote the answer on the blackboard. "Cube root to two decimal places, Gentlemen," he said.

"Ten point five three," called out Bouncer again.

"Correct again," smiled Brompton as he added that to the blackboard.

"How did you do that?" Spindle wanted to know.

"With pen and ink," laughed Bouncer.

"That was a bloody hard class, Bouncer," said Spindle, sipping from a cup of tea at break time. "I'm beginning to get square roots but cube roots have got me baffled."

"It's the same as multiplying a number by itself three times," explained Bouncer.

"You mean, three times three is nine, and three times nine is twenty-seven? So, the cube root of twenty-seven is three?" asked Spindle.

"You've got it now, Spindle," said Bouncer.

Spindle thought for a moment. "How did you get the answer for one hundred and eleven? I can get to a hundred, but no more."

"That's easy," said another student who was just sitting down at their table and overheard them. "You then go through the numbers after the decimal point."

"Do what?" exclaimed Spindle.

"Multiply ten point one by itself three times. Then ten point two and so on until you reach the number," explained the student.

"Sounds complicated," said Spindle, frowning.

"Or you can use one of these," said the student, producing a tube computator and placing it on the table.

"Where did you get that?" asked Bouncer.

"I import them from Germany. They are for engineers and scientists."

"How much?"

"Five shillings," smiled the student.

"That's a lot of money," said Spindle.

"It will make it easier for you. It's a good investment."

"I'll ask my dad for the money," said Spindle.

"I'll ask my aunt," said Bouncer.

"My name is Rupert Squires," said the student picking up the computator. "I'm in my last year here, then I'm going to Sandhurst for officer training."

"I'm thinking about joining the Army," said Bouncer.

"It's better to go for officer training. Once you are trained, you enter as an officer. If you go directly into the Army, you start as a private, and it takes a long time to become a non-commissioned officer," said Rupert.

"Squires? That name is familiar," said Spindle.

"You don't happen to be related to someone who drives a Bristol Bomber?" inquired Bouncer.

"My dad drives the only one in Bridgefield," said Rupert.

Spindle and Bouncer glanced at each other. "So, you are Susan Davenville's cousin?" asked Bouncer.

"That's right. Susan is my cousin."

"We were at Susan's sixteenth birthday party last year," said Spindle. "Understand she is up in London living with her uncle and studying to be a nurse."

"Yes, that's correct. Her uncle is a Harley Street surgeon, you know. Quite successful."

"Have you seen Susan recently?"

"No, I haven't seen her since last Christmas before she left for London. My mother was up in London staying with Aunt Mary for a couple of weeks last month while Lord Davenville had to be away on business. Aunt Mary is not well... never got over Paulina's death, I'm afraid. Lord Davenville moved her up to their London house in May as he didn't want her to be alone," explained Rupert.

"Such a tragedy about Paulina and George," said Bouncer. "We met them at Susan's party. They had just become engaged and were talking about their wedding plans and the honeymoon trip on *The Titanic*."

"I know. We were all devastated, of course," said Rupert sadly. Then he drew himself up. "Well, it's nearly time for class. Good to meet you chaps. If you want to buy a computator, let me know."

"What's the next class, Bouncer?" asked Spindle, as Rupert stood to leave.

"Science in Laboratory Six," said Bouncer.

"Mr. Cook is the science teacher," said Rupert. "He likes to talk about the solar system."

"Solar system," joked Spindle. "The only stars I know are the ones I see when I get hit on the head."

Spindle and Bouncer rose from the table and shook hands with Rupert before heading down the hall to Laboratory Six.

Professor Cook was already at the front of the room looking at his lecture notes when they entered and found seats together. He was a tall, gaunt man with thick bristling salt and pepper eyebrows and a shock of unruly steel gray hair. Exactly at the appointed moment for class to begin, he looked up from his notes, and without any preliminaries, abruptly announced, "My first lecture will be about air. Have pen and paper ready to take notes."

"Cubes and now air," whispered Spindle picking up his pen.

"The composition of air was first ascertained in 1774. It is composed of seventy-seven parts of nitrogen and twenty-three parts of oxygen. Candles go out when the percentage of oxygen falls below eighteen point five. Each adult inhales a gallon of air per minute, and consumes thirty ounces of oxygen a day. Horses require sixteen hundred cubic feet of air space to function properly."

"What about automobiles, Sir? How much oxygen do they need?" asked Spindle.

"Interesting question, young man. What is your name?" said Cook peering at Spindle from under his bushy brows.

"Brian Adams, but my friends call me Spindle."

"Well, Spindle, cars use either steam or combustion engines. But let's talk about that later. Cars move because of the explosive energy given off by the fuel. Like a candle, the fuel needs oxygen to burn. Without going into the physics of combustion too much, Spindle, a rough estimate of air needed would be the cubic inch displacement of the engine."

"That means I multiply the volume of the cylinder by the number of revolutions per minute to obtain the volume of air used per minute. Then I multiply that by point seven seven?" asked Spindle.

"Perfect, Spindle. You have the makings of a scientist," declared the professor with the hint of a smile.

"What was that all about, Spindle? I didn't understand anything you said," whispered Bouncer.

"You know numbers, I know about air," Spindle laughed.

After science class, Spindle, Bouncer and James Taylor joined the rest of the students in the lunchroom where they sat at long tables. Ladies in white aprons passed out plates containing the student dinners. The air smelled heavily of cooked cabbage.

"I don't like boiled cabbage," said Bouncer, looking at his plate and wrinkling his nose.

"I like the mashed potatoes," said James. "By the way, Spindle, you sounded just like a scientist in Cook's class. How did you know about that air stuff?"

"I don't know. It sort of happened. I opened my mouth, and the words came out. I didn't actually think. It just came out that way."

"Must be Daisy," said Bouncer, grinning wickedly at Spindle. "Bet she's been teaching you a thing or two about air exchange."

Spindle reddened.

"Who's Daisy?" asked James.

"Daisy Summers, Spindle's new girlfriend," said Bouncer.

"Oh?" asked James, looking inquiringly at Spindle.

"What do we have next?" asked Spindle, changing the subject.

"Geographical Studies," replied James looking at a sheet of paper.

"Like colonies in the British Empire?" asked Spindle remembering Alwood's quiz.

"Lots of statistics involved," replied James looking at the class summary.

"I thought statistics were used in accounting or something like that," said Bouncer "They are numbers, aren't they?"

"Not cubes again!" said Spindle.

"The size and populations of countries, that sort of thing," said James.

"I'd rather have a science lesson," said Spindle.

After lunch, the three boys found seats together in the assigned lecture room where a rather rotund, ruddy-faced gentleman stood behind the lectern.

"I am Professor Henry, your geographical teacher," he announced. "During this school year you will learn geographical statistics for the British Empire and the rest of the world. You should find this course very interesting." He paused and looked around the classroom.

"Is statistics something that accountants use?" asked James.

"Yes, that's correct. Without statistics, British business would not operate efficiently and perhaps there would be no Empire."

"Can you give us an example of what you mean?" asked another student.

"You will understand better later on," smiled Professor Henry.

"My father is an accountant. I've never heard him talk about statistics," said Spindle.

"Where does your father work?"

"At the gas works, in the billing department."

"A good example. Gas is produced according to customer demand. The amount of coal used to produce the gas is relative. The gas company orders the coal according to the demand for gas. In cold weather more coal is needed, in hot weather, less. The billings your father makes for gas are according to the gas produced. Just a question of statistics."

"Sounds complicated," called out a student sitting in the back row.

"Let me get on with the lesson, and perhaps you will understand. To begin with, we will examine the 1891 Census for England and Wales. In England and Wales there are twenty-nine million persons. Of these, fourteen million are males and fifteen million are females."

"That means there are one million single women to choose from," called out Spindle laughing.

"You're getting the idea of statistics now, but your observation is not correct. There are eight point seven million men and eight point nine million women who are unmarried, which means there are just enough to go around," said the professor with a broad grin.

A small moan emanated from the classroom.

"Talking about marriage," continued the professor, "Five thousand five hundred men and twenty-eight thousand eight hundred women are identified as being married at the age of fifteen."

"What about babies?" asked Bouncer.

"There are seven hundred fifty-four thousand babies under twelve months old."

"What are their names?" asked James.

Professor Henry thought for a moment. "They begin with 'A' and continue through 'Z,'" he said, straight-faced.

"That's not fair, Sir. He wanted to know the actual names," called out Spindle over the laughter that filled the classroom.

"Now you understand statistics," smiled the professor.

\* \* \*

On Saturday night, Spindle walked into The White Horse and joined Freddie and Bouncer who were seated at the bar.

"How are you tonight, Spindle?" asked Ben as he began pouring the usual half-pint of bitter.

"It's been a tough first week at the Poly," said Spindle.

"It will pay off in the end," said Nan, who was assisting Ben behind the bar.

"Let me buy that drink," offered Freddie.

"Thanks, Freddie. How was Commerce School?" asked Spindle as he picked up the glass of bitter and took a sip.

"Money is the article agreed upon as a common denomination of value, in terms of which all commodities may be expressed," parroted Freddie.

"You learnt something of importance Freddie," said Ben handing him his change.

"Bloody hell, Freddie, you're being clever again!" joked Bouncer.

"Leave nothing for tomorrow that should be done today," quoted Freddie.

"Pack it in, Freddie. We've had enough," laughed Spindle.

"I thought you were going dancing with Daisy?" asked Bouncer, looking at Spindle.

"Meeting her at the hotel at nine o'clock," said Spindle. "Are you going?"

Freddie and Bouncer shook their heads.

"Saving my money to buy that computator," said Bouncer. "I've got to use my weekly allowance. My aunt can't afford to pay for it."

"I told my dad about it. He says he will buy it as long as he gets to use it," smiled Spindle.

"What's a computator?" Freddie wanted to know.

"Rupert Squires is selling a machine that calculates numbers. Square roots, that type of thing," explained Bouncer.

"I need one," laughed Spindle.

"Rupert Squires? Susan Davenville's cousin, son of Bristol Bomber Squires?" asked Freddie with a raised eyebrow.

"The very same. He says he is going to Sandhurst for officer training when he finishes at the Poly," said Bouncer.

"Three half bitters, please, Ben," said Spindle looking at the clock. "I'm buying. Then I have to go to meet Daisy. By the way, where is Sam tonight?"

"I think he is meeting Rose for more dancing lessons," said Freddie. "Seems to really fancy dancing, or maybe it's his teacher," he joked. The others laughed, and Spindle looked at the clock again as he drained his glass and plunked it down on the bar top.

"Getting anxious to see Miss Daisy?" teased Bouncer. "Better keep an eye out for Sidney Chapel. He should be back in town," he added.

"Daisy said he's not her boyfriend. I am," said Spindle confidently as he turned to leave. "See you later," he said as he walked away.

The next morning, Bouncer ran into Spindle at the newsagent's shop. "What happened to you?" he asked, observing the patch Spindle was wearing over his left eye.

"That bloody Daisy lied. Sidney Chapel is her boyfriend, and he punched me in the eye," said Spindle mournfully as he raised the patch to reveal his eye, which was black and blue and swollen shut.

"Tried to warn you," said Bouncer.

"I know," said Spindle, grimacing. Then he grinned. "Had a good time, though, for a couple of weeks. Maybe the black eye was worth it."

Bouncer was frowning at a newspaper headline. "You may have had a good time, but the news doesn't look too good," he remarked.

"What do you mean?" asked Spindle peering over his shoulder.

"The Germans are building more battleships," answered Bouncer reading the small print.

"What's wrong with that?"

"They are jealous of our Empire," responded Bouncer looking concerned. "They want an Empire as well."

"They have one, don't they?"

"Not as big as ours," said Bouncer, continuing to read the paper. "Remember what Lord Davenville said?" He read on. "They have a large army already, so why are they building more battleships?" he wondered.

"It's a question of statistics," said Spindle.

\* \* \*

# Chapter 6

## *The Bridgefield Volunteers*

"**B**RITAIN DECLARES WAR on Germany! Goes to Aid of Belgium," proclaimed the August 4, 1914 newspaper headline that was posted above the bar in The White Horse pub.

"Damn Germans," said Spindle, who was sitting with Sam at the bar on a Saturday evening in late August. They were waiting for Bouncer to appear.

"We'll take care of them all right, now that Kitchener's been appointed Minister of War," commented Ben as he wiped the bar with a towel. "He's raising an army of 500,000. Wants the first 100,000 right away."

"Been reading about that in *The Times*," said Sam. "I hear Major General Wallis is sponsoring The Bridgefield Battalion – paying for it out of his own pocket. Recruiting starts Monday."

"A brave man, General Wallis. Kitchener still remembers what he did for him in Khartoum. They say when Kitchener was appointed Minister of War, he gave Wallis a special assignment," said Ben. "What'll it be today, Harry?" he asked as a new customer walked up to the far end of the bar. When Ben had walked down to the end of the bar out of earshot, Sam turned to Spindle.

"I'm going down to volunteer for the battalion on Monday," he said in a low voice. "It'll be a chance to get out of the butcher shop."

"Thought you have to be nineteen," said Spindle.

Sam shrugged. "It's worth a try anyway. If I wait till I'm nineteen, the war will be over. They say it'll be over by Christmas now that we're in it."

"From what I read, Kitchener doesn't think so. Thinks it's going to be a long war. That's why he convinced Parliament to pass the bill to raise the New Army."

"Hello, Bouncer. Want the usual?" called out Ben from the other end of the bar. Spindle and Sam turned. Bouncer and a young man dressed in an army captain's uniform were walking toward them.

"Look who I ran into on the street," said Bouncer, as they joined them. "Spindle, you remember Rupert Squires. Rupert, this is Sam Baldwin."

"Rupert!" laughed Spindle. "See you are Captain Squires now. What are you doing in Bridgefield? Thought you were stationed in Maidstone."

"On leave for five days, then I leave for France. My regiment, The Royal West Infantry, is part of the Expeditionary Force," said Rupert.

"Sit down and let us buy you a drink. What will it be?" said Spindle.

"A pint of Tetley's if they have it," said Rupert drawing up a stool next to Spindle.

"Ben, a pint of Tetley's for our friend here. I'm buying," called out Spindle.

"No, you're not. It's on the house," said Ben. "Honored to serve an officer in our Army." He beamed at Rupert and held out his hand.

"Rupert, this is Ben Ashley, landlord of The White Horse," said Bouncer. "Ben, meet Captain Rupert Squires."

"Wish I was going off to fight the Germans," said Bouncer after they were all settled with their drinks and Ben had gone off to serve

133

other customers. "I was going to join the Army when I was eighteen, but they raised the age to nineteen, and I won't be nineteen until January. Now, that my aunt is gone, I have no one to sign the papers – not that she was willing to sign anyway."

"Well, if you want to fight, you'd better go in now," said Rupert. "With Kitchener in charge, this war will be over by Christmas."

"I'm going down to the drill hall and volunteer for The Bridgefield Battalion on Monday, and I'm younger than you," said Sam quietly. "Why don't you come with me?"

"Is your dad signing the papers?" asked Bouncer.

Sam shook his head. "No. Haven't told him, but if I get in, he'll be proud. Then I won't have to work in the butcher shop. There's got to be more to life than making sausages. I made fifty pounds this morning."

"What kind of sausages?" asked Spindle.

"Not German sausages, I can tell you," smirked Sam. They all laughed.

"If you get into the Army and get sent to the front, then you can make German sausages," quipped Rupert.

"I'll go with you to volunteer on Monday. Maybe we'll both get in," said Bouncer, draining his glass and signaling to Ben for another. "What about you, Spindle? Going back to the Poly, I suppose."

Spindle held up his glass and studied it. "I was thinking of going into officer training school after the Poly, like Rupert here," he said slowly. "But that will definitely be too late to get into this war – three more years." He paused, took a sip from his glass and suddenly banged it down on the bar. "Sod it! I want to fight Germans, too. I'll go with you to volunteer on Monday as well!" he cried.

"Volunteer for what? Can I come, too, if I promise to share my sandwiches?" queried a familiar voice behind them.

Spindle spun around on his stool. "Freddie! Didn't see you come in. Where've you been?"

"On holiday in Wales. Just got back and thought I'd find all of you here," said Freddie, drawing up a stool next to Bouncer.

"Good to see you, Freddie. Meet Rupert Squires, or I should say, Captain Squires. Rupert, this is Freddie Simpson."

Rupert and Freddie shook hands. "Son of Barrister Simpson?" asked Rupert.

"That's right," replied Freddie. "And you are Susan Davenville's cousin, son of Frederick Squires? You were at the Poly with Bouncer and Spindle?"

Rupert nodded.

"Remember, we told you about meeting him when we were in our first year," said Spindle. "Rupert saved our lives with those computators. Never would have passed without them," he added.

Rupert laughed. "Those computators saved a lot of lives and made me a tidy sum into the bargain. Well, I must be going now. Only five days before I leave for France," he said, placing his empty pint glass on the bar and standing up. "It was good to see all of you. Perhaps I'll see you on the front." He touched his cap in a mock salute and turned to leave.

"Good luck, Captain Squires! Kill a Hun for me and come back for another Tetley's!" called out Ben from behind the bar.

Cheers filled the room as other customers turned to see who Ben was addressing.

"Kill a Hun for me, too!" cried out the customer at the end of the bar, holding up his tankard of beer.

"And me as well!" yelled another, raising his glass.

"We'll be right behind you, Captain! Joining up on Monday!" yelled another man, who was sitting at a table with four comrades. They all jumped to their feet and saluted.

Rupert stopped and saluted in return. "Pleased to hear it. We need all the men we can get to stop the Germans."

After Rupert had departed and the commotion died down, Freddie poked Spindle on the arm. "What did you say about volunteering? Are you volunteering for the Army?" he asked.

"Yes, we all are," said Spindle indicating Bouncer and Sam with a sweep of his hand. "Major General Wallis is sponsoring The Bridgefield Battalion to help meet Kitchener's quota for the New Army. They start recruiting Monday morning at the drill hall."

"Oh, good-o. Then, I'm volunteering, too," announced Freddie with a huge grin on his face.

"What about your father? He'll never agree to you leaving Commerce School, will he?" asked Bouncer.

"Oh, bother. He won't know about it until I'm in, and then he won't be able to do anything about it, will he? Besides, I can always finish Commerce School after the war," said Freddie, unperturbed. "What about you, Banger? What does your dad say about you leaving the butcher shop?"

Sam reddened and grinned sheepishly. "Haven't told him I'm volunteering, but if I get in, I think he'll be proud of me. King and Country and Duty, you know."

"Right! That's the spirit! I'm not telling my dad, either. He still wants me to apply for an accountant position at the gas works. Thinks my brother being in the Navy is enough contribution for our family," said Spindle. He raised his glass. "Here's to The Bottom Five! We stick together through thick and thin, peace and war!"

"That's right. We're all here except Pete," said Bouncer, raising his glass and clinking it against Spindle's.

"Where is Pete? Have you heard from him?" asked Freddie.

"Still in the Merchant Navy somewhere in the Mediterranean, the last I heard," said Bouncer.

"What about Ginger?"

"Still in London working as a projectionist at The Odeon," said Spindle.

\* \* \*

At eight o'clock on the last Monday in August, the front door of the Bridgefield drill hall was already surrounded by men of all ages clamoring to be recruited.

The door opened a crack, and a sergeant looked out. "Men, it will be a lot easier if you would form a line of four abreast," he yelled in order to be heard over the din. "Be patient and hold the line and the quicker we can process you for enlistment," he added when the men had quieted and had begun forming the four-abreast line.

When the door finally opened at 8:30, a cheer went up from the group outside.

"Step inside, the first four, and stop on the green line," ordered the sergeant.

The first four recruits walked in and stopped on the line.

"Step forward to be interviewed," said another sergeant. The four men walked forward and took seats at wooden tables facing uniformed interviewers, and the next four stepped up to take their place on the green line.

By the time Spindle arrived at nine o'clock, the four-abreast line circled the drill hall and extended up the road for some distance. He could see the line getting longer as he walked a way up the line looking for Bouncer, Freddie and Sam, but he couldn't find them.

As he was walking back toward the end of the line, a man he knew who was a regular customer at The White Horse called out to him. "Better get in line quickly, Spindle. They only want a thousand men for the battalion."

Spindle nodded and hurried to the end of the line where he joined the queue, becoming the fourth man in the last row.

"Must be over a thousand men here," commented the man who was standing next to him. "If it wasn't for my friend Bert here, I would have missed enlisting."

"That's right. Harry was on his way to work, and I told him this was the day to enlist," said Bert, who was standing next to Harry.

"What about your job?" asked Spindle.

"Dropped everything. I'm going to fight Germans," responded Harry.

"It's going to take a while," said the man standing at the end of Spindle's row. "My name is Percy Johnson, and I come from Toadhill," he added as he extended his hand to Spindle.

Spindle reached over and shook his hand. "They call me Spindle, but my real name is Brian Adams."

"Pleased to meet you, Spindle," said Percy. "I hope we pass the medical exam. They say you have to be in perfect condition."

"I'm Bert Bolcomb, and this is Harry Phillips, and we're in perfect condition," said Bert with a grin.

"Pleased to meet you, too," smiled Percy, and shook hands with the other two.

"Now here's a welcome sight," said Harry, pointing up the line where ladies pushing carts were passing out hot tea and bread rolls to everyone. The sound of men laughing and joking created a carnival atmosphere.

"If they don't hurry up the war will be over!" called out someone at the back of the line.

"I want to kill Germans, not stand in line," yelled someone else.

Up and down the line, hundreds of voices roared in agreement.

"Settle down, men!" yelled a sergeant. "There will be enough Germans to go around."

It was three in the afternoon when Spindle's four reached the green line. He could hear the recruits being questioned. After two or three minutes the recruits stood up holding a piece of paper. "This way." said a sergeant, directing them to a medical doctor.

"Next," said a recruiter, looking at Spindle. Spindle sat at the table across from him.

"Name, address and age," demanded the recruiter in a clipped tone.

"Brian Adams. Ivy Terrace. Bridgefield. Eighteen."

The recruitment sergeant squinted at Spindle and winked. "Nineteen, you say?" He wrote that down. "Occupation?"

"Want to go to officer training school."

"Occupation?" asked the recruiter again.

"Am attending Bridgefield Polytechnic and want to go on to officer training school."

"Carpenter," said the recruiter, filling in the form. "Qualifications?"

"Two years at the Polytechnic."

The recruiter finished writing down Spindle's particulars and gave him a form. "That way, medical inspection next," ordered the recruiter, pointing over his shoulder.

"This way," said a sergeant opening a door.

"Strip to the waist," said the doctor. "Need to check you over."

The doctor examined Spindle without speaking to him.

"Average, average," whispered the doctor as he filled out the form. Suddenly, he spoke to Spindle. "What do we have here? Your chest size is below average for your height. It should be at least thirty-six inches. Yours is only thirty four."

The doctor wrote Spindle's chest size on the form shaking his head.

"Am I rejected?" asked Spindle looking worried.

"Drop your trousers," ordered the doctor, ignoring Spindle's question.

"Cough, and cough again," commanded the doctor as he held Spindle's genitals. "I thought so. You have a hernia, young man," said the doctor. "You've done some heavy lifting. Better take it easy or it will get worse later on."

"A rifle doesn't weigh very much, Sir," said Spindle pulling his trousers up.

"It's not a rifle I'm worried about. It's your reproductive organ."

"Have I passed, Sir? Have I passed the medical?"

"Afraid not. Your chest is too small to meet our specifications."

"Please, Sir, I want to fight the Germans."

"We have over seven hundred men already. We will have more than enough recruits," said the doctor stamping 'Rejected' on the form.

A depressed Spindle walked dejectedly out of the front door of the drill hall where hundreds of men were still waiting their turn. The other three men in his row were standing just outside.

"Did you pass the medical?" asked Percy.

"Rejected," said Spindle, turning red.

"Rejected for what?" asked Harry.

The men in line went silent and looked at Spindle in disbelief.

"I have a hernia," said Spindle.

"They shouldn't have rejected you for that so long as you can fire a rifle," said Bert indignantly.

"Hear, hear," said a group of volunteers who had overheard the conversation.

Later that evening, Spindle was perched on his usual stool at The White Horse, attempting to drown his sorrows.

"Bloody shame you were rejected," said Ben as he poured him another half-pint of bitter. "Why don't you try again next week? Will be different doctors then. Maybe they'll pass you."

"I heard they filled their quota. Don't suppose I'll have another chance to try again, at least here in Bridgefield," said Spindle. "Anyway, classes begin at the Poly next Monday, so guess I'll go back to school and see if I can get into officer training early."

Suddenly there was a great deal of commotion, raucous laughter and cheering as a group of men walked into the pub. "Pour drinks all the way round on me, Ben! We're celebrating. All of us are members of The Bridgefield Battalion!" yelled Bouncer above the hubbub.

"Oh, no, you don't!" cried Ben. "Drinks are on the house for all our fighting men!"

More cheers filled the room.

"Look, there's Spindle," said Sam as he and Freddie emerged from the group and walked toward the bar.

"Hello, Spindle," said Freddie. "Did you go down to volunteer today? We didn't see you."

"Yes," said Spindle with a dejected look on his face. "I got there about nine o'clock and the line was clear around the building. I looked for you, but didn't see you, and I decided I'd better get in the line before it got longer."

Bouncer walked up to join them just in time to hear Spindle's remark. He clapped him on the shoulder. "Well, we're all members of Kitchener's Army, now. How about you, Spindle?"

"Rejected," muttered Spindle, looking down miserably into his half empty glass.

"What? Rejected? For what reason?" asked Sam.

"Didn't pass the medical. I have a hernia," mumbled Spindle.

"Oh, bloody hell. What's that got to do with it? A hernia won't prevent you from carrying a rifle," said Bouncer, shaking his head.

"I know. Tried to tell the doctor that, but he said they had plenty of men who were in good physical condition to fill the quota, so he rejected me," said Spindle mournfully.

"You could try again next week," said Freddie. "Maybe you could go to Cranbrook and get in there. They got their thousand volunteers today for the battalion – had to turn away about two hundred men who were still waiting in line."

Spindle shook his head. "No, I think what I'll do is go back to the Poly and see if I can get into officer training early. School starts next Monday."

"Sorry about your rejection, Spindle. Let me buy you a drink to cheer you up," said Bouncer.

"No, I don't want to put a dampener on your celebration. I'm happy for all of you that you got in. Just wish I was going with you. Think I'll go on home now," said Spindle. Freddie, Sam and Bouncer looked at each other as Spindle downed the rest of his drink and stood up to leave.

141

"It's a bloody shame, Spindle. Wish there was something we could do to cheer you up," said Sam.

"I'll be all right in a couple of days. Just don't feel like celebrating right now. We'll get together later."

"Think of the bright side," said Bouncer. "With so many men gone, there'll be plenty of single women about. You'll have free range!"

Spindle smiled weakly and waved his hand as he strode out of the pub.

"Too bad about Spindle," commented Ben as he came to replenish their drinks.

"Right," said Freddie. "Who'd have thought he'd be rejected for medical reasons? We were more worried about age and height requirements, and Spindle stood a better chance than either Sam or me on both of those counts."

"How did the three of you manage to get in, being underage and all?" asked Ben.

"Oh, Bouncer here had no problem. He simply told them he's nineteen and they believed it because he looks older," said Freddie with a grin.

Bouncer shrugged. "Well, it wasn't really a lie. I'm nineteen if you count the nine months my mother carried me." He ducked good-naturedly as Freddie took a swipe at him.

"Now who's being clever?" demanded Freddie.

"At least I didn't have to buy me way in, like somebody I know," teased Bouncer, chuckling and warding off another attempted swipe at his head.

"What's this about buying your way in?" Ben wanted to know.

Freddie grinned. "Well, I decided not to lie about my age because I look younger and I thought they might reject me on that account. So, when I told the sergeant I'm eighteen and three months, he looks at me and says with a straight face, `Two bob will get you another nine months.' I slipped him the two bob, and, presto! here I am, nineteen and in the Army!"

Ben howled with delight.

"But Sam's is the best story," said Freddie, after the laughter had died down. "You might say he got in by following in Bouncer's footsteps."

"What's this?" asked Ben, looking at Sam who reddened and grinned mysteriously.

"We were worried Sam might be rejected because of his height. You have to be at least five foot three, and Sam's just short of that," explained Bouncer. "Then, some of the men who had already gone through the process came out an told us they measure you with your boots on because they had so many men they didn't have time to have you take all your clothes off." He looked at Sam and nodded for him to pick up the story from there.

"Right. So, Bouncer told me to get in line several rows behind him, and when he came out, he gave me his boots, and several of the blokes I was in line with packed the insides with paper. Then, I began to worry that they'd reject me because I was walking funny, but I passed all right, and they put down on my papers that I'm five foot three and a half!" said Sam.

Ben chuckled and shook his head in amazement at Sam's story. Then, he hefted a beer tankard. "Well, here's to Kitchener's Army," he said. "With that kind of cunning, we're sure to send the Germans packing in no time."

"That's right," said Bouncer. "We'll be home by Christmas."

\* \* \*

By the end of September Kitchener's 500,000 men had been recruited. The Bridgefield Battalion containing most of the town's young men was quickly organized, but because of the lack of officers, basic training had been delayed.

Meanwhile, Spindle, James Taylor, and two other students sat in their science class on the last Monday in September waiting for the teacher to arrive.

"It's a pity we were rejected. Otherwise, we wouldn't be here," said Spindle.

"I know what you mean," said Roger Smith. "People think we are cowards."

"We can still try for officers' school," responded Spindle.

"We could bribe the sergeant," suggested Andrew Butler. "That's how my friend's brother got in. He was rejected the first time because of his age and he was one inch too short. The next time he gave the recruiter two shillings and he was in."

"Wouldn't work for me," said James, shaking his head. "If my father found out I lied or cheated to get in, I would have to do penance for the rest of my life. My father's a vicar, you see," he added for Roger and Andrew's benefit. "Has his heart set on my going to the seminary when I finish at the Poly, but I really don't want to. If I could just get into the Army, it would save me from becoming a man of the cloth."

"Wonder where Mr. Cook is. Maybe he's enlisted, too," said Roger. "There are very few teachers left. Even Mr. James, the headmaster, volunteered."

"Some didn't even bother to resign. They just went down to the drill hall and signed up and never bothered to show up when school started," said Spindle.

At that moment, a short, balding gray-haired man wearing bib overalls walked into the classroom hesitantly. "Is this Mr. Cook's science class?" he asked.

"Yes, it is," said James. "We're the only students left who aren't in the Army."

"Well, I'm here to tell you that there is no science teacher today. Mr. Cook and the other few teachers who were left have answered Kitchener's call for men to serve as officers for the New Army. My name is Bill Foster. I'm the maintenance man here at the Poly."

"Does that mean classes are canceled?" asked Andrew, joy registering on his face.

"I guess it does," Bill said slowly.

"Oh, good-o! I'm leaving, then. Got other things to do," cried Andrew, grabbing his books and bolting out of the classroom.

"There's something else. You might want to stay," said Bill rubbing his unshaven face, and pulling an envelope out of the back pocket of his overalls.

"What do you mean, Bill?" asked Spindle. "If there aren't any teachers, how can we have class?"

"Some army men delivered this letter this morning," replied Bill holding up the envelope. "I was the only one around so they gave it to me. Said it was urgent and that they had important war business to take care of."

"What does it say?" asked Roger.

Bill handed him the envelope. "You'll have to read it."

"Why is that?" asked Roger, taking the envelope from him.

"Can't read. Never learnt how," said Bill, his face flushing with embarrassment.

"Come on, Roger, read it. What does it say?" asked Spindle excitedly.

Roger unfolded the letter and scanned it. "It's from the War Office. Says 'Due to the shortage of officers for the New Army, the War Office is asking for young gentlemen to apply for commissions. It's signed by Lord Kitchener himself!"

"Young gentlemen – that mean us?" asked Spindle, breaking out into a wide grin, his eyes sparkling.

"Says you have to be twenty-one and have graduated," said Roger slowly, peering at the letter.

"That's no good," said Spindle, his grin fading.

"What a shame. We all want to fight the Germans for the King and the Empire. If it wasn't for the age requirement, I'd be in a uniform right now," said James.

145

"Too bad," said Bill, rubbing his face again. "Strapping lads like you. Now, me, they definitely won't have. I'm too old and too short and have a bum knee into the bargain."

Spindle frowned. "There must be a way... ," he said slowly, almost to himself. Then he snapped his fingers. "I know! It's all got to do with statistics," he announced, the grin returning to his face. "They must mean the average age of twenty-one."

Roger looked at the letter again. "It doesn't say anything about averages," he said slowly.

"There you are! We meet the age requirement!" said Spindle.

"What about being graduated?" asked James.

"We passed the exam last June, so we are graduates," said Roger, with a grin spreading over his face as well.

"I see what you mean," said James. "I do believe we qualify. Don't have to lie to get in, either. My father would never stand for that, you know."

"Bill, we need your help. Since you're the one they gave the letter to, we need you to write to them and give them our names, addresses and qualifications. Then, they'll contact us," said Spindle.

Bill hesitated and shook his head sadly. "Sorry, lads. I can't write, either. Can one of you do it?"

"I will," called out Roger. "Find me some Polytechnic stationery, and I will do it now."

Bill looked uncomfortable. "I won't get into trouble and lose my job, will I? All I do is stoke the boiler, do repairs and a bit of gardening."

"Don't worry, Bill. They're in such a hurry to recruit officers that they won't bother to check on your position here. As long as the letter is on Poly stationery, that should be enough. Can you find some?" asked Spindle.

"Well, all right, then... if you think I won't get into trouble. There's some stationery in the headmaster's office. I'll be right back." Bill left and returned shortly with Polytechnic stationery and envelopes, which he handed to Roger. He crossed his arms and leaned against the desk at the front of the room, watching as Roger began to write.

"We are twenty-one, right?" said Roger, dipping pen into ink.

"On the average, yes," said James. He winked at Spindle.

"What did we graduate in?" asked Roger.

"Statistics," said Spindle.

"Science," said James.

"Write down your addresses and give them to me," said Roger.

After copying their addresses onto the letter, Roger passed it to Bill. "Sign here," he said, indicating with his index finger where Bill should sign.

"Can't write me name, either," mumbled Bill looking at his feet.

"Make one of these," said Spindle, drawing a wavy line on the blackboard. Bill picked up the pen and did his best to reproduce the wavy line on the letter.

"That takes care of that," said Roger, writing the War Office address on the envelope.

"Do you have a penny for a stamp?" asked Spindle looking at Bill.

Bill pulled out a penny and gave it to Roger.

"We owe you for this, Bill," said Spindle gratefully.

"The penny or the letter?" Bill asked over his shoulder as he walked out of the classroom chuckling to himself.

"This calls for a celebration," said Spindle elatedly. "Let's go and have a drink at The White Horse."

"It's too early to drink," said Roger looking at the classroom clock.

"By the time we post that letter, the pub will be open," Spindle reminded him.

"What are you so happy about, Spindle?" inquired Ben as Spindle, Roger and James marched up to the bar laughing and joking. "The last time I saw you, you were down in the dumps."

"The Polytechnic has recommended us for Commissions," Spindle announced.

"Commissions!" exclaimed Ben.

"That's right, the three of us."

"Drinks on the house," called out the landlord, with a huge grin on his face.

"You are lucky we're the only three here," laughed Roger.

"Word will travel fast," said Ben.

"Has the battalion found a camp yet?" asked Spindle.

"Not yet. They don't have uniforms or rifles either," said Ben as he drew a pint glass of beer from the tap. "Every day they assemble at the drill hall and march off for training. They expect to have the camp ready by next week."

"Where do they train now?'" asked James.

"Some on the football field, some on the common," answered Bill.

"What do they use for rifles?" asked Roger.

"Shovels and garden rakes," laughed Ben.

"What about uniforms? What do they wear?" Roger wanted to know.

"Anything they have. It doesn't make any difference."

"It sounds like going to work, or practicing for a football game," joked Spindle

.

* * *

The Bridgefield Battalion assembled on the town's football field the following Monday morning. They were wearing civilian clothes as army uniforms had not yet arrived. Each man was holding a small bag containing his personal items. They had been told to limit the things they could bring.

A small platform had been erected at one end of the field. On it sat the Mayor, Town Council members and other local dignitaries, including high-ranking army officers. The men were standing at ease in front of them.

"Attention!" called out a sergeant.

The order echoed down the line as other sergeants repeated it. The sharp thud of shoes and boots clicking together in unison filled the air. Then, there was silence. Only the sound of birdsong remained.

"Men, my name is Lieutenant-Colonel Adrian Harcourt, your commanding officer," announced a silver-haired man in a crisply-pressed uniform who stood up behind the podium on the platform. "Thank you for enlisting in The Bridgefield Battalion. As you know, our camp is now ready at Wadhurst, and after another three weeks of training, we will be going to the front in Northern France. Our Expeditionary Force has fought bravely and due to overwhelming odds urgently needs our help. I know how anxious you are to fight, and fight we shall. Remember, men, we are fighting for King and Country, to protect the Empire against German aggression."

"Hear! Hear!" called out the Mayor and Town Council members.

"On this occasion, I would like to thank Major General Phillip Wallis for his sponsorship of The Bridgefield Battalion. I would like all of us to be able to thank him personally, but due to urgent matters at the War Ministry, he is in London and unable to be here today."

"Three cheers for Major General Wallis!" bellowed a second lieutenant.

The men cheered enthusiastically, and it was several minutes before Lieutenant Colonel Harcourt could resume.

"It is our mission to get you men fully trained before we embark for the front," he continued when the cheers had died down. "All that remains is for you to learn how to fire your rifles... now that we finally have rifles."

This brought laughter and more cheers from the men.

Lieutenant Colonel Harcourt nodded to his lieutenants, and the lieutenants nodded to their second lieutenants, and then a small Army band began to play a military march.

"Quick March!" called out a sergeant, and the first column of men followed the band past the platform where the dignitaries stood at attention.

Crowds lined the streets of Bridgefield anxiously waiting for the volunteers to march by on their way to camp.

"Here they come!" yelled Ben who was leaning out of his bedroom window over The White Horse pub. He heard the faint sounds of a band over the noise of the cheering crowd.

"Can you see Bouncer and the rest of them?" called out Spindle who was standing next to Roger and James on the street below Ben's window. Rose and Elizabeth were standing near them, holding Union Jacks and bouquets of flowers.

Ben shook his head. "Can't see them yet."

The cheering increased as the first column of men passed The White Horse. Women and children waved white handkerchiefs and Union Jacks. Some women ran up to the column and kissed their men as they marched by.

"There's Bouncer!" yelled Ben pointing to the next column that was advancing toward them.

"See you in France, Bouncer!" yelled Spindle, waving.

"The war will be over by the time you get there!" called back Bouncer.

"Good luck with your Commission, Spindle!" called out Freddie who was marching in the same column, five rows back from Bouncer.

"Good luck to you, Freddie! Save a German for me!"

Elizabeth ran up to the passing column and threw a bouquet and a kiss at Bouncer, and then at Freddie. "God bless you both, Bouncer and Freddie!" she cried. "Come back safely!"

"We'll be back in time to take you to the New Year's dance! Save the first one for me," called back Bouncer.

"I will!" cried Elizabeth, waving at them with the Union Jack as they passed on down the road.

Rose had anxiously been looking at faces in the approaching rows. "There's Sam!" she cried. She ran to his line and kissed him on the cheek as he marched by. "Take care of yourself, Sam," she said with tears in her eyes. "I'll wait for you."

Sam blushed as the other men in his line grinned at him. "You stay well, Rose. I'll be back for more dancing lessons." Then, he spied Spindle and the others on the side of the road in front of The White Horse. "If you need any sausages you know where to go!" he yelled.

"Bring us back some German sausages!" yelled Spindle. "Good luck, Banger!"

The crowd slowly dispersed after the last of the lines had marched by.

* * *

When the battalion reached camp, groups of men were assigned to tents that would be their homes for the next three weeks. Bouncer, Sam and Freddie managed to get assigned to the same tent.

"Private," said an officer. "You will be in charge of this tent."

"You mean me, Sir?" asked Bouncer.

"Yes, you, Private," replied the officer. "What is your name?"

"Private Russell, Sir."

"Got promoted already," joked Freddie when Bouncer entered the tent.

"It's not fair, I'm much older than him," said Harry who was twice Bouncer's age.

"Better him than me. I don't want the responsibility," said Percy.

"I want to kill Germans, not be in charge of a tent," said Sam.

The men who had been assigned to Bouncer's tent continued to laugh and joke as they unpacked their belongings.

"Did you see who I saw sitting on the platform?" asked Freddie.

"I saw him, too," said Sam.

"Bloody Alwood dressed as a captain," responded Bouncer. "I wonder if he noticed us."

"Shouldn't think so. He wasn't wearing his glasses," noted Freddie.

"He's a bit old," said Bouncer, "but then again we're under age."

"It doesn't matter how old you are as long as you can fire a rifle," laughed Harry.

Bouncer blew out the lantern after all the men had climbed into their cots.

"Let's make a promise that everyone in this tent will do his best to help each other," said Freddie. "And that we'll do our very best to stay together throughout the war."

"Good idea," whispered Harry.

"I agree to that," said Sam. "Let's call ourselves Bouncer's Seven."

"We all agree," whispered Percy.

The sound of men talking quietly could be heard outside the tent. "Quiet in there!" ordered a sergeant who was passing by. "You'd better get some sleep. You'll be firing rifles tomorrow."

The sound of the bugle woke them.

"Wake up, wake up," called out Bouncer. "It's time for breakfast."

The men quickly dressed and went outside to join the breakfast line.

"Don't dally, get your bread and dripping. You have ten minutes before falling in," said their sergeant, noticing the men looking at loaves of bread and a container of beef fat.

"I thought we were going to have eggs and bacon," bemoaned Sam, holding up a thick slice of bread covered with brown fat.

"You're in the army now, and you eat what is given you," said the sergeant.

"What's all the fuss about, Sergeant?" asked a lieutenant who appeared on the scene.

"The men want eggs and bacon, Sir," replied the sergeant.

"Eggs and bacon!" exclaimed the lieutenant. "They won't be having that until the Germans are beat."

"Then, it will be scrambled eggs on toast!" joked Freddie. The men in the breakfast line laughed at the comment.

"What's all the laugher about?" asked a captain who had just walked up.

"It's a joke about the Germans, Sir," said the lieutenant.

Freddie, Bouncer and Sam looked at the newly-arrived captain and then quickly looked away.

"Bloody hell," whispered Bouncer. "It's Alwood."

"Did he recognize us?" asked Sam.

"Is that John Russell, Sam Baldwin and Freddie Simpson?" called Alwood before anyone could reply.

"Yes, Sir!" shouted Bouncer, as the three of them drew themselves up to attention before Alwood.

"Pleased to see you all again. It must be at least four years since you left King Charles," declared Alwood.

"Pleased to see you too, Sir," said Freddie.

"Glad to see many of my former students in the ranks," said Alwood. He saluted and strode away.

Bouncer, Freddie and Sam relaxed their stance and looked at each other in relief. "Whew! I thought he'd give us away," said Sam.

"Me, too," said Freddie. "But he added a year to our ages. He surely remembers we were in his class just two years ago, not four. Wonder if he did it on purpose?"

"Can't be sure, but I think he probably said it on purpose," said Bouncer. "There are other chaps here who were behind us at King Charles."

After breakfast the men gathered on an open field and were divided into companies. Each company was then broken down into platoons and finally into sections. Bouncer and his seven managed to stay together throughout the process.

"Good news," said Bouncer smiling. "Alwood will be in charge of our company and I have been promoted to lance corporal."

"Bloody hell, Bouncer! They put you in charge of a tent for one night, and now you are a lance corporal?" laughed Freddie.

"Shortage of qualified men," said Bouncer modestly. "Now I have responsibility for two tents and fourteen men."

"Yes, but just think, you'll get an extra three pence a day," said Sam. "We only get a shilling."

"You could be filthy rich by the end of the war!" roared Percy, and everyone laughed loudly.

"Lance Corporal! Keep the men quiet!" demanded a sergeant.

"Men, be quiet!" repeated Bouncer, trying to look stern.

* * *

On the Friday evening after the Bridgefield Brigade had departed for their camp in Wadhurst, Spindle, James Taylor and Roger Smith burst through the door at The White Horse.

"Set 'em up, Ben! We got our commissions!" shouted Spindle. "We leave next Wednesday."

"Congratulations!" smiled Ben. "Where are you off to?"

"Don't know yet, but I'm going to be a statistician," said Spindle with a broad grin on his face.

"What does that mean, Spindle?" asked Ben's wife Nan, who had emerged from the kitchen when she heard the shouting.

Spindle hesitated. "Well... , if there are more women than men, it doesn't mean men can have their pick. It means there are just enough to go around."

"That's right, Spindle," laughed James.

"Never did understand statistics," grinned Roger.

"What about you, James? What are you going to do?" asked Ben.

"Signal Corp, I believe, because of my science background."

"And you, Roger?"

"Logistics," replied Roger laughing.

"Why logistics?"

"I graduated in history," he said.

"I don't see the connection," said Ben scratching his chin.

"Napoleon lost because he didn't have enough hay to feed his horses," said Roger.

"You mean logistics is about horse feed?"

"Yes, Ben, it's about hay," Roger chuckled, picking up his beer glass.

"Statistics, logistics... I don't understand it," said Ben, shaking his head. "As long as the Germans don't have them, it will be a short war."

"I'll drink to that," called out the customer at the end of the bar, holding up his beer tankard.

* * *

# Chapter 7
## *A Change in Assignments*

THE TRAIN STATION was filled with enlisted men either going to camp or to the front line. Many well-wishers were at the station to see them off. Spindle, Roger and James had been issued lieutenants' uniforms, and it took Spindle a bit to get used to being saluted by other men in uniform.

"Best of luck, Sir," said the ticket master when Spindle showed his first class ticket. "Give the Germans hell."

Spindle looked for Roger and James amongst the crowd. They were all going to London together. He spotted them standing by the train talking with Ben Ashley and his wife Nan, who had come to the station to see them off.

"Good luck, Spindle. Keep the statistics from the Germans," said Ben, as Spindle walked up to them.

"Give us a kiss, then," said Nan. "My, but you are handsome in your uniform."

Spindle grinned and pecked her on the cheek. "Keep the home fires burning and the ale flowing. Statistics will save the day, and we'll be back before the end of the year to celebrate in The White Horse," he said.

"What about logistics?" asked Roger.

"And the Signal Corp?" added James.

"I've got the message," said Nan. "You are both very handsome in your uniforms, as well." She smiled and gave both of them a kiss on the cheek.

"I was worried that you were not going to make it," said Spindle.

"My father held a prayer vigil for me this morning in the chapel, and it took longer than I thought," said James.

"Well, at any rate, we're here, and we'd better find a compartment. The train is going to be full," said Roger.

"Well, all the best to you," said Ben shaking their hands.

"I will miss you," said Nan, tears welling up in her eyes.

"We will be back at Christmas, so keep those kegs full," Spindle reminded her again as he followed Roger and James onto the train and into a first class carriage.

"Give my love to the others if you see them," called out Nan.

At each station the train passed through enroute to London, crowds of well-wishers lined the platforms. They were waving Union Jacks and holding up placards that wished the troops well and a safe return.

Spindle and his companions shared their compartment with a gentleman who was wearing an expensive top hat and a black overcoat. Initially, no one spoke. They gazed out at the passing countryside, each caught up in his private thoughts about the war and the future.

After the third railway station, the gentleman rose from his seat.

"My name is Charles Morton, and I'm pleased to be in such good company. There is nothing more pleasing then seeing three fine officers going off to war. I am honored to be in your company, gentlemen," he said, with a small bow.

"Thank you, Sir. You are very gracious to make such a statement," said Roger.

The three lieutenants stood up and each introduced himself and shook Morton's hand.

"I fought in the Sudan and in South Africa," remarked Morton. "Seeing you dressed in uniform has brought back many memories."

"I met Major General Wallis a few years ago," said Spindle. "I understand he was a hero in the Sudan?"

"You did? You were very lucky. Major General Wallis became a recluse after returning from the Sudan. He didn't want to see anyone. Shut himself away on his country estate, you know. Only came out when called upon to serve his county," said Morton.

"Why did he lock himself away?" asked James. "He was adored by so many."

"Legs. It was his legs. They are wooden you know. Felt guilty about living. He thought he should have got back to Kitchener sooner."

"But he saved Kitchener's column. If it wasn't for him Khartoum would not have been relieved," said Roger.

"That's right, but the column was six days late due to lack of fresh water. Wallis thought if he had brought the water sooner, Chinese Gordon's life would have been saved."

"It was a logistics problem," said Roger.

"And statistics," added Spindle.

"Communications, too," added James. "Without that nothing works."

"How right you are, James, but without the other two, wars cannot be won. From what you are saying, you are familiar with all of these aspects," said Morton with animation in his voice.

"Yes Sir, we have been assigned to carry out these responsibilities," replied Spindle.

"How did you meet Major General Wallis?"

"Four friends and I stopped his horse from bolting. If the horse had bolted, he could have been hurt."

"You mean you could have saved Wallis's life?" asked Morton.

"May have, Sir. He gave my friends and me a half sovereign each."

"Do you still have it?"

"Yes, Sir. I have it here. I keep it as a good luck charm." Spindle retrieved the gold coin from his uniform pocket and showed it to Morton who examined it closely and then smiled.

"Yes, it's one of the General's, all right," he said, handing the coin back to Spindle. "Special issue, you know. The Government was pleased with what the General had done, so they paid him a bonus in sovereigns and half sovereigns in the amount of ten thousand pounds."

"How do you know the half sovereign is one of them?" asked Roger.

"If you look closely, you'll see the coin has been marked on the head side with the small letters 'MFW' which means 'Minted for Wallis,'" smiled Morton. "You are very lucky to have such a coin. The General would not have parted with it unless he felt you deserved it. It is now a very valuable collector's item."

"I also got a caning for helping him, but that's another story," said Spindle noticing Saint Paul's Cathedral through the train widow.

"Did the General know that?" asked Morton.

"No, Sir, but the caning wasn't hard."

The train stopped at Charring Cross Station, and everyone got off the train and merged into the crowd of well-wishers.

"Can I have your names, rank and serial numbers?" asked Morton, pulling a pencil and a small diary from inside his topcoat. The three gave Morton the information he requested. After writing down the information, Morton hesitated, frowning at the diary.

"We're not in trouble, Sir?" asked James, noticing the concerned look on Morton's face.

"To the contrary gentlemen. Not only have you been good travelling companions, but you have also exhibited talents that our country needs."

"Thank you, Sir," smiled Spindle.

"You said you and four friends helped the Major General? What are their names and did they volunteer?"

"Yes, Sir. John Russell, Freddie Simpson and Sam Baldwin were all accepted into The Bridgefield Battalion that Major General Wallis is sponsoring. The other is Peter Court who is in the Merchant Navy."

"Interesting man," said Roger as they strode along the platform, watching Morton walking quickly away ahead of them.

"Seems to be in a hurry," said James. "Must be a banker."

"He knows a lot about Major General Wallis," observed Roger.

"I think he knows more then what he is saying," commented Spindle.

The three made their way through the crowd waiting to meet arriving passengers, and then stopped to say goodbye to James who was catching another train.

"Good luck, James. Keep those signals in order," smiled Roger. "Logistics needs them."

"Same with statistics," added Spindle shaking his hand.

"We'll all write to Ben, and Ben can write us back to keep us posted on each other's whereabouts," said James, smiling and turning to get on his train.

"Good luck, James," Roger and Spindle said again as they walked away.

"Let's walk to the War Office. It's such a nice day. Besides, it will take forever to find a hackney," said Spindle.

Roger nodded and they began walking along Charring Cross Road. A coach drawn by a team of four matched black horses pulled up beside them.

"Can I give you gentlemen a lift?" asked Morton peering out of the coach window.

Spindle and Roger looked at Morton, noticing the coat of arms painted on the door beneath the window.

"Thank you, Sir," answered Spindle as he and Roger climbed into the coach.

"Where are you going?" asked Morton.

"To the War Office, Sir."

"War Office," said Morton to the driver. He turned to Roger and Spindle. "Are you going to get your assignments there?"

"Yes, Sir. We are to speak to General Armstrong."

"Know him well," said Morton.

"You know a lot of people, Sir," commented Spindle.

"A few," replied Morton. "It's my job, you see. It's my job to know."

"I hope you don't think I am being forward, but what is your job?" asked Spindle.

"Difficult to say what it is," said Morton, "but I can say it is something to do with statistics and logistics."

"And the war?" asked Roger.

"And the war," Morton confirmed.

The coach pulled up in front of the War Office, and Spindle and Roger disembarked. They said goodbye to Morton and watched the coach move off down the road as the driver cracked his whip.

"Morton seems to be a man of mystery," commented Roger as they walked into the War Office building.

"Did you notice the coat of arms on the coach?" asked Spindle, as he handed his credentials to a guard at the door.

"Somebody important," answered Roger as he handed over his papers.

"This way. gentlemen," said the guard, after reviewing their papers and returning them. He led them up some stairs and down a long corridor until they reached a small meeting room.

"Please be seated. General Armstrong will be with you shortly," the guard instructed them and then left, closing the door.

Roger and Spindle surveyed their surroundings. The meeting room was sparsely furnished with a table and four chairs, and a blackboard occupied one wall.

"Not what I expected," whispered Roger observing the plainness of the room.

"He's only a general," joked Spindle.

At that, General Armstrong walked into the room from a side door. Spindle and Roger stood at attention, and Spindle wondered if he had overheard his comment.

"At ease, gentlemen," said the general. "Please be seated." He opened a document file he had carried into the room with him and looked at Spindle and Roger. "Who is Second-Lieutenant Brian Adams?"

"I am, Sir," replied Spindle.

"And you must be Second-Lieutenant Roger Smith?"

"Yes, Sir."

"You come with excellent credentials," smiled the general looking at documents in the file. "To give me some idea of where you should be assigned, I am going to ask each of you several questions about your specialties."

Roger leaned forward in his chair, and Spindle gave a nervous little cough.

"Second-Lieutenant Smith, your specialty is logistics. Give me an example of how Britain has lost a war because of logistics."

Roger tensed. He hadn't anticipated being questioned on the topic and knew he had to come up with a knowledgeable answer. He looked around the room for a clue, his eyes coming to rest on the blackboard. "Black," he thought. "Black...African slaves. . America..."

"Do you have trouble in answering?" asked the general, who had been expecting a quick response.

"The American Revolution, Sir," said Roger.

"What did logistics have to do with that, Second-Lieutenant?"

"The French, Sir."

"I need more details than that, Second-Lieutenant," said the general, sounding exasperated.

"Britain didn't have enough troops to send to America, because we were fighting the French at the same time, Sir."

"Any other logistical problem?"

"Yes, Sir. Our troops were wearing the wrong uniforms, Sir."

"Uniforms? What do uniforms have to do with it?"

"Wrong color, Sir."

"What do you mean, Second-Lieutenant?" asked the general sounding even more exasperated.

"They were wearing red, Sir. The Americans could see them coming. They should have been wearing green so they would blend in with the countryside, Sir."

The general sat back and analyzed Roger's answer. After a few moments he smiled. "Reasonable answer, Second-Lieutenant. I never thought losing America was because of our red uniforms."

Roger breathed a sigh of relief as the general turned his attention to Spindle.

"Now, Second-Lieutenant Adams, what did statistics have to do with losing America?" he asked.

Spindle sat frozen in his seat, trying to think of a suitable answer.

"I need an answer," demanded the general.

"Weights and measures, Sir," Spindle blurted out.

"Weights and measures? How did they cause the Americans to win?"

"Liquid measure, Sir. America's is different from the English," said Spindle hesitantly. "The Americans didn't get drunk like the British, Sir."

"What are you talking about? Are you aware of the question, or should I repeat it?"

"I understand the question, Sir. Statistics suggest we lost America because of liquid measure, Sir."

"Poppycock, Second-Lieutenant! You don't know what you are talking about. Liquid measure, indeed!"

"I'd like to hear the lieutenant's explanation in detail, Sir," interjected Roger.

"Very well, explain the detail of your analysis."

Spindle was thinking of Ben pumping a glass of ale at The White Horse Pub. "It was caused by ale, Sir."

"Ale, indeed!" sneered the General impatiently.

"Yes, Sir. The British pint is bigger than the American. The night before fighting, the British Officers challenged the Americans as to how much ale they could drink. After eight pints, the British were tipsy, but the Americans were not. The British kept on drinking to beat the Americans but they never did. Of course, the next day the Americans won the battle because their heads were clearer. The British didn't realize they had been drinking more ale, Sir."

"That's the most ridiculous thing I have ever heard!" shouted the general. "Do you think I am stupid to accept such an answer?"

"No, Sir," replied Spindle hanging his head.

"Is that what statistics are about? Making stupid assessments that would accuse our Red Coats of losing because they drank too much ale?"

"That was a poor example, Sir. Please ask me another question, Sir."

The General thought for a moment and then smiled. "Well, I have to say you were creative with your answer. It was a difficult question, especially following Smith's answer. For that reason, answer the following statistical question. Who will win this war?"

"Please understand, Sir. My answer will be based upon statistics and nothing else," said Spindle.

"Agreed, but hurry up."

"The German Empire Army has over four million men including reserves. Britain had one million, but it has been increased with Kitchener's five hundred thousand. The French have two and a half million. On the surface, it appears France and Britain match the Germans in army personal," Spindle said slowly.

"Well?" prompted the general.

"However, the German army has more at its disposal. The population of Germany is fifty-two million. Every year, one million males reach the age of eighteen. So Germany can sustain its army if a million are killed. The British population is twenty-two million and using the same basis four hundred thousand males are available."

"What about the Empire? Our colonies can provide recruits?" said the general looking concerned.

Spindle paused and thought for a moment. "Those with British ancestry, Sir. The climate will affect the others, Sir."

"What about the French and the Russians?"

"The French, Sir, have been invaded. They are demoralized. It is difficult to say if they will carry on fighting. The Russians are more concerned about their own country than they are about fighting in France, and France is where the war will be won or lost, Sir."

"You still haven't said who is going to win the war, Second-Lieutenant."

"If the war lasts more than six months, Sir, it will be the side that can sustain the casualties. As I said, Germany can provide an additional one million a year. Britain can provide only four hundred thousand. That means a British soldier must kill an average of five Germans to be even. Ten to win, Sir."

"No question about that," said the general. "Our men can do that." He wrote notes on plain white paper, occasionally looking at Spindle or Roger, who fidgeted in their chairs.

"Well, gentlemen, here are your assignments," said the general, putting down his pen. "Second-Lieutenant Adams, you will act as liaison between Headquarters and Woolwich Arsenal."

"Woolwich Arsenal, Sir?"

"Yes, your knowledge of ale should suit you well. They make munitions there. Second-Lieutenant Smith, you are assigned to the Household Cavalry logistics section."

"Cavalry, Sir?"

"Logistics for horses, saddles, that type of thing," said the general. "Their bear skin hats won't cause a problem will they?" The general laughed at his own joke, then closed his file, told them he would return, and left the room.

"Not a bad assignment, Roger, taking care of horses," said Spindle when the general was out of earshot.

"And yours is just as good. You'll be counting bullets."

"What's taking the general so long?" asked Roger after they had sat there for some time. "He must have been gone for at least half an hour."

"Can't find someone to type our orders, I guess," laughed Spindle

"Perhaps he has found out we fiddled our ages and qualifications," whispered Roger.

"Quiet," whispered Spindle, raising his finger to his lips. "Rooms have ears."

Another hour dragged by.

"Should we go and find the general? Perhaps he has forgotten about us," said Roger.

"You go, Roger. He liked your answer about the Red Coats," said Spindle.

As Roger stood up to leave, the general suddenly came back into the room.

"Sorry to have kept you waiting," he said, appearing to be in a better mood. "My delay was caused by a visit from a gentleman from Section Z. For some reason, which I cannot explain, Section Z is interested in you, and you are to be promoted to the rank of lieutenant and assigned there. I have no option but to do as ordered."

"Section Z, Sir? What do they do?" asked Spindle.

"Don't know, will not ask. Sort of hush-hush," replied the general.

"Hush-hush, what does that mean, Sir?" asked Roger.

"Nobody knows, except our King and Prime Minister. That's all I can say, gentlemen. You are assigned to them. Here are your orders. Get to your assignment quickly."

"Milford Lane," said Roger to the hackney driver, looking at the letter. "Chad House."

"Doesn't sound like a military barracks," commented Spindle.

"It's not, Sir. It's a large Georgian mansion," said the driver.

"What is it used for?" asked Roger.

"Can't be sure, Sir. Gentlemen go in wearing uniforms and few people come out. When they do come out, they are wearing regular clothes," said the driver.

"Could be a tailor's shop," joked Spindle.

"Too big for a tailor's shop," laughed the driver. "Besides there are sentries outside and it is surrounded by sand bags and barbed wire."

"Papers please, Sir," said the guard who was posted outside the iron gates of Chad House.

The guard examined their letter carefully. Then he called over to a sergeant.

"These papers are different, Sir," said the guard. "They have a different stamp."

The sergeant looked at the papers, then at Spindle and Roger.

"Special designation. They make three today," said the sergeant and saluted the two lieutenants.

The gate opened and the sergeant escorted them to the front door. The sergeant whispered something to another guard, and he opened the door. Inside, yet another guard examined their papers, and they were led to a large sitting room.

"It's like a palace," whispered Spindle, observing the oil paintings and gilded mirrors on the walls.

"It is," whispered the guard. "It belongs to Princess Alice, and it's on loan."

"To whom?" asked Spindle.

"Can't say, Sir," replied the guard looking uneasy. "Take a seat. It may be a while before somebody is able to see you."

"What was all the fuss about?" asked Roger looking at his papers for a clue.

"The sergeant said the stamp was different," said Spindle, examining his own papers.

"Special Designation," said Spindle looking at the initialed stamp. "Can't tell whose initials. Looks more like numbers to me."

Before Roger had a chance to say anything, a gentleman walked into the room.

"My name is Alfred Bottoms, but my military rank is general. Please remain seated, gentlemen," he said as Spindle and Roger started to get up from their seats. "First of all, I'd like to explain where you are and what you are doing here. This house is headquarters for Section Z, and you have been chosen by high authorities to become members of its staff. Before I go any further, you must have questions. I understand you were originally assigned to go somewhere else?"

"What does Section Z do?" asked Spindle, gazing about at the opulent surroundings.

"Can't tell you very much detail, but I can tell you Section Z is responsible for evaluating the war. It examines all military and other operations. It's sort of a shadow war cabinet."

"Why do the people wear civilian clothes instead of uniforms?" asked Roger.

"For security. When you leave, you will change clothes."

"What do clothes have to do with security?" inquired Spindle.

"Good question," laughed the general.

"What does Special Designation mean?" continued Spindle.

"It means that someone in high authority has selected you," replied the general. "You must know someone in high government."

"We have no idea who that could be, unless...," said Spindle, remembering their ride in the coach with the crest on its doors.

"Before we go any further, there is somebody you should meet," said the general, opening a side door. "You can come in now, Lieutenant."

Spindle and Roger looked towards the door. "Good God, what are you doing here?" Spindle blurted out upon seeing James Taylor walk into the room.

"The same thing as you. Special Designation," said James. The three shook hands, pleased to see each other. It seemed to them that their morning parting had been several days past.

"Each of you has been assigned a small office and you will work on your individual specialties," said the general. "You will be briefed later today on the overview of the war so far. You will then do your own analysis and make recommendations to Five-0-One."

"Five-0-One, Sir? That's a strange name," said Roger.

"Security code name for the chief," explained the general.

"Will we get to meet him?" asked Spindle.

"In due course," said the general standing up. "Well, we'd better get you started. We have a war to evaluate, you know."

They followed the general along mirrored corridors, then down an ornate staircase to a landing where a guard was standing in front of a small door.

"This is the operations room," said the general as he opened the door.

The four walked through the door onto a balcony that surrounded a very large room.

"Used to be the banquet hall," whispered the general. "Down there is the contoured map of Europe. This is where the war is analyzed."

They looked down at the map. It showed England and Western Europe. Mountains and valleys and other features were depicted in precise scale.

"The Union Jacks show our positions and so on," continued the general. "Every aspect of logistics and communications is on the map. Because of scale, the map is broken down into sectors. Each of these sectors is depicted in larger scale in a separate room. Your sector will be D-17."

The three were speechless. They hadn't seen anything like it before. After walking around the balcony and admiring the map, they left by the same door.

"And now to room D-17," said General Bottoms. He led them to another smaller room where a detailed contoured map of Sector D-17 was laid out below. Instead of Union Jacks, battalion markers were placed on one side of a red line, with German counterparts on the other side.

"The black cotton thread indicates our communications, and the various markers show logistics," explained the general.

"Is a battle being fought now?" asked James, noting the men below who were moving markers on the map.

"Personnel work on the map twenty-four hours a day. We are holding on to our positions until reinforcements arrive. That's where you come in. Five-O-One wants you to analyze the current situation in this sector and make recommendations," said Bottoms.

"You mean we get to evaluate the war in Sector D-17?" asked Spindle.

"Somewhat. You could say 'evaluate.'"

"If it wasn't for your bloody letter, Roger, we wouldn't be here," said James after the general had left them in a small conference room.

"We are responsible for the lives of thousands of men," said Spindle nervously.

"Well, you wanted to be officers," said Roger defensively.

"It was Morton's fault. He got us in this mess," said Spindle. "It's the only explanation."

The three sat in glum silence for a moment, each contemplating the critical implications of their assigned tasks.

"What should we do?" asked Roger. "Should we own up and tell them I faked the letter?"

"Could be court martialed and finish up in prison," Spindle moaned.

"Shouldn't have lied about our age," added James.

Their conversation was interrupted by a soft knock on the door.

"Come in please," said Spindle, looking at Roger and James with a warning expression.

"Corporal John Harvey at your service," said a smiling youngish-looking man. "I'm your assistant for D-17."

"Take a seat, Harvey," said Spindle. "We were just discussing the situation. This morning we left Bridgefield expecting to be in some barracks. This evening we discover ourselves about to evaluate a battle."

"I know, Sir. It happened the same way with most of us here," said Harvey. "I graduated from the University of Plymouth expecting to join the Royal Navy, but instead I was assigned here."

"What is your specialty, then, Harvey?" asked Roger.

"Physiological Science, Sir."

"Bloody hell, Harvey! Sounds as bad as statistics," cried Spindle laughing.

"Don't let the responsibility issue get you down," said Harvey. "After a couple of battles you will get used to it. By the way, you all look young for your age."

"Another story," said James.

"Same as me," said Harvey.

"Let's go to our war room," said Spindle. The atmosphere in the room had lifted considerably with Harvey's confession.

Corporal Harvey led them back to the balcony of the Sector D-17 room. Below were women and men dressed in civilian clothes, each wearing a set of ear phones and a mouth piece.

"This is how it works," said Harvey, waving a hand at the map spread out below them. "Sector D-17 is divided into twenty sub-sectors. Each sub-sector is one mile wide. Like the large map, the British and

171

German positions are indicated by flag markers. The markers depict the Regimental Battalion, the number of troops, and their specialty. If you want to know specifics, you use the headsets. Think of the map as a chess board. Men and equipment are moved by giving instructions to the movers below."

"It's difficult to see the detail on the markers," said Roger, squinting at the map below them.

"Use these," said Harvey, producing a set of field glasses for each of them.

Roger looked through the field glasses. "I can see everything now – the flag numbers as well as the writing on the map."

"All geological features are identified in accurate detail. The hills are very important as they hold strategic advantage. This map represents two hundred square miles. Twenty miles of front line and five miles on either side," said Harvey, continuing his explanation.

"How do they know where to place the markers?" asked James.

"Information is relayed from G.H.Q. Montreuil, France, by telephonic. Their location is accurate within fifty yards in a twenty-four hour period."

"I see D-17 covers the front line from Ypres to Armentieres," observed Spindle. "There seems to be a lot of flags around Ypres."

"Yes, there is a major battle brewing there," replied Harvey. "That's where we need to prevent the Germans from completely over-running Belgium and reaching the Channel. It's important that we hold the line there; otherwise, the Germans could cut our soldiers off."

"Battle," said James with trepidation. "I never examined a battle before. I have no experience with fighting or knowledge of military strategy."

"Don't worry, you will be observers for this one. After a few battles you will be able to take over," said Harvey, trying to reassure them.

"Bloody hell! I can see The Bridgefield Battalion marker five miles from the front line!" exclaimed Spindle.

They all quickly focused their glasses on the area Spindle pointed to.

"Reinforcements. They will be held in reserve just in case," said Harvey, gazing at the Bridgefield Battalion marker.

"Just in case of what?" asked Roger.

"In case they are needed by the Royal West Infantry to hold the line."

"Royal West Infantry – that's Rupert Squires's regiment," commented Spindle.

Roger, James and Spindle looked at each other with trepidation. Harvey looked from one to the other. "Appears you know some of the men at the front," he said.

The three lieutenants only nodded. The lumps that had risen in their throats prevented them from speaking.

\* \* \*

# Chapter 8
## *Battle!*

"QUICK MARCH, MEN!" yelled Bouncer as he set the pace along the side of the column where his section was marching.

The Bridgefield Battalion had landed at Boulogne and was on its way to join the Royal West Infantry at the front near Ypres, Belgium. The road the soldiers marched along was congested with Belgian civilians fleeing from the German encroachment. Horses, carriages, carts piled high with household belongings, dogs, cattle, goats, and an occasional automobile steadily streamed westward past the columns of soldiers.

"Our gear is too heavy to carry, Sir," said Harry who was struggling to keep up the fast pace under the weight of his kit bag.

"Mine weighs the same," responded Bouncer. "We'll just have to put up with it. Must get to our camp by the end of the day, and that means keeping up a fast march."

"Is everything all right, Lance Corporal?" asked Captain Alwood who had ridden up on horseback beside the marching column.

"Our kits are too heavy, Sir. The men are having trouble keeping up the pace," said Bouncer.

Alwood looked at the men and thought for a minute. "Have your men stop and make them lighter, then," he said. "Keep only what is essential – rifles, shovels, ammunition. The rest is up to them. Don't take long. Remember, we must reach camp by sunset."

"Thank you, Sir!" yelled Bouncer as Alwood spurred his horse and loped on up the column. Then he turned to his men. "All right, lads, you heard the captain. Fall out along the side of the road and get rid of as much as you can. Hurry!" he ordered.

Bouncer's section dropped out of the column, threw their kit bags on the ground and rapidly began sorting out items with which they could dispense. These they either left along the side of the road or gave to passing refugees who expressed their gratitude with tears in their eyes.

"They're happy to see us," commented Sam.

"Of course, they're happy to see us. Most of their country has been overrun by Germans," said Bouncer.

"They'll be even happier when you make them some German sausages, Banger!" winked Freddie.

"What's this about sausages?" Percy wanted to know. "I haven't had any since leaving England."

"Shut up, Perce! Stop complaining about the wonderful food!" laughed Bert, as he handed one of his tins of bully beef to an elderly woman who was riding atop a horse-drawn cart.

"This is much better!" said Harry, as he shouldered his lightened kit bag.

"Right!" said Bouncer. "Let's go!" He led his men at a run until they caught up with the column where they resumed their places at a quick march.

When they reached camp, near the town of Ypres, the sun was just dipping below the western horizon. Bouncer's Seven were again assigned to the same tent, with his other seven charges in the next tent. The men made short work of settling in for the night.

"My feet are killing me," said Sam, collapsing on his cot and pulling off his boots.

"Better than being hit by a German bullet," said Bouncer as he sat down on his cot and opened a tin of corned beef.

"I can hear guns in the distance," said Harry nervously.

"They are at least five miles away, and it's not long-distance shelling," Bouncer reassured him.

"When are we going up to the front?" asked Harry.

"Don't know yet. Waiting for orders from G.H.Q."

The men looked at each other nervously as they took off their boots and dug in their kit bags for food. No one spoke as they listened to the guns, which seemed to grow louder. Suddenly, they heard a voice calling from outside the tent.

"Lance Corporal Russell!"

"Here, Sir!" responded Bouncer. He jumped to his feet, lifted the tent flap and went outside. He peered blindly into the darkness.

"Over here, Lance Corporal," said the voice.

Bouncer looked in the direction of the voice. In the feeble light of the half-moon that had risen, he could make out the outline of a man in an officer's uniform standing a small distance away from the tent among some oak trees. He could not see his face, and he didn't recognize the voice. He started to walk towards him, but the man held up his hand in warning. "Don't come any closer Lance Corporal," the officer said in a low tone. "I've got some important news for you."

"Who are you, and what's the news?" asked Bouncer curiously.

"I'm an officer who knows of you. I cannot disclose my identity because what I have to say is confidential. If you knew my identity and mistakenly disclosed it, I could be court martialed," said the officer, his voice reduced to a near whisper.

"What is it?" asked Bouncer softly.

"You must swear that you will not repeat what I'm about to tell you. It must remain secret. Never repeat it," the officer demanded.

"Yes, Sir, I swear."

"You are John Russell from Bridgefield?"

"Yes, Sir, the only one in The Bridgefield Battalion."

"Lance Corporal, in the next day or so a major battle will be fought. The Bridgefield Battalion will take part in this, and there will be many casualties."

"Casualties, Sir?" asked Bouncer.

"Yes, there will be many dead and wounded, and that's the reason you have been given an option,"

"What sort of option, Sir?"

"You have two options, John Russell. Either you and your men stay and fight, or..." the officer paused.

"Or what?" prompted Bouncer, somewhat impatiently.

"Or you can go back to England and serve your county in another way."

"Another way, Sir?"

"Yes, you and your men can serve your country in England without firing a rifle."

Bouncer stood silently considering the options. "Do you have to know my decision right now, Sir?" he asked.

"Tomorrow morning at the latest. After that it will be too late. The battle will be on."

"I can't decide now, Sir. There is too much to consider. I would need to discuss it with my men."

"No! You may not discuss it with your men. No one must know except you. You must make the decision for all of you," warned the voice in a slightly alarmed tone. "Remember, it may save your life as well as your men's if you choose to go back to England," said the officer.

"I'll let you know in the morning," replied Bouncer.

"You will have to give me a sign," said the officer. "If you want to go to England, spill a cup of tea at breakfast. I'll be watching you."

"Very well. Spilled tea means England. Unspilled tea means we stay and fight."

"That's right," said the officer. "Until tomorrow morning, then. No later."

Bouncer watched as the outline of the man faded away into the darkness that was not penetrated by the faint moonlight. He shivered in the frosty October night air, and then turned to return to his tent.

"Who goes there?" called out a guard as he returned to the tent line.

"Lance Corporal Russell!" said Bouncer. "Just taking a piss."

"Right, Sir!" said the guard, saluting, and Bouncer stepped back into his tent.

"What was that all about?" asked Sam.

"Someone wanted to know if we wanted to trade bully beef for chocolate," smiled Bouncer.

"Didn't you?" asked Freddie.

"No, the beef is in tins. The chocolate is wrapped in paper."

"What? What's that got to do with it?" asked Harry.

"Won't melt in your pockets when the battle heats up," grinned Bouncer.

"That's our Bouncer! Always thinking about his Seven," exclaimed Percy. "Why would we want chocolate when we can have this tasty tinned beef?"

"Speaking of battle, do you really think we'll be in it tomorrow?" asked Freddie when the laughter had died down.

"Yes, I do," said Bouncer quietly. "If not tomorrow, then most certainly the next day. We'd best get as much sleep as possible tonight. I'm turning out the lantern now."

"Right, but don't think I'll get much sleep just thinking about getting into the war," said Sam with a small quaver in his voice.

Bouncer turned out the lantern and crawled into his cot. After a few minutes, he said in a low voice, "You know. I was just thinking. We all volunteered to fight the Germans, and now here we at the front and hearing German guns and facing an actual battle – a battle in which there's the possibility that some of us might not make it. What if we had a chance to do it over again? Would you still volunteer?"

There was a short silence, and then Percy's voice came out of the darkness in the tent. "Bloody hell, yes. It beats being down in the coal mine where I used to work in Durham... if I'm going to die, I'd rather die out in the open air."

"I know what you mean," said Sam. "As scared as I am about tomorrow, I'd still volunteer to fight. That's how bad I want out of the butcher shop. Besides, Rose would think I was a coward if I stayed home."

"As for us, we'd both do it again, wouldn't we Harry?" said Bert.

"That's right. No question. Quit my job the minute Bert told me they were recruiting. Proud to do my duty for the King and the Empire," said Harry.

"What about you, Ned?" asked Bouncer. Ned Jones had been a hod carrier before he volunteered for the Bridgefield Battalion and ended up in Bouncer's section. A short, muscular red-headed man who had left school to work at thirteen, Ned rarely spoke and kept mostly to himself.

There was a silence as the others waited to hear Ned's response. Bouncer began to wonder if he was asleep and hadn't heard the question. Then Ned's raspy voice broke the silence. "Never would be a question with me. I signed up to fight the Huns and that's what I'm going to do. There'll be some sorry Huns when I get to 'em, and the sooner the better."

"That leaves you, Inky. Would you do it again?" asked Bouncer.

"Of course I would. A few bullets from the Germans can't be worse than those canings from Alwood and Nicholson, and I survived those. Wouldn't want The Bottom Five thinking I'm a coward, now would I?" said Freddie in his usual cheerful voice.

"That's the spirit," said Bouncer. "Pleased you lot are in my charge. Get some sleep now, and Bouncer's Seven will give those bloody Germans hell tomorrow."

* * *

"Not bread and dripping again," complained Freddie as Bouncer's Seven joined the breakfast line the next morning.

"Oils your ass," called out a soldier who was standing down the line.

"Mine is loose enough!" joined in another.

The breakfast line broke into raucous laughter.

"Come on, Bouncer, don't look so serious," said Freddie noticing that Bouncer had not joined in.

"Just concentrating on getting a cup of tea," commented Bouncer holding out his tin cup to a private who was pouring from a large teapot.

"One tea coming up," said the private, beginning to pour the strong tea into Bouncer's cup.

"Lay flat!" yelled an officer. "Incoming! Keep your heads down!"

There was a whistling sound, then a large explosion as Bouncer fell to his knees holding onto his cup with both hands. The ground shook and dirt spewed around them.

"Three cheers for Lance Corporal Russell!" yelled Harry, when the crisis had passed. "He didn't even spill a drop of his tea!"

"Stupid idiots," said Freddie, getting to his feet and brushing dirt off his uniform. "That was one of ours."

"Got their coordinates messed up again," said a nearby officer, who was picking himself up off the ground and shaking his head in disgust. Bouncer looked closely at him trying to ascertain if his voice matched the one he had heard the night before in the oak grove.

"Lance Corporal, report to Captain Alwood's tent for a briefing. We are going to fight Germans! We don't have time to drink a second cup of tea!" said the officer, and Bouncer realized the voice wasn't the same.

When he returned from the briefing, Bouncer led his section on a quick five-mile march to the front line. "Here's the battle plan," he said as they huddled outside a deserted farmhouse. "The cavalry will go in first and break through the German line and we will follow on foot. They will ride fast, so we will have to run to keep up. It will be a surprise attack and we have the advantage."

"What time will it start?" asked Sam nervously.

"At eight o'clock. The cavalry should be coming any minute now."

The words were barely out of his mouth when hundreds of horses thundered past their position at the farm house and onward to a passage between two small wooded hills. The dust from the horses' hooves was so thick they couldn't see up ahead. Suddenly the air was filled with a loud tat-tat-tat followed by the sound of horses shrieking and men shouting and screaming in pain.

"Bloody hell! It's a trap. The Germans are in those hills!" exclaimed Bouncer. He and his men watched in helpless horror as more of the Cavalry rode into the crossfire.

"Get ready to charge!" yelled Captain Alwood, who rode up to their position at a gallop, leapt from the saddle and whacked his horse on the rump. He held a whistle in the air in preparation for the signal.

"Don't want to charge into that lot!" said Sam, visibly shaking.

"We don't have any choice! Follow me!" yelled Bouncer as Alwood blew the whistle and began leading the charge. With bayonets drawn, Bouncer and his men followed at a run over the rugged terrain towards the jumbled men and horses lying on the ground ahead.

"Keep your heads down and fall to the ground!" yelled Bouncer above the roar of bullets cutting through the air. The ground was wet, and the bullets were like a hailstorm around them. They lay flat and slithered along, pulling themselves by their elbows.

"Crawl to the horses for cover!" yelled Alwood who was up ahead of them. Then, they heard him scream as a bullet pierced his chest. Seconds later, they saw Alwood's head explode like a pumpkin that had been thrown from a tall building.

"Alwood! Oh, my God! Alwood!" screamed Freddie as he started to stand up.

Bouncer grabbed Freddie's arm and roughly pulled him back down on the ground. "Keep down! You can't help him now. Come on! Our only chance is getting to those horses!" He resumed crawling along the ground with the rest of his men following him.

Sam felt something under his belly as he slithered along. "What's that?" he cried. "Oh, bloody hell! It's somebody's arm!" he said, looking at the bloody bullet-riddled sleeve and the mass of red pulp where the arm had once been attached to a shoulder.

"It's a bastard! Fucking slaughter! Let's go back!" cried Percy. He was frantically trying to wipe off the warm sticky blood and bits of flesh that covered his hands, face and uniform.

"Don't stop, men! Don't think about it. We can't go back. Our only hope is getting to the horses. We're almost there," yelled Bouncer over his shoulder as he continued to inch forward through the gore on the ground beneath him. He could hear Freddie sobbing and Sam retching as they crawled along behind him.

Shells exploded and bullets pierced the ground around them. "Come on men it's not far now!" screamed Bouncer. Suddenly a shell exploded close to them. "Fuck!" screamed Bert, feeling a hot pain in his back. "I'm hit!"

Harry, who was crawling next to his friend, stopped and grabbed Bert's arm, attempting to drag him forward. "You'll be ok. Hang on, Bert. We're nearly there."

Harry heard a small gurgling sound and then he felt Bert's body go limp.

"Bloody bastards," moaned Harry. "They've killed Bert!"

Suddenly, Ned jumped to his feet. "Fucking Huns!" he shouted, as he charged forward over the dead bodies with his bayonet drawn. "I'll make 'em pay for this!"

They watched in horror as Ned charged into the melee. They saw his body jerking spasmodically as hundreds of bullets ripped into him. He continued to charge, almost making it over the pile of horses before he finally fell.

There was a moment of stunned silence, and then Bouncer pulled himself together. "Just a little further, men!" he said as he gritted his teeth and resumed the crawl toward the dead horses and bodies of soldiers that had by now stacked up into large heaps.

The men moved forward as best they could through the dead and wounded and at last reached the dead horses.

"Get cover under anything you can," called out Bouncer, grunting as he hefted a horse's leg over him. He lay there as wave upon wave of soldiers rushed over him and were cut down. He groaned under the weight as bodies piled up on top of him. He could see nothing for the dirt and blood that seeped down upon him. He felt a sharp pain in his left side. Then he felt nothing.

The onslaught continued all day. At last the pounding of the bullets and the explosions stopped as the sun set. The silence that fell was broken only occasionally by the feeble moans of the wounded.

As dusk settled over the carnage on the battlefield, a British voice speaking through a megaphone echoed through the hills. "We want to collect our dead and wounded!"

After a short silence, a German voice responded in broken English. "Yah, English, you can recover your wounded and dead. Ve vill gif you thirty minutes."

Men carrying lanterns appeared.

"Good God, the bodies are six foot deep!" exclaimed a British sergeant as he walked towards a mass of bullet-ridden bodies. "I can't see the horses, the men are piled so high!"

Men carrying stretchers loaded as many bodies as they could carry and walked quickly back to the English side of the line.

"Help me, help me," said a weak voice from a stack of bodies.

"Quick!" called out the sergeant. "There's a live one over here."

More men with stretchers arrived. Most of the top layer of soldiers was dead, their bodies cut to ribbons by scores of bullets. The procession of stretchers continued.

"We need more light. Bring more lanterns," instructed the sergeant.

"English, your time is up!" yelled the German voice.

"We need more time. We've only moved half," responded the English voice through the megaphone.

"OK, English. You haf another hour, but zat is all," said the German voice in a slightly softer tone.

"Thank you," said the English voice gratefully.

"We need more stretchers! Quick!" yelled the sergeant.

"There are no more stretchers, Sir," responded a private.

"Then get anything you can find to carry the dead and save the stretchers for the wounded," ordered the sergeant.

Stretcher bearers wrapped handkerchiefs around their faces to ward off the stench of seared horse flesh and the dead. Their uniforms were thick with blood, and millions of insects swarmed around them, attracted by the lantern light and the blood.

"Getting close to the bottom now," called out a corporal who was examining a vast pool of body parts and blood.

"Are they men or horse parts?" asked a stretcher bearer holding his lantern over a mangled pile next to a dead horse. He used a rag to wipe the blood and horse flesh away from the faces of several men, then stood up and yelled to other stretcher bearers who were examining another pile some distance away.

"There are some alive here!" he yelled. "Bring the stretchers!"

The wounded soldiers were carried back to waiting horse-drawn wagons that bore them to a field hospital away from the front.

Two days later, Bouncer awoke and as his eyes focused, he saw the kindly face of an army surgeon anxiously peering down at him.

"How do you feel?" asked the surgeon.

Bouncer tried to move and winced at the sharp pain in his left side. "I feel fine except for my arm and my side," he said weakly.

"A bullet went through your arm and broke some ribs. It will take at least ten weeks before you can fight again," the surgeon explained.

"Where am I? What happened?" asked Bouncer, frowning and trying to clear his foggy memory.

"You were in the battle at Ypres. They found you buried under a pile of dead soldiers and horses – unconscious, but alive."

"Oh, now I remember," said Bouncer slowly. "I remember trying to make it to the horses for cover."

Then he started up and quickly collapsed back onto the bed as the sharp stabbing pain from his broken ribs wracked his body. "What about my men?" he asked anxiously after he caught his breath. "Must find my men."

"Out of your battalion more than half were casualties, I'm sorry to say," said the doctor, looking down and shaking his head sadly.

"Who survived?"

The doctor looked up at him and shook his head again, and Bouncer could see that there were tears in his eyes. "I can't be sure, but I have a list of the wounded who were brought into the hospital. I'll get it for you if you feel up to looking at it. It's very tragic, I'm afraid. More than half our men were killed or wounded. The whole thing was a terrible disaster. The Germans had the high ground and were waiting in ambush, you see. Our cavalry and infantry didn't stand a chance. Sure you feel up to looking at the list?"

Bouncer swallowed hard and nodded, and the doctor went off to get the list. He returned shortly with sheets of paper attached to a clipboard.

"No, don't try to raise up," said the doctor, holding up his hand when he saw Bouncer beginning to struggle. "Just tell me the names of the men you want to know about, and I'll look for them on the list. Give me their last names first."

"Simpson, Freddie?"

"Has a throat wound and a broken nose," said the doctor after flipping through the sheets of paper.

"Baldwin, Sam?"

The doctor flipped back towards the front part of the list.

"Broken shoulder bone and a mild concussion."

"Johnson, Percy?"

The doctor flipped through the list, then paused as he read. Then he looked up at Bouncer. "He was brought in to the field hospital with massive chest wounds. Sorry to say he expired last night – had lost too much blood. We couldn't save him. I'm very sorry."

Bouncer gulped and tears welled in his eyes.

"Do you want me to go on?" asked the doctor.

"Yes," said Bouncer after a short silence. "What about Phillips, Harry?"

"Not on the list."

"Balcomb, Bert?"

The doctor flipped through the list again, and frowned. "Not on the list," he said.

Bouncer swallowed hard and lay back on his pillow. He couldn't bear to go on. "What happens now?" he asked after a moment, tears streaming down his face.

"You will be going back to England tomorrow. When you are fit again you will be coming back," said the doctor. "You are lucky. You can spend Christmas with your family away from the war."

"I don't have a family. All I have is...my men," said Bouncer. "Where are they? Can we be together?"

"I can see to it that the wounded in your battalion are all taken to the hospital in Bridgefield," said the surgeon compassionately. "You'd best try to rest now. Tomorrow will be a long day."

"Thank you," said Bouncer, as he closed his eyes and tried to block out the battle scenes that kept replaying in his head like a moving picture reel. Again and again, his thoughts returned to the options he had been given in the oak grove the night before the battle.

"Did I do the right thing?" he wondered. "If I had chosen to be transferred back to England, Bert and Ned and Percy would still be alive," he reminded himself miserably. Then, he remembered Percy's words: "If I'm going to die, I'd rather die out in the open air... ," and he was somewhat comforted. At last, he drifted off into a troubled sleep.

The next morning horse-drawn Red Cross wagons were lined up outside the Field Hospital ready to transport the wounded British soldiers to Boulogne for passage to England. Stretcher bearers were bringing out those who could not walk, and those who could were hobbling along and slowly and painfully climbing into the wagons.

"Sorry about the bandages, lads," remarked an orderly, noticing that most of their bandages were blood-soaked and had not been changed. "We just didn't have enough, you see. You'll get fresh ones on the ship."

"In six hours we'll be back in Blighty," remarked Bouncer from his stretcher to Freddie and Sam who were walking along beside him.

"Soon enough for me," said Freddie hoarsely, rubbing tenderly at the wrappings around his neck.

"Looking forward to some bitter and sausages," added Sam whose right arm was in a sling.

"Watch out!" said Bouncer, seeing  an officer rapidly approaching on horseback.

"Is Lance Corporal Russell here?" shouted the officer as he reined in his horse near the wagons.

"Well, if it isn't Captain Squires!" said Bouncer. "Over here, Sir."

Squires looked down at Bouncer and grinned. "Oh, there you are, Bouncer. Who's that with you? Is that Freddie and Sam?"

"Pleased to see you, Captain," said Sam. "It seems a long time since we had that drink together in The White Horse."

"Heard you were wounded," said Squires. "Got news for you, Bouncer."

"News?" asked Bouncer, squinting up at Rupert.

"Yes, you are a corporal now."

"Bloody hell, Bouncer!" exclaimed Freddie. "Laying down and still climbing the ladder!"

"Don't be insubordinate, Private!" said Rupert with a straight face.

"Insubordinate? Not me, Sir. No, Sir!" exclaimed Freddie with a wicked grin.

Rupert brought his horse's head up with the reins and saluted at his three friends. "Remember me when you are having a pint back in Blighty at The White Horse," he said.

"That reminds me. You owe us a round," said Bouncer.

"All I can offer right now is a round of ammunition, I'm afraid. Got to get back to the front. The battle is still on," said Rupert, grinning and tapping his horse with his spurs. The horse wheeled and he rode off in the direction from which he had come.

"Good luck, Captain!" shouted Sam as Squires galloped off.

Boulogne Harbor was full of supply ships and troop carriers. Disembarking troops had smiles on their faces, enthusiastic about fighting the Germans. The wounded were loaded on Red Cross ships, happy to be going back to England.

"Easy does it," said the stretcher bearer as he placed Bouncer's stretcher on the floor in the converted cruise ship's dining room. Freddie and Sam sat down next to Bouncer.

"Never thought I would be going back wounded after one battle," remarked Freddie.

"I know. I feel embarrassed... never fired my rifle once," said Sam.

"We never had the chance, couldn't fire when we were crawling," said Freddie.

"They shouldn't have used the Cavalry. The Germans had bigger targets to aim at. Once they had them in their sights, they just had to keep firing. Horses didn't stand a chance," said Bouncer.

"Did you hear their guns? They continued firing for minutes at a time, not like our single shot rifles," said Freddie.

"Yes. They were using some kind of automated rifles. I don't know how we're going to win against that," said Bouncer.

"Now, now men, no more talk about fighting. You are going back to England," said a passing sailor, who had overheard their conversation and was looking into the room through a porthole.

"It's all right for you," said Bouncer. "You haven't been fired at."

"Where do you blokes come from?" asked the sailor.

"We come from Bridgefield. We're volunteers," said Freddie with pride in his voice.

"Bridgefield! I come from Bridgefield," exclaimed the sailor, straining to see their faces.

Bouncer looked up at the face in the porthole. "Bugger me! Is that you, Pete? What are you doing on a Red Cross ship?" asked Bouncer as he recognized their old school chum.

"Yes, it is. Who's that?" asked the sailor.

"It's Bouncer, Freddie and Sam!" exclaimed Bouncer. "The Bottom Five."

"Blimey! Can't be!" Pete's face disappeared from the porthole, and seconds later he walked into the dining room. "Christ Almighty! I never thought I would see you in bandages!" he said.

"Better than being in a coffin," retorted Sam.

Pete beamed from ear to ear as he looked at each of his former classmates. "I can't believe it!" he exclaimed. "I'll be back after we've set sail. Have work to do right now," he promised as he turned on his heel to leave. "It's three hours to Sheerness," he added as he hurriedly walked out the door.

In about a half hour Pete returned. "Well, we're on our way. Won't be long before you're back in Bridgefield."

"Bridgefield?" asked Sam.

"You're going to Bridgefield hospital. I asked a nurse," Pete explained.

"How did you manage to get a job on a hospital ship, Pete?" asked Bouncer.

"I was working on this cruise ship in the Mediterranean. When war broke out, it was converted from a cruise ship to a hospital ship, and I stayed on and joined the Navy."

"Have you been back to Bridgefield lately?" asked Freddie.

"No, the last time I was there was when I was going to King Charles with you blokes."

"Why did you leave, Pete?" asked Bouncer.

"Wanted to join the Merchant Navy, but I had a family problem as well. Had an argument with my mum," replied Pete.

"What was the argument about?" Bouncer quizzed.

"It was over that shawl, the one I gave Susan. Remember?"

"Sure, I remember. You and Spindle and I all ended up giving Susan shawls," he chuckled. "But why was your mum upset about that?"

"It was hers. She hadn't been wearing it, so I nicked it and gave it to Susan."

"I thought you bought it with that half sovereign – the one Major General Wallis gave you."

"No, I still have that," said Pete. "Did you ever hear from any of those girls at the party or find out who we were with in that blindfold game? That was the strangest party. Never been to one like that since."

"I know what you mean," chuckled Bouncer.

"And now, I know what you mean as well!" laughed Freddie.

"We've seen Martha, Elizabeth and Rose," added Bouncer. "Have gone dancing with them a few times... in fact, Sam and Rose are courting. Isn't that right, Sam?"

"Is that so?" asked Pete looking at Sam, who was blushing and grinning slyly.

"Guess so," he said. "She's been giving me dancing lessons," he added.

"Oh, fiddle! It's more than dancing lessons!" burst out Freddie. "She ran right up to you when we were marching off to camp and kissed you and said she'd wait for you right in front of everyone! Think she likes your sausage, Banger," he teased.

"Why, Sam, you sly dog," said Pete. "Was Rose the one you were with at Susan's party, then?"

"Don't know," said Sam, who had turned bright red from Freddie's teasing. "She won't tell me."

"Spindle tried to pry it out of Elizabeth, but she wouldn't tell either," said Bouncer.

"So, where is Susan? Has anyone heard from her?" asked Pete.

"Last we heard, she's still in London, living with her uncle, the surgeon, and learning to be a nurse," said Bouncer. "We heard that from her cousin, Rupert Squires, who is a captain in the Royal West Infantry."

"Squires?" asked Pete, with a raised eyebrow. "That name sounds familiar!"

"That's right," said Bouncer. "Rupert's dad is Susan's Uncle Frederick who was driving the Bristol Bomber the day we helped the Major General. Spindle and I met Rupert when we were going to the Poly," he explained.

"Speaking of Spindle, what's he doing? Did he volunteer for the Army?" inquired Pete.

"He tried to volunteer, but was rejected, and then he wangled an officer's commission," said Freddie.

"Don't know where he is. The day we left with the Bridgefield Battalion he was waiting for a posting," added Sam.

"Finished up at H.Q. somewhere away from the front, I expect," grinned Pete. "That's where officers finish up. They don't do any fighting, just give orders."

"We heard Ginger is in London. Left Bridgefield around the same time as you," remarked Freddie.

"That's right. I bumped into him in Oxford Street about six months ago. He works at The Odeon. He is the projectionist there," said Pete.

"Sees a lot of pictures for free," joked Sam.

"He says the organ music is making him deaf," laughed Pete.

"Still the comedian, I take it," said Freddie. "Wonder if he volunteered for the Army."

Their conversation came to an abrupt end when a naval officer walked into the room. "What are you doing in here?" asked the officer, looking pointedly at Pete.

"Just keeping our boys company, Sir."

"You'd better get back to your station, Sailor. We're getting close to Sheerness Harbor."

"Aye, Aye, Sir!" said Pete, saluting as the officer walked away. "Better get going," he muttered, and turned to leave.

"Come down to Bridgefield," said Freddie. "You can find us in The White Horse."

"Don't have anywhere to stay. Can't stay at my mum's," responded Pete over his shoulder.

"You can stay with me," called out Bouncer. "You know where I live. My aunt died last summer, and I have the house all to myself."

Pete paused at the door. "I might take you up on that. Would be fun to get The Bottom Five together again. Pleased I ran into you. You lads take care and get well soon," he said with a wave of his hand as he went back to his duties.

* * *

# Chapter 9

## *Statistics, Logistics and Communications*

A T CHAD HOUSE, Spindle and the other D-17 evaluators were watching the movers who were rapidly placing additional markers around Ypres. At Boulogne on the French coast, battalion markers depicted arriving reinforcements.

"The whole exercise was a disaster," said General Bottoms looking down on the Sector D-17 map. "We lost nineteen hundred men and the Germans have maintained their positions. Despite our efforts, not an inch was gained. I need you to analyze what went wrong and make recommendations. This will be your first opportunity to prove your individual specialties."

Roger, James and Spindle glanced at each other nervously. Spindle cleared his throat. "We need information, Sir, all types of information," he said.

"Make a list of what you need, then, and I'll see that you get it. I will contact G.H.Q. Montreuil and order them to supply it."

The three lieutenants and Corporal Harvey returned to their meeting room, each wearing a somber expression on his face.

"I wonder how many of the Bridgefield Battalion survived," said Spindle glumly.

"Doesn't look good if we lost nineteen hundred men," said James, shaking his head sadly.

"Guess we'll soon find out," said Roger. "We'd best get on with our task and report to the general. Need to get the information as fast as possible."

"Right," said Spindle, turning to Corporal Harvey who was prepared to write down what they needed. "For my part, I need to know the types of wounds inflicted on our men and the cause of death."

Harvey nodded and wrote that down.

"I need information about what sort of weapons the Germans are using," said Roger. "And I need to know how many bullets and artillery shells were fired by both sides."

Harvey looked at James who was deep in thought. "Ask for the battle log," James said slowly. "After the battle started, how often were orders issued, and how long did it take to get those orders to the front, that type of thing."

"That's a tall order, Lieutenant," said Harvey writing down his request. "You may not get that."

"You heard what the general said," interjected Roger. "He's going to order it."

"But the Commander of the Expeditionary Forces has a higher rank than General Bottoms," Harvey reminded them.

"Well, we'll just have to give our requests to Bottoms and see if he can deliver, won't we?" said Spindle impatiently. "This information is important if we're to do a proper job of analyzing what went wrong."

Harvey left, feeling somewhat chastened and looking downcast. "I only hope the general can get all this information," he muttered to himself. "Never been asked for these types of things before. Wonder if these lieutenants know what they're doing."

Three days later General Bottoms delivered the data they had requested, and by the next morning, they were prepared to present their analyses to him.

"Here's my analysis of the casualties, Sir," Spindle said as he stood next to the blackboard in their meeting room where he had written a number of facts.

The general looked at Spindle's list of injuries, stroking his left ear. "I see sixty percent of the wounds were inflicted on the shoulders and the head."

"Of that, forty percent were above eye line," added Spindle.

"Interesting," remarked the general.

"Each of the nineteen hundred casualties had sustained an average of ten bullet wounds, and the first bodies that were recovered had twenty percent more bullet wounds than the last," noted Spindle, pointing at the blackboard.

"Do you have an explanation for that, Lieutenant?" asked the general.

"The Germans were prepared for our attack and all they had to do was set up their guns in the hills and keep firing at the same target area. It was just a question of how much ammunition they had to keep the guns going, Sir. The first bodies that were recovered had more bullet wounds than the last because they were lying on top of the others."

"What else have you determined, Lieutenant?"

"Estimates say the Germans fired two million rounds. We fired two hundred and fifty thousand. That is a ratio of eight to one. Estimates show the Germans had two hundred casualties. They had the advantage with a kill ratio of nine and a half to one, Sir."

"How was that possible?" asked the general frowning at the blackboard. "We outnumbered them by five thousand troops."

"They had the high ground and were in fixed locations. Our men were running. It is difficult to fire and load rifles when you are running, and it was never hand-to-hand combat for which our men were trained."

"How long does it take to fire a bullet, Lieutenant?"

Spindle tried to remember. He had only fired a gun once and that was when he was hunting for pheasants a number of years ago. "If you have practice, about five rounds a minute, Sir."

"That's if you are good," remarked the general. "How could the Germans fire that many rounds of ammunition?"

Spindle shrugged his shoulders. "The only explanation is that the Germans are using some kind of automated rifles – something like the Gatling guns used in the American Civil War, Sir."

The general paused, considering this explanation. "Well, do you have any recommendations, then?" he asked.

"Just two, Sir. First, our soldiers need head protection – something similar to what the knights wore in medieval times to protect them from flying arrows. It needs to be something light, but strong enough to prevent bullets from entering the skull. That alone might have prevented about four hundred casualties in this battle," said Spindle. He paused and the general nodded for him to go on. "Second, to increase our kill ratio, our men should fire from fixed positions rather than on the run, Sir."

"Right. Your points are well-taken, Lieutenant," said the general as he wrote down Spindle's recommendations in a leather-bound notebook. Spindle sat down next to James.

"Now, what about logistics, Lieutenant Smith?" asked the general, turning to Roger.

Roger went to the blackboard and erased Spindle's lists. "It boils down to one word, Sir," he said as he wrote that word on the board. "Cavalry."

"Cavalry? What do you mean?"

"Horses are easy targets, Sir. The Germans had larger objects to aim at, Sir."

"Is that all, Lieutenant?" asked the general raising his eyebrows.

"When the horses were shot, our troops couldn't run through them. They blocked the way, causing a jam. That's why we had so many casualties, Sir."

"The reason we used the Cavalry was to rapidly inundate the German line and pave the way for the infantry," said the general somewhat defensively.

"Yes, Sir. That tactic used to work well, but not with automatic guns firing down from higher ground. Our Cavalry was trapped in crossfire," explained Roger.

The general sat back in his chair and digested Roger's comments.

"There's a connection between what Lieutenant Adams said and what you are saying," said the general slowly. "It's difficult to aim and fire when you're riding a galloping horse, especially if your target is above you. Interesting, Lieutenant. I hope Lieutenant Taylor's analysis is just as intriguing."

He looked at James, who remained seated. "Once the battle order had been given, the orders were never changed even though it was obvious our Cavalry had ridden into a trap," said James. "Little or no communication took place between the front and H.Q. The generals viewed the battle through field glasses at some distance from the front, and they just kept sending in more and more of our men into the slaughter. The only orders given were for more reinforcements."

"Is there something wrong with that?" asked the general, sounding defensive again.

"The problem was with communications, Sir," said James hastily. "If H.Q. had known the Cavalry strategy had failed, they could have changed the battle plan. As it was, no adjustments were made, and our generals just kept sending our men right into the German trap."

"How would the communications take place, Lieutenant? There were no telephonic wires, and H.Q. is twenty miles from the front."

"Well, Sir, I thought about using everything from blinker lights to messengers or even motorized bicycles, but I think the best solution would be hot air balloons."

"Hot air balloons! You mean those contraptions people go up in at fairs?" asked the general incredulously.

"Yes, Sir. From a height of five hundred feet in a hot air balloon, observers can see for five miles. At a thousand feet, fifteen miles. The balloons could be fixed to the ground by ropes with telephonic wire attached. These wires could go directly to H.Q. as well as to the front, and instantaneous communications would be possible."

The general slapped his knee and grinned broadly. "Splendid idea, Lieutenant! In fact, all of you have done an excellent job. I will inform Five-O-One of your analysis and recommendations right away. Perhaps he will pass them along to the War Committee. I will keep you informed." With that, General Bottoms stood up quickly, tucked his notebook under his arm, and strode purposefully out of the meeting room.

"Do you think we made an impression?" asked Spindle, after the door had closed behind the general.

"I would say so," said Harvey. "I've never seen him that excited before. I'll bet he is on his way to talk to Five-O-One right now."

Spindle, Roger and James were fine-tuning their analyses of the data later that afternoon, when Harvey burst in upon them excitedly. "General Bottoms wants to see us in his office right away! Says it's urgent!"

"Have we done something wrong? Isn't he happy with our analysis?" asked Roger with a worried frown.

"I don't know, but he wants to see us now," replied Harvey.

"It's the first time he's called us to his office," said Spindle, glancing at James. "Perhaps he has found out about the letter."

"What letter?" inquired Harvey.

"A letter of recommendation," said Roger hastily.

"Don't worry about that," smiled Harvey conspiratorially. "I had one of them, too."

"Be seated gentlemen," said the general who was sitting behind a large ornate desk, holding a telephone painted bright blue. They noticed two other telephones on his desk, one painted red, the other dark green.

"I will bring them up to date, Sir," said the general and then put the hand piece back on the hook. He turned his attention to Harvey and the three lieutenants. "Five-O-One is pleased with your analysis. He is impressed with your conclusions about the relationship between the number and type of casualties and the use of the Cavalry, and he believes your recommendation for the employment of metal helmets is an excellent suggestion. He has already ordered war supply to collect hats from coal miners to send to the front as a stop-gap measure until we can design and produce our own style. He is somewhat resistant to the balloon idea, but he is willing to give it a try."

The general smiled at them and propped his elbows on the desk, steepling his fingers in front of his chin. "Because of your outstanding performance, Five-O-One has ordered me to promote each of you to the rank of captain and to give you additional help to further analyze the war and make recommendations. What do you need?"

"We need more men, Sir," said Roger.

"You've got it, so long as they bring some type of expertise that we are lacking," replied the general.

"You mean we can choose anyone we want?" asked Spindle.

"Yes, it's up to you as long as they can contribute to your work."

"What if our choices are already enlisted?" asked Roger.

"Special Designation will be given. There's nothing more important than Section Z. Has top priority over everything else," explained the general waving a hand. "Just give me a list of names, and I will see to it."

"We will need time to get our list together, and we may need to visit some old friends," said James.

The general slapped his desk with his hand. "Get cracking then, men. Get your list together as fast as you can. It's urgent. Get on with it!"

"Yes, Sir!" they responded in unison, jumping to their feet and saluting.

"By the way, Corporal Harvey," said the general, as Spindle, James and Roger were leaving the room.

"Yes, Sir?"

"You are now Sergeant Harvey. You've been promoted as well," said the general. "That's all, you're dismissed," he said as he turned his attention back to the papers on his desk.

"Yes, Sir! Thank you, Sir!" said Harvey with an enthusiastic smile. Then he hurried off to share the news with his captains.

* * *

"Pleased to see you back!" roared Ben as Spindle, Roger and James walked into The White Horse two days later. They had come down to Bridgefield by train for a short visit with their families and to see if there were any of their old school mates about to recruit for their Sector D-17 work.

"It's only been a month, but it seems a year since we saw you off at the station," said Nan who had come into the bar from their living quarters when she heard Ben shouting. "Where are your uniforms?"

"We don't have spare uniforms to wear on leave," said Roger smiling. "We were issued only one apiece, but we've all been promoted to the rank of captain."

"Let's have a drink, Ben. Fighting Germans makes us thirsty," laughed James winking at Spindle and Roger.

"Were you in the battle at Ypres, then?" asked Ben as he filled three pint glasses.

"No, we haven't been to the front yet," said Spindle. "We're all assigned to supply depots up in London. What about the Bridgefield Battalion? Heard they were at Ypres."

"Bouncer, Freddie and Sam were in here yesterday. They just got out of the hospital – all of them were wounded, but they'll be ok. They're home for a while, probably till after Christmas, before they have to go back to the front," said Ben.

"We lost a lot of men, though," said Nan with tears welling in her eyes. "The Bridgefield Battalion lost three hundred, but they broke the German line."

"Three hundred and broke through?" repeated Spindle, raising his eyebrows and exchanging glances with Roger and James.

"That's what the newspaper said. Look here," she said, retrieving a copy from a pile of old newspapers behind the bar.

Spindle and the others looked at the headline and glanced at each other again.

"It's very sad," said Nan, wiping away a tear that had trickled onto her cheek. "So many of our customers gone – Percy Johnson, Bert Balcomb..."

"Percy and Bert were killed?" asked Spindle. "I was in the same line with them when we were volunteering. What about Harry Phillips?"

"No one knows. He isn't on the wounded list or the death list, either. Percy, Bert and Harry were all under Bouncer's command. You see, he was put in charge of a section and has now been promoted to corporal. Freddie and Sam were in his section as well," said Nan, still wiping tears from her cheeks. There was a moment of glum silence as they all thought about the men who had so recently been alive and regular customers at The White Horse.

"Well, free drinks for our three captains!" yelled Ben, attempting to brighten the gloom that had descended on the bar.

"I'll drink to all our boys in uniform!" called out Ben's regular customer as he held up his tankard.

"Oh, Barney, you'll drink to anything!" joked Ben, and everyone laughed.

"That's not right, Spindle. There were more than three hundred killed, and they didn't break the German defenses. It was more like six hundred," whispered Roger after Ben and Nan were preoccupied with serving other customers.

"Wonder why the newspaper is reporting a lower number of casualties?" Spindle murmured.

James shook his head, still poring over the newspaper article.

"Has anyone seen John Russell?" called out a voice from the pub door.

"Who wants to know?" asked Ben, looking toward the door where a tall, blond man in a sailor's uniform was standing.

"Peter Court. I went to school with him."

Spindle spun around on his seat and looked toward the door, grinning widely. "Pete! What are you doing here? Come over here and let me buy you a drink! It's been a long time!"

"Blimey! Is that Spindle?" cried Pete as he walked towards the bar.

"Sure is," said Spindle. "Where have you been, Pete?"

"I was working on a cruise ship that got converted to a hospital ship when the war broke out," said Pete, shaking Spindle's hand. "I stayed on and joined the Navy."

"Hospital ship!" grinned Spindle. "I'll bet there are plenty of nurses on board."

"Not too many young ones, mostly older ladies," said Pete in a mournful tone.

"I'll buy you a drink, Pete. What will it be?" said Ben. "Good to see you again. Anyone who takes care of our wounded deserves a free drink."

"I'll drink to that!" responded the regular, hoisting his tankard in the air again.

"There goes Barney again, regular as clockwork!" said Ben, rolling his eyes, as he drew a pint for Pete.

"Pete, meet Roger Smith and I think you remember James Taylor who was in the same class with us at King Charles," said Spindle.

Pete shook hands all around. "Sure, I remember you, James. Got in trouble with Alwood for smoking in the toilet, didn't you?"

"Yes, that's me," laughed James. "I not only got a caning at school, but my father also made me do penance for half a year. Cured me of smoking. Haven't tried it since."

Pete laughed, and then his face suddenly sobered. "Oh, speaking of Alwood, don't know if you've heard...he was killed at Ypres."

"What? Alwood? How did you know that?" asked Spindle.

"Bouncer told me. My ship transported the wounded from the Bridgefield Battalion back here, and I ran into Bouncer, Freddie and Sam. Alwood was their captain, and they saw him get killed as he was leading the charge."

"Oh, God! That's bloody horrible!" cried James.

"Yes, it is," said Pete sadly.

"Let's drink one to Alwood," said Spindle raising his glass. "If it hadn't been for him, I'd have never made it into the Poly."

They all raised their glasses in a silent tribute and took a drink.

"What about you?" Pete asked. "Are you in the Army?"

"Yes," replied Spindle. "We're all captains."

"Why aren't you in uniform then?"

"Only issued us one uniform apiece, so we don't wear them when we're on leave," explained Roger. "We're stationed at HQ in London."

"Meaning you haven't fired a rifle yet?" asked Pete, grinning.

"Nah, they're in statistics, logistics and something else," interrupted Ben, who had returned to their part of the bar. "Something the Germans don't have."

"That's good," laughed Pete, and Spindle grinned.

"You say your ship evacuated the wounded from Ypres?" he asked quietly after Ben had gone off to serve another customer.

"Only the casualties from the first battle," replied Pete in a low voice.

"How many do you think were killed and wounded?" whispered James.

"I know there were two hundred wounded, and an officer said there were six hundred killed," answered Pete.

"Something doesn't add up. Look at this," said James pointing to the newspaper headline. Roger, James and Spindle watched Pete's face for a reaction as he scanned the newspaper article.

Pete frowned and looked up at them with a puzzled expression. "There's something fishy here. It doesn't add up."

"Still reading that article?" asked Ben returning to their end of the bar.

"I haven't read a local paper for years," Pete commented.

"They're advertising for women workers. All the men have gone to war," said Ben.

"What about your Missus? Send her out to work," joked Spindle, seeing Nan approaching out of the corner of his eye. She took a playful swipe at his ear, and he ducked.

"I work enough cleaning up after you lot," she said, picking up two pints of ale to deliver to two men who had just taken seats near the door of the pub.

Spindle turned back to Pete. "What kind of job do you have on the ship?" asked Spindle.

"I'm a signalman," Pete replied. Spindle, James and Roger looked meaningfully at each other.

"You know how to use telephonics, then?" inquired James, his eyes lighting up with interest.

"Sure do," said Pete. "I'm the fastest one on the ship relaying messages by Morse Code."

"What about semaphores?" asked James.

"Oh, sure. That's the first thing a signalman on a ship has to learn – sending signals by flags as well as by lights. I'm fast at that, too, but the best way is by Morse Code."

"Do you have any other kinds of expertise?" asked Spindle.

"I'll bet the only expertise Pete has is chasing women in foreign ports," joked Ben. "That's the kind of expertise sailors have. Probably has a girl in every port from Tilbury to Casablanca."

"Lucky for him!" called out the customer with the tankard.

"Did you want to drink to that, too, Barney?" chuckled Ben. "Here, I'll bring you a refill," he added, and went off down the bar to serve Barney.

"Other than women, Pete, are you good at anything else?" asked Roger after the laughter had died down.

"Good at fixing things, electrical wiring, that type of thing," said Pete.

"For telephonics?" asked James.

"Somewhat. I can lay the wires and hook up telephones."

"What ship will you be going back to?" asked James.

"Used to be called *The Queen of the Nile* before it was converted to a hospital ship. Now, it's the *Saint George*. It's docked at Sheerness, and I'm on leave for a week. I decided to come to Bridgefield for a few days – Bouncer said I could stay with him." He paused and took a sip of his ale, then looked at Spindle. "By the way, I bumped into Ginger about six months ago when I was in London."

"I heard he works at The Odeon," commented Spindle.

"That's right. He's a projectionist. Says he's having a good time playing with the lenses."

"Projection lenses?" asked Roger.

"Yes, he's figured out how to make pictures larger by projecting them on a wall using mirrors or something," said Pete putting his empty glass on the bar.

"Fascinating." said Roger.

"Pretty clever, I would say," added James.

Spindle laughed. "Doesn't surprise me. Ginger's always been pretty inventive. Remember the postcard he gave Alwood as proof that he'd been visiting his aunt in Great Yarmouth?"

James chuckled. "I remember that," he said. "No one could figure out what the joke on the postcard meant, but we all laughed as if we knew!"

"Well, I'm off to see Bouncer. Going to stay at his place tonight," said Pete, standing up.

"I'll go with you," said Spindle, jumping to his feet. "I haven't seen Bouncer since he left for the front."

"We have to leave, too," said Roger. "We want to spend time with our families before we have to go back on Monday."

"I'll see you at the station, then, " said Spindle, waving at James and Roger as he walked out of the pub with Pete.

As they walked along the streets in mid-afternoon toward Bouncer's house, many passers-by stopped to talk to them, attracted, it seemed, like magnets to Pete's uniform.

There was a girls' school on the corner where they turned to go to Bouncer's house, and the little girls were outside on the playground, dressed in their uniforms that resembled sailor's attire – white middy blouses with square collars and navy blue trim over white pleated skirts. One little blond-headed beauty was skipping rope while two companions twirled the rope for her and chanted: "Kaiser Bill went up the hill to see if he'd take France; Kaiser Bill came down the hill with bullets in his pants!"

Spindle and Pete laughed with delight. "Is that what they're teaching them in school these days then?" Spindle commented as they shook their heads and walked on up the street to Bouncer's house.

Bouncer's house was in the middle of a row of attached two-story dwellings. They walked up the three steps to the door that was painted black and rapped on it with the brass doorknocker.

A few seconds later, the door flew open and Bouncer looked out and then grinned broadly. "Well, blow me down! Pleased to see you two!" He looked over his shoulder and announced, "It's Pete, and Spindle is with him!"

"Freddie and Sam are here, too, as well as Rose," he explained, turning back to Spindle and Pete.

"A Bottom Five reunion!" laughed Pete.

"Pleased to see you survived the battle!" said Spindle, clapping Bouncer on the left shoulder.

Bouncer winced. "Go easy on that side, Spindle," he said. "Still tender where the bullet went through, and I've still got bandaged ribs."

"Oh, sorry," said Spindle, pulling his arm back gingerly.

"That's all right," said Bouncer grinning. "You can beat on the other shoulder all you want. Bloody hell, but it's good to see you lads. Come on in."

Bouncer started to step aside so they could enter when a woman's voice called out, "John Russell, are you in there?"

"Who's that?" asked Bouncer, looking out the door, and Spindle and Pete turned as an elderly heavy-set woman came puffing up the steps bearing a huge covered pot.

"It's Mrs. Graham with a meat pudding, that's who," said the woman, trying to catch her breath as she thrust the pot at Bouncer.

"Oh, Mrs. Graham, not again – that's the third time this week!" exclaimed Bouncer as he took the pot from her.

"Well, you've got to eat, don't you? Need to get strong if you're going to go back and fight those Germans. I know what you bachelors eat – just bread and cheese and lots of ale," she said.

"Thank you so much, Mrs. Graham. You're so nice."

She turned and put her hands on her hips and examined Pete and Spindle. "See we've got a sailor here," she remarked. "What's wrong with you, young man? Why aren't you in uniform?" she inquired, looking indignantly at Spindle.

Spindle reddened and started to speak, but Pete jumped in. "Oh, Brian here is in the Army all right. He's just not wearing his uniform today."

"Hmmmph!" snorted Mrs. Graham, shaking her finger at Spindle. "You'd best wear your uniform when you're out in the town. Don't want people thinking you are a coward, do you?"

"No, ma'am," said Spindle meekly, hanging his head.

"Well, John Russell, you enjoy that meat pudding. Should be plenty to go around... and not too much of that hard cider, mind you!" she said as she turned to leave.

"Thanks again, Mrs. Graham," said Bouncer as she walked back to her house next door. After she had gone inside, he grinned at Pete and Spindle. "Come on in, then, before another neighbor shows up. I've got enough meat puddings to feed an entire platoon!"

Pete and Spindle followed Bouncer into the front room where Freddie, Sam and Rose were gathered around the coal fire.

"There you are!" cried Freddie advancing toward them with a wide grin. "What took you so long?"

"Mrs. Graham showed up with another meat pudding," explained Bouncer, who went off to the kitchen to deposit the pudding in the cupboard and bring back some cider.

"Good to see you, Inky!" said Spindle, clasping his hand. "But what's this, then?" he asked, indicating the bandage across Freddie's nose and the wrappings around his neck.

"War wounds," said Freddie proudly. "Broken nose and shrapnel in the neck. Should be all healed up soon. Sam has a broken shoulder bone." He pointed to Sam who was seated by the fire with his right arm in a sling. Rose was holding his left hand with her arm tucked under his.

"Pleased to see you, Spindle. You, too, Pete," said Sam, grinning at them.

"See you are being well taken care of, Banger," Spindle laughed. "How are you, Rose? Do you remember Pete? Peter Court, who was with us at Susan Davenville's birthday party?"

Rose smiled up at them, but didn't let go of Sam. "Of course, I remember. Nice to see you again, Peter, and Spindle as well. It's good to see you all together again. Sam is blessed to have such good friends." She looked up at Sam with a quiet smile, and he returned her gaze with adoration in his eyes.

The others glanced at each other, and Freddie rolled his eyes as if to say 'ooh-la-la!'

"Yes, well, I'm pleased to see the three of you made it through the battle at Ypres," said Spindle after an awkward pause.

"No thanks to the generals," said Freddie bitterly.

"What do you mean?" asked Spindle as he and Pete drew up chairs around the fire.

"Bloody generals sent the cavalry in first and never changed the plan of attack when they rode into a trap. They were mowed down, and those of us who followed couldn't get over the dead horses and men. Germans were in the hills on either side and had us in a crossfire, you see, but the generals never changed the battle plan - just kept sending more and more of the infantry right into the trap."

"It was fortunate in one way," remarked Bouncer who had just come back into the front room from the kitchen. "If it hadn't been for the dead horses, the three of us wouldn't be alive."

"What about the waves of men who followed us? They were cut down like a field of wheat," said Freddie indignantly and started to say more, but Sam intervened.

"Let's not relive it all right now, Freddie. What's done is done, and we're alive," he said, nodding his head slightly toward Rose, whose eyes had grown wide with concern.

"Right. Let's all have a drink," said Bouncer hastily. He began to pour hard cider into glasses on a sideboard. "It's time for a toast to the reunion of the Bottom Five."

"I'm for that!" said Pete enthusiastically. "Sailors can't stand to get too dry, you know."

They all laughed and went over to the sideboard to pick up a glass, while Bouncer brought glasses of cider to Sam and Rose.

"When are you going back to the front?" asked Spindle, after they'd had their toast and taken a few sips.

"The Bridgefield Battalion is no more," said Bouncer sadly. "It's been incorporated into the 34th Division. Not enough survived to make up the full battalion, you see."

"How many did you lose?" asked Spindle.

"Can't be sure," said Bouncer. "All I know is that Freddie, Sam and I are the only ones from my seven tent mates."

"Did you see the paper?" asked Pete.

"Oh, I saw that," said Rose. "So sad. The paper said the Bridgefield Battalion lost three hundred, but that we broke the German line and killed over a thousand Germans," she said proudly.

"What? I haven't seen the paper," said Freddie.

"That's what it said all right. I read it, too," commented Sam, glancing at Freddie and Bouncer who were frowning at each other with puzzled expressions.

"So, do you know where you're going to be stationed when you go back?" interjected Spindle

"Be going back in a month's time to a place called Albert close to the Somme River," responded Bouncer.

"River Somme. That's at the end of the British Sector where the French line begins, near Amiens," mused Spindle.

"They say there isn't much action there. Quiet end of the front to give us a rest, I expect," said Freddie.

Bouncer regarded Spindle with a quizzical expression. "How do you know where the French line begins, Spindle? How did you know where the Somme River is?"

Spindle hesitated, searching for a plausible explanation. "Mr. Underwood," he stated.

"Mr. Underwood?" asked Freddie with a puzzled look.

"Yes. He was a geography teacher at King Charles."

The five burst out laughing.

"You have a good memory," said Sam. "I don't remember a Mr. Underwood."

"Neither do I, but I do remember Alwood. Too bad about him," said Pete, and the room suddenly went quiet.

"Poor Alwood," said Bouncer sadly. "Shot by the bloody Germans. He was our captain," he added for Spindle's benefit. "We saw it happen."

"Pete told me about that," said Spindle. "Terrible thing. Sorry to hear it."

"He was a good teacher," said Sam softly, squeezing Rose's hand.

"Let's have another drink of cider – a toast to Alwood. It will make us feel better," said Bouncer, as he got up to get the cider and refill their glasses.

"Do you want to go back to the front?" asked Spindle, after they had drunk a toast to their former teacher.

"Sure, we want to go back. It's our duty to fight the Germans, and besides we have to get our revenge. They killed many of our friends. It's the only thing to do," said Bouncer.

"There are ways to fight the Germans other than firing rifles," said Spindle. "You could get a posting out of the war zone."

"You mean, transfer to another unit away from the front?" asked Bouncer, looking at him curiously.

"Something like that," answered Spindle.

"We don't want that. We want to fight together. Sam, Freddie and I are the only ones left of my original seven, and we've promised to take care of each other and take revenge for those who were killed. Bert Balcomb, Percy Johnson and Ned Jones were all killed, and no one knows what happened to Harry Phillips. We want to kill Germans, unlike the generals," he added bitterly.

"What's wrong with the generals?" asked Spindle.

"Didn't see one on the day of the battle. They were living a life of luxury away from the front," said Freddie disgustedly.

"Eating the best food and drinking the best wine," added Sam.

"They gave the order to attack, then sat back waiting for the result," continued Freddie.

"Didn't I tell you that's what officers do?" joked Pete.

Spindle pondered the information about the generals as they each drank from their glasses of cider. He dreaded the question he knew was coming, and he didn't have to wait long.

"Where are you stationed, Spindle?" asked Bouncer.

"At Army HQ in London. My job is counting bullets. Bloody boring, but someone has to do it," said Spindle, fearing the reaction to this news.

Freddie laughed. "Ended up being an accountant after all, just like your dad wanted, didn't you?"

"Guess you could say that. Ironic, isn't it?" said Spindle, raising his glass to them and feeling relieved.

"Well, I think it's time for you to quit talking about the war and enjoy your reunion," said Rose. "I'll go heat up the meat pudding, and there's treacle tart for dessert."

"Rose made the tart," added Sam proudly.

"And I have plenty of cider," said Bouncer. "We'll have a regular party."

"Sounds great," said Spindle, and the others nodded enthusiastically in agreement.

"I'll just go off to the kitchen, then," said Rose, rising from her chair. "No, Bouncer, stay where you are. I can find everything," she added as she saw Bouncer start to get up. She gave Sam a fond smile and left the room.

"Didn't want to say anything in front of Rose," said Bouncer softly after he was sure she was out of earshot, "but that newspaper report you were talking about has been bothering me."

"Been bothering me, too," said Freddie, in a low tone. "As far as I know, our troops most certainly didn't break the German line, and I can't think how it is possible that we killed a thousand Germans when they were mowing us down like that."

"We never even had a chance to fire our rifles being on the run as we were," commented Sam with a puzzled frown.

"Well, it bothered me, too," said Pete. "How many men do you think the Bridgefield Battalion lost, Bouncer?"

"I can't be sure," said Bouncer slowly, "but when I woke up in the field hospital, the surgeon told me that the battalion lost more than half, and I know that there are only three of us who survived from my section of fourteen. Of course, we were in the first wave of infantry, right after the cavalry had gone in."

"It just doesn't add up," said Pete, shaking his head. "I know that we transported two hundred wounded from the Bridgefield Battalion, and an officer told me that six hundred were killed."

"Good God! If that's right, it means there's only two hundred men out of the thousand volunteers who weren't killed or wounded!" exclaimed Freddie.

"That's a far cry from the three hundred the newspaper reported," said Pete.

"Curious," remarked Spindle.

* * *

Back at Section Z the following Monday, General Bottoms confronted them. "Do you have your list?" he asked.

"Can't think of any one suitable," said Spindle.

"I have one candidate," said Roger. "Mr. Patrick Murphy. He's a projectionist at The Odeon, and specializes in photographic enlargements."

"Why do you need him?" asked the general.

"The maps, Sir. He can project them on a wall. Will be easier to see what's going on when they are enlarged."

"Fascinating. I see what you mean," responded the general.

"I have a candidate too, Sir," said James. "Signalman Peter Court who is a crew member aboard the hospital ship *St. George.*"

"A signalman?" queried the general.

"Yes, Sir, he's a specialist in telephonic."

"Gentlemen, these men are not in the Army. I expected that you would choose from Army ranks," said General Bottoms with a frown.

"You didn't say that, Sir. You said Five-O-One had asked you to get whomever we wanted," James reminded him.

"Yes, Captain, he did. The sailor shouldn't be a problem. He can be transferred easily enough over to the Army. The civilian, however, is a different matter. He would have to be willing to enlist. Would he?"

"I don't believe that will be a problem, Sir," said Roger with a confident air.

"Well, all right, then. Now, do you have other needs?" asked the general.

"I need at least three assistants who are good with numbers – accountant types," said Spindle. "And several computators as well."

"Computators?" asked the general raising his eyebrow.

"Yes, Sir. They are devices that speed up the process of doing mathematical computations."

"I see," said the general. "Well, I'll see to it, then."

"We have a question, Sir," said Spindle hesitantly.

"Well, let's have it then," said the general as he wrote down their requests.

"Why are the newspapers reporting incorrect information about the battle of Ypres, Sir?"

The general's head jerked up. "Incorrect information? What do you mean?"

"They are reporting that we killed over one thousand Germans and broke the German line, and they are reporting a much lower number of casualties for us."

The general waved his hand. "It's government policy to state the numbers of our casualties lower. Better for morale, you know, and we always kill more Germans."

"But, Sir, that doesn't sound right. Surely, it's not fair to the families?" commented Spindle.

"Well, that's the way it is," said the general in an impatient tone. "Policy is made by much higher authorities – not for you or even me to question. Our job is to evaluate, and you'd best remember that the information you're dealing with here is to be kept secret! Now, you'd better get back to D-17 and get on with your jobs!"

"Yes, Sir!" said the three captains, jumping to their feet and saluting.

"Dismissed!" said the general with a stern look.

Back in D-17, Sergeant Harvey briefed them on the current situation as they looked down on the map from the balcony above. "The Germans have taken a defensive position. They have dug trenches from the North Sea to Switzerland. They are going to hold on to the land they have taken. We have also dug trenches parallel to theirs, and so have the French, because neither side has been able to outflank the other," he informed them.

"That means it's going to be a long war. The army that can sustain the most casualties will win," commented Spindle.

"Unless there is a full frontal assault," said Roger, peering at the map through his field glasses.

"Where and when?" whispered Spindle.

"It's not for us to say," winked James. "We're only evaluators, remember?

"Let's find the German weak spots. We need to gather some information," continued Roger in a low voice.

"I'll get anything you need," Harvey whispered.

\* \* \*

"I never thought I would be a lieutenant in the Army," said Ginger as he projected a D-17 map onto a large white sheet hanging on the wall, two weeks later. "Tried to volunteer, but they wouldn't have me. Said I had flat feet," he grinned. "Guess they don't care if officers have flat feet, eh?"

"I certainly didn't expect to be a lieutenant in the Army, either. I enlisted in the Navy," laughed Pete who was adjusting a telephone head piece.

"That's better," said Spindle as Ginger brought the projection into focus. "I can see the detail much better now."

"Move marker six to DD-22, " said James through his head piece.

A mover used a long stick to shift the marker, casting a momentary shadow on the projected map.

"Brilliant!" said General Bottoms who walked into the room and stood looking at Ginger's projection. "Why didn't we do this before?"

"We didn't have Lieutenant Murphy, Sir," said Roger.

"What other inventions do you have to show me?" asked the general.

"Come to our enlargement room, Sir," said Spindle.

"Remember the photographs you got from GHQ, Sir?" asked Roger smiling. "Lieutenant Murphy has made them larger, and it's amazing what we've discovered."

The general bent over a large table where enlarged photographs of the front had been laid out. "My word! You can see the German artillery pieces!" he gasped.

"That's not all, Sir. You can also see the German fortifications and machine gun emplacements," Spindle pointed out.

The general looked up at them with a wide grin on his face. "You know what this means, gentlemen? We know exactly where the Germans are and the equipment they are using!"

"I counted one hundred six-inch guns, twenty machine gun emplacements, and ten horses in one mile of front," said Spindle.

"They have made a barbed wire maze in front of their trenches, and they have used four miles of wire," said Roger.

"Brilliant, just brilliant!" exclaimed the general. "Anything on telephonic?"

"No, Sir, we are working on that," smiled James.

"I must inform Five-O-One right away. Your inventions will be of interest to him," said the general as he hurried from the room.

"I should say we've impressed Bottoms with Ginger's projection and enlargements. Now, let's get Pete to work on the telephonic," said Spindle enthusiastically.

"What do you want me to do?" asked Pete eagerly.

"I don't know," replied James scratching his head.

"I know," said Ginger. "In the attic of The Odeon there is a large telephone cable. Must contain a thousand telephone lines. Maybe Pete should have a look at it and see if it would be useful."

"No, I wouldn't advise that, Sir. Would be trespassing and that's illegal," said Sergeant Harvey with an alarmed expression.

"You're quite right, Sergeant. Would you go and check to see if the computators have arrived yet?" asked Spindle.

"Yes, Sir!" said Harvey and left the room in search of the computators.

After he had gone, Spindle turned to the rest of the group. "It would be best if Harvey doesn't know everything we're doing. He seems to want to do everything by the book. What he doesn't know won't hurt him," he cautioned.

The rest of them nodded their agreement and turned their attention back to the photographic enlargements.

* * *

# Chapter 10

## *In the Trenches*

T HE SUN HAD just risen behind the German trenches near La Boisselle, France when Bouncer came down from the fire-step in the trench his section of men were occupying. He walked along the duckboards lining the bottom of the trench, squeezing past other soldiers and trying to avoid kicking the legs of those who were curled up under waterproof sheets trying to sleep.

After several yards, he came to a small indentation carved into the side of the trench where Freddie was heating water over a small fire. Sam was sitting cross-legged on the floor, squinting into a mirror hanging on a peg and scraping his face with a razor.

"Another quiet day on the Western Front," remarked Bouncer, dropping down on the ground beside them. "Can't remember the last time we had morning hate, can you?"

Sam snorted derisively. "Morning hate, indeed. This has been the most boring year of my life – I've only fired my rifle once, outside of training, that is."

"Shouldn't complain," said Freddie, handing Bouncer a tin cup of tea. "We're lucky to have the Saxons on the other side. If they were

Prussians, we'd have morning hate all the time and then some, I've heard."

"You're right, there," said Bouncer, grinning. "A real friendly lot, those Saxons. I'd have a hard time trying to kill one of them."

"Don't know how this war is ever going to end if all we're going to do is sit in these trenches and stare at each other," grumbled Sam. "I'd rather be back in Bridgefield in the butcher shop." He laid down the razor, put on his tunic and began buttoning it.

"I know what you mean," said Freddie. "I'd rather be in a battle dodging bullets than digging bloody trenches and constantly filling bleeding sandbags."

"No rain today," said Bouncer, trying to change the subject. "You can see the Golden Virgin." Nearly a year ago, in January 1915, just after Bouncer and his men arrived at the front, a German shell had struck the tower of the basilica in Albert, which was two miles west of the front line. The statue of the Golden Virgin atop the tower nearly plunged to the ground and was left leaning at a right angle over the square below. On a clear day, the statue in its precarious position was visible to both German and British troops at the front line.

"Still hanging there, I guess," said Sam. "Just like us. They say the war won't be over until she falls."

Bouncer chuckled. "I've heard the Germans think that whoever shoots her down will lose the war."

"I've heard just the opposite – whoever shoots her down will win the war," said Freddie, shaking his head.

"Well, I wish somebody would shoot her down and get some action started," groused Sam, and they all laughed.

Their laughter was interrupted by a German voice booming through a loud-hailer. "Hey, English Bouncer, you want to trade eggs for chocolate?"

"It's Fritz, again," laughed Bouncer looking in his kit bag for chocolate. "One pound of milk chocolate for a dozen brown eggs!" he shouted through cupped hands.

"Hard deal, English. Dozen eggs for chocolate too much. Nine eggs for chocolate."

"Dozen eggs for three quarters chocolate!" called back Bouncer

"Ok, English. Dozen eggs for chocolate."

Bouncer wrapped the chocolate in a sock and launched it via a crude catapult he had made out of a plank of wood, some nails and a bit of elastic. The sock sailed up out of the trench and across the fifty-yard stretch of No Man's Land toward the German trench line. Freddie, Sam and Bouncer watched the sock's journey in a mirror mounted to a post behind their trench.

"Bugger! It's short!" commented Freddie seeing the sock land between the barbed wire and the trench on the German side.

"Bad throw, English! Need to climb out to get it!" yelled Fritz.

"What about our eggs?" called back Bouncer.

"Get ready, English! Here zey come!"

Bouncer, Sam and Freddie stood with their hands in the air, looking in the mirror over their shoulders.

"There it is!" yelled Freddie as they saw a small sandbag hurtling towards their trench.

"Good catch!" laughed Bouncer as Freddie managed to snag it out of the air. "Good throw, Fritz!" he yelled.

"English, I vill go for chocolate now," called out Fritz over the loud-hailer.

"Hold your fire!" yelled Bouncer, his order reverberating up and down the line of trenches. As they watched in the mirror, they saw a figure quickly climb out of the trench, scuttle toward the sock, and race back.

"Did you get it, Fritz?" called Bouncer.

"Yah. Danke, English. Ve haf singing tonight, zen ve play football Sunday, and ve beat you this time, yah?"

"Don't bet on it!" yelled Freddie, examining the eggs to see how many were broken.

"If you win, English, you come stay with me in Dresden after war!"

"Keep the noise down," commanded an officer from a nearby dugout. "We are trying to take our morning nap."

"Yes, Sir!" said Bouncer, grinning at Freddie and Sam and nodding toward the officer's dugout. "Sorry to disturb your sleep, Sir."

On the following Sunday Bouncer recruited eleven men for his football team and met the Germans half-way between the opposing trench lines in No Man's Land. Both the British and German soldiers had shed their tunics and hats and wore only their undershirts, army trousers and combat boots for the occasion.

"We need a referee," said Bouncer, shaking hands with a tall blond man with pale blue eyes and a pockmarked face.

"Your turn to provide referee, Corporal Bouncer," replied the German with a smile.

"Right you are, Captain Fritz," laughed Bouncer. Then, he turned and called to Freddie who was standing near the British trenches. "See if you can find an officer to referee for us, would you Freddie?" he shouted.

Freddie nodded and, in turn, shouted back to the trenches, "We need a lieutenant to referee!"

After a few moments, a short dark-haired lieutenant named Barlow climbed out of the trench nearest to Freddie's position. He strode quickly across No Man's Land, holding a whistle above his head. When he reached the half-way point where the men were gathered, he looked at Bouncer and Fritz who appeared to be serving as captains of their teams. "Lieutenant Barlow, here," he announced. "I'll referee. Are you ready?"

Bouncer and Fritz looked at their men who were in their positions and nodded at Barlow. "Then let the game begin!" yelled Barlow, and he blew the whistle.

At the sound of the whistle, soldiers on both sides climbed out of their trenches to cheer their respective teams. The pitch was littered with spent cartridges and large artillery craters, making it difficult to play. Pairs of army boots served as the goal posts.

After forty-five minutes of play, Lieutenant Barlow blew the whistle, signifying the half-time break.

A couple of German soldiers walked toward them from the sidelines bearing tin cups and wine bottles.

"You play well, English," said one of the soldiers as he handed a tin cup to Bouncer.

"Thank you," said Bouncer. "You Jerries play well, also."

"We offer you German wine from the Moselle Valley," said Fritz as the other soldier poured white wine into Bouncer's cup.

"Have an English biscuit," said Freddie holding out an opened tin of shortbread.

"Danke, English. You are kind," said Fritz taking a biscuit and holding it up to examine it before taking a bite. Just as he was preparing to bite into it, an earth-shattering shriek cut through the air.

"Fuck! Take cover!" screamed Sam at the top of his lungs. "It's one of ours!"

Germans and British alike flung their cups aside and scattered in all directions, diving into the nearest craters or onto the ground with their arms over their heads for protection.

A massive explosion shook the ground where they had been standing, sending a great cloud of black smoke, dust and white chalky earth rocketing skyward. Then huge clods of earth and rock rained down upon them. There was a stunned silence before anyone moved. Slowly, Bouncer lifted his head and crawled on his stomach to the lip of the crater where he had taken cover. He cautiously peeked over the top and noted that all the sideline observers had disappeared into their trenches. There was a great smoking black hole where the football players had been standing.

"Gott in Himmel! Zat was close!" said a voice behind him. Bouncer looked over his shoulder and saw Fritz crawling toward him, his face smeared with chalky dirt. "Why would English shoot at own men?"

Bouncer slowly shook his head. "I don't know," he said. "Hope everyone is all right. We'd better see and then get back to our trenches."

When Fritz and Bouncer emerged from the crater, they discovered that all the men had managed to survive. Aside from minor cuts and scratches, they had not been harmed except for the unlucky Lieutenant Barlow who had to be dug out from under a pile of debris and had suffered a mild concussion and a broken leg.

When Bouncer and his men arrived back at their trench, carrying Lieutenant Barlow in a makeshift stretcher, Captain Squires was waiting for them. "Corporal Russell, report to my dugout when you have seen to your men," he said sternly.

"Yes, Sir!" said Bouncer, surprised at Rupert's coldness which seemed quite out of character.

When he arrived at the officers' dugout, Bouncer found Rupert pacing up and down, hands behind his back, deep in thought.

"Corporal Russell reporting as ordered, Sir," announced Bouncer, standing at attention.

Rupert abruptly stopped pacing, looked about to see if they were alone, and then smiled at Bouncer and waved his hand, "At ease, Bouncer," he said in his usual friendly tone. "We need to talk." He motioned for Bouncer to sit on a crude bench at the back of the dugout.

"What's up, Sir? Why did our artillery fire on our game?" asked Bouncer as he sat down.

"That's what I need to talk to you about," said Rupert, drawing up another bench to sit on, facing Bouncer. "There's been a change in command. General French has been recalled, and the new C-in-C of the B.E.F is Sir Douglas Haig. General Haig has issued direct orders to stop this friendliness with Jerry. I believe he means to launch an offensive in the near future."

"Firing on our own men without warning seems quite extreme, Sir," said Bouncer, shaking his head. "Lucky none of us were killed. As it is, Lieutenant Barlow was injured."

Rupert glanced around to make sure no one was in earshot before responding. "I agree with you, Bouncer," he said in a low voice. "The bloody communications between GHQ down to us in the trenches is horrible. Too many chains of command to get through, you see. That's why we didn't get the message before they fired on us. Nothing to be done about it now, I'm afraid, except to alert everyone that any further chumminess with the Jerries will be quickly and severely dealt with. Make sure the men in your section understand that."

"Right, Sir. I'll have a talk with them at once," said Bouncer. "Is that all, Sir?"

"One more thing," said Rupert. "Our company is scheduled to return to the rear at the end of this week. Our battalion commander, Lieutenant-Colonel Hastings-Jackson, has ordered me to select one of my platoons to serve as an honor guard for some visiting dignitaries in two weeks' time. I'm going to use Lieutenant Barlow's platoon, which is the one your section is in. Because Barlow is now out of commission with a broken leg, I'm appointing you to step in and act as leader of the platoon."

"Yes, Sir," said Bouncer hesitantly. "May I ask who these dignitaries are, Sir?"

Rupert shook his head. "I wasn't told, but they must be important. Hasty Jack said the order came right down to him from the divisional commander, Inky Bill himself."

"Never served in an honor guard before," said Bouncer tentatively.

"Don't worry, Bouncer. There'll be plenty of time for practice. I'm sure you and all the men will do us proud. Besides, it's a chance to get some better uniforms and some of those new trench coats from London." Rupert grinned, and Bouncer chuckled with relief as he went off to share the news with Freddie and Sam and the other men in his section.

The rest of the week was anything but quiet in the trenches. The British shelling of the football game had provoked retaliation from the Germans, and, in turn, the British stepped up their bombardment of the German lines. Each morning, all the men were aroused for "stand-to" before dawn, and unlike the many mornings preceding, these were accompanied by morning hate, in which both sides fired large quantities of rifle and machine-gun ammunition at each other. Night-time activity was stepped up, with patrols going out into No Man's Land to repair damage to the barbed wire barriers, spy on the enemy and dig tunnels under enemy trenches to lay explosives. By the end of the week, when Captain Squire's company was scheduled for relief, the company had lost twenty of its two hundred forty men – fifteen wounded and five killed. Bouncer's section of fourteen lost two men who were spotted in the light of a flare sent up by the Germans during a night raid and were gunned down.

As Bouncer and his men slogged along in a heavy downpour toward their billets in Albert, Captain Squires rode up beside them on his horse. "Corporal Russell, the platoon will spend the night in Albert. Then, we'll board the train tomorrow at seven o'clock for Montreuil. There'll be plenty of good hot food tonight and tell your men to get as much sleep as possible."

"Yes, Sir. Thank you, Sir," said Bouncer, saluting as Squires rode on up the line of marching men.

"Can't believe they'd pick the likes of us for an honor guard," said Sam. "Not exactly turned out for a tea party are we?" He pointed to his uniform which was crusted over head to toe with caked mud.

"Never been so cold and wet and grimy in my life," groused Freddie, blowing his nose on a dirty handkerchief. "Think I'm coming down with pneumonia."

"Could be worse," said Bouncer, trying to be cheerful. "Could be like Jack and Billy."

"Oh, God! Those poor blighters – caught like rabbits in the light from that flare. Nothing anyone could do – no place to take cover," said Sam, shaking his head miserably, tears filling his eyes.

"Bloody awful," said Freddie. "Better to have pneumonia than be like that."

"Well, brace up, lads. Won't be long till we're out of these uniforms and having our smoke and tot of rum. Not sure I fancy being in an honor guard, but it's got to be better than digging trenches and filling sand bags for two weeks till we go back to the front," said Bouncer.

"You're right there," said Freddie. "If I have to dig one more trench, I think I'll just lie down in it and let them cover me up. I'm not cut out for that kind of hard labor – don't have the build for it."

The following Saturday found them outfitted in their newly-issued uniforms, standing rigidly at attention outside the chateau in Montreuil that served as General Headquarters for the British Expeditionary Forces. As acting platoon leader, Bouncer stood at the left end of the front row of soldiers, with Freddie and Sam next to him. Standing at attention in front of them were Captain Squires and Lieutenant Colonel Hastings-Jackson, commander of the Royal Kents battalion, and in front of them, standing by himself, was Major General Ingouville-Williams, commander of the 34$^{th}$ Division.

"Here they come. Look sharp, lads," muttered Bouncer as he saw the group of dignitaries approaching to review the troops.

"Bloody hell, it's King George!" murmured Freddie. "And that must be General Haig right behind him with the French General."

"Who's that behind them?" whispered Sam. "Looks familiar..."

"I think the short one is the French president, what's his name... Poin something," said Freddie.

"Quiet!" hissed Bouncer. "They're almost here." Then he gave a low chuckle. "Blow me! That's Lord Davenville with the Frenchy. That's why he looks familiar."

Freddie and Sam grinned slightly with recognition but didn't have time to say anything further because the party had reached the line of soldiers and the King was speaking to Major General Ingouville-Williams.

Bouncer and his men stood rigidly, staring expressionlessly straight forward as the King, the two generals and the French president passed, each giving them a small nod. Lord Davenville brought up the rear, and when he reached Bouncer's position, he paused.

"You look familiar, corporal," he remarked, peering at Bouncer's face. "Do I know you?"

"Yes, Sir, Lord Davenville, Sir," responded Bouncer. "John Russell from Bridgefield. I was at your daughter's sixteenth birthday party."

"Of course! Son of the heroic Captain Russell. I remember quite well," said Davenville with a smile. "Oh, and these two lads were with you as well," he added, noticing Freddie and Sam. "Let's see... Freddie Simpson, son of the barrister, and Sam, the butcher's son."

"Right you are, milord," said Freddie with a slight grin, still staring straight ahead at attention.

"Pleased to see you are well and serving the Empire. Are they treating you well? Have all the equipment you need?" asked Davenville.

"Can't complain, my lord," said Bouncer.

"Well, carry on, then. Must catch up with the rest of them. Don't want to delay the King, you know," said Lord Davenville, winking at them and moving on.

"Fancy running into Lord Davenville after all these years," remarked Freddie when they were back at their quarters.

"A pleasant surprise," said Bouncer, unbuttoning his tunic. "He looks just the same as he did at Susan's party. Hasn't aged a bit."

"Never thought I'd ever be in the presence of the King," said Sam, who was sitting on his cot rolling a cigarette.

"Corporal Russell, are you in there?" called a voice from just outside the door.

"Yes, Sir," said Bouncer, and Rupert walked in. Bouncer, Freddie and Sam started to get up to salute him, but Rupert waved his hand.

"At ease, mates," he said. "Just came by to congratulate you on your performance. You did our company proud."

"Pretty nerve-wracking, being reviewed by the King, himself," commented Sam.

"Not to mention General Haig and the head of the French government and army," said Freddie.

"Well, they must have been impressed," said Rupert. "Hasty Jack sent me over to tell you that you've been promoted to second lieutenant, Bouncer. Now, you're officially the leader of this platoon."

"Promoted? I can't think why," said Bouncer. "Didn't do anything special."

"Hasty Jack was somewhat puzzled, too," said Rupert. "Said the order for the promotion came down from GHQ."

"GHQ? You mean from General Haig?" exclaimed Freddie.

Rupert shrugged as they all looked at each other with surprise. "That's all I know," he said. "Anyway, congratulations, Bouncer."

"But all I did was stand at attention," said Bouncer, shaking his head.

"Shouldn't be surprised that you'd get promoted for standing," said Freddie. "You got the last one lying down!"

They all laughed as Bouncer good-naturedly took a swipe at Freddie's ear.

"Well, have your tot of rum and get some sleep," said Rupert. "We head back to the trenches next week. By the way," he said, pausing in the doorway on his way out. "It was a real surprise to see Uncle Alfred today. Know he's on the Privy Council and a friend of King George, but didn't know he had that kind of prestige."

"We were surprised to see him, as well," said Bouncer with a fond smile. "He recognized us and stopped to say a few words."

\* \* \*

"It's the Transatlantic Telephone Cable!" said Pete excitedly, adjusting his headset in the basement of The Odeon moving picture theatre. Spindle, James, Roger and Ginger were anxiously hovering over him.

"The what?" asked James.

"It's the cable that carries the telephonic to America."

"How do you know that?"

"I can hear the American Embassy sending cables to Washington."

"How do you know it's the American Embassy?"

"By the number of messages and the way they tap the keys. I worked in the ship's radio room for a while. American operators are trained to tap differently than British operators. They dwell on the A's," explained Pete.

"What are they saying?" asked Spindle.

"Can't be sure. They're using a code. I did make out the word `helmet,' but that's all."

"Can you hear anyone else?"

"Lots of cables being sent each way, some are easy to make out. No codes being used. Just a question of understanding the keys and being quick to write down what is being sent."

"Let's keep this to ourselves," whispered Spindle.

"I wish I knew of someone who could help Pete decipher the messages," whispered James.

"There are hundreds of cables. Would take a lot of time," added Pete.

"Concentrate on the American Embassy for now, Pete. If you find the GHQ in France, listen to them as well," said Spindle.

"You mean listen to the generals?" said Pete with raised eyebrows.

"Until we can get translators for the codes," said Spindle.

"Translators... I know some - retired radio operators mostly," said Pete.

"Make a list, Pete. We'll tell Bottoms we need them to translate the German markings on Ginger's enlargements," said Spindle in a conspiratorial tone. "If we can translate fifty messages a night, it won't take that long."

"It's going to be a big job to splice into the cable," said Pete holding up a lantern.

"We can run the spliced cable upstairs to the attic. Less likely we'll be discovered up there," suggested Ginger.

"What about the translators?"

"Plenty of room. They can listen in shifts."

"How do they get in and out?"

"They buy a ticket to the cinema in the evening, and during the picture show they go to the toilet. There is a hatch in the ceiling there where they can get into the attic. The only problem is the cinema doesn't open until afternoon, so they would have to stay up there until the next day."

"That means we'd need another shift to come in the next afternoon," said Spindle.

"That's good," said Pete. "Most transatlantic cables are sent in the morning, so we'd have people there to listen every morning."

"When you get anything that sounds interesting, let me know. We will meet at my digs in the evening. Don't say anything at Z, especially to Harvey," cautioned Spindle.

They all nodded their agreement.

One afternoon in early December, Spindle drew Roger and James aside in the D-17 map room.

"Let's meet at my room tonight before we go for a pint at Nell Gwynn's," said Spindle, glancing over his shoulder to make sure they weren't being overheard. "Pete and Ginger will be there."

"Do you have any beer or cider?" asked Roger.

"I'll bring the refreshments," said James with a grin, and they quickly returned to their work as they saw Corporal Harvey enter the room.

At seven o'clock that evening, Pete, Roger, Ginger and James were all crowded into Spindle's small rented room in Soho. Pete was sifting through a pile of handwritten papers. "Got some unusual traffic," he commented.

"How many messages do you have?" asked Roger.

"Over one hundred from the American Embassy alone, but there are two of those in particular that seem to be odd."

"What are they about?" asked Spindle.

"We have deciphered the American code. Our War Supply Department has ordered one million steel helmets from an American company in Chicago. A few minutes later another cable was sent to Berlin relaying the message about the helmet order."

"The cable is connected to Berlin, Pete?" asked a surprised James.

"Of course. All telephone traffic from Europe goes through the same cable."

"Why would the Germans want to know about the helmets?" asked Ginger.

"Could change their strategy. The helmets will protect our troops from head wounds. Knowing that, the Jerries could try something else," Spindle surmised.

"Why would the American Embassy pass along that information?" wondered Ginger.

"Someone in the Embassy is working for the Germans!" exclaimed James, snapping his fingers.

"The Americans are supposed to be neutral. It's our job to find out who is passing information to the Germans from their Embassy," said Roger.

"What will you do when you find out?" asked Pete.

"Was it a man sending the cable?" asked James, ignoring his question.

"Can't be sure," said Pete.

"Do your best to identify this person, Pete. We need a name," said Spindle.

"Perhaps I can. There are ten telephonic lines coming from the Embassy. All I need to do is find out where they go. Then it's a question of elimination."

"Don't get caught doing it, Pete. If you do, it would be the end of us working at Section Z," Spindle warned.

"What we need to do is to set a trap. We'll make a special request for something the Americans have. Then Pete can listen for the message to be sent to Berlin," said James.

"Give me a week before you do that," said Pete, thinking of the work involved in preparing for this venture.

"What do the Americans have that we want?" asked Roger, scratching his head. "I know! Baseballs!"

"You bloody fool!" laughed James.

"Not a bad idea," said Spindle, smiling. "We will ask Bottoms for baseballs."

"Why baseballs?" asked Pete.

"Cheaper than artillery shells and easier to throw!" said Spindle with a snort.

The next day, Spindle, Roger and James requested a meeting with General Bottoms.

"Will cricket or tennis balls do?" asked the general. "They are immediately available."

"We could try cricket balls, but baseballs would be better, Sir," said Roger trying to maintain a deadpan expression.

"It's a good idea if it works," said the general, considering. "If we could knock down the Germans, we could recover their guns undamaged. We need the machine guns."

"We need five thousand baseballs, just to try the principle, Sir."

"Very well. I'll mention it to Five-O-One. You will get your balls."

"Thank you, Sir!" said Roger. The general left the room in his usual hurried, pompous manner. The three looked at each other and burst into side-splitting laughter.

"Leave it to Bottoms to take the bait!" laughed Spindle, then they promptly stopped laughing when Corporal Harvey appeared with a new batch of photographs from the front.

"Hmmmm. Very good, Harvey. Get these to Corporal Murphy right away for enlargements," said Roger, pretending to examine the photographs.

"Right, Sir!" said Harvey, saluting and walking hurriedly out of the room.

"That was close," said James in a low tone. "Hope he hasn't overheard us. We must be more careful."

"That's right," whispered Spindle. "Must not talk about anything here. Save it for our after-hours meetings."

They all nodded and returned to their work.

Two weeks later, they were gathered in Spindle's room to hear the latest report on the listening operation.

"Any luck Pete?" asked Spindle.

"It's frustrating. Too many operators at the Embassy. We have tried our hardest to isolate the German contact. In the last two weeks, he has made contact ten times, but we haven't manage to find out who he is. Even the baseballs didn't catch him."

"There must be another way," Spindle replied thoughtfully.

"Why don't we watch the Embassy and find out who works there. Then we can eliminate those who are on the up and up," suggested James.

"Good idea, James. We can follow them and pick up clues," said Roger. "Whoever it is might make a mistake."

"I'll see to it," said Pete.

"Anything else?" asked Spindle.

"Lots of German traffic to Mexico from someone named Zimmermann. Seems the Germans want to make a deal with the Mexicans," said Pete.

"What sort of deal?"

"Can't be sure. The Germans have changed their code again, but we are working on it."

"That may be important, Pete," continued Spindle.

"I know. All that communication between Berlin and Mexico seems quite out of the ordinary."

Nearly three months passed while they were attempting to ascertain the names of all the personnel at the American Embassy and, at the same time, attending to their duties at Section Z. Then, one morning in late February, they were called to a meeting in General Bottoms' office.

"There's going to be a big push in the near future," announced the general, after they were all seated. "The Prime Minister has ordered General Haig to join with our allies in a major offensive designed to break through the German lines and end this stalemate."

"The Germans are well dug in, Sir. Photographs show they have four or five parallel trenches from the front line," said Roger. "Each trench line is protected by miles of high barbed wire."

"They also have the high ground, Sir. They can fall back easily and entrap our men," added Spindle.

"Well, we have thousands of soldiers. Some will make it through," replied the general impatiently, waving his hand in dismissal.

"The Germans have more artillery and they can fire it with great precision, Sir," said Spindle.

"The location of the push has not yet been determined, but there are several options," said the general, ignoring Spindle's comment.

"What are the options, Sir?" asked James.

"At present, it's either D-17 or H-42, but that could change."

"Where is H-42, Sir?" inquired Spindle.

"It's in the Fourth Army Sector, close to the river Somme near Albert," said the general.

"What do you want us to do, Sir?" asked Spindle.

"Analyze both D-17 and H-42, captains. Look at every aspect and make recommendations as to which sector would give us the most strategic advantage in a frontal assault. If we can break the German lines and take back some important territory, it will put the Germans on the defensive and hasten the end of the war."

"Yes Sir!" the captains answered enthusiastically.

"Good. Get to it, then. We need your analysis by the end of this week. You're aware that the Germans have launched an attack on the French at Verdun. Keep that in mind as you prepare your evaluation." The general returned their salute, and they marched out of the room, anxious to begin.

"Gentlemen, what are your findings for D-17 and H-42?" asked General Bottoms later that week.

"D-17 and H-42 are comparable in many ways, logistically speaking, Sir," said Roger. "Both have the same disadvantage. The Germans hold the high ground and they have four lines of parallel trenches for defense, Sir."

"H-42 is easier to make fortifications in, Sir," interrupted Spindle. "The ground is chalk and easier to dig."

"Could you dig tunnels in it, Lieutenant?" asked the general.

"Without difficulty, Sir," replied Roger confidently. "Our sappers could dig under No Man's Land and under the German trenches."

"And attack the Germans from their rear?"

"Possibly, Sir, but if we can do it, so can they," added Spindle. "On the other hand the Germans have fewer machine-gun emplacements in H-42 than in D-17, and No Man's Land is only fifty yards across at the front near La Boisselle. There is, however, a large German redoubt on the hill just across from that point."

"Our men could fill the tunnels with explosives and detonate them right before we attack, Sir," said Roger. "The explosion would destroy their trenches. The crater would make cover for our infantry."

"What about the communications aspect?" asked the general, turning to James.

"H-42 is situated on the main road, which the Germans occupy from La Boisselle to Pozieres and on to Bapaume. If we could recapture that territory, we could do serious damage to their communications with the front while, at the same time, increasing our own communications capabilities," said James. "If we had command of the main road across Pozieres Ridge, we could launch our balloons there and really be able to see what the Germans are up to."

"Splendid! I will relay your analysis to Five-O-One, especially the information regarding the chalk and the short distance between the trenches. It might influence the decision as to where to launch the attack."

"The chalk may be the influencing factor?" asked Spindle uneasily.

"There are many. Political circumstances override everything else, but this chalk thing may make a difference," said the general as he got up to leave.

"Sir, there are the other negative factors about H-42 to consider..." said James, but the general cut him off.

"I've got enough information, Captain. I've got to get back to another meeting." He strode hastily from the room.

"I wish I'd never said anything about the chalk," said Spindle shaking his head in dismay after the general had gone. "The Germans hold all of the high ground. A hundred tunnels filled with explosives won't make much difference, and we'll still lose thousands of men."

Roger shook his head sadly. "The generals don't seem to care how many men we lose," he said, disgust registering in his voice.

"I must remind you, Sir, that these decisions are made by high authority, and who's to question them?" piped up Sergeant Harvey, who, until that point, had remained silent.

Spindle, James and Roger looked meaningfully at each other, and Spindle cleared his throat. "Suppose you are right, Sergeant," he said. "Our job is simply to evaluate, not to question the decisions that are made."

Harvey nodded smugly. "Yes, Sir, that's correct," he said. "If you have no further need of me, I'll just pop over to the map room and see if there have been any changes in positions."

"Good idea, Sergeant. You're dismissed then," said Roger.

They watched Harvey as he walked out of the door and closed it behind him, then Spindle turned to Roger and James.

"Would you like to have supper at my place tonight?" he asked.

"Sure thing. Do you have something special you're serving?" asked Roger.

"Yes, I do. It's an American dish. Pete got the recipe from a friend in the American Embassy." Roger and James grinned knowingly as Spindle winked at them.

That evening when they met in Spindle's room, Pete had news for them. "Here's what we've discovered," he said, reading from a sheet of paper. "There are seventy-five people working at the Embassy. Twenty-four are British, doing office work. The remaining fifty-four are American. Out of these, there are ten who are transmitting telegraphic messages."

"What do you know about these ten telegraph operators?" asked James.

"For one thing, they are all under the age of thirty," replied Pete.

"How do you know that?" asked Roger.

"Because the signals indicate their age. Each message has distinct characteristics, dwells before words, that type of thing. The older a person gets, the longer the dwell. Listening to the signals tells me there is no one using the machine who is over thirty."

"Can you tell the difference between men and women?" asked Roger.

"Yes, there are four women among the ten, and possibly it's one of them."

"Go for the women first," smiled Spindle, with a wink. "We will have more luck dealing with them."

"Well, some of us have more luck with women... namely you, Spindle. I think you should give it a go first," said Pete, winking at the others.

"Sure. Be happy to give it a go. Give me a name and an address," said Spindle with a grin.

Ginger laughed. "That's our Spindle. Always willing to give all for King and Empire! A dangerous job, but someone's got to do it!"

They all chuckled at Ginger's joke, while Pete looked at the list of names. "Here's one," he said after a moment. "Name's Abigail Richards. Rents a house in Stanhope Mews West in Kensington."

"Married or single?" asked Spindle.

"Single, of course, you bleeding lecher," howled Pete, rolling his eyes.

"As I said, a dangerous job...," said Ginger with a straight face.

The next evening Spindle walked into The Stanhope Arms on Cromwell Road in South Kensington. He strode up to the bar and ordered a half-pint of bitter. "That's three-pence," announced the barman when he returned with Spindle's bitter. "Anything else I can do for you, mate?"

"As a matter of fact, there is," said Spindle as he counted out the three-pence. "Can you give me directions to Stanhope Mews West?"

"That's easy," said the barman. "You're practically there. Stanhope Mews West is just behind the pub. You can walk right through the alley beside the pub and that puts you in the Mews."

"Thanks, mate," said Spindle as the barman picked up the three-pence. He downed his bitter and headed out of the door and down the alley the barman had indicated.

When he arrived at Number Two, he saw that there were lights on inside. He walked up the three steps to the front door and banged on it with the doorknocker. He saw a curtain part on the window to the left of the door and then after a few seconds, the door swung open. A pretty blond woman in her twenties stood facing him with a questioning look in her hazel eyes.

Spindle took off his hat and smiled at her. "Good evening. Are you Miss Abigail Richards?"

The woman nodded, still looking at him quizzically.

"My name is Brian Adams. I understand you work for the American Embassy, and I wonder if you might be able to help me," continued Spindle, still smiling politely.

"How can I help you, Sir?" she asked in a low timbre.

"I'm trying to locate an uncle who immigrated to America twenty years ago. I want him to know that his sister has just died and that he has been left a large estate in Cornwall."

"Really? Well, why don't you come in and give me more details about your uncle and I will see what I can do for you?" said Miss Abigail Richards with a smile that brought a sparkle to her eyes. She stepped aside so Spindle could enter.

Spindle's smile broadened as he stepped past her into the small foyer. "I can't tell you how much this means to me, Miss Richards," he said as the door swung shut behind him.

"It wasn't her," said Pete, shaking his head, when they were gathered in Spindle's room the next evening. "Your request went through, but it didn't have the same key patterns as the one we are looking for."

"One down and three to go," laughed Roger.

"Good old Roger, it's your turn next," said Spindle. "Time for someone else to take on this dangerous assignment."

In the following weeks, Roger, James and Ginger each had their turn at contacting one of the remaining women to seek their help in sending various contrived messages to America. When Pete analyzed the messages, however, he found that none of the styles matched that of the Berlin sender.

"We'd better try another way," said Spindle, frustrated by the lack of results.

"There are six men left," said James.

"I agree, we need to try another way," added Roger.

"Is the operator sending the messages at the same time of day, Pete?" queried Spindle.

Pete looked through some papers and then smiled. "Normally sends to Germany at 10:30 in the morning."

"There we are. There's a clue!" said Spindle. "We can watch the Embassy to see who is in there at that time."

"Good idea, Spindle," said James.

"The Embassy has ten telegraph operators, as you know. There are three shifts of three each, and one is on standby," said Pete when they were gathered in Spindle's room later that week.

"Do you have their names and which ones work in the mornings?" asked James.

"The ones who normally work in the mornings are William Shoals, Abigail Richards and Mary Grimes. Since we've already eliminated the women, it would seem that Shoals is our man," said Pete, looking at his papers. "Of course, there's always the possibility that it could be the standby is a chap named George Hayes."

"Well, the best thing is for me to try to get to know Shoals and see if I can get him to send a message for me. Then Pete can analyze it to determine if he is our spy," said Spindle."

They all agreed, and the next morning found Spindle and Pete standing across the street from the gates of the American Embassy.

"That's him, the tall one wearing the bowler hat," Pete said, indicating a tall, lean man with silver blond hair, dressed in an expensive black suit and carrying a walking stick. The man had come out of the gates of the Embassy and had walked off in the direction of Regent Street. Pete and Spindle followed him at a discreet distance down the crowded street where he stopped frequently to look into shop windows.

"Seems to be looking for something," observed Spindle.

"What kind of shops is he looking in?" asked Pete.

"They all seem to be bookshops," said Spindle.

"Wonder what he's looking for?" wondered Pete.

They continued to follow Shoals until he entered Bartlestone's Book Sellers.

"I'll go in and see if I can find out what he's up to," said Spindle. "You wait here."

Spindle entered the bookshop just as the shopkeeper approached Shoals who was examining a book-lined shelf.

"And what can I do for you, Sir?" he asked.

"I'm looking for an English dictionary," said Shoals, turning from the bookshelf.

"Oxford's, Sir?" asked the shopkeeper, pulling a large volume off the shelf.

"That's the one I want. How much is it?'

"Two shillings, Sir."

"Thank you," said Shoals as the shopkeeper started to go to the counter to wrap up the purchase.

"I'd like a dictionary, too," interjected Spindle. "I need an American one to understand American spelling."

Shoals looked at Spindle and smiled as the shopkeeper turned to a different bookshelf. "We Americans take short cuts with English you know."

"Ah, you're American? I wonder if you could help me understand some of your words?" asked Spindle.

"I will do my best," said Shoals.

"Perhaps you can tell me why Americans leave out the 'u' when they spell words like 'labour' or 'neighbour,' for example," said Spindle curiously.

Shoals thought for a moment. "I frankly don't know, and I'm puzzled, too. It's an interesting question," he said.

"I've never heard of the reason for that either," said the shopkeeper, who handed Spindle a Webster's American dictionary. "Must have something to do with the way Americans streamline things. After all, the 'u' isn't really necessary because it's not pronounced in 'neighbour' and 'labour'."

"We English do the same thing with 'ballet.' We drop the 't' when we say the word," said Spindle.

"It's not the same," Shoals pointed out. "Americans still spell it with the 't'; even though the 't' is silent. Besides, 'ballet' is really a French word, and they do not pronounce the 't' on the end. Rather, the spelling indicates that you pronounce the 'e' as a long 'a.'"

"Fascinating!" laughed the shopkeeper.

"Well, then, why do we English spell theatre 't-h-e-a-t-r-e,' but the Americans spell it 't-h-e-a-t-e-r'?" asked Spindle.

"Americans spell most things the way they actually sound. You English don't pronounce it 'thea-tray,' do you, even though that's the way you spell it?" said Shoals.

Spindle laughed. "You're quite right. Wonder why we do spell it that way?"

"Now, I have one for you," said Shoals opening the Oxford dictionary. "What are 'pitcher enlargements?' Are they oversized water jugs?"

"Could be," said Spindle, starting slightly and frowning as in thought. "Possibly you have the spelling wrong. Maybe, it's 'picture' – like a photograph, or painting, that type of thing."

"That's about right," said the shopkeeper. "Depends on how you spell the word. We English pronounce them the same."

"Do you have photographs you want to enlarge?" asked Spindle.

"No, no, nothing like that. I'm a telegraph operator at the American Embassy. Just want to be sure I am sending the right word in a cable," said Shoals.

"Ah, a telegraph operator at the American Embassy? Perhaps you can help me with another matter," said Spindle. "I have an aunt who is visiting friends in Boston, and I need to contact her. Need to let her know that my mum – her sister – is quite ill," said Spindle. "By the way, my name is Bernard Atkins," he added, holding out his hand.

"Pleased to meet you, Mr. Atkins. My name is William Shoals, and I would be happy to send a message to Boston for you," said Shoals shaking Spindle's hand. "If you'll write down the message and the address, I'll send it tomorrow morning."

"Shoals is our man," beamed Pete the following evening at the gathering in Spindle's room. "I matched your message with his key strokes. They are the same as the Berlin telegrams."

"What do we do now? Report him as a spy?" asked James.

"No, not right now. We might be able to use him to our benefit," said Spindle.

"How do you mean?" asked Roger. "If he is a German spy working out of the American Embassy, the Americans should be told."

"False information," said Spindle with a cryptic grin.

"There you go again, Spindle. What do you mean by false information?" asked Roger shaking his head.

"We can use Shoals to relay false information to Berlin," replied Spindle.

"Information which we will supply..." said Roger, snapping his fingers.

In early May, the custodians of the map rooms were called to a meeting where General Bottoms was going to brief them on the latest offensive plan.

"The decision has been made," announced the general, pointing to a map on the wall behind him. "The Somme region has been chosen for our next offensive. The French are having difficulty holding on at Verdun and have petitioned our government to launch an attack to distract the Germans. General Haig has given orders to launch the attack on June 25, and has placed the main part of the attack in the hands of the Fourth Army which, as you know, is commanded by General Rawlinson."

General Bottoms turned to the map on the wall and used a pointer to illustrate his explanation. "The Fourth Army occupies approximately twenty-six miles of the British front line from Serre in the north to Montauban in the south where our line meets the area of front occupied by the French Sixth Army."

General Bottoms turned and looked sternly at the group in the meeting room for a moment and cleared his throat. Then, he pointed to a section of the British front line that had a heavy red mark around it. "This, gentlemen, is where the center of our attack will take place. It is known to you as Section H-24, and it is occupied by the 34th Division. You will note that the Germans occupy the small villages east of Albert as well as the highest point of ground at Pozieres, known as the Pozieres Ridge.

He paused and looked at the group again, allowing this information to sink in. "Section H-24 is vital because of the main road running from Albert to Bapaume and because of the Pozieres Ridge. It is essential that we capture both. Our strategy will be to heavily bombard the German trenches with our artillery before the attack. Then, after the front trenches are cleaned out and the barbed wire destroyed, our infantry will attack, taking and securing one trench line after another. After our troops have broken through and secured the trenches, Lieutenant-General Gough's Reserve Army, consisting of three cavalry divisions, will be sent in to take Bapaume. Altogether, our force will consist of eighteen divisions with thirteen battalions each and 10,000 artillery. That is over half a million men, giving us superiority over the Boche by seven to one."

"Sounds like a suicide mission," commented Spindle when he and his cohorts were back in their meeting room discussing the general's briefing. "The infantry won't stand a chance. The Germans have thousands of machine guns, and they have the high ground. And, God damn it, the 34th Division is where the rest of the Bridgefield Battalion is – Bouncer, Freddie, Sam, and Rupert Squires..."

"What do you think the casualties will be, Spindle?" asked Roger looking glum.

"There's a lot of variable, but I would say up to sixty percent," estimated Spindle.

"It sounds bloody horrible," said James agitatedly.

"Can we stop it? Can we stop the offensive at the Somme? There must be a better place to fight the Germans," asked Roger.

"Don't know if we can. You heard the general. The decision has been made. We evaluate, we don't make the plans," said Spindle.

"Surely they know how many men could be killed!" said Roger. "Isn't there anything we can do?"

The three sat dejectedly around their small table wondering how they could prevent the high casualty numbers that seemed inevitable.

"It's a terrible feeling knowing what we do," said James nervously. "Knowing how many men are going to be cut down."

"There may be a way to cut down on the number of casualties," said Spindle thoughtfully. "We could use Shoals to tell Berlin the offensive will be somewhere else. If the Germans thought it would be somewhere else, they would move some of their troops and artillery to that area."

"How would you get Shoals to do that, Spindle?" queried James.

"We will make up false documents and post them to him, saying they are from a German sympathizer. He either takes the bait or rejects it. At least we will have tried," said Spindle, shrugging his shoulders.

"Who is going to prepare the documents?" asked James.

"Roger. He's good at writing letters," laughed Spindle.

"OK, I'll do it," said Roger. "Where should we say the offensive is going to be?"

"Armentieres?" suggested Spindle.

James and Roger nodded their agreement.

"Good. I will send Shoals a package by the end of the week," said Spindle, and they all sat looking solemnly at each other until Corporal Harvey brought in their afternoon tea.

* * *

# Chapter 11
## *The Glory Hole*

"SHOALS HAS TAKEN the bait," said Pete, one evening in early June. He held up a hand-written transcription of a telegram. "He sent this message to Berlin this morning saying that the British will be launching an attack on June 25 at Gommecourt."

"Gommecourt? Are you sure that's what it said?" asked Roger with a surprised expression.

Pete examined the message again. "That's what it says, all right. No mistake," he said.

"Can't be right," said Spindle, with a frown. "Our bait was Armentieres."

"That's right. Armentieres and Gommecourt are like worms and maggots. One is used for catching pike, the other for perch," said James.

"There is something fishy here," said Spindle, smiling at the fishing analogy. "Nonetheless, Shoals has informed Berlin that the attack is going to be somewhere else. I'm concerned that Shoals may be up to something. Perhaps he knows more than we think. Better take special care, Pete, in the translations and make sure your listeners are on their toes. A slipup could endanger the operation."

"I know," said Pete, hanging his head and looking at the transcription again.

"Great show, Pete," said Ginger, trying to cheer Pete up. "When you go fishing, it doesn't matter what bait you use as long as you catch a fish."

"That's right, Ginger. As long as we have Shoals on the hook, we have caught one," grinned Spindle. "We have identified Shoals as the German spy. Good show, Pete!"

"Now that Shoals has sent the message, there's a good chance that the Germans will move men and equipment before our attack on June 25$^{th}$," said Roger excitedly.

"Hope so. Every gun, every Hun moved will save the lives of hundreds of our men, so we are counting on it," said Spindle. "The French are taking a beating at Verdun. Our attack is necessary to take the pressure off there. If the Germans break through the French lines and reach the channel, they will win the war."

"Is there enough time?" queried Ginger. "There is just under a month before the attack."

"Should be. The Germans can move their men and equipment quickly, not like us. We have the channel to cross," replied Spindle. "Let's hope Shoals's masters take notice and do what we expect."

"Better have a drink now. We deserve it," said Ginger, getting up and going to a table where there were a number of pint bottles of beer.

"Don't bother with glasses, Ginger," laughed Spindle. "Let's drink to discovering Shoals. If this works, we may have saved the day for our troops!"

"Hear! Hear!" called out the five as they raised their bottles in a toast.

* * *

Meanwhile, Bouncer and his platoon were coping with the cold, torrential rain in the trenches. The mud was knee-deep, their only footing the duckboards that emitted slurping sounds as the men walked and stood on them.

"Come on, Freddie, use your shovel and help get rid of this muck," said Sam, lifting a shovel full of runny white soup and throwing it over the lip of the trench. The murky water ran back into the trench splashing him in the face. "This is a bugger," commented Sam, pausing to wipe the muck off his face.

"This works much better," grinned Freddie, holding up a latrine bucket. He dipped it into the swirling water, then climbed up on the fire step and threw the bucket's contents as far as he could from the trench. "You see," he said. "No back flow when you do it with the bucket."

"Bloody hell! Get down from the fire step!" yelled a private who was shoveling next to Sam. "Don't want to see you shot emptying a shit bucket!"

"Better than being drowned in this muck," groused another private who slapped the muddy water in the bottom of the trench with his shovel.

"It's all right for you, Freddie. You're in charge of the latrine bucket today. Glad I used it earlier this morning," laughed Sam.

"I know you did, Sam," joked Freddie, holding his nose.

The surrounding men burst into laughter.

"Better check that bucket, Freddie. You might find a floater," called out a private further down the trench line.

"Nah! I saw it floating south twenty minutes ago," shouted another voice, and the laughter increased.

"Sod it!" shouted Freddie above the din. "It's still better than trying to scoop up this stuff with a shovel!"

"What's the joke?" asked Bouncer, emerging from a nearby dugout.

"We need more buckets, Sir. They work better than these shovels," responded a private, pointing to Freddie.

"I see what you mean," said Bouncer, smiling at Freddie, who was scooping up more muck with the latrine bucket. "I'll see if I can get the quartermaster to supply some."

"Lieutenant Russell, report to Captain Squires, Sir," said the private standing next to Bouncer. The order had been relayed from man to man down the trench from the captain's headquarters until it reached Bouncer.

"Perhaps another promotion, Sir?" asked Sam, breaking the silence that had fallen among the men.

"Shouldn't think so. We haven't fired a shot today. Been too wet for that," joked Bouncer.

"Are promotions based upon firing rifles, Sir?" asked Freddie as he dropped his bucket in the mud and grabbed his gun.

"Put your rifle down, Private Simpson. You'll just get it rusty," retorted Bouncer as he turned to go to Captain Squires's quarters. He squeezed past the men in his platoon and tried to keep his balance as he sloshed through the muddy water in the bottom of the trench.

"Come in, Lieutenant Russell," said Squires when he saw Bouncer's water-soaked figure appear at the entrance to his dugout.

Bouncer stepped over a small wall of sandbags and entered the makeshift room carved into the side of the trench.

"At ease, Lieutenant, and take a seat," said Squires, pointing to a folding canvas stool. Bouncer sat down and looked questioningly at Rupert.

"It's most unusual, Bouncer," said Rupert, pacing up and down in front of him with his hands clasped behind his back. "We'll be informal. I've been told to relay an order for you to report to Lieutenant Colonel Hastings-Jackson at battalion headquarters at eleven o'clock tomorrow morning." Rupert stopped pacing and faced Bouncer, who looked up at him in surprise.

"I have to tell you I'm somewhat baffled," continued Rupert with a frown. "There was no reason given, and I can't understand why Hasty Jack would want to see you alone, except that the message said it involves an urgent private matter."

"Urgent private matter?!! Can't think what that would be," exclaimed Bouncer.

"I know. Even more mysterious is the fact that the Colonel doesn't ordinarily meet with lower-ranking officers. Procedure is for orders to come down through the chain of command."

"I know," mused Bouncer. "Very odd, isn't it?"

"As your commanding officer, I should be going to the meeting with you, but the order was specific that you should come alone," Rupert went on in a puzzled tone.

"I'm not in a position to request your presence at the meeting am I?" asked Bouncer.

"No, you're not," said Rupert slowly. Then he drew himself up to his full height and announced, "So, here it is. Lieutenant Russell, you are to report to Lieutenant Colonel Hastings-Jackson at eleven o'clock tomorrow morning."

Bouncer jumped to his feet, stood at attention and saluted. "Yes, Sir!"

"Best to leave now, Lieutenant. Weather conditions are expected to worsen by morning, and traveling will be difficult enough anyway – mud up to your waist, that type of thing," continued Rupert.

"Yes, Sir!" responded Bouncer.

"Be sure to wear a clean uniform when you meet with the Colonel. You can get one from the quartermaster at HQ when you arrive, and here is your trench pass," said Squires, handing Bouncer a slip of paper. "You're dismissed, Lieutenant!" he added.

"Yes, Sir!" Bouncer saluted again and turned to leave. As he was climbing back over the sandbags, he heard Rupert say in a low voice, "Good luck, Bouncer. Hope it's not serious and that you come back to us."

The rain came down harder. Soldiers used what they could to keep up with the rising water. Rats were flushed from their nests, and men screamed as they swam past them. Bouncer went back to his dugout with the words 'private matters' ringing in his ears. He gathered his belongings and packed them in his kit bag, pausing occasionally as he looked at them.

"Where are you off to, Lieutenant?" asked Freddie as Bouncer squeezed past him trying to maintain his balance on the swaying duckboards.

"No, not where -- between us and the sea – a bastard place called HQ," answered Bouncer, grinning ironically.

"Blimey, Lieutenant," chimed in Sam. "You're going for champagne and caviar."

"I don't know the reason why. Just following orders."

"Don't be talked into moving. We need you here to help us kill Germans and win this lousy war," said Sam.

"Yes, that's right. Don't be talked into another promotion. That would mean we'd be separated. Remember our promise: The Bottom Five...," said Freddie.

"I know, I know. The Bottom Five sticks together," said Bouncer putting his hand on Freddie's shoulder. "Don't worry mates. We joined up together to fight Germans and so we shall. Been through too much. Not leaving you lot now."

"Three cheers for our lieutenant," called out Sam. The cheers could be heard over the sound of splattering rain as Bouncer continued on his way through the trench. He followed the maize of trenches showing his travel pass at each junction. Each trench like his own was knee deep in muddy clay, men using anything they could to keep the sickening water at bay. Bouncer smiled and hiked up his kit bag when at last he came to the communication trench that led to the west and the town of Albert, where both the division and battalion headquarters were located. The going would be easier now as the communication trench was sheltered from the rain by a corrugated tin roof.

The next morning Bouncer awoke feeling refreshed. The officer's billet was warm and dry, and the cot upon which he had slept seemed like a luxurious feather bed compared to the miserable damp ground in the trench. As he sat up and stretched and surveyed his surroundings, he noticed a young lieutenant dressed in the uniform of a highland regiment observing him. Bouncer grinned and nodded at him.

"Understand you were in a front line trench," said the lieutenant in an unmistakable Scottish brogue.

"That's right," said Bouncer smiling up at him. "Just got in last night. Have orders to report to HQ."

"My name is Glenn Forbes, and I come from Scotland," said the lieutenant, stepping forward and extending his hand to Bouncer. "Arrived yesterday. Haven't seen any action yet, but soon expect to be in the thick of things. The Big Push, you know."

"Pleased to meet you Glenn," responded Bouncer. "My men call me Bouncer. Real name is John Russell, and I come from Bridgefield. You say you're from Scotland?"

"That's right – near Aberdeen," said Glenn, shaking Bouncer's hand. "Bridgefield. Where is that?"

"Down in Kent, about thirty miles south of London."

"I've heard of that, but I can't think why," said Glenn, pausing for a moment. Then he smiled. "Now I remember. That's where they have the water that cures hangovers."

Bouncer laughed. "Oh, that old story! I've heard that, too, but that water never cured my hangover, I can tell you."

"Nothing like a real Scottish hangover," laughed Glenn. "Best thing for that is to have another dram the next morning."

"I'd drink to that, if there was something to drink," said Bouncer. "Wish I could have a dram right now. Have to see the top brass this morning. Need to be prepared. A drop of whiskey would do the trick."

"I'm here for an assignment, waiting for orders. Should get them by this afternoon. They need me to inspire our men when the Big Push begins," chuckled Glenn. "It's the kilt you see. Will just flip it up and show my ass. That scares the life out of the Huns, you know. The Jerries call us Scots the 'ladies from hell!'" Glenn turned and illustrated by bending over and flipping up his kilt.

Bouncer howled with laughter. "That would scare the shit out of me! With an ass like that, a fart would blow the Huns away. No need for a Big Push." After they had stopped laughing, Bouncer looked up at him with a serious expression. "What about this 'Big

Push,' Glenn? Do you know when it will begin? No word has come down to us in the trenches. It's been relatively quiet in my sector."

"Don't really know. All I do know is that the French are getting a beating at Verdun, and if we don't attack soon, the Germans will defeat the French and the war will be over. No official word yet, but I can tell you thousands of men are being prepared. The channel ports on both sides are full of troop transports and supply ships. It must be a logistic nightmare in getting everything ready."

"Any idea where the attack will be?" asked Bouncer, nodding at Glenn's observations.

"Just guesses, that's all. Many officer types say it's going to be in the Gommecourt sector. Personally, I believe it could happen in the Armentieres region."

"Not the Somme?" asked Bouncer, somewhat wistfully. "My men are champing at the bit wanting to fight."

"It doesn't look like it. Intelligence says the Huns have many machine guns and artillery and that they hold the high ground here at the Somme."

"Intelligence? What is that?" asked Bouncer, raising his eyebrows.

"The back room boys in London who analyze the war. They say there would be too many casualties if we attack at the Somme."

"Any guesses as to what your assignment is going to be, Glenn?" asked Bouncer.

"Going to the front. Have to report to Captain Squires. Do you know him?"

"Captain Squires!" exclaimed Bouncer. "He's my commanding officer."

"What a coincidence," smiled Glenn.

"Didn't know he needed another lieutenant," said Bouncer with a puzzled frown.

"Not official yet. Won't know for sure until later today. Hasty Jack needs to make room for me."

"Room for you?" asked Bouncer.

"Yes, a family thing. Between you and me, Hasty Jack is my uncle, married my mother's sister. He didn't think I was doing enough fighting. I was stationed at Regimental HQ. He pulled some strings, and now I'm here headed for the front line. A matter of family honor, you see."

"Bugger me, Glenn, I would keep quiet about that. If word gets out that you're related to the Colonel, you'll get English asses in your face. Top brass is not liked much, you know. All they seem to do is live in fancy houses, eat and drink fine food and wine, and send us poor blighters out to be killed." Bouncer looked at his pocket watch. "Bloody hell, must get going. Have a meeting with Hasty Jack meself at eleven."

Bouncer hastily finished dressing, and after saying goodbye to the Scot, strode up the street to the chateau that served as headquarters for the Royal West Kent battalion. A captain was seated at a small table just inside the door.

"Lieutenant Russell reporting to Colonel Hastings-Jackson," said Bouncer, saluting and handing the captain his papers.

The captain scrutinized the papers with a frown and looked sternly up at Bouncer. "Where's your commanding officer, Lieutenant Russell?"

"The orders were for me to come alone," explained Bouncer with a shrug.

"Unusual, Wait here, Lieutenant," muttered the captain getting up from his seat. He walked quickly down a corridor hung with fine paintings and disappeared into a door at the end of the passageway.

A few minutes later, Bouncer saw the captain emerge from the doorway and walk back toward him. He was still holding the papers and his face was flushed. "Be back at one, Lieutenant. The Colonel will see you then," he said abruptly.

"Do I need to bring my commanding officer?" asked Bouncer with an innocent grin.

The captain scowled at him and his face grew redder. "Off with you, Lieutenant! Don't go nosing around the restricted areas. Be back here at one sharp, and don't keep the Colonel waiting!"

Bouncer walked out of the headquarters building and began strolling up the street toward the basilica where the "hanging virgin" was still jutting out over the street at its precarious angle. Bouncer looked up at the statue, musing about the morning's events. Suddenly, someone calling his name interrupted his thoughts.

"Is that you? John Russell from Bridgefield?"

Bouncer swung around and saw a private walking towards him. The walk seemed familiar, and when the private drew closer, Bouncer smiled with recognition.

"Bloody hell! Is that Harry? Harry Phillips?" cried Bouncer, surprise registering all over his features.

"Private Dirty Face, reporting, Sir!" said Harry, snapping to attention in front of Bouncer. "See you are a lieutenant now, Sir!"

"At ease, Harry," said Bouncer, waving his hand. "Great God, it's good to see you Harry. Thought you were dead. Killed at Ypres."

"Me killed? No, no, I'm here in the flesh as you see," said Harry with a broad grin.

"You wasn't on the casualty list or on the body count. What happened?"

Harry's face began to twitch, his eyes blinking rapidly and uncontrollably. Bouncer noticed that his hands were shaking as well. "What's the matter Harry? What's wrong? Are you all right?" he asked in alarm.

Harry opened his mouth to speak, but no words came out. Bouncer took his arm and looked around. "Let's find somewhere to sit so we can talk about it," he said. He led Harry a short distance up the street where he found a bail of empty sandbags. He helped Harry to sit down, and gradually Harry's shaking subsided.

"All right Bouncer, I'll tell you... , I'll tell you what happened," he said when he had managed to regain his composure. Bouncer rolled a couple of cigarettes and handed one to Harry while he waited for Harry to collect his thoughts. After he had taken a puff of the cigarette, Harry began to speak.

"It was after the battle, at sunset that I woke up. I passed out after reaching the horses during the battle. I had managed to pull Bert Balcom with me. The weight of the dead piled on top of me caused me to pass out. The smell of human blood and dead horseflesh was horrible.

"After waking up, I didn't know where I was or who I was. Confused, Bouncer, confused as hell. Bert was dead; I was still holding his arm. I felt I was going mad. My head began thumping, my heart was in my mouth."

Harry paused and shook his head as if to think more clearly. "I had to run, Bouncer. Had to get away from that dreadful place. I saw flickering lanterns, and I thought the people carrying them were going to bury me alive. I ran and ran, through the barbed wire, stumbling into shell craters, falling over bodies. The bodies were everywhere! I heard voices telling me to stop. I felt bullets flying around me, but I kept on running. I must have run all night! Finally, I was exhausted and I fell to the ground. The next thing I remember was the sound of running water and warm sun rays. I awoke with a pleasant feeling, as if I was having a dream. It was as if I was back in Bridgefield and there was no battle. My head was not thumping, and I felt at ease."

"What did you do next, Harry?"

"I wandered around a bit, and then I remembered there had been a battle. I looked down at my uniform. It was covered with blood, and it stunk. I washed my face in a stream, and it was wonderful. I took off my clothes and bathed and soaked my clothes in the water trying to get the blood out. I must have lain in the water for hours. Then I heard giggling, and looked up and saw two young girls, one with blond hair the other with black, walking beside the steam.

"They were sisters who took me back to their home and took care of me. I stayed there, Bouncer, with those girls who were living alone because their parents were stranded behind the German lines. I was still in Belgium, fortunately on our side of the line. I was lucky enough to have run in the right direction. I was happy there, Bouncer, with those girls, and I did not want to go back to the front. Every time I heard gunfire, I would go berserk, couldn't control myself. Even now, Bouncer, my head thumps and my hands shake so bad I can't pull a trigger. I'm ashamed of myself. I'm not a coward, Bouncer."

Bouncer looked into Harry's eyes where he could see tears forming. " You're no coward, Harry," he said reassuringly. "You're no different from the rest of us. Harry, I remember Ypres. I remember the battle. It was nothing more than a slaughter. Our men were cut down like grass at hay time. Never want to go through that again."

Harry pulled out a dirty piece of rag and blew his nose. After putting the rag back into his pocket he looked at Bouncer and gave him a weak smile.

"What happened next, Harry?" asked Bouncer in a gentle voice.

"Can't be sure how long I stayed with the girls. One day a British patrol came by. I just gave myself up, said I'd lost my memory and didn't know who I was. It was true, Bouncer. I didn't know. The patrol took me back, and the next thing I remember, I was in a convalescent home in England. Could have been an officer as far as the authorities were concerned," said Harry, winking at Bouncer with a chuckle. " Doctors said I was suffering from something they called shell shock. Said I needed lots of rest. My memory came back gradually. Now I am here. Supposed to report to Captain Squires's company in the Royal West Kents."

"Bloody hell, Harry! I'm in Squires's outfit on the Somme, and so is Freddie Simpson and Sam Baldwin. Not many left from the Bridgefield Battalion, Harry. Most were lost at Ypres. The survivors have been absorbed into the Royal West Kents. You remember Sam and Freddie, don't you?"

"Certainly do," grinned Harry.

Bouncer suddenly remembered his meeting with Hasty Jack. He looked at his watch. "Must get going, Harry. Have a meeting with Colonel Hastings-Jackson. See you at the front. Perhaps you'll be assigned to my platoon."

"Oh, I do hope so, Sir. So good to see you again, Sir," said Harry as Bouncer turned to walk back toward headquarters.

When Bouncer arrived, the captain was waiting impatiently. "Come with me, Lieutenant Russell," he said, jumping up from his seat the moment Bouncer walked through the door. "One more minute and you'd have been late. The Colonel doesn't tolerate tardiness – he'd have sent you right back to the front!"

Bouncer grinned sheepishly at the captain's scolding and followed him down the corridor toward the ornately carved door where the captain paused and tapped lightly. He heard a muffled voice from within, and the captain opened the door and went in, then quickly returned.

"The Colonel will see you now," he announced, opening the door wider for Bouncer to enter.

"Lieutenant Russell reporting!" Bouncer said, standing at attention before Lieutenant Colonel Hastings-Jackson who was seated behind a huge carved mahogany desk.

"Yes, indeed, Lieutenant. Be at ease," said the Colonel, waving his hand toward a chair in front of his desk.

"Yes, Sir!" responded Bouncer, taking the seat the Colonel had indicated.

"I'm mystified, Lieutenant, and no doubt you are, too," said the Colonel, looking closely at Bouncer.

"Oh, yes, Sir, I'm quite puzzled," said Bouncer, sitting on the edge of the seat.

Hasty Jack frowned, then picked up a telegram from the desk in front of him and held it up for Bouncer to see. "Lieutenant, I received this message from GHQ. It presents a quandary for you. The message states you have a choice of assignments."

"Choice, Sir?"

"Please wait till I have finished, Lieutenant. You'll have ample time to say your piece," said the Colonel somewhat sternly.

"Yes, Sir," said Bouncer in an apologetic tone.

"GHQ indicates you can stay in your present sector or... " Hasty Jack paused and looked at Bouncer, then he looked back at the telegram. "Or you can take an assignment with the Second Army at Armentieres." The Colonel went silent waiting for Bouncer's reaction.

"I can choose to be transferred to Armentieres?" asked Bouncer in surprise. "Is that where the attack is going to be, Sir?"

"The location is a secret and won't be revealed till right before the battle, Lieutenant."

"But I won't know how to choose unless I know where the offensive is going to occur, Sir," said Bouncer.

"Well, all right then...," said the Colonel hesitantly. "Can I trust you to keep the location secret if I tell you? There would be severe consequences if word leaked out."

"Oh, yes, Sir! I would not say a word. I understand the consequences," said Bouncer, leaning forward in his seat.

"All right. I will trust you, Lieutenant. The offensive is going to be here at the Somme, and the 34th Division as well as the Royal West Kents will be at the very center of the attack." The Colonel leaned back in his chair and looked somberly at Bouncer. "Now, Lieutenant, knowing this information, what do you want to do? It's your quandary."

"What about my men, Sir?"

"They stay. Only you have this opportunity to choose. Either stay and fight with the Royal West Kents or transfer north to Armentieres."

Bouncer sat motionless, his mouth agape. "What the hell is going on?" he thought, as he remembered the choice he had been given before the battle at Ypres.

"Lieutenant, I don't have all day," said the Colonel impatiently. "What is your decision?"

"Please give me another minute, Sir. I have to think. Can't understand why I'm being given this option."

"Very well, Lieutenant. Another minute, that's all." The Colonel looked down at some paperwork on his desk, and when he heard Bouncer clear his throat, he looked up at him. "Well?" he asked.

"I will stay with my men, Sir! We all volunteered to fight the Germans for King and Country. I will not take the easy way out. My men and I want to fight!"

"I thought as much, Lieutenant. I have heard about your heroism at Ypres and your capabilities in leading the men assigned to you."

"Is that all Sir? I would like to get back to my men now."

"No, Lieutenant, there is something else."

Bouncer looked at the Colonel with raised eyebrows.

"I have your record here, Lieutenant, You have risen in the ranks quickly. Your battle experience at Ypres was exemplary. You are, Lieutenant, an example of what our army needs." The Colonel paused, stood up and stretched his back, then turned to point at a large map pinned to the wall behind his desk. "Here, Lieutenant Russell, is the map of the Somme sector. Come closer."

Bouncer walked behind the mahogany desk and stood next to the Colonel, looking at the map that showed both British and German trench lines, the geological features, and most of all, the German positions on the high ground directly across No Man's Land from his trench line.

"This is my quandary, Lieutenant. My orders came down from GHQ through the chain of command."

The Colonel cleared his throat and hesitated. "As a military man, I know I can confide in you. If I had anything to do with it, the Somme would not have been my choice for the offensive. Look here and here." The Colonel used a stick to point to the German markers on hills in front of the British line. "These German redoubts are well fortified, built to withstand attacks from all directions, riddled with dugouts and passages."

The Colonel paused again. "Without taking these high positions from the Germans, our offensive will collapse and we will have thousands of casualties. My quandary, Lieutenant, knowing the outcome of our attack, is whether I should simply obey orders without question, or whether I should tell my superiors about the fallacy of centering the offensive at the Somme."

Bouncer thought for a moment, surprised that the Colonel seemed to be seeking his advice in what was obviously a highly confidential military matter. Then, he said, slowly and thoughtfully, "Begging your pardon, Sir, but I don't think it is a quandary. Our men are ready to fight. In that, there is no doubt. The French, Sir, are taking a beating at Verdun. If we don't attack, the French will be overrun, and our forces will be cut off from the channel. The Germans will win the war, Sir! If we can beat the Germans back from the Pozieres Ridge and secure the main road to Baupaume, we will deal them a serious blow that could turn the tide of the war." Bouncer pointed to the area on the map directly across the German line from where his men were stationed.

"Yes, Lieutenant," smiled the Colonel, "You're quite right. It's a political decision, not a military one."

"Orders are orders, Sir! It's not for me to question them."

"Thank you Lieutenant. You not only solved my quandary but also have convinced me that you can be entrusted with the responsibility for saving thousands of our men."

"My men and I will do our duty, Sir!"

"Look here, Lieutenant." The Colonel tapped his stick on Hill Fifty-One. "This hill juts out between the two valleys across from your sector. If the German redoubt atop that hill can be taken, it will give us some strategic advantage when our forces attack."

"Yes, Sir, I can see that. That's the hill that separates Sausage from Mash."

The Colonel looked at him with a puzzled expression. "Sausage and Mash?"

Bouncer chuckled. "Yes, Sir. That's what the men call the two valleys. They named the one on the left 'Sausage' because of the sausage-shaped observation balloon that the Jerries usually fly there. It was only natural to call the other one 'Mash.'"

The Colonel laughed. "I see what you mean. Well, if we can knock out the German redoubt atop Hill Fifty-One, the Germans won't be able to fire directly down on our men as they charge up the two valleys – 'Sausage' and 'Mash,' as it were."

"Yes, Sir! That's correct, Sir!"

The Colonel looked at Bouncer and thought for a moment. "Lieutenant, I want you to take Hill Fifty-One. Take it before the offensive begins. If you can do that, we will surely be able to weaken the German advantage and save some British lives." He smacked his stick on the map for emphasis.

"Yes, Sir! My men are ready," cried Bouncer with great enthusiasm. "You can count on us to take that hill, Sir!"

"Easy said, Lieutenant." The Colonel sat down in his leather chair and began to write, and Bouncer returned to his chair in front of the desk. After the Colonel finished writing he looked up at Bouncer, and leaned back in his chair. "This is your assignment, Lieutenant. You will lead your platoon on attack and take Hill Fifty-One in the early morning hours on the day the offensive is to begin. This order will come down to you through the chain of command. Be on the alert for it, and don't tell any of your men, or your commanding officer, that you know about it in advance. The command must come down through the proper channels. We must follow procedures, Lieutenant. I'm sure I can trust you with this confidentiality?"

"Yes, Sir!" said Bouncer, jumping to his feet and standing at attention.

"That's all, Lieutenant. You may return to your platoon now," said the Colonel. "Remember, you must wait for the order to come down to you. If you talk about it beforehand, or about where the offensive is to take place, it will be denied by this office, and you will be charged with insubordination."

Bouncer nodded and saluted, then turned towards the door.

"Tell your men that they are doing well, Lieutenant Russell, and good luck to all of you," said the Colonel, as Bouncer put his hand on the doorknob to exit the room.

"Yes, Sir!"

The door suddenly burst open, and a captain rushed in unannounced. "What is the meaning of this, Captain?" said the colonel rising angrily from his seat.

The captain came to a screeching halt in front of Hastings-Jackson's desk and saluted. "Sorry, Sir, but it's bad news, Sir!" he exclaimed trying to catch his breath.

"Bad news? Out with it then, man!"

"Sir, we just received a telephonic message – Lord Kitchener was killed. He was on the *Hampshire* headed for Russia, and a U-boat torpedoed it just off the Orkney Islands," said the captain breathlessly.

Hastings-Jackson put a hand up over his eyes. "Oh God! Lord Kitchener... that is bad news. When did this happen?" He took his hand down. Tears stood in his eyes.

"Just yesterday, Sir – June 5."

Bouncer stood riveted to his spot by the door, trying to digest this news. Finally, he drew himself up and said quietly, "I'm very sorry, Sir. It is a great loss."

Hastings-Jackson's eyes focused on Bouncer whom he had forgotten was in the room. Then a look of defiance came over his face. "Good luck, Lieutenant, with your mission. Kill a thousand Huns for Kitchener!"

"Yes, Sir! For Lord Kitchener, Sir!" Bouncer left the room and walked slowly back to the officer's billet with a heavy heart.

Forbes was there when he arrived. "You're off, Bouncer, back to the front?" he asked. Bouncer nodded, swallowed the lump in his throat and told him the news.

After they had commiserated over the loss of England's hero, Forbes announced, "I will come with you. My assignment was confirmed a few minutes ago. I'll be reporting to Captain Squires. HQ is boosting his company strength. I will have a mixture of new recruits and experienced men in my platoon. The experienced men are all Scots. It will be up to us to show these New Army recruits how to fight."

"Being given a quiet assignment then?" asked Bouncer with mischievous grin.

"Oh, yes! I'm lucky to have an uncle who is a Colonel."

Forbes and Bouncer loaded up their kit bags and Bouncer led the Scot back through the maze of trenches to where Squires's company was positioned. When they arrived at their section of trenches, they parted company, Forbes going toward Captain Squires's dugout to report to him, and Bouncer making his way in the other direction toward his dugout and his men.

"Pleased to see you back Lieutenant," called out Sam, when he saw Bouncer sloshing through the ankle-deep water towards them.

"At ease, Private," said Bouncer with a grin. "Bloody hell, but I'm pleased to see you lot again."

"How was the champagne and caviar?" asked Freddie.

"About as good as the shine on your latrine bucket, Freddie."

This brought guffaws of laughter from the other soldiers who were within earshot. "At least you haven't lost your sense of humor, Lieutenant. HQ is known to do that," called out one of them.

"HQ and the top brass have no humor when it comes to us," said Sam bitterly. "Just issue orders expecting us to do the dirty work."

"Private Baldwin, stop being insolent. You will be reprimanded if you keep talking that way. We all follow orders here," said Bouncer, loud enough for all his men to hear. The men went silent and returned to their never-ending task of bailing water out of the trench. Satisfied that his men had comprehended his warning, Bouncer made his way back to his dugout. He had just finished unpacking his kit bag when Captain Squires appeared.

"Welcome back, Lieutenant. Hope everything went well at HQ."

"Yes, Sir! Colonel Hastings-Jackson said to tell our men they are doing well."

Rupert hesitated; Bouncer knew what he was going to ask. "Was the meeting about 'private matters,' Bouncer?"

"Yes, Rupert, nothing to be of concern. He wanted to know how our men are doing, are they ready to fight, that type of thing."

"Strange thing to ask you. He should have asked me that," commented Rupert with a frown.

"There was something else, Rupert, but I am not at liberty to say what it was. You will find out soon, though."

"You are not being reassigned are you? Rumor had it you were going to be posted somewhere else."

"Why would I want to be reassigned, Rupert? I'm part of the 34th and always will be," replied Bouncer trying to alleviate Rupert's curiosity.

"Pleased to hear that, Bouncer. You are a good soldier. We need you here."

"By the way, I take it you've met our Highlander – Lieutenant Forbes. He's a real character," said Bouncer, attempting to change the subject. " He showed me the Scots' secret weapon."

"Weapon? I thought the Huns feared their war cry and the sound of the bagpipes," said Rupert with a puzzled look.

"And their bare asses," laughed Bouncer. "Asses. They flip up their kilts and show them when they give the war cry."

"I just hope they point them at the enemy, and not at us," chuckled Rupert. "That was a strange thing. Forbes just suddenly showed up with papers saying he is assigned to my company. I never received word from HQ by normal channels that he was going to be assigned here. Last minute assignment, he says. Going to boost my company's strength. I can't see why – I already have a full complement of officers and men. Was afraid you were going to be transferred and he was going to be your replacement."

"Lots of troops at HQ, coming in by train loads, never seen so many," said Bouncer. "Maybe we are getting ready to attack the Germans. Forbes said there are lots of new recruits who've never seen action and that he and some of his experienced Highlanders are in charge of training them."

"That's what he told me, too. But rumor has it, Bouncer, that the attack is going to be at Armentieres, not here."

"I heard that, too. There are many rumors. Who knows where it is going to be."

Rupert looked at Bouncer and shook his head. "Communications with HQ stinks!"

"Yes, Rupert, I know. I've been there. I know what you mean."

"Such a pity, Bouncer. Here we are ready to fight, and no orders to do so."

"Saw Harry Phillips wandering around at HQ. You remember him?"

"Of course, lost track of him after the battle at Ypres. Thought he was dead."

"Very much alive. Suffered shell shock after the battle, but seems to be all right now."

"Not many left from the Bridgefield Battalion, Bouncer. Pleased to hear about Harry. I've heard about this shell shock. Damn brain gets shaken up. No cure they say. Bound to be a lot more of it before this war is over."

A private stuck his head inside the dugout and interrupted their conversation. "Captain Squires, Sir, come quick, we have an important visitor."

Rupert and Bouncer quickly brushed off their uniforms, went outside and squeezed their way through the packed men standing in the trench.

"This must be the Company Captain," said a soft-spoken blonde-haired man who was dressed in a general's uniform.

"Yes, Sir! Captain Squires, Sir!" said Rupert, saluting and standing at attention.

"How are conditions here, Captain? Do your men have enough to eat and drink?"

"Apart from the rain, everything is as good as can be expected, Sir!"

"Must be used to the rain, Captain Squires, coming from ..." The general inclined his head and one of his aides whispered into his ear. "Bridgefield," he continued, raising his head and smiling at Rupert. This brought a volley of cheers from the soldiers who were standing shoulder to shoulder in the trench.

The General smiled at the men, then looked at Bouncer. "What is your name, Lieutenant?" he asked.

"Lieutenant John Russell, Sir!" responded Bouncer.

"From Bridgefield?"

"Yes, Sir!"

The General looked at Bouncer again more closely, and his smile broadened. " Not related to..." The General paused as if to search his memory. "Captain Henry Russell, one of our heroes of the Boer War?" he asked.

"He was my father, Sir!" said Bouncer, surprise and pleasure registering on his face.

"Looking forward to seeing your name in dispatches, Lieutenant Russell. With men like you fighting on our side, we're sure to win the war." An aide whispered something into the General's ear and he began to move further along the trench. The men squeezed together and did their best to make room for him to pass.

"Anyone like a cigarette?" called out the General, opening a gold cigarette case.

"Here, Sir, here, Sir," came back a chorus of voices.

The visitor extended the case towards the soldier nearest him. The soldier took a cigarette from the case and held it up for his mates to see. "Abdullahs!" he exclaimed excitedly. "Thank you very much, Sir!" Soon there were more hands than cigarettes in the case. An aide came quickly to the rescue, opening a brief case full of the expensive cigarettes and distributing them to each waving hand.

"God save the Prince of Wales!" called out a private, and the other soldiers joined in as the son of King George and heir to the throne walked on through the trench, shaking hands with the men as he                                                                                         passed.

"Fancy that! The Prince of Wales coming down to the trenches," said Sam after the Prince had disappeared on down the line. "He's our man. He's actually concerned about us, God bless him!"

"Haven't seen a regular General yet in all the time we've been in the trenches. They wouldn't sully their hands, but here's the Prince shaking our hands and mixing with the likes of us," said Freddie.

"And that's saying a lot, Freddie, since you use the shit bucket to ladle water," said Sam.

The men around roared with laughter. Captain Squires and Bouncer let the men have their fun. It wasn't every day they saw Royalty, especially in the trenches.

In the last week of June 1916, the prelude to the battle began. The British started a non-stop artillery bombardment that was to go on seven days and seven nights, in the hopes of knocking out the barbed wire barriers and the Germans in the front line trenches before they attacked. Thousands of reinforcements had been marched to the front line trenches to join the soldiers who were already stationed there, and more continued to join them as each day passed. The weather conditions were miserable, the rain coming down in torrents night and day. The trenches were now so crowded that men were squeezed in shoulder to shoulder, having to sleep, if they could, standing up in knee-deep water, leaning on each other, and trying to keep their heavily-loaded kit bags dry. As day after day of the artillery bombardment passed, the men grew deaf from the pounding of the guns, and the artillery gunners themselves suffered powder burns and were bleeding from the ears. The offensive had been scheduled to begin on June 26, the date known only to the top command, but because of the weather, the date was postponed. The soldiers huddled miserably in the trenches waiting, waiting.

Finally, on June 30, word came down to the commanding officers in the trenches that the offensive would begin at sunrise the next morning, July 1. Rupert gathered his platoon leaders together for a briefing. After explaining that the attack would begin at sunrise and that they were to take their men and charge the enemy lines upon receiving his order, Rupert announced sadly, "Unfortunately, I won't be allowed to go in with you men. Orders are for all officers from captain on up to stay here and make sure our troops are being sent in as assigned. High command assures us, however, that our artillery barrage has knocked out the barbed wire and the front-line trenches so we'll be able to march right across No Man's Land and secure the enemy trenches one after another. After that, the cavalry will be ordered in to ride in and take Baupaume. Any questions?"

"No, Sir, seems perfectly clear," said Lieutenant Forbes. "Should be a cake walk with all the artillery that's been fired. My men are ready – anxious to get out of the trenches and fight. You can count on us, Sir!"

The other lieutenants nodded their agreement.

"All right, then. You're dismissed. Get back and prepare your men, and good luck, lads," said Rupert. Then, he turned to Bouncer. "Lieutenant Russell, I need to speak to you."

Bouncer nodded and stayed behind as the other lieutenants rushed out of the dugout, excited to be facing action at last and getting out of the miserable conditions in the trenches. After they had gone,

Rupert motioned for Bouncer to join him in front of the map that was tacked to a board at the back of the dugout.

"Bouncer, I have a special assignment for you and your platoon," said Rupert, pointing to the map. "You and your men will go over the top at three a.m., and take Hill Fifty-One. Our artillery will stop firing for twenty minutes beginning at three. This should give you time to reach the bottom of the hill. After that the artillery will begin again and will avoid firing in this area."

"Yes, Sir!" said Bouncer. "My men will be ready."

Rupert pointed with a stick at Hill Fifty-One. "You must take the hill, Bouncer. It is crucial. Otherwise, the Germans will be firing down on us from all sides and God knows what havoc they will cause."

Bouncer looked at the map closely. It had more detail than the one he had seen in the Colonel's office, depicting the German trench lines and artillery positions.

"What's on top of the hill?" asked Bouncer.

"A well-fortified redoubt, made of concrete, full of machine gun emplacements, riddled with passages. Enough room for two hundred and fifty well-armed men. Must get inside, Bouncer, and destroy the machine guns. Hold on to it until reinforcements arrive. It's our only hope."

"Yes, Sir!" responded Bouncer.

"There will be another signal, Bouncer, to let you know our attack has begun. We have dug a tunnel under the German trenches and planted a mine. It will explode at precisely 7:30 a.m. That is the cue for our men to go over the top. You must have Hill Fifty-One secured by that time."

"Yes, Sir! You can count on us," said Bouncer.

"Better get back to your men, then. You and your men had better try to get some sleep, if you can."

At that moment an artillery shell exploded a few yards in front of the trench. After the blinding flash and the deafening sound of ignited explosive, the ground shook, and mud and white clay rained down.

Rupert looked at Bouncer as the lantern flickered. "You don't have a family, Bouncer, so just in case, is there someone you want me to write to?"

"No, Sir!" said Bouncer. "All I have is my men."

"Well, someone needs to know of your gallantry. I'll write to my own family about you. Will send a letter to Lord Davenville and my cousin Susan."

Bouncer looked at him in surprise. "Me, gallant? I don't think so. Just following orders, Sir," he said modestly. "Can't imagine that Susan or Lord Davenville would be interested."

"I have some suspicions, Bouncer," said Rupert, looking closely into Bouncer's eyes. "I know you haven't given me the full story of your meeting with Colonel Hastings-Jackson. It must have been a very private matter?"

Bouncer looked directly back into Rupert's eyes, and then looked down. "Yes, Rupert, it was something that I don't really understand myself. If we survive the war, I will tell you about it, and maybe you can help me solve the mystery. I'm really not at liberty to talk about it right now."

"Very well, Bouncer. I'll not pry any further," said Rupert, putting a hand on Bouncer's shoulder. "You'd better get back to your men, now, and may God be with you on your mission."

\* \* \*

The pounding of the artillery continued. The troops tried to rest, but the excitement of the next day's action kept them awake. Each of Bouncer's men had smeared their faces and helmets with lantern soot.

"Take only what is necessary," ordered Bouncer to his men who were tightly gathered together.

"No extra underwear, Freddie," said Sam, poking Freddie on the arm.

"Just your rifles with bayonets drawn and as many grenades as you can carry."

"I'm for that," called out a private over the sound of exploding shells.

"Get ready. We're over the top in five minutes," said Bouncer looking at his pocket watch by the flash of an exploding shell.

Without warning silence fell. The world seemed to stand still. Men pulled on their ears trying to alleviate them of the ringing noise caused by the deafening barrage they had been subjected to for an entire week.

"All right, mates. Over the top and follow me," said Bouncer waving his arm in a forward motion. "Freddie, hold on to my trouser leg and crawl on your elbows like me. The rest of you hold on to the one in front, keep your heads down and crawl!"

Bouncer climbed the ladder and the rest followed. They crawled from one shell crater to another. A German flare went up, and Bouncer and his men waited for it to fade before moving again. Another flare went up. Luckily, the group was below the rim of a large crater.

"I can see barbed wire," whispered Sam.

"Pass the word. Wire twenty yards ahead," whispered Bouncer. "Keep low. When the flare goes out, we'll make for that large crater, the one closest to the barbed wire."

Freddie and the others looked ahead, saw the crater Bouncer indicated, and nodded.

"Then we'll follow the wire north using shell craters for cover," continued Bouncer.

"I hear Huns laughing," said Sam.

"I hear them, too," said Bouncer, raising his hand to his lips in a warning signal. "Quiet everyone."

The light of the flare went out. The men crawled to the crater closest to the wire and had just made it into the crater when another flare lit up the sky.

"Fuck!" whispered a private. " Damn bloody flares."

"Shut the fuck up," said another.

"What in the hell are those?" asked Sam, pointing at thousands of shell canisters lying on the pocked ground next to the barbed wire.

"Jesus, unexploded shells! The barbed wire is still intact. No wonder the Huns are laughing," said Freddie, raising his head slightly to see what Sam was talking about.

"Bloody hell! All that talk by the brass saying the barbed wire is destroyed was a lie! The men that follow us will be massacred!" said Sam. "Should we send word back?"

"No way to send word back right now," said Bouncer. "The sooner we take the hill, the better."

Darkness fell again, and the platoon inched its way from crater to crater, as quietly as they could. Bouncer knew the artillery would soon begin again and that the roar of the guns would cover any noise they would make. However, when they reached the section of barbed wire that they needed to breach, the barrage had not yet resumed.

"We will cut the barbed wire here," whispered Bouncer, lying on his side and retrieving a small pair of cutters from his tunic pocket. The snap of the wire when he cut it broke the silence, and the men froze. "Need to muffle the noise," muttered Bouncer, taking off his tunic and wrapping the cutters with one of its sleeves. He cut through the wire, and after a short pause to see if any German ears had picked up the noise, the men crawled through the opening to the second line of wire. Again, Bouncer cut the wire, muffling the sound of the cutters with his tunic.

As the men prepared to crawl through the opening in the second line of wire, Bouncer warned them in a low voice, "At the next wire line, there will be trenches with Germans in them."

Suddenly, the sound of incoming artillery broke the silence. The barrage had resumed, and the flashes and thunderous roar of thousands of shells exploding filled the air.

"Now's our chance!" shouted Bouncer. "Run for the wire!"

Unexploded shells fell around them as they ran, and occasionally, one would explode a distance away from the fence line, doing no damage to either barbed wire or the Germans' front line trenches. When they reached the last line of barbed wire, Freddie and Sam helped Bouncer cut it, and they all dropped to the ground waiting for Bouncer's orders.

"The Germans are keeping their heads down. Now's the time to attack. Follow me and use only your bayonets!" said Bouncer, jumping to his feet and leading his men through the hole in the wire. The men rushed through the hole and swarmed into the trench, surprising the Germans, many of whom were comfortably asleep in their deep, well-built dugouts. Their screams could not be heard over the thunder of artillery.

After the last German had been dispatched, Bouncer gathered his men. "Is everyone all right?" he asked, and was gratified to learn that all his men were accounted for and that there were no casualties.

"Well done, men!" said Bouncer. "Now, exchange uniforms with the dead Germans, and do it quickly," he ordered. "More Germans are likely to show up any minute. Corporal Conway, be sure to put on an officer's uniform," he added, addressing the only one of his men who spoke fluent German.

"Now, men, follow me," whispered Bouncer after the men had exchanged uniforms with the dead soldiers. "Conway, stay close behind me."

After walking fifty yards along the trench, they could see the silhouettes of German guards against the faint skyline.

"Who goes there?" called out a guard.

"Been attacked by English, killed many," said Conway in perfect German. "Need more ammo."

"Sure, we have plenty," responded the guard.

Bouncer and his men concealed their bayonets behind them as they approached the Germans. Quick work was made of killing them.

Bouncer led the way again through the trench that began to rise steeply. "Must move quickly now," he said. "Time is running out. We must take the hill before sunrise. Do not use your rifles until I say so. Use the bayonets. It won't be long before the Huns discover us. Our best bet is to get on top of the hill before they do."

After encountering and disposing of several Germans along the way, they finally saw the outline of the redoubt atop the hill.

"Impossible task," whispered Sam. "There are machine guns slits all around it."

Bouncer thought for a moment. "There is a way, Sam," he said slowly. "Pass the word back. We need glass bottles, lantern oil and anything else that is fluid and will burn."

The men quickly gathered bottles and lantern oil and filled the bottles with the oil. The filled bottles were quickly distributed to each of the men.

"Now, when I give the word, we must all throw the bottles at the rifle and machine gun slits," instructed Bouncer.

The men held the bottles as if they were preparing to throw cricket balls.

"Throw!" yelled Bouncer.

The bottles sailed through the air, striking the concrete around the gun slits. They shattered, splashing the lantern oil into the openings.

"Now, fire your rifles at the gun slits!" shouted Bouncer.

The men fired, and the heat from the bullets ignited the lantern oil. Flames and black smoke engulfed the concrete bunker.

"Now, the grenades!" shouted Bouncer. "Follow me and throw them into the slits --- fast! Before the Huns have a chance to figure out what's going on!"

Bouncer led the charge up the hill to the bunker where the men hurled their grenades as well as they could manage into the gun slits. Flames and blue smoke issued from the redoubt, and they could hear men screaming in pain.

"More grenades, quick!" ordered Bouncer.

More flames and smoke emitted from the bunker. The screaming inside intensified and Bouncer's men continued to throw. After each volley, the screaming decreased until no human sound was heard. All that remained was the cracking sound of bullets being ignited by the intense heat.

"That's enough grenades. They've done their job," announced Bouncer.

His men stood in silence watching the smoke and listening to the bullets exploding. After a few minutes the smoke began to clear and the explosions ceased. A steel door opened on the side of the bunker and a white flag appeared.

"We surrender!" called out a German, his hand frantically waving the flag.

"Come out with your hands over your heads!" yelled Conway in perfect German.

The steel door opened and the Germans walked out in single file, their hands clasped atop their heads.

"Hell, there must be over fifty of them," commented Sam over his shoulder to Freddie. There was no response, and Sam looked around and saw Freddie lying on the ground some distance away, his trousers smoldering.

"My God! Freddie has been hurt!" screamed Sam.

"Someone take care of him!" shouted Bouncer, not daring to look around and take his eyes off the Germans.

Sam and two other men ran to Freddie's aid, while Bouncer and the others held their guns on the Germans. Sam held Freddie's head while another man tore off his tunic and beat on Freddie's trousers until the smoldering stopped.

"Prisoners lay face down over here," ordered Conway. The Germans did as ordered and lay down with their hands behind their heads.

"Remove the dead from the bunker, and check every room and passageway," Bouncer commanded. Leaving Conway and a couple of others in charge of the Germans, Bouncer ran to Freddie.

"Freddie is badly burnt. Below the knees his legs are like cinders," said Sam with tears in his eyes.

"Get him inside the bunker and take care of him, Sam," ordered Bouncer. He ran back to Conway.

"There are sixty-two prisoners, twenty-three German dead and four German wounded, Sir!" reported Conway.

"How many casualties do we have?" asked Bouncer.

"Just Simpson, Sir!"

The men cleared out the dead and the mangled remains of equipment from the bunker.

"Everyone inside, and be quick about it! The Germans will be here soon to counter attack," yelled Bouncer.

"What about the prisoners, Sir?" asked Conway.

"Get them inside as well, and be quick about it!"

Bouncer climbed to the top of the bunker. He could see the soft glow of the sun rising. Below him he could see lines of trenches on both sides of No Man's Land. He reached into his tunic pocket and brought out a pair of field glasses. Looking through the glasses he could make out men crammed into the British line. "Poor buggers," he muttered. Then, without warning, there was a loud explosion. Bouncer focused his glasses on the massive explosion that had occurred close to the German trench. "That's the signal. The battle has begun," he whispered to himself.

Men rushed out of the British trenches, and the sound of German machine guns and exploding artillery shells soon followed. Wave upon wave of British soldiers climbed out of their trenches and ran with their rifles held in front of them into the spray of machine gun bullets and exploding shells. Bouncer shook his head. "They don't stand a fucking chance," he winced. Soon, huge clouds of black smoke obscured the battlefield from his view. He put the field glasses back into his tunic and went into the redoubt.

"Found many passageways, Sir, but no more Germans," said Conway as Bouncer entered the bunker. "We've secured the prisoners in a dugout over there. Has a steel door. Must have been their commanding officer's quarters."

"How's Freddie?" asked Bouncer looking at Sam.

"He needs urgent medical attention, Sir!" replied Sam. "If not, infection will set in and he will die."

"We're stuck here until reinforcements arrive," answered Bouncer. "Can anything be done?"

Sam shook his head. "Blood is clotting at the knees. Could lead to gangrene, and after that ... ," Sam choked and looked down at the floor.

Bouncer stood looking at him in silence for a moment. Then, he turned to Conway. "Need to inform HQ we have taken the hill. Send a pigeon. At the same time, ask for British uniforms. If we are caught wearing this lot we will be shot."

"Yes, Sir!" responded Conway. He wrote a short message on a small piece of paper, rolled it up, and put it into a small wooden capsule. The homing pigeon clacked as the capsule was attached to its leg. Conway released the pigeon from the bunker. It flew up into the sky, circled twice, then honed off into the direction of HQ at Albert.

Bouncer walked over to where Freddie lay unconscious on the floor. Sam was mopping his brow. "Freddie has a fever now," he said.

"Must do something. It will take a while for reinforcements to reach us. Our message will take a while to get through," muttered Bouncer, looking down at Freddie with concern in his eyes.

"There is one thing," said Sam hesitantly. "Saw a farmer do it to a prize bull once."

"What was that? Willing to try anything to keep Freddie alive, Sam," said Bouncer.

"Cut off his legs below the knee," said Sam, grimacing.

"Can you do that Sam? Can you do that to Freddie?"

"I don't know. I have cut up meat in the butcher's shop. Cutting humans is a lot different."

"Just think Freddie's legs are legs of lamb and you will be all right," said Bouncer, trying not to sound insensitive.

Sam looked up gravely at Bouncer. "I don't know... ," he began, but was cut short by movement under his hand. He looked down and saw that Freddie's eyes were open.

"Freddie, Freddie, are you awake? Can you hear us?" asked Bouncer leaning down over him.

"I can't feel my feet," croaked Freddie. "My legs are burning up."

"Your legs are burnt Freddie, burnt bad," said Sam.

"The pain is horrible. I feel as if I'm going to die."

"Die, Freddie, and leave The Bottom Five? Not if I can help it! We stick together, remember? No more talk of dying and deserting us," said Bouncer, a small tear trickling down his face.

"Besides, Freddie, you have to catch Jack the Ripper, remember?" added Sam, trying to sound cheerful.

"That's right, Freddie. Hang in there my friend," added Bouncer, wiping the tear off his cheek.

Freddie's eyes closed and he began to moan. "It hurts, it hurts," he breathed.

Bouncer looked at Sam, and Sam looked at Bouncer, each with anguish in their eyes.

"You have to do it, Sam. You have to save our Freddie," said Bouncer in a muted voice.

Sam looked at Freddie's legs, then at his face, which was extremely pale where the lantern soot had rubbed off. Beads of sweat dotted his forehead.

"I can't just do it, Bouncer. I must tell him first. I must let him know that I'm the one who took his legs away," whispered Sam.

"Tell Freddie I ordered you to do it, Sam," said Bouncer quietly. "If he wants to blame someone, he can blame me."

Sam nodded his head reluctantly. "All right, then, Bouncer. I'll do it. I will need a sharp knife and a saw and lots of whiskey," he said, looking down at Freddie who had passed out again.

"Conway will get you whatever you need, Sam. I'm going outside to see how the battle is going."

Sam nodded again and choked back the lump that had risen in his throat. He could see tears streaming down Bouncer's face as he turned and walked out of the bunker.

Bouncer climbed to the top of the bunker and looked at the battlefield through his field glasses. A small westerly breeze was blowing; the smoke was well over the German line. Bouncer had a clear view of the slaughter. The British continued to leave their trenches by the thousands, only to be shot to pieces by German artillery and machine gun bullets. Bodies of those who had been massacred covered No Man's Land. "The stupid bastards!" exclaimed Bouncer. "Why don't they stop sending men into this nightmare? Hasty Jack knew this was going to happen."

Bouncer continued to observe. Then Freddie's agonizing scream came from inside the bunker. Bouncer closed his eyes and muttered, "Hang in there, Freddie. The Bottom Five stick together." After a while Bouncer went back into the bunker.

"How is Freddie now?" he asked, walking over to where Sam and a couple of assistants were crouched over Freddie's body.

"Did a clean job, Sir," answered Sam, wiping his bloodied hands on his tunic. "Just have to seal the cuts now."

Using a needle and thread Sam began sowing together the loose skin below each knee. "Must make sure no air is trapped inside. Then I'll undo the belts on the thighs. If there is no bleeding, then I'll know I've done a good job. After that it's up to Freddie to pull himself through."

Bouncer marveled at Sam's work – the neatness of the surgery and now the stitching. Bouncer watched until Sam finished. Freddie now had neatly sown stumps where his legs use to be.

The buzzing sound of telephonic telephone startled everyone.

"Lieutenant Conway, better answer the damn thing," ordered Bouncer.

Conway confidently picked up the receiver hanging on the wall.

"Post Forty-Seven," he answered in German.

The men standing around looked at Conway in disbelief. Bouncer smiled.

"Our position is held," said Conway. "Had a surprise attack at sunrise. Many English killed; they retreated back down the hill. We suffered no casualties, no action since then."

A loud laugh reverberated from the receiver. Conway smiled as he pointed to the earpiece. After the laughter stopped, the men could hear the crisp voice of the German crackling through the receiver.

"Yes, Sir, Captain," replied Conway trying not to laugh. "Have many rings and watches to share with you, Herr Captain. Will bring much money back in the homeland."

Laughter one again echoed from the earpiece.

"We have orders from a German Captain," smiled Conway after he had replaced the receiver. "We are to hold our position at all costs. The British are attacking below. No relief until the British attack is over, and he says it could last all day."

"Splendid," responded Bouncer grinning. "Where did you get 'Post Forty-Seven'?"

"Above your head, Sir."

Bouncer and the men looked up. Written above, in red paint, was the number forty-seven.

Everyone laughed and shook Conway's hand.

"Men, get to it. Fire your rifles and the machine guns through the slits. We must do our duty for the fatherland," joked Bouncer. "But, for God's sake, don't hit any of our lads!"

The men cheered and stuck their rifles and working machine guns through the slits and fired into the air.

"Must let the Germans know we are alive and well," laughed Bouncer.

Back at the $34^{th}$ Division Headquarters in Albert, Major General Ingouville-Williams, along with his battalion commanders, was observing the battle on a large map in his war room. Accurate information was not available. Once the order to attack was given, it was a waiting game. Over one hundred thousand troops were to attack and break the German line. Field commanders witnessed the events through field glasses from observation platforms placed well away from the battle itself. Success to the generals, at that early stage, was measured in terms of how many troops went over the top and into No Man's Land.

"Just received a message from Lieutenant Russell for Lieutenant Colonel Hastings-Jackson, Sir!" announced a captain who walked hurriedly into the war room.

Hastings-Jackson turned from the map and walked over to the captain, who drew himself up to attention and saluted.

"What does it say Captain?" asked the Colonel.

"Hill Fifty-One has been taken, ... taken before our attack!" exclaimed the captain.

"Good news, that! I knew Russell would do it!" exclaimed the Colonel, rubbing his hands together in satisfaction.

"He needs reinforcements, Sir, and ... ," The captain looked at the paper closely.

"Out with it Captain!" demanded the Colonel impatiently.

"New uniforms, Sir!"

"For what reason?" asked the Colonel looking puzzled.

"Doesn't say, Sir!"

"See to it, Captain. Get the Corp to drop them at sunset and tell them not to make it obvious. A few uniforms for Hill Fifty-One – best news today."

"What about the reinforcements, Sir?"

"See to the uniforms, Captain. That is all."

"Congratulations, Colonel. Taking Hill Fifty-One is a great success. It lessens the German advantage and will make it easier for us to advance," remarked another colonel who had been standing nearby.

"Bollix!" hissed Hastings-Jackson. "You know as well as I do that our advance is nonexistent at present. We are simply sending in men to use up German ammunition. If we have enough men to outlast their ammunition, then we will advance."

The other colonel stared at him, surprised at his outburst. Then the two colonels joined the other officers at the map to continue to observe the progress of the battle.

* * *

Bouncer watched in tormented anguish as the horrible slaughter continued below. The barbed wire fences still intact on the German side slowed the soldiers down and made them sitting ducks for the German gunners. Heaps of dead and wounded piled up in front of the wire, and the bodies of men who attempted to climb over were hanging in the wire riddled with bullets. Bouncer focused the field glasses on the British line and saw that despite this slaughter, the troops continued to climb out of the trenches and rush headlong into the carnage. "May God have mercy," he mumbled.

He refocused the glasses to see more detail, making it possible to make out the faces of individual soldiers. He saw that their faces were frozen in blank expressions and that they marched forward obeying orders like so many automatons. Bouncer knew that they surely realized there would be no hope for them. They could see the twisted bodies of those who went before littering their path and the barbed wire ahead. They had to know that certain death awaited them.

Bouncer shuddered as he scanned the British trench line. Then he gasped; he could see his sector of the line. There were no men's faces he knew. He watched as unknown officers climbed out of the trench, their men following. "When will this carnage end?" he muttered. Then a familiar face appeared. It was the Scot lieutenant, Glenn Forbes. Bouncer watched him climb the ladder and then saw Forbes turn and lift his kilt, waggling his backside at the Germans. The men following him raised their bayonets and appeared to be cheering.

Then, Forbes quickly led his men in and out of shell craters, over the dead and wounded, across No Man's Land toward the German line. Bouncer saw Forbes reach the barbed wire and climb up on the mangled heap of dead and wounded to take hold of the wire. With cutters drawn, Forbes proceeded to snip the wire. Bouncer marveled at the Scot's heroic feat, and then he heard it – a salvo of British artillery shells. The area where Forbes and his men were attempting to break through the wire became an inferno of flames, hurled-up earth and black smoke. When the smoke cleared, Bouncer saw that Forbes was no longer there. He and his men had been blown to smithereens. Bouncer felt ill. "Fucking artillery," he muttered. "First, the shells don't explode, and then when they do, they blow away our own men. Some bleeding Glory Hole, this is!"

He climbed down from the top of the redoubt and ran to the door. "Fire your guns again and let the Germans know we are still here!" he screamed as he yanked open the steel door.

His men opened fire with their rifles and sprayed the surrounding area with long machine gun bursts. The bunker filled with smoke from the burning gunpowder.

For the rest of the day the men continued to fire, being careful not to hit any English troops, but keeping up their ruse as German soldiers.

Just before sunset Bouncer climbed to the top of the bunker again and focused his field glasses on the battlefield below. There were no more troops running forward, no more artillery shells exploding. He winced at the sight of thousands of shell craters and bodies littering the ground between the British and German lines. Not a tree stood, not a blade of grass, no sign of human life. Black smoke from cordite fires provided an eerie backdrop to the hellish scene. Bouncer focused the glasses on the German trenches. The barbed wire was still intact. Mounds of English lay dead in front of the wire, and he could see Germans using long poles to knock down the dead soldiers who had made it that far.

The sound of a biplane interrupted Bouncer's thoughts. Conway ran out of the bunker and other men followed. "It's the flying corps. Must be our uniforms," he cried.

The plane appeared, then disappeared towards the east, its engines fading in the distance. Then there was a swishing sound, indicating that the pilot had cut his engines and was returning at a low altitude. Parachutes opened and large wicker baskets floated down and landed close to the bunker.

"Take the baskets into the bunker and change uniforms on the double," ordered Bouncer.

The last rays of the sun of that July day faded away and the light of a full moon gave a silver glow. A casualty truce was negotiated, and men carrying lanterns and stretchers began moving among the dead and wounded on the battlefield.

Bouncer went to the top of the bunker again, this time in his British uniform. He needed to be alone, knowing that he and his men had been lucky. If they had been part of the regular battle, they would surely have been slaughtered. Once again, fate seemed to have intervened on his behalf.

"Hey, English! Thought you were German until I saw the brass buttons shining in the moonlight."

The German voice, speaking in broken English, came from somewhere below the bunker in the direction of the trench Bouncer and his men had come through to get to the bottom of the hill.

"Greetings, German," called back Bouncer, grabbing his rifle.

"You took me by surprise English. We thought we still held the redoubt."

"Took it at sunrise. Have many German prisoners, some dead and some wounded," replied Bouncer cautiously, holding his rifle at the ready.

"Your voice sounds familiar, English. Ve haf spoken before, ya?"

"Don't see how. Never been to Germany," replied Bouncer. "But I'll soon be there when we break through your lines!"

"Ya! Ya! English. You are funny," laughed the German voice. "You English are such comedians. Pity you can't play football as well as telling jokes."

"Pity you Germans don't have any chocolate," laughed Bouncer, recognizing the German's voice.

"In the name of the Kaiser, you must be English Bouncer!"

"In the name of King George, you must be Fritz the Saxon!"

"Ya, ya, English Bouncer."

"What is to be done, Saxon Fritz? We hold many of your men as well as the redoubt."

"How many, English Bouncer?

"Sixty-two total, twenty-three dead and four wounded."

"How many English? How many dead and wounded?"

"I have a sufficient number of men to hold this redoubt – no dead, and one seriously wounded who needs medical help or he will die. Can we bargain, Saxon Fritz?"

"Ya! Ya! I'll bargain with you, English Bouncer. We Saxons have no quarrel with the English. We are related to you. If not for the damn Normans, we would be brothers. Now we have to fight each other. Damn French are responsible for it all."

"I'm not a historian, Fritz. I just follow orders."

"Let's bargain, English Bouncer. What do you propose?"

"Take my wounded man and one other to the English line to be picked up for medical treatment by the British, and I will release your four wounded men," said Bouncer.

"Hard bargain, English. What about the rest of my men?"

"They will be taken care of, Fritz. If you attack us, everyone dies."

"Too many English killed today – more tomorrow."

"If you don't attack us, many lives will be saved, Fritz – both English and German."

There was a silence while Bouncer waited for Fritz to consider his proposition and give his answer.

After a couple of minutes, Fritz spoke up again. "Very well, English Bouncer. We will take your wounded man and one other to English line, and you will release our wounded. I will not attack you as long as I am in command here and as long as you take care of the rest of my men."

"We will need food and water, Fritz. Supplies will soon run out with so many to feed," replied Bouncer, trying not to let the relief show too strongly in his voice.

"Ya, ya. We will do the exchange tonight, and I will see that food and water are delivered in the morning, but you must promise not to attack us either, or harm the prisoners."

"Agreed. You have my word, Fritz. I am a man of honor."

"Then it is done. You have my word, also. We Saxons are men of honor, too, English Bouncer. High command still thinks you are German. I will let them think that as long as possible, but you and your men must stay in the redoubt. If you come out, you must wear German uniforms."

"All right, then. I'll have the men ready for transfer in fifteen minutes. You will need to bring five stretchers."

"We will be ready, English."

Bouncer went back into the bunker with a lighter heart knowing that Freddie and Sam would be saved and that he and the rest of his men had a reprieve for the time being.

* * *

"No further than the wire," warned a German voice, as English orderlies carrying stretchers and lanterns approached the German side of No Man's Land. The orderlies piled bodies onto the canvas stretchers until they were barely able to lift them. Then, they passed the stretchers back along a chain of men toward the British line.

"Remember, English, you have till midnight to recover your casualties," continued the German. The orderlies acknowledged this warning with indiscernible grumbles and continued with their gruesome task.

Suddenly, an English voice called out from the German line. "Over here, over here! I have a seriously wounded man!"

Two orderlies held up their lanterns and saw a private carrying another man across his shoulders through an opening in the barbed wire.

\* \* \*

# Chapter 12
## *Hill Fifty-One*

THE FIELD HOSPITAL was overflowing with wounded men lying on stretchers. Most had been waiting for medical treatment since sunset. Orderlies and nurses shook their heads in alarm; they were not prepared for the onslaught of so many men needing urgent care. They had run out of bandages many hours ago, and now they were reduced to using torn up bed sheets.

The inventory of the wounded continued as orderlies went from stretcher to stretcher asking questions and writing information down on paper attached to clipboards.

"How do you feel, Private?" asked a gray-haired orderly, stopping by a stretcher where a dark-haired youth lay, his face smudged with soot. "See you are in the $34^{th}$," he commented, noticing the insignia on the lad's uniform.

"Afraid he can't hear you. He's unconscious," said a short sandy-haired private who was hovering nearby.

The orderly looked up. "Do you know this soldier?" he asked.

"Yes. His name is Freddie Simpson of the Royal West Kents."

The orderly nodded and wrote this information down. "What is the nature of this man's wounds?" he asked, looking up again.

The private drew the army blanket back so the orderly could see Freddie's amputated legs. The orderly peered down at the legs, frowned, and looked up again. "This man has already been treated. Can't understand why he is waiting here."

"Legs need to be cauterized," explained the private.

The orderly looked down at Freddie's legs again. "You're quite right, Private," he said. "Come and look at this!" he called out, motioning to a doctor who was standing by a stretcher two rows away.

An elderly man wearing a white bloodstained apron leaned over Freddie and looked to where the orderly was pointing.

"My word!" he exclaimed. "Who in God's name did this?" He looked up in surprise at the orderly, and then both he and the orderly looked questioningly at the sandy-haired private.

The private hesitated. "I did," he said, hanging his head. "Had to or he would have died..."

"You? You were responsible for this?" asked the doctor in an incredulous tone. "What is your name, Private?"

"Yes, Sir. My name is Sam Baldwin, Sir, also with the Royal West Kents.

"Son of a surgeon, no doubt?" asked the doctor, with a smile.

"No, Sir. I'm a butcher's son. Did the best I know how."

"No need to be nervous, Private Baldwin," said the doctor, clapping Sam on the shoulder. "What you did saved his life, and I haven't seen better work from a Harley Street surgeon – certainly not under these conditions."

Sam blushed and wiped the beads of perspiration from his forehead. "Well, you see Freddie here is a close friend – a very close friend. Don't know if he will understand the reason I did it..."

The doctor looked at Sam with a kindly expression. "Yes, Sam, he will understand. This man will be grateful to you for the rest of his life. He was lucky to have a butcher's son for a friend. Very lucky, indeed."

Sam's eyes began to water, the reality of what he had done beginning to hit him. His face went pale and he staggered. The doctor grabbed his arm to steady him. "That's all right, lad. Sit down. I'll see to it that Private Simpson is sent to Lunbury Hospital in London right away, and you, Sam Baldwin, will go with him. As far as the Army is concerned, you're on the casualty list. I'm going to write a letter to the head surgeon. Going to tell him that Sam Baldwin is wasting his time in the trenches and that he would serve his country much better if he could practice his talents as a surgeon."

The doctor wrote a note, glancing up occasionally at Sam who was sitting on a canvas stool with his head down between his knees.

The doctor finished writing a note, then looked at Sam.

"No reason why the surgeon should not accompany his patient, is there, Sam?"

Sam raised his head slowly, mopped his brow and nodded in gratitude at the doctor. The doctor smiled at Sam, then turned to the orderly. "This one goes on the next ambulance train to Boulougne, and from there on the first ship back to England, along with his friend here."

"Most certainly, Doctor. It will be a pleasure," answered the orderly, grinning broadly. He signaled to another orderly, and without further ado, they lifted Freddie's stretcher between them and carried him to the waiting ambulance train with Sam following close behind.

Within five minutes of settling Sam and Freddie on the train, the orderlies stood watching as the train pulled out, gathering steam for its sprint to the channel port. In another hour, the train reached its destination, and its occupants were quickly transferred to ferries waiting to transport them across the channel back to England.

Eight hours later, a motorized Red Cross ambulance pulled up outside Lunbury Hospital in the outskirts of London. "Emergency wounded!" shouted the driver as he jumped out of the driver's seat and rushed to the rear of the vehicle to open the doors.

Orderlies exploded out of the hospital doors and rapidly unloaded the ambulance. Then, two orderlies to a stretcher, they rushed the wounded men to operating rooms where surgeons and nurses waited.

Sam was nearly forced to run to keep up with the orderlies bearing Freddie's stretcher. "You can't go in. No one allowed except the medical staff," said one of the orderlies over his shoulder to Sam as they raced toward double doors at the end of a hallway.

"He's my friend!" cried Sam. "Came over from the front with him, and I'm not leaving him!"

"Wait over there, Private," said the orderly nodding his head toward a small area with a few chairs to the left of the doors. "I'll see that the doctor talks to you after he has examined your friend," he added hastily as they disappeared through the doors with Freddie.

Sam sat down in one of the empty chairs as he had been directed and tried to catch his breath. He gave a great sigh, closed his eyes and rubbed his temples. Within minutes he was fast asleep, his head slumped down on his chest.

"Undo the bandages. Let's see the wounds," commanded a tall dark-haired man in a surgeon's gown when the orderlies had transferred Freddie from the stretcher to the operating table. The orderlies unwrapped the bandages covering the stumps of Freddie's legs, and the surgeon examined them closely. "Clean cuts and perfect stitching. No bleeding," he commented as he probed gently around the wounds.

He handed the dirty bandages to a red-haired nurse who was standing at his side. She disposed of them in a bin and returned to the operating table.

"All we need to do is cauterize the wounds," the surgeon told her. "If this soldier has the necessary fortitude, he should recover nicely."

The nurse nodded and looked more closely at the wounded man's face. "I think I know this fellow," she said in surprise.

"His name is Freddie Simpson," replied the doctor, looking at the papers that had been attached to Freddie's stretcher.

"I do know him!" exclaimed the nurse. "He lived very close to us in Queen Anne's Gardens and is Martha's cousin! I haven't seen him since my sixteenth birthday party."

"There is something else here," said the surgeon, opening an envelope clipped to the papers. "There's a letter here."

The nurse continued to look at Freddie, tears welling in her eyes as the surgeon read the letter.

"Well, I never! This man's legs were amputated by a butcher's son!" exclaimed the surgeon.

"A butcher's son?" inquired the nurse, looking up at him.

"Yes, a Sam Baldwin. This is a letter from the doctor at the field hospital. He is recommending that we take Baldwin on as a surgeon."

"Oh, Uncle Tommy, I know Sam, too. He came to my birthday party with Freddie. Brought me sausages...," said the nurse with misty eyes and a fond smile.

"Really? Sausages for your birthday?" laughed the surgeon. "Too bad I wasn't able to be there. I would have liked to see that."

"One of the best gifts I ever had," said the nurse. "I'm pleased they're both here. I'll give extra care to Freddie."

"Now, Susan, you know we give extra care to all our patients," said the surgeon, gently chastising her.

"You're right, of course, Doctor Davenville," said Susan. "It's just nice to be able to give that extra care to someone you know."

* * *

The sun was rising above the fog that filled the valley below. Hills and ridges poking up above the fog reminded Bouncer of islands in a calm sea. He and his men were peering warily out of the gun slits in the bunker, rifles at the ready.

"Awfully quiet out there, Sir," remarked Conway who was standing at Bouncer's side.

Bouncer nodded. "Strange, isn't it? Hope Sam and Freddie got through all right." He was about to say more when a German voice from outside the bunker broke the silence.

"Hey, English Bouncer! I haf water and food!"

"I'll be there!" yelled Bouncer out the gun slit, and then he turned to Conway. "It's Fritz," he said.

"Do you think it's a trick?" asked Conway anxiously.

"Only one way to find out," said Bouncer, pulling on a trench coat. He picked up a slat of wood to which he had attached a white handkerchief and stuck it outside the door of the redoubt. Then, he cautiously opened the door wider and stepped outside holding the flag high above his head.

Down the hill, he saw a white flag appear from a German trench, and then Fritz climbed out and began walking toward him, carrying his flag, which was attached to the bayonet of his rifle.

As the two met halfway between the redoubt and the trench, Fritz silently produced two cigarettes and handed one to Bouncer. They lit up and stood silently gazing at the valley below as they smoked. Finally, Fritz said in his broken English, "It will be a quiet day today. Still many English dead hanging in the wire and on the ground. Because of this, ve haf agreed to a cease-fire for today to allow more time for you British to remove your dead. It is the proper thing to do, English Bouncer."

"What about my wounded man?" asked Bouncer, turning to look at Fritz.

"I kept my word. He and the other soldier were taken to the barbed wire. From there, the English took them. I watched to make sure."

"Thanks, Saxon Fritz. You are indeed honorable."

Fritz smiled and nodded his head. "Remember, English Bouncer, ve are kindred. Sad to see so many of our kindred killed." He cleared his throat, turned and pointed to some oak barrels and wooden crates that were stacked near some rocks a few yards away. "Come. I haf water for you," he said.

Bouncer followed Fritz to the barrels, and the German filled a tin cup with water from one of the barrels and offered it to him. Bouncer took the cup, put it to his lips, and then hesitated, looking at Fritz questioningly.

Fritz laughed. "Don't worry, English. The water is good. See?" He took the cup from Bouncer and drank out of it.

Bouncer laughed, took the cup and drank deeply. "Thanks for the water. My men and our prisoners will appreciate it."

"And the food, too," said Fritz, pointing to the wooden crates stacked beside the barrels.

Suddenly, the crack of a rifle split the air. Both Bouncer and Fritz dived to the ground.

"What the hell? You gave your word you wouldn't attack us!" said Bouncer angrily.

"I did!" said Fritz as more shots rang out from the trench below. "Don't know what's going on!" Before he could say more, Bouncer's men began to fire from the redoubt.

"Are you all right, Lieutenant?" screamed Conway above the roar of the gunfire.

"I'm all right!" yelled Bouncer as Fritz jumped to his feet waving his arms at the German trench line. "Cease fire! Cease fire!" he roared.

The firing stopped. Bouncer got to his feet and brushed the dirt off his uniform.

"I gave my word, English Bouncer," said Fritz angrily. "Must have been one of those trigger-happy Prussians in my company. I will deal with him when I get back!"

"Well, I'm grateful for what you have done," said Bouncer. "I'll make sure the prisoners are treated well so long as you don't attack."

Fritz looked back down at the valley below and shook his head. "You English have lost thousands. It is madness," he said sadly.

"Let's at least keep our pact, Fritz," said Bouncer. "No point in further killing."

Fritz looked back at Bouncer. "Yes, English Bouncer. I will keep my word. You are surrounded and hold no advantage. You hold my men as prisoners, and you and your men are my prisoners. There is no escape for you..."

"If you attack us, your comrades will be killed," Bouncer reminded him.

"I understand the consequences, English. That is why I will keep my word. For how long I can't be sure, but for as long as I am in command here." He turned to walk back down the hill, then stopped and looked back at Bouncer with a wry grin. "Besides, we need to finish our football game, remember?"

"Bloody right. Without being shelled by the Brits next time, eh?" said Bouncer with a chuckle.

"Ya! Or the Germans either!" returned Fritz with a wave of his hand as he headed back down the hill.

Bouncer watched until the Saxon disappeared into the trench at the bottom of the hill. Then he went back to the redoubt where he was besieged by questions from his men. After filling them in on his meeting, he dispatched a small detail to collect the provisions supplied by the Germans.

Bouncer flopped down on a pallet and fell into an exhausted sleep knowing that he and his men were safe - for the time being, at least.

* * *

Susan Davenville leaned over Freddie and mopped his brow. Sam could see she had tears in her eyes.

"How did this happen, Sam? Why did you amputate his legs?"

"We were with the Royal West Kents at the Somme in Captain Squires's company - your cousin, I believe?" began Sam, watching as Susan continued to minister to Freddie.

Susan looked up in surprise. "Rupert?" she asked.

Sam nodded.

"I knew he was a captain in the Royal West Kents, but I never knew exactly where he was stationed, although Daddy did say he saw him when he accompanied King George to France last year when General Haig took over," said Susan.

"Oh, yes. Lord Davenville. I remember seeing him," said Sam. "Our platoon was chosen as the honor guard for that event. Our platoon leader is John Russell, by the way... you remember Bouncer? He's our lieutenant."

Susan stared at Sam, a sparkle of recognition lighting up her green eyes. "Oh, yes... I remember Bouncer... ," she said with a smile and a faraway look. Then she started slightly and quickly added, "I remember all of you who came to my party - you and Freddie, Bouncer, Spindle and Pete. You say you were in Bouncer's platoon? Where is he? Is he all right?"

"Last I saw of him, two days ago - but can't be sure for how long. You see, he and the rest of the men in our platoon are trapped behind the German lines."

Susan listened intently with great concern as Sam told her about their mission, the capture of the redoubt and how Freddie had been wounded.

"So you see, Bouncer was forced to order me to take off Freddie's legs for fear that he would die otherwise," concluded Sam sadly. "Later in the day when there was a cease fire, Bouncer was able to negotiate an exchange of wounded German prisoners for Freddie and me, and that's how we came to be here."

He paused and looked at Freddie who still lay in a comatose state. "I did what I had to do at the time, but what bothers me is I'm afraid Freddie will blame me for the rest of his life for the loss of his legs," he said, looking down quickly as he felt the sting of tears in his eyes.

Susan came to him and put a comforting hand on his shoulder. "Don't think that way, Sam. Both the field doctor and my uncle said that if it weren't for your skill, Freddie would not have survived. He will be grateful and not blame you after he's gone through the adjustment time. You must not think that way or blame yourself, Sam."

Dr. Thomas Davenville walked up as Susan was comforting Sam. He looked at Susan questioningly over Sam's head. "How's our patient today?" he asked.

"Still in a coma and still has a fever," replied Susan, nodding her head meaningfully at Sam who still sat looking down at the floor with a dejected expression.

"The fever will take its course. Our biggest concern will be shock when he wakes up."

"There are so many men, Doctor," said Susan shaking her head. "It's dreadful to see so many without limbs."

"Yes, Susan, we were not prepared for this many," said Dr. Davenville gently. "Thanks to this young man, however, your friend Freddie had the best possible treatment before he reached us." He looked at Sam and then went over to the bedside and held Freddie's hand. "Poor fellow. It will be a couple of days before the fever breaks, but perhaps that is a blessing in disguise," he said.

"But he is going to get better?" asked Sam, finally looking up at the doctor.

"Oh, yes, Sam. He will recover physically, but how long it will take him to adjust to not having legs is another matter. He will be in shock, you know, and will go through some depression." Dr. Davenville paused and then added, "You know, you would make a good surgeon. We have a major shortage of men with your skills, Sam." He paused again and smiled at Sam. "How would you like to stay here and become my assistant?" he asked.

"A surgeon, Doctor?" asked Sam incredulously. "I have no experience in cutting on humans. Just worked in our butcher shop, that's all. Freddie is the only person I've ever cut on, and I was ordered to do that!"

The doctor put his hand up to allay Sam's fears. "I said 'my assistant,' Sam. You will work under my direction, and we'll have Susan as our nurse to assist us both. What do you say?"

Sam looked at the doctor, then at Susan. "Well, I don't know..."

"It's a splendid idea!" interrupted Susan enthusiastically. "You don't have to go back to the front. We need you here."

"But I'm a private in the Army, signed up to fight Germans," said Sam slowly.

"You can serve your country better here," countered the doctor.

"Yes, Sam. The doctor is right," urged Susan. "Think of all the lives you can save working here with us."

Sam thought for a moment and then he smiled. "Yes, I see what you mean," he said. "Besides, I promised Bouncer I'd see that Freddie is safe."

"Good. It's done, then," said Dr. Davenville. "I'll see to it that you are transferred immediately to the Medical Corps. With the letter from the field doctor and one from me, there's no doubt the transfer will take place. Can't be sure what rank you'll get, however."

Sam grinned. "I don't care about rank as long as I can be of service. Bloody hell!" he exclaimed, scratching his head. "Didn't think I'd end up as a surgeon's assistant. Wanted to be a vet, but the furthest I got was being a butcher."

Susan and Dr. Davenville laughed along with Sam at the ironic turn of events.

"Well, it's settled, Sam. Pleased to have you with me. I'll just go and write that letter right away," said the doctor.

After he left, Susan smiled at Sam. "Just think, Sam, after the war is over you can still go back to the butcher's shop or be a veterinarian or even become a surgeon, whatever you want. Besides, now you will get to see Rose - imagine she's frantic with worry wondering where you are."

Sam looked up in surprise. "How did you know about Rose?"

"Martha writes to me. Keeps me posted on all the news about my friends back in Bridgefield," said Susan, grinning wickedly. "Said you and Rose had become quite an item. You'd better write to her and let her know you're here..."

Before Susan could say more to make Sam's face even redder, there was a movement in the bed. Freddie moaned weakly and tried to roll to his side. "Come on, Sam, you can begin assisting right away. Help me strap Freddie in. We don't want him moving about and doing further damage to himself," she said, placing her hand on Freddie's forehead. "It may be a while before he wakes up, and when he does, he'll have his friends here to help him cope."

\* \* \*

Chad House had grown high sandbag walls, and slats of wood covered its windows. German Zeppelin bombardments were evident – several craters marred the road outside the entrance, and young men dressed in Army uniforms were shoveling the debris back into the craters.

Inside Chad House Spindle and his cohorts were in the map room.

"The whole attack was a disaster. Not a hope in hell for our men," said Spindle looking up at the projected map. "Too many machine guns, too many artillery pieces. Our men didn't stand a chance."

"And the barbed wire too. Don't forget that," added Roger.

"They should have listened to us. They should have taken into account our recommendations in not attacking at the Somme," said James. "How many casualties Roger?"

"On the very first day one hundred thousand went over the top, and fifty thousand were either killed or wounded," said Roger as he read mournfully from a tally sheet.

"How many German casualties?" asked Harvey.

"Less than four thousand," answered Roger.

The four stood on the balcony in silence, staggered by the numbers Roger had read.

"At this rate the war will soon be over. The Germans will outlast us! By the grace of God, the generals shouldn't continue this slaughter!" cried Spindle passionately slapping his hand on the balcony railing.

"Look there, Spindle, "said Roger pointing at the map. "In between Hill Fifty and Fifty-Two. We have taken a position from the Germans."

"The only one," added James.

The four focused their field glasses on Hill Fifty-One.

"Bugger me, Roger!" exclaimed Spindle. "A platoon of the Royal West Kents took the bloody thing -- the only success of the whole disaster! I wonder if Bouncer, Squires, Sam and Freddie came through it all."

"Squires, I'm sure, made it through all right. Officers - captain and above - were ordered to stay in the trenches. Just the lieutenants and the lower ranks went over the top," replied James.

"And the bloody generals sat back and watched," retorted Roger sarcastically.

"Sir!" said Harvey in an alarmed voice, looking around to see if anyone had overheard Roger's outburst.

Spindle turned to Harvey with a stern expression. "Sergeant, get the latest dispatches and bring them to us. On the double!" he ordered.

After mumbling a barely audible "Yes, Sir!" Harvey exited quickly.

"Must be careful about him," said Spindle in a low voice after Harvey was out of earshot. Roger and James nodded their agreement, and they all turned their attention back to Hill Fifty-One.

"Those men on the hill are cut off. They're surrounded by a Saxon regiment," observed James.

"Yes. If they're not reinforced, the Germans can easily take that hill back," commented Roger.

"Won't happen. They won't be reinforced for a while - if at all. Certainly not now. Just read a command from HQ. The plan is for another frontal assault to try to drive the Huns back from their positions around the hill," said James. "Perhaps they are counting on our men to hang on until we can break through the German lines."

"How detailed is your information, Roger? Do you know who is on that hill?" asked Spindle.

"No. All I have is numbers, no names," replied Roger, shaking his head.

"Can we find out if Bouncer, Sam and Freddie are all right?" asked Spindle. "Just to put my mind at ease. Must let Pete and Ginger know."

"I'll do my best, Spindle," replied Roger. "Give me a couple of hours. I will send a telegram to the Royal West Kent headquarters."

The three captains left the map room and were walking back to their office when Harvey met them in the narrow corridor.

"General Bottoms wants to see the three of you immediately, Sirs," said Harvey with a smug expression. He handed Spindle the day's dispatches, saluted, and went on down the corridor to the map room.

"Wonder why? Our scheduled meeting with the general was not to be for another hour," murmured James as the three of them looked at each other in surprise at Harvey's pronouncement.

"Bloody Harvey is up to something," opined Roger. "Never did trust him."

"Let me do most of the talking," whispered Spindle as he gently knocked on the general's office door. After hearing a muffled "Enter!" the three captains went in to face General Bottoms who was seated at his desk holding a file marked "Top Secret."

"Well, gentlemen be seated," he said in a brisk voice. "Just a few words to say to you." He put the file on top of a stack of others. "There is the tendency to be critical when things go wrong, especially of those in command, those whose job it is to win this war."

Spindle opened his mouth to speak, but on second thought, quickly shut it again.

The general looked sternly at them as if to let this sink in before continuing. "We have suffered heavy losses and we will suffer many more. A word to the wise, Captains: do not be verbally critical. You can think it, but you must not say it. There are many who think the same as you and there are many who think otherwise, myself included. We are bound by duty to go along with it all. Unity is what will ultimately win this war. Dissention spreads quickly, and if it is not controlled, it will shatter that unity. Do I make myself clear?"

"Yes, Sir," said Spindle in a humble tone. "But please understand, Sir, that we were quite overwrought this morning when we saw the high casualty numbers and learned that our only success was in taking Hill Fifty-One."

"Yes, Captain Adams, that is correct. Hill Fifty-One is the only position that we did take, and the rest was a total disaster. But remember, the major objective of this battle has been achieved. We have forced the Germans to concentrate on The Somme thereby relieving the French at Verdun."

Again, the general looked sternly from one captain to the next. "Now, do you have anything further to say?" he asked.

"Yes, Sir. Hill Fifty-One is of great strategic value. Can't you recommend that reinforcements be sent in to help our men hold it?" asked Spindle.

"I quite realize the significance of Hill Fifty-One, Captain Adams," said the general waving his hand at the file he had been holding when they came into his office. "I have read the dispatches on the situation. The platoon on Hill Fifty-One is hopelessly surrounded. They have sent only one message shortly after they took the hill. For all we know, the Germans have overrun them and retaken the hill. No point in sending in more men under those circumstances. Besides, what we have to say has no bearing. We only evaluate. We do not make strategic decisions."

"How many of our men are on the hill, Sir?" asked Spindle.

The general reached for the file, opened it, and squinted at the first page. "Sixty-four, one severely wounded. They also held sixty German prisoners," he noted.

"A very heroic feat! Only one casualty despite the overwhelming odds!" exclaimed Roger.

"Yes," said the general. "The lieutenant in charge will most certainly get a medal, no doubt about that. He is mentioned in the dispatch." He peered again at the contents of the file. "A Lieutenant Russell."

"Excuse me, Sir. Not Lieutenant John Russell?" asked Spindle, sitting straight up on the edge of his chair.

"Just says Lieutenant Russell of the Royal West Kents Battalion. You think you know this officer, Captain?"

"Yes, Sir, if it's John Russell from Bridgefield, I – we all – went to school with him, Sir."

"Well, you can all be proud that one of your classmates has so distinguished himself," said the general, as Spindle and the others looked at each other with mixed emotions.

The general picked up a dark blue file from his desk, hesitated, then put it down again. "There are other matters to discuss, but they can wait. No need to discuss them now. Just poppycock, I suspect..." The general cut himself off abruptly and started again. "Yes, well... Five-O-One is very pleased with your work, Gentlemen. Your casualty forecasts have proved accurate, and because of those predictions we were prepared with additional field hospitals, ambulance transport, and pre-dug grave sites. Reports say the wounded are being treated within six hours, and the severely wounded transported back to hospitals waiting to receive them in the home counties."

The general paused and looked at his pocket watch. "Now, then, Gentlemen, that is all for today. No need for a further meeting. I'll expect your observations tomorrow morning at eleven. Remember: you can think what you like about the strategic decisions that are being made, but you must not say it," he admonished, a little less severely this time, with the hint of a smile playing around his mouth.

"That bastard Harvey! He's the one who opened his mouth," spouted James when they were alone in the corridor. "Ran right to the general and repeated Roger's words. I imagine that dark blue file contains other Harvey tales."

"The general said they were 'poppycock'," said Roger with a grin.

"Harvey is that!" laughed James scornfully.

"Must be careful," whispered Spindle. "We know he is an asshole creeper. Must be careful what we say in front of him."

"Yes, and isn't it comforting to know that our predictions helped the generals prepare enough graves to accommodate all the dead?" said Roger bitterly.

"Enough of Harvey and enough of their bloody decisions!" said Spindle. "We must find a way to help Bouncer. If the generals won't do it, we will!"

"I'm for that," said James.

"Me, too," said Roger.

"All right. Any ideas about how to get Bouncer and his men off that hill?" asked Spindle when they were settled back in their office.

"Well, first, we can't be sure that he still holds the hill or even if he and his men are still alive," remarked James.

"That's the first thing we have to do, then. We have to find out, and then we need to get Pete and Ginger in on this. They might have some ideas. Let's go see them at The Odeon this afternoon," said Spindle.

James and Roger nodded their agreement and the three of them turned their attention to the high piles of papers stacked on their desks.

* * *

The men in the redoubt on Hill Fifty-One were breakfasting on tinned food supplied by the Saxons, and the prisoners locked up in the officer's dugout were doing the same.

"How are the prisoners?" inquired Bouncer when he saw Conway emerge from the dugout and close the door behind him.

"They're fine, Sir. Pleased to be alive, I expect," said Conway. "Talked to their lieutenant in there – a chap named Heinz. Seems they're from the same Saxon regiment as our friend Fritz. He remembers when we used to catapult eggs and chocolate back and forth to each other."

Bouncer and the other men laughed in fond remembrance of quieter days on the Western Front.

Bouncer downed the rest of his tea and stood up, motioning with his hands for the men to gather round him. "Listen up, men!" he announced. He waited for the men to quiet down, then he continued. "You realize, of course, that we are surrounded by Germans. Our only hope is for reinforcements to show up. If no reinforcements arrive, then it's up to us to hang on for as long as we can. This hill is very important to our men below. Without this redoubt, the Germans can't fire down on our men after they break through the trench lines and come up the two valleys on either side – Sausage and Mash."

There was a murmur of understanding and some muffled laughter at the use of the nicknames the English had invented for the two valleys.

"The battle day before yesterday cost us many lives. From what I could see, the numbers must be in the thousands. But what we did - in taking this hill - has to have saved many lives. Of that, you should be proud."

The men gave a short cheer, and then a private raised his hand.

"Yes, Private Benson?" asked Bouncer.

"Do we have any choices, Sir?" asked the private.

Bouncer looked around. The men had grown serious, each looking at him in silence, awaiting his response.

"There are three, as I see it," said Bouncer slowly. "If no reinforcements are sent, then our first option is to fight our way back to our line. As I said before, we are surrounded, and the chance of any of us getting through is very slim. A second option is to surrender and spend the rest of the war in a German prison camp."

There was a general chorus of boos and "No bloody way!" when Bouncer announced this option.

"The third," said Bouncer after the men had quieted, "is to stay neutral for as long as we can and fight back if we are attacked to try to hold this redoubt. The longer we are able to hold on, the more likely the chances that our mates below will be able to break through the German lines in the next assault."

Bouncer looked from face to face. The men remained silent, weighing the choices Bouncer had outlined. "Any questions?" he asked.

"For me, I take the third, Sir!" proclaimed a loud voice from the rear.

"Me too!" called out another voice.

The rest of the men demonstrated their agreement with a loud cheer.

"Right! Stay and hold on it is!" said Bouncer with an approving grin.

"How long will we be here, Sir?" queried another private.

"Can't be sure. If reinforcements are on their way, shouldn't be long. If not, then we may have to hang on for days. For right now, we have a truce with the Saxon officer in charge of this sector. But he is only a captain and may be ordered by higher command to do something else at any moment."

"Does HQ know we are here?" asked another.

"Yes," replied Bouncer. "We sent our only pigeon yesterday morning, and we know the message was received because we got the uniforms we requested."

"So we have no further way of communicating with our side, Sir?" inquired another private.

"That's correct, Private. Not at the moment. We are completely cut off," answered Bouncer, not mincing his words.

A murmur went through the group as they shifted uncomfortably upon hearing this news.

"Now, then, men, there are things we can do. We don't have to just sit here thinking about what could happen," said Bouncer attempting to draw their attention back to the positive side. "I want you to split up into groups of six and search every inch of this redoubt – every room, every passageway, every hole. Perhaps there's already a way out or a way to create one if the time comes that we need it."

The men did as he ordered and quickly dispersed, disappearing into rooms and passages.

"Do you trust the Saxon officer, Sir?" asked Conway in a low voice when the rest of the men were out of hearing.

"I've no reason not to," said Bouncer quietly. "We are still here, and the Germans could take us out anytime they feel like it. A few well-aimed artillery shells would blow us all to smithereens. Besides, he assures me that he got Sam and Freddie out, and he followed up on his promise of food and water for our men."

"Including his own men," added Conway.

"True, but the Saxons are more amenable – concerned about saving lives, not only on their side, but ours as well. Comes from our shared ancestry, I guess."

"Ancestry? Oh, yes, I do remember that Alfred the Great was a Saxon from my history lessons in school," said Conway.

"Yes, if it wasn't for those damn Normans, we wouldn't be in this bloody mess today," laughed Bouncer. "Once again the French are to blame!"

"You're right there, Lieutenant!" returned Conway. "You've become quite the historian, I see."

* * *

Back at Chad House in London, Spindle, James and Roger were gathering and analyzing information about the first day of what would go down in history as the Battle of the Somme.

"Have you found anything, James?" asked Spindle.

"Nothing other than it's confirmed that there has been no communication from Hill Fifty-One since nine a.m. on July 1 – two days ago," said James, looking up and shaking his head.

"Here's something, Spindle," said Roger excitedly holding up a sheaf of papers attached to a clipboard. "It's a casualty list for the Royal West Kents."

"Well done, Roger!" cried Spindle grabbing the clipboard. He anxiously scanned the list that presented names in alphabetical order by last name. "Oh no! Here's Baldwin, Samuel! Says he was wounded, sent back to England," he cried, running his finger down the "B's." He flipped quickly to the "R's" and traced his finger down as Roger and James hovered over him. "No Russell," said Spindle, breathing out a sigh of relief, and Roger and James gave a small cheer.

Spindle began to scan the "S's." Halfway down the list he stopped. "Uh oh, here's Simpson... Freddie," he said, pointing to the name.

"What does it say? Not dead, I hope?" asked James anxiously.

Spindle read, "Says `seriously wounded, transported to Lunbury Hospital.'"

"Does it say how he was wounded?" asked Roger.

Spindle looked down at the list again and shook his head.

"Lunbury Hospital...," said James thoughtfully. "Lunbury specializes in amputees. Could be Freddie has lost a limb..."

Spindle frowned. "Could be... Well, I see there's no `Squires' on the list either," he said and handed the clipboard back to Roger.

"Should we go to Lunbury? Try to see Freddie?" asked Roger.

"No, not now," said Spindle. "We know Freddie's in good hands. Must see what we can do about Bouncer and his men on that hill." He looked at his watch. ""We've got everything we need for our meeting with Bottoms tomorrow morning?" he asked.

Roger and James nodded.

"Good," said Spindle. "Let's go to The Odeon and see Pete and Ginger."

Dressed in civilian clothes, the three captains made their way along the crowded streets. Women passed them possessively clutching wicker baskets containing what food they had been able to find. Sentries stood watch outside government buildings where broken sandbags had spilled onto the pavement. Workers wielding picks and shovels hurriedly filled in last night's bomb craters.

"Look at that headline," said Spindle as they passed a news agent's shop.

"What a pack of lies!" muttered Roger. "'British have broken line. Heavy losses inflicted on Germans.'" He shook his head in disbelief.

"Now, now, Roger, we can think it, but we must not say it," said Spindle, mimicking General Bottoms. "How they can get away with this, I shall never know. It's despicable."

"Well, they have a problem, don't they? How can they tell the people that their stupidity caused over fifty thousand casualties?" said James.

"Before this is over, millions will be killed or wounded. They won't be able to cover that up with lies," said Spindle.

A cold drizzle began to fall, and the three picked up their pace. They stopped at the corner of Regent and Piccadilly Streets to wait for the traffic to pass before crossing the busy road.

"Could you spare a penny, Sirs?" asked a plaintive voice.

The captains looked down and saw three young children huddled under a tattered blanket on the pavement. They were barefoot.

"Could you spare a penny, Sirs?" asked the voice again, and they saw it came from a little girl with thick curly hair and huge brown eyes. She sneezed and wiped her nose and mouth with the sleeve of her tattered coat.

"Who are you and where do you live?" asked Spindle in a compassionate tone.

"We are orphans, Sir. This is my little brother and my baby sister," the tyke replied, hugging her brother and sister closer to her on either side. "We live under London Bridge. We have no place else to go."

"Why are you orphans, young lady?" asked Roger, concern written on his face.

"Our dad got drowned in the Navy, and mum was taken away by policemen."

"You have no other family to take care of you?" questioned James.

"Don't think so, Sir. Remember dad saying we have a granny in Ireland."

"Why was your mum taken away by policemen?" asked Spindle.

"Can't be sure, Sir. We were playing at a friend's house when they took her away." The girl paused, trying to remember. "Mrs. Laird, our next door neighbor, said it was because she is German. Said the police were rounding up Germans and shipping them to Canada."

"Utter madness," muttered Spindle to Roger and James who had looks of disgust on their faces. They had heard rumors about Germans being interned, but they had not given it much thought.

"Can't believe they would do this – taking a mother away from her children," said James sadly.

"Can you read, young lady?" asked Spindle, directing his attention back to the children.

"Only if you print big, Sir," said the little girl, sniffling.

Spindle withdrew a pen and a bit of paper from his pocket to write a note to his landlady. He printed her name and his address below the note in big block letters. He handed the paper to the little girl. "What is your name?" he asked.

"Annie, Sir, and this is Tommy and Betsy," said the little girl, indicating her brother and sister who sat staring up at them with wide eyes, sucking their thumbs.

"Well, Annie, take Tommy and Betsy and go to the address printed here. Give the paper to the lady who answers the door. Her name is Mrs. Thatcher. She is a very nice lady, and she will take care of you," directed Spindle.

"Thank you, Sir!" said Annie. The three children stood up, covering their heads as best they could with the blanket. Then, they turned to walk away, holding hands.

"Just a moment," called out James, holding out a three-penny piece.

The children turned and Annie accepted the money with a grateful smile on her pinched face. "God bless you, kind gentlemen," she said.

Just then a large horse-drawn coach clamored by, its wheels thundering through a large puddle. The water rolled over the children knocking them to the ground as if they had been inundated by an ocean wave. Spindle and Roger started to rush toward them, but they quickly got to their feet and toddled on their way, their blanket dripping murky water.

"See that man in the bowler hat walking behind the children?" commented James as they watched the children walking down the road. "I think he was following us."

"What makes you think that?" asked Roger as he and Spindle observed the man walking a short distance behind the children.

"He's been behind us ever since we left Chad House, and while we were talking to the children, he stopped and stood in the doorway of the tailor's shop," said James.

"Well, he isn't following us now," shrugged Spindle. "This cloak and dagger stuff is getting to you, James. If we thought there was someone following us all the time, we'd soon be in the loony house."

"I think we're already in one – Chad House!" joked Roger.

Still chuckling at Roger's comment, the three captains crossed the road and walked two roads down to The Odeon.

They entered The Odeon, purchasing tickets to the cinema. Then, one by one, they went to the toilet and on up to their secret operations room in the attic.

"How's the telephonic traffic today Pete?" asked Spindle, looking about at the various men who were listening through headsets and jotting down messages.

"The busiest day so far. The American Embassy is sending messages by the hundreds, and GHQ Montreuil is jamming up the lines. There are too many to decode."

"We have news," said Spindle. "Bouncer and his platoon have taken Hill Fifty-One – the only success of the assault on the Germans – and Freddie and Sam have been seriously wounded. Freddie's at Lunbury Hospital. We don't know where Sam is other than he's back in England."

Pete nodded and picked up a piece of paper. "Knew about Hill Fifty-One and Bouncer," he said. "Ginger read a dispatch about it this morning. Seems to be a dispute going on between London and GHQ Montreuil about whether or not to send in reinforcements."

"That's right," added Ginger, who had taken off his headset and joined them. "Didn't know about Freddie and Sam being wounded though."

"Any communications between Shoals and Germany?" asked James.

"Yes, some very strange messages," said Pete. "Had to have them double-checked to see if they had been deciphered correctly. Shoals is telling Germany that the attack at the Somme is a British ploy and that the real attack is going to be at Gommecourt in ten days."

"That's news to us," said Roger, raising his eyebrows in surprise. "The Somme is the major thrust. They won't change that. They'd lose face if they called it off now."

"Gommecourt? You're right, Pete. That is a strange thing for Shoals to say," said Spindle with a frown. "Has he been sending anything interesting to America?"

"Yes. Those messages are odd, too. He says the British have broken through the German lines and are now attacking the Huns from the rear. Says the Germans have suffered many casualties."

"Same as the headline we saw in the newspaper this morning...," said James, looking at Spindle.

"What the hell is going on? It's all a pack of lies!" exploded Roger.

Spindle scratched his chin thoughtfully. "Appears that whoever is supplying Shoals with his information has got it all wrong."

"We must be grateful for that small mercy, then," said James with a grin.

"Right you are," said Spindle. "Shoals isn't doing us any damage at the moment. We need to concentrate on finding out if

Bouncer and his men are still alive and if they're still holding that hill. Anything else on Hill Fifty-One?" he asked, turning to Pete.

Pete shuffled through the pile of decoded messages on his table and nodded his head. "There have been several messages about reinforcing Hill Fifty-One. London Army HQ wants to send in a rescue mission. GHQ in France does not. Seems to be a tug of war going on. Who is going to end up top dog is difficult to say. GHQ Montreuil says it doesn't have the men to spare. They want to concentrate their forces on another direct assault on the German line. They believe their first attack weakened the German defenses and that a major breakthrough is imminent. London HQ, however, says the hill is of strategic importance and must be held at all costs."

"Sounds like a political tussle to me," said Spindle. "Appears General Haig is flexing his muscle. Doesn't want to be questioned or overridden by London."

"Interesting telegram here," said Pete, picking up another decoded message. "Remember Lord Davenville, Susan's father?"

"Of course. Who could forget that birthday party?" asked Spindle with a grin.

"You remember he's on the King's Privy Council?" asked Pete.

Spindle nodded. "I remember. Went to school with King George. Sits on the council that advises the King."

"Well, listen to this," said Pete, holding up the decoded message and reading it. "'It would be a great boost for the morale of our country and our fighting men, if we relieved the platoon on Hill Fifty-One. In times like these, and particularly with the loss of Kitchener, the country needs a hero.' It's signed 'Lord Alfred Davenville, Privy Councilor.' But that's not all," said Pete, smiling and raising his hand. "There's a postscript at the bottom. Says 'Churchill thinks it's a marvelous idea.' What do you think of that?"

"That's great, but unfortunately Bouncer is not Chinese Gordon. He's only a lieutenant. Lord Kitchener would have ordered that they send in reinforcements and they would have listened to him. Too bad he had to get killed before the offensive," said Spindle. "Sod them! We can't wait for the generals to make up their minds. We must do something ourselves. Let's figure out what we can do to rescue them."

"Provided they still hold the hill..." said James. "We need to find out somehow. No communication from them since the first day...."

They were all silent for a moment, each one pondering the situation. Suddenly, Spindle snapped his fingers. "I know!" he exclaimed. "Pete and Ginger can go to France and find out if Bouncer is still on that hill. If he is, then we'll have to figure out how to help him. We can't go," he added, waving his hand at Roger and James, "but there's no reason Pete and Ginger can't go. How about it?"

"Bloody right, we'll go!" exclaimed Ginger. "We can hitch a ride on a medical ferry at Sheerness and be at the front by sunset if we hurry. I have a new invention. Should be just the thing to make contact with Bouncer if he's still on the hill. Come on, Pete!"

"Right! I'll be right with you," said Pete, getting up from his table. He went over to one of the men who was decoding messages, spoke to him briefly and returned. "We'll get word to you about what we find out. Bert over there will listen for our message and get it to you," he told the captains.

"Come on, Pete! We need to go by my place and collect a heavy box, and we don't have much time," urged Ginger.

"If Bouncer and Sam are alive, we must find a way to encourage GHQ Montreuil to send in reinforcements, or...," mused Spindle. He paused, and then his eyes lit up.

"Or what?" asked Roger.

"Or barter!" said Spindle with a grin. "We can barter with the Germans to exchange their spy for Bouncer and his men!"

"Brilliant!" responded Roger.

"Trade a German spy for our own men? What a grand idea, Spindle. A spy must be worth at least a hundred of our men," joined in James.

"Two hundred if they come from Bridgefield!" laughed Spindle.

\* \* \*

The road from the channel port to the front was congested with military transports, marching troops and Red Cross vehicles. Pete and Ginger, dressed in their lieutenant's uniforms, hitched a ride on a wagon carrying medical supplies to a field hospital near Albert. Once there, the wagon driver would unload the urgently needed supplies, then pick up another batch of seriously wounded soldiers and take them back to the channel port. As the wagon wended its way along the road to Albert, it passed thousands of fresh troops marching toward the front, all eager to fight the Germans. The stream of wagons carrying the wounded in the opposite direction toward the port stretched as far as the eye could see. Many of the wounded who were able to do so reached out from their stretchers to yell to the passing troops, "Give the Huns hell for me!"

After an hour or so, the wagon pulled up at the field hospital just outside Albert. Pete's and Ginger's eyes grew wide at the sight of row after row of seriously wounded men lying on stretchers outside the hospital, waiting to be taken to the channel port and from there, each hoped, to an English hospital close to home.

"This is as far as I go, Sirs," announced the wagon driver, hopping down from his seat.

"Thanks for the lift," said Ginger as he and Pete climbed down from the back of the wagon. "Can you tell us the quickest way to the front?"

"Front?" repeated the driver in an incredulous tone. "Bloody idiot officers, ain't you? All you have to do is follow the empty stretchers. If you fired a rifle, you'd know where the front is. Damned officers don't know the front from their mother's ass!"

"Hold off there, driver!" yelled a sergeant who was marching by with a column of new recruits. He left his column and came up to them. "Can't you see these men are lieutenants? They fight like the rest of us. Not like the fucking generals!" He stopped abruptly and saluted Pete and Ginger. "Beg your pardon, Sirs," he said as the chastised wagon driver slunk off toward the field hospital. "My men and I are going right up to the front. You can march along with us if you want. It's about five miles."

"Thank you, Sergeant. We'd be honored to march along with our fighting men," said Pete.

As Pete and Ginger fell in with the group, the sergeant saw that they were struggling under the weight of a heavy wooden box.

"Here, Sirs," he said. "I'll help you put your box in our supply wagon. Will make the going much easier."

"Most grateful for your help, Sergeant," said Ginger after they had deposited the crate in the wagon.

"Quite all right, Sirs," remarked the sergeant, standing back and looking at them. "Pardon me, but I don't recognize your insignia, Lieutenants. What outfit are you with?"

Ginger and Pete glanced at each other. "The Signal Corps," blurted out Pete, and Ginger nodded.

"Signal Corps? Hope you are here to improve communications with the high command back behind the front. They don't seem to know or care how many of our men are being killed," said the sergeant with a bitter edge to his voice.

"We're here to test out some new equipment," said Pete.

"So that's what's in the box? What sort of equipment is it?" queried the sergeant.

"Secret for now. Just here to test it and see if it works before we make more of them," explained Ginger. "It has the potential for saving many lives, though."

The sergeant looked about and sidled closer to Pete and Ginger, out of earshot of his men. "That's what I like to hear. About time someone thought of testing out the new equipment before using it in a battle. Bloody shells they used to destroy the barbed wire and drive the Germans back before our assault didn't go off – most of them anyway. Generals told us it would be a cakewalk after a week of shelling, but when our men went over, the barbed wire and the Germans were still there. For the Germans it was like shooting fish in a barrel, and the generals never changed the orders. Just kept sending our men in to be slaughtered. I'd be pleased to assist you – anything to help save our men's lives."

"That's useful information, Sergeant," said Pete. "We'll see that it's made known to people who can do something about it." He paused for a moment. "Perhaps you could help at that," he said slowly, considering the sergeant's offer. "However, you must not say anything. It's secret, and we don't want the word to get out until we know for sure that it works."

"You can trust me, Sir. I'll keep the secret," said the sergeant with a serious look.

At sunset the column reached their encampment near a communications trench that connected to the front-line trenches.

"Tomorrow morning we hook up with the Royal West Kents and go over the top," said the sergeant. He jerked his head over his shoulder toward the soldiers who were eating, smoking and telling jokes. "Poor blighters. Don't know what they're in for. They still think it's all glory for King and Country."

Pete and Ginger looked at each other meaningfully, and then Pete put his hand on the sergeant's shoulder. "Sergeant, we need to get on with our mission. We need to walk up a little further toward the front and take the box with us. Still want to assist us?"

The sergeant affirmed his willingness to help, and together they carried the box about a quarter of a mile further where they set it down. They were just behind the British front line trench, looking east across No Man's Land, which at this point was only about fifty yards.

"Now, then, Sergeant. Can you point out Hill Fifty-One to us?" asked Pete.

"Sure can," responded the sergeant. He pointed to a hill directly across from them that jutted out between two valleys. "Jerries have a well-fortified redoubt up there. As you can see, they can fire down on all sides. Rumor had it that we sent in a platoon to take that hill before the battle started, but there's no sign of that."

"Well, Sergeant, that's what we're here for," explained Pete, focusing his field glasses on Hill Fifty-One. "Part of our mission is to find out what happened to that platoon. But," he cautioned, "no matter what we find out, you must not say anything about it, understand?"

"Yes, Sir. You can trust me. I won't say a word," said the sergeant.

"Good man. Now, you can help by mounting these field glasses on this tripod and focusing them in on the hill," said Pete.

"We'll have to wait until it gets dark. Still too much light to test out the equipment," said Ginger, unpacking a large spotlight from the crate.

The sergeant had finished setting up the field glasses on the tripod, and he came over to examine the light Ginger was setting up. "Seen one of those before," he said. "Navy men use them, don't they?"

"That's right, but they're not like this," grinned Ginger. He turned a handle that was attached to the light causing shutters to open and close in front of the light.

"That's interesting, Lieutenant, but what is the point of that?" asked the sergeant scratching his head.

"Well, you see, when I turn the handle I can send a prearranged Morse Code message over and over again," explained Ginger as he made adjustments to the contraption.

"See these, Sergeant?" said Pete, holding up some metal disks with small holes punched in them. "Each hole in these disks represents a specific letter or number."

"I see," said the sergeant, fingering one of the disks.

"Each disk has a message that's already been punched into it," explained Ginger. "All I have to do to send the message is put the disk in this slot here and turn the handle."

"It's a lot easier than working the shades by hand," added Pete.

"Well, I'm knackered!" laughed the sergeant. "Never seen anything like it. I can see how you can send messages this way, but how do you receive them?"

"Haven't got that far yet, Sergeant. Pete here will still have to write any return messages down and decipher them," said Ginger.

While they had been showing the sergeant Ginger's invention, it had grown dark enough that they could now see the light of a star or two in the night sky.

"Can you see any lights on the hill?" asked Pete as Ginger peered through the field glasses mounted on the tripod.

"I think I do see one," said Ginger after a moment. "It's very dim."

Pete and the sergeant trained hand-held field glasses on the hill.

"I see it, too," said the sergeant. "Looks like it could be a candle or a lantern."

"We'd better be sure before we turn on our light and try to send a message. We'll have to do it quick or the Huns will target us," remarked Pete.

"Now I can make out three dim lights," said the sergeant. "They must be shining through the gun slits in the redoubt.

313

Someone's in there all right. Just hope it's our men and not the Germans."

"I confirm that. There are three lights. Quick, Ginger, send the message!" exclaimed Pete.

Ginger flipped a switch, and after a few seconds the light reached its maximum intensity. Ginger began to turn the handle. The shutters opened and closed causing the light beam to go on and off.

"They should be able to see that," said Pete, staring at the hill now through the field glasses on the tripod.

"The Germans, too ...," remarked the sergeant.

* * *

Up on Hill Fifty-One, Bouncer and his men had just finished their supper of bully beef and German black bread.

"Lieutenant, Sir!" called out a private who was standing watch at one of the gun slits. "There's something different out there tonight – a bright light shining from the west."

Bouncer and Conway went over to the gun slit and peered out into the darkness.

"It's not a normal light. Too bright for that, and it's also blinking," said Conway.

"You're right, said Bouncer. He paused for a moment watching the light, and then he smiled and turned back to his men. "Anyone here who can read Morse Code?" he asked.

"Here!" called out Private Benson. "I can, Sir."

Bouncer motioned for him to join him at the gun slit. Benson peered out at the light. "It's Morse Code all right," he said after a moment.

"What does it say?" asked Bouncer.

"Seems to be a message that keeps repeating, every minute or so, Sir."

"Out with it, Private Benson! What does it say?" asked Bouncer impatiently.

"Just a moment, Sir," said Benson, straining to read the message. "That's strange. It says... What did you give Susan for her birthday...What could that mean? Doesn't make sense," said Benson, scratching his head.

"Bugger me!" laughed Bouncer. "I know what it means! One of my mates is trying to find out if we're up here on this hill. Anything else?"

"No, just the same words over and over," said Benson as he continued to stare at the light.

"All right. Extinguish all the lights except this lantern," ordered Bouncer. The men quickly doused the lights, and Bouncer brought the lantern up to the gun slit.

"Send this message back," said Bouncer, whispering in Private Benson's ear.

"Yes, Sir," said Benson with a puzzled look. He began to pass his helmet up and down in front of the lantern.

\* \* \*

"There's only one light on the hill now, and it's flickering," called out the sergeant excitedly. "They must be sending a message!"

"Turn off the light, Ginger!" said Pete, looking through the field glasses on the tripod.

"Is it a message? Can you make out what it says?" asked Ginger.

"Slow in coming, but it's Morse Code all right," said Pete. "Says... blue shawl... Bloody Hell! That's Bouncer up there! Quick, Ginger, send the next message!"

Ginger quickly inserted another disk that read: "Mauve shawl here. Green shawl, sausages, music box in England. Bottom Five planning another party. Hope to send hand-delivered invitations soon."

He turned on the light and began cranking the handle. Then, he quickly flipped the switch to douse the light and anxiously waited while Pete watched through the field glasses. After a couple of minutes the light on the hill began to flicker again.

"Here comes the response," said Pete. "Says 'Look forward to invitations. Need immediately. Also need birds to RSVP'."

Pete jotted down the message and turned to Ginger. "Ok, tell them 'Message received. Hang on for invitations'."

Ginger turned on the light, but just as he started to send the message, an artillery shell exploded near the trench line in front of them.

"Douse the light!" yelled the sergeant. "The Germans are lining their sights up on us!"

Ginger quickly flipped the switch on the light and dropped to the ground along with Pete and the sergeant. They lay on the ground in the darkness and waited, but after several minutes, no further shelling took place. They cautiously got to their feet, packed up the equipment, and moved back to the encampment.

"That was close!" said the sergeant, mopping his brow, after they had set the equipment down. "Pleased to see your invention works. Too bad you couldn't finish your mission."

"We got what we came for, and as far as we're concerned, the mission is a success," said Pete, who was busily jotting down a message on a piece of paper.

"Want to thank you for your help, Sergeant," said Ginger, shaking the sergeant's hand.

"Quite all right. Was my pleasure. Just want to reassure you that I won't breathe a word about anything," said the sergeant.

"Thanks, Sergeant. We appreciate that," said Pete as he folded the piece of paper. "Have one more favor to ask. Can you see that this message is sent by telegram? We have to head back to England right away."

"Sure. I'll take it to communications right away. How are you going to carry your equipment?"

Ginger shrugged. "We'll just have to carry it between us back to Albert and see if we can hitch a ride from there."

"We have a wheelbarrow I can loan you. Just leave it at the field hospital outside Albert, and tell one of the wagon drivers to return it to me next time he comes to the front," said the sergeant.

"That would certainly help," said Pete. "Thanks again, Sergeant. You've been most helpful. By the way, what is your name? Need to say who to return the wheelbarrow to. Need to write it down."

"No need to write it down. It's a name no one forgets!" The sergeant saluted. "Sergeant Butterchad at your service, Sir!"

Pete and Ginger burst into laughter. "You're right, Sergeant. We won't forget that name, or you, either!" said Ginger.

* * *

# Chapter 13
## *Think But Don't Say*

THE NEXT MORNING Sergeant Harvey rushed up to Spindle. "Have a message for you, Sir." He handed Spindle a small brown envelope. "It was delivered by Army courier early this morning."

"Thank you, Sergeant. That will be all," responded Spindle. He waited until Harvey left before opening the envelope.

"Great news!" he said to Roger and James. "Bouncer is safe. He's holding out on Hill Fifty-One. Says he needs reinforcements right away. Also needs carrier pigeons."

Roger and James gave a small cheer and patted Spindle on the back upon hearing this news.

"How can we take care of that, Spindle? We're not supposed to know that Bouncer is still up there," said Roger.

"I'll speak to Bottoms. Will be careful about what I say. I'll have to come up with a reason to talk to him. Hold on," said Spindle, looking more closely at the message. "Here's something. Perhaps I could use this... Pete says the barbed wire on the German side was still intact. Says the shells didn't explode."

General Bottoms was meeting with senior members of his staff. A large map of the front was spread out on a table and he was leading a discussion on the Somme offensive.

"The whole thing was a balls up. Nothing but a disaster. Captain Adams's group forecast this would happen. Five-O-One tried to persuade C in C not to attack at the
Somme but the politicians had the final word. The only consolation is that the French have been relieved at Verdun."

A soft knock on the door interrupted him. He frowned and rolled his eyes. "Come in!" he said impatiently. "What is it now?"

One of his staff sergeants poked his head in the door. "Sorry to interrupt, Sir, but Captain Adams is here. Says it's urgent."

The general's face brightened. "Ah, Captain Adams. Show him in." He turned to his staff. "We'll see what he has to say. Should be enlightening."

Spindle strode purposefully into the room, noting the morose atmosphere that seemed to visibly hang over the staff officers' heads. He came to attention in front of General Bottoms.

"At ease, Captain. What is this urgent matter?" asked the general.

"I've just learned there is a major problem, Sir. We have been firing dud shells at the German lines. The barbed wire is still intact, preventing our men from breaking through. We must get artillery shells that work and quickly. If not, many more will be killed."

"Is this true? We have been firing artillery shells that don't explode?" exclaimed the general, looking at his staff officers. The officers looked at each other and shrugged their shoulders.

"Is it true or not?" the general demanded. Again, he received no response and his face conveyed his displeasure. He turned his attention back to Spindle. "How is it you know this and my staff officers don't, Captain?"

"Statistics, Sir. I've reviewed the casualty lists, and the huge numbers can mean only one thing. The artillery bombardment didn't do its job. It didn't take out the barbed wire nor did it destroy the Germans in the front line trenches as had been intended. I can only conclude from the vast numbers of shells fired during the bombardment that more than half didn't explode."

"I see," said the general. "Go on."

"Well, Sir, if the shells had destroyed the barbed wire, we would have sustained fifty percent fewer casualties. As it was, the men who made it across were trapped trying to breach the wire, making them easy targets for the Germans."

The general nodded and looked around at his staff officers. "There, Gentlemen. That is what I expect. That's the kind of analysis we need." He turned back to Spindle and smiled approvingly. "Is there anything else, Captain?"

"Hill Fifty-One, Sir! We need to find out if our men are still holding that hill. It is very important, Sir, to know this before reinforcements are sent in."

"No decision on reinforcements yet, Captain. C in C thinks it's better to rush the German line than waste men reinforcing that hill."

"Wrong strategy, Sir!" Spindle blurted out. "We need that hill to keep the Huns from firing down on our men. That alone would save at least thirty percent of our troops!"

The general frowned sternly at him. "It's not your responsibility, Captain, to make that decision. Remember, your task here is to evaluate and nothing else!"

The staff officers looked at the ceiling, then at the floor, embarrassed at Spindle's dressing down.

"I have had occasion in the last week to remind you and your group that if you have any private thoughts on military matters you should keep them to yourselves! Once more, you have violated this rule!" shouted the general.

"But, Sir! Those men are surrounded and there is no escape! Reinforcements are their only hope!" cried Spindle, ignoring the general's warning.

"Captain! No more talk of reinforcements! It's not up to us to make that decision, so keep your thoughts to yourself!" The general's face had turned an angry red.

Still, Spindle persisted. "Can't we at least find out if they are still alive, Sir?" he asked in a pleading tone.

The general looked down at the map in exasperation. He took a deep breath and looked back up at Spindle who was staring at him expectantly. "All right, Captain Adams," he said slowly, trying to compose himself. "Because you and your group have been such a valuable asset to Section Z, I'll take the matter up with Five-O-One, but I can't promise anything. How would you propose that we find out if those men are still in command of the hill?"

"Carrier pigeons, Sir," responded Spindle without hesitation. "Get the flying corps to drop some pigeons. If they are still there, they could send a message to GHQ."

"Seems a good idea. I will suggest it to Five-O-One, then, but remember, I can't promise anything," he said holding up his hand in warning. Then he turned to his staff again. "You see, Gentlemen, when I ask a question I expect a quick response. Captain Adams is always quick to respond."

"I have one more request, Sir," said Spindle cautiously.

The general turned back to him, his face beginning to flush again. "No more asking for reinforcements!" he exclaimed, throwing his hands up in the air.

"No, Sir," said Spindle humbly. "Would like to have permission to visit Lunbury Hospital tomorrow. I have a friend there who was seriously wounded on the first day of the battle."

"All right, Captain. Permission granted," said Bottoms in somewhat of a relieved tone. He waved his hand in dismissal.

* * *

The following day at Lunbury Hospital, ambulances bearing wounded men waited in line at the emergency entrance. Haggard-looking orderlies lifted stretchers from the ambulances and carried them to waiting areas around the operating rooms. With charts in hand, nurses went from stretcher to stretcher confirming each man's identity and nature of wound.

"Another seventy-five patients are waiting for admittance," reported the senior orderly to the sister in charge of the emergency ward. "Twenty legs, forty-five arms and ten hands."

"Never seen so many wounded men," said the sister, shaking her head sadly. "The surgeons are operating day and night, many without sleep."

The orderly shook his head. "I know, and now we are getting low on wheelchairs, and the carpenters are having trouble getting enough of the right kind of wood to make the artificial limbs."

The sister looked alarmed. "It's urgent that we get the men out of bed as soon as possible. The sooner they start using their artificial limbs, the quicker they will recover mentally."

"I'll do my best," said the orderly. "I'll go around to local hospitals and see if I can round up more wheelchairs. The oak problem is a different matter," he said, hesitating and scratching his unshaven face. "Maybe I can go around the village and see if I can get people to donate furniture that we can use for the wood."

"That's a good idea. The people will certainly do everything they can to help our wounded men," said the sister as she noticed three tall young men in civilian clothes approaching the information desk on the other side of the room. "Now, I wonder why those three aren't in uniform, strapping lads like that," she said, shaking her head and returning to her paperwork.

"We're here to see Private Freddie Simpson," said Spindle, addressing the middle-aged lady at the information desk.

"All three of you?" asked the woman, looking at Pete and Ginger who were standing behind Spindle. They nodded.

"Visitors must sign in," she said, smiling kindly and nodding at a registration book on the corner of the desk.

She watched as they signed the visitor's register, then nodded her approval and looked through an alphabetized list of patients. "Simpson, Simpson," she murmured as she traced her finger down the list. "Ah, yes - Simpson, Freddie. He is in Ward 26." She looked back up at Spindle and pointed down the hallway. "Go down this hallway and through the back door, turn right, then right again along the path. Ward 26 is the single-story building. You'll see the number over the door," she instructed.

"Thank you, ma'am," said Spindle, turning to go.

"One other thing, gentlemen," said the lady. "There isn't recognition of rank or title here. Our patients are treated the same by everyone, so please address the wounded only by name."

Ward 26 was a long ordinary looking building. The London brick walls, small pained windows and tarred corrugated roof did not prepare Spindle, Pete and Ginger for what lay within. When they entered, their noses were immediately assaulted with the strong odor of disinfectant and the stench of something else that was indefinable. They could clearly hear the agonized cries and moans of wounded men coming from behind the swinging doors at the far end of the reception area. Spindle tapped a bell sitting atop a podium near the door, and they waited in silence and awe as if they had entered a sacred and holy chapel.

"We're here to see Freddie Simpson," said Pete when a young nurse entered through the swinging doors in response to the bell.

"Freddie is not having visitors today – doctor's orders," said the nurse in a crisp voice.

"We came all the way down from London. Isn't it possible that we could see him just for a few minutes?" asked Ginger in a pleading tone.

The swinging doors parted slightly. "What's wrong, Helen?" asked a feminine voice.

"These gentlemen want to see Freddie Simpson. I told them the doctor says no visitors today."

"That's correct," confirmed the voice, and the door opened wider to reveal a redheaded young woman in nurse's uniform. She looked out at Freddie's would-be visitors.

Spindle started. "Susan? Susan Davenville?" he asked.

"Good Heavens! Is that Spindle?" cried Susan, rushing into the room. "Oh! And Pete, too!" she exclaimed. "It's so good to see you!"

Spindle and Pete each shook Susan's hand, grinning hugely and rendered speechless with surprise.

"I don't believe I know this gentleman," said Susan, noticing Ginger who was standing behind Pete.

Ginger stepped forward and grasped Susan's extended hand. "Name's Patrick Murphy, known as Ginger. Have heard a lot about you and your birthday party from the lads here," said Ginger with a sly grin.

Susan blushed slightly and laughed. "Oh, don't let's talk about that party right now! Very pleased to meet you Ginger. All here to see Freddie, then?" she asked, stepping back to look at the three of them.

"Yes, Susan. We heard he was wounded. Can't we see him? Just for a moment? We came all the way from London," wheedled Spindle.

Susan smiled up at him and shook her head. "Oh, I do wish you could, but you see Freddie is sedated and he must rest. The doctor wants him to get all the rest he can in order to help prepare him for the shock when he wakes up."

"Shock? What do you mean?" asked Spindle.

Susan hesitated and looked from one face to the other, a tear forming in her eye. "Of course... I guess you don't know. Freddie has lost both of his legs below the knee," she said as gently as she could.

Spindle, Pete and Ginger stared at her in horror.

"Oh, my God! We knew Freddie had been seriously wounded and might have lost a limb. But both legs? That's horrible!" choked Spindle.

"How was he wounded? Do you know?" asked Pete with a tremor in his voice.

"Sam Baldwin says Freddie's legs were badly burnt during an attack on the Germans on July 1."

"Sam! You've seen Sam?" exclaimed Ginger incredulously.

"Yes. Sam came to the hospital with Freddie. He was the one who saved Freddie's life. He amputated his legs. Now Sam is assistant to my Uncle Tommy, who is the chief surgeon here."

"My God! Sam cut off Freddie's legs? Was he wounded, too?" cried Spindle, grabbing Susan's arm roughly. She looked up at him, the tears now running down her cheeks. Spindle quickly released her arm and collected himself. "Sorry," he mumbled.

"It's all right, Spindle. I understand," said Susan, patting him on the arm. "No, Sam's not wounded. The doctor at the field hospital sent Sam back with Freddie, along with a note recommending him to my uncle for his surgical skills."

"What are Freddie's chances? Is he going to be all right?" asked Pete.

"He should be. Sam told him before he did it that he was going to amputate his legs. So, he should be prepared for it when he wakes up... if he remembers." Susan's voice began to falter. "The only concern we have is that Sam wasn't able to use any anesthetic. He got Freddie drunk before he did the amputation. The shock to his system may have been too much. He has been unconscious ever since he arrived and has a fever. We are keeping him sedated for another day or so. The doctor says the fever should diminish by then."

There was a short silence as all of them looked down at the floor contemplating the horrible thing that had happened to Freddie.

Spindle looked up at Susan with watery eyes. "Where is Sam? Is he here now?"

"He is in the operating room. Another seventy-five patients arrived this morning, and he will be busy for the rest of the day. He and the doctors have been working around the clock. I don't think Sam has had any sleep for two or three days now," said Susan.

"Such a pity. Would have like to have seen Freddie and Sam," said Pete wistfully.

"I know. It's a shame," said Susan with an understanding smile. "Perhaps you can come back next week?"

Spindle looked at his watch and then at Pete and Ginger. "We'd better get back to London. We have some bartering to do, remember?"

"Why aren't you all in the military?" asked Susan, pointing to their civilian clothes. "And what's this about bartering?"

"All we can say is that we're involved in the war effort and doing some important work," responded Spindle.

"Yeah! We're going to barter German sausage for English Tommies," said Ginger with a snort.

Susan looked puzzled.

"Oh, that's Ginger – always the comedian," said Pete quickly, jabbing Ginger in the ribs with his elbow.

"Well, whatever you're up to, I'm sure it's worthwhile," said Susan with a smile.

"That's right," said Spindle. "Must go now. Would you please tell Sam and Freddie that we were here and that Bouncer is still holding the hill? We managed to get a message from him."

Susan's eyes widened joyfully. "Oh, you've heard from Bouncer? He's alive? Oh, I'm so pleased to hear that! Sam said they were surrounded by Germans and that Bouncer was their leader," she began. Then she stopped and looked at Spindle with an odd expression. "If Bouncer's surrounded by Germans, how did you manage to get a message from him?"

"Oh, we have a sausage balloon," said Ginger cryptically, winking at Spindle.

Susan looked even more puzzled. Spindle shrugged and smiled at her. "I see – don't ask, right?" she said with a sparkle in her eyes. Spindle grinned and nodded.

Just then, a nurse called to Susan from the ward doors. "Nurse Davenville! Aaron Flannery in bed eighteen just woke up and we need your assistance!"

"I'll be right there!" called out Susan. She turned back to Spindle, Pete and Ginger. "I must get back to my patients. It was good of you to come. So pleased to see you again. Freddie and Sam will be thrilled that you were here," she said.

"We will try to come again soon," said Pete. "Maybe next time we'll get to see Freddie and Sam, and we can all talk about old times."

"Yes. That would be fun, and you can tell me what all of you have been doing the last five years. I especially want to hear more about your sausage business," responded Susan with the old mischievous twinkle in her eyes.

Spindle, Pete and Ginger each kissed Susan on the cheek and said goodbye. On their way out, they passed the lady at the information desk, who gave them a sweet smile. "Do hope your friend is recovering well?" she asked as they smiled back at her.

"Oh, he's in very good hands – very good hands, indeed!" replied Spindle, winking at Pete and Ginger as they left through the main doors of Lunbury Hospital.

* * *

On July 5, Bouncer and his men spent most of the day observing the battle that raged below. They stood at the gun slits watching as wave after wave of British troops rushed forward, bayonets drawn, across No Man's Land. British shells exploded in front of them, German shells amongst them. The soldiers zigzagged their way across, diving into craters and attempting to avoid the hail of machine gun bullets as best they could. Those who were lucky enough to reach the barbed wire and breach it found the front-line German trenches empty. They discovered that they had to do it all over again, the Germans having retreated to the second line of trenches behind yet another razor-sharp wall of wire.

Occasionally, Bouncer and his men would fire volleys of ammunition from the gun slits to keep the German high command thinking that their men still held the redoubt. In the dusk just after sunset, the droning of aero planes caught Bouncer's attention. He looked out and saw a squadron of five BFC biplanes passing overhead at a low altitude.

"What is it, Sir? Ours or theirs?" asked Conway who was standing behind Bouncer.

"Ours," said Bouncer excitedly. "There are three... no five of them. Must be on their way to knock out the Huns' observation balloons. Bloody Hell! Everyone get down! They just dropped a bomb!"

The men dropped to the floor in the bunker, hands over their heads, anticipating the explosion, but it never came. After a few minutes, Bouncer cautiously got to his feet and peered out of the gun slit through his field glasses.

"Can you see anything, Sir?" asked Conway.

"Yes... there's something out there about twenty yards away. Looks kind of like a bomb, but I don't think it is. Appears to be made out of leather or something... ," said Bouncer, straining to see better.

Conway got to his feet and Bouncer handed him the field glasses. "I think you're right, Sir. Doesn't seem to be a bomb. It's almost dark. Do you want me to go out and see what it is?"

"Wait until it's dark, then take Private Benson with you," ordered Bouncer.

Ten minutes later, Corporal Conway and Private Benson, wearing German uniforms, cautiously exited the bunker and crawled toward the object. Bouncer watched anxiously through the gun slit but could see nothing in the pitch-black darkness. A few minutes later, a private opened the door upon hearing the one long, two short, two long knocking code they had devised. Conway and Benson burst into the redoubt. Benson was carrying a bomb-shaped object about the size of a beer keg. He brought it over to Bouncer and placed it carefully on the floor.

"Well, what is it?" asked Bouncer, kneeling down to examine the object.

"As you can see, Sir, it's not a bomb. It's made out of leather, and it has all these holes in it. I think there's something inside," said Conway.

Bouncer took out a knife. "We'll soon find out," he said. "Better take cover, men, just in case."

He waited until the men had gotten as far back as possible, and then he slit the object open along a seam line. Then he began to laugh. "Come here, Corporal Conway," he ordered.

Conway rushed over to Bouncer and the rest of the men crept up behind him. Conway looked down at the bomb Bouncer had opened. "Well, I'm blowed! It's carrier pigeons!" he exclaimed. He knelt down and began to take the individual pigeon crates out of the container. "There's four dead and two alive," he said.

"Is there anything else in there – a message or anything?" asked Bouncer.

Conway examined the object further, and then he shook his head. "No, just the pigeons."

"Bollix!" cursed Bouncer. "No message about reinforcements? Well, at least we have two pigeons... more than we had before," he said, trying not to raise his men's anxiety.

The buzzing of the telephonic device reverberated throughout the bunker. The men all looked up in fear. Bouncer looked at Conway. "Answer that, Corporal, and remember to speak in German," he said.

Conway nodded and went over and picked up the receiver. After a moment, he looked at Bouncer and motioned him over. "It's a German asking for you, Sir. I think it's Fritz," he said.

Bouncer picked up the device and said cautiously, "Fritz?"

"Ya, English Bouncer. Vat is going on? I saw your flying corps drop something near the redoubt just before dark. Am afraid my commander might have seen it and I'll be questioned," said the voice.

"I understand, Fritz. Bloody British flying corps dropped a bomb, but it didn't go off. We checked it out and found out it is a dud – the fuse didn't work. Thank God, or they'd have blown us up!"

"I see," replied Fritz. "I will tell my commandant, if he asks, that the English are still using shells and bombs that don't explode. I will talk to you again before sunrise."

"Right!" said Bouncer and replaced the receiver. He turned to his men. "Now, then, men. We'll use one of the pigeons to send a message to HQ – let them know we are still alive and holding on. Then we still have one live pigeon left."

"What about the dead pigeons? I know! Let's pull straws for roast pigeon!" called out one of the privates, breaking the tension in the room.

"You can pull mine any time!" joined in another private.

"Only if you pull mine first!" yelled another.

The men burst into raucous laughter. Bouncer laughed along with them. It was the best laugh they had had since taking the hill.

After the laughter died down, Bouncer motioned for the men to gather round him.

"Now, men, it's possible that HQ might send in reinforcements when they get the message that we're still here," he began, looking around from face to face. "But I don't think we can rely on that. We must come up with a plan to get ourselves out of here. Even though the Saxon's truce is holding, his commander may discover any moment that we are here, and he'll be ordered to attack us. We must be prepared for an attack at any moment."

He paused and looked around again at the men's sober faces.

"Here's what I want you to do. Step up the search of the passageways again for a way out, and make an inventory of all the weapons, explosives and other materials we have. Do it now and do it quickly, men! The Saxon said he'd talk to me again before sunrise. We need to have a plan by then, because our ruse may have been discovered. Let's get cracking!"

With a chorus of "Yes, Sirs!" the men jumped to their feet, assembled into their small groups and disappeared into the passageways, each group carrying one lantern for illumination.

Bouncer stood watch at a gun slit and attempted to think of all the options for a plan as the night wore on. Just after Midnight, the men began drifting back from the tunnels and Conway rushed over to him with a piece of paper.

"Here's a map of what we found, Sir," he said handing Bouncer the sheet of paper. "This hill is riddled with blind tunnels, but this one goes down ten feet and then directly west, and there's another that goes the same distance directly east."

"How far west?" asked Bouncer, his eyes lighting up.

"About a hundred yards, Sir," answered Conway.

"Is the tunnel finished? Did the Germans finish digging it?"

"No, Sir. Looks as if they abandoned it quickly. Picks and shovels are lying around."

Bouncer looked again at where Conway was pointing on the crude map, and then he smiled. "Looks as if we have two chances to get out, Conway. Get all the explosives you can muster and make the biggest bomb you can. Then plant it at the end of the west tunnel. Block the tunnel off so the explosion goes upwards. Use a ten-minute fuse. Have another detail of men take the extra picks and shovels to the other tunnel that heads east."

"What about the Germans, Sir? If we break out of either tunnel, we'll be right in the middle of them. They'll gun us down."

"It's a risk worth taking, Corporal. Would be worse staying here and being sitting ducks if they attack. Let's have all this ready by sunrise."

Conway had all the bullets gathered up and issued fifty to each man for ammunition. Then the men carefully dismantled the rest and collected the black powder. Then they gently poured the gunpowder into a dry empty water barrel. By sunrise, they had manufactured the bomb and placed it per Bouncer's instructions in the west tunnel.

Just as the rays of the rising sun lit up the clouds on the eastern horizon, the telephonic buzzed. Conway answered in German.

"It's Fritz again," he said to Bouncer.

"He does keep his word," said Bouncer with a grin, reaching out for the receiver. "The sun's just beginning to rise."

"Fritz?" he said into the receiver.

"English Bouncer. Great difficulty. HQ saw the English planes dropping something near you. I told my colonel we saw them and checked it out. Told him it was a bomb, but he didn't believe me – wanted to know why there was no explosion. Told him we retrieved it and found out it didn't explode because of a faulty fuse."

"What did he say then?" asked Bouncer.

"Still sounded suspicious, but when I said it was like the unexploded British shells we found all around our trenches, he laughed and made jokes about English manufacturing. It was very close, English Bouncer. He believed me this time, but I don't know for how long. No more aero plane drops, ya?"

Bouncer sighed with relief and grinned at Conway. "No, Fritz – I promise. No more unexploded bombs."

* * *

Pete, Ginger, James and Roger spent that night at Spindle's digs contriving a scheme to induce Shoals to meet with Spindle so he could be kidnapped. They decided the abduction would take place the next evening at Nell Gwynne's pub near Charring Cross Road. The major difficulty in trading the spy for Bouncer and his platoon was how to let the Germans know they had Shoals. After many hours of devising a plan, they all agreed with Pete's idea of sending a telegram to Berlin. The telegram would be sent after Shoals had been whisked away.

"So," said Spindle, "This is our only hope in rescuing Bouncer. Are we all agreed that this is the best plan and that we have considered everything? If we've made a mistake or overlooked some detail, I'm afraid we can say good-bye to Bouncer."

James, Pete, Roger and Ginger somberly nodded their approval.

"We'd better get going to Chad House, then. Don't want Harvey to get suspicious. Remember I'll be at Nell Gwynne's to meet Shoals at eight tonight," added Spindle.

The four left Spindle's lodgings separately and made their way to Section Z by different routes. When it was Spindle's turn to leave, his landlady met him at the bottom of the stairs.

"Mr. Adams, just wanted you to know that the children are comfortably asleep and they have had plenty to eat. They have clean clothes, too, as well as shoes. I went through my things and found articles of my children's old clothing."

"Thank you, Mrs. Thatcher. I felt sorry for them, having no mum or dad to take care of them. The eldest girl said she had a granny in Ireland. Maybe you can contact her and they can go to live with her."

"Yes. I plan to go around to where they used to live and find out more," said Mrs. Thatcher with a misty smile, and then a serious look crossed her face. "I've been meaning to tell you – an odd thing happened. Just after the children arrived, a gentleman came to the door looking for a Mr. Atkins. He looked rather official - bowler hat, pinstriped suit, expensive overcoat - the lot. I wondered if he might have had the name confused with yours."

"Did he leave a name or a card?" asked Spindle, a chill running down his spine.      "No, he said he wanted to speak to Mr. Atkins on an urgent confidential matter, and when I said that no Mr. Atkins lived here he went away."

"Did you tell him I did?" asked Spindle with alarm.

"No, no. Not to be concerned. He didn't ask about anyone else, and it wasn't until later that I wondered if he might have had the name wrong," said Mrs. Thatcher quickly, trying to ease Spindle's anxiety. Then she frowned. "It was odd, though. The children said the same gentleman came up to them in the street and asked to see the piece of paper you had given them - the one on which you had written down my name and address."

Another chill went down Spindle's spine as he remembered the man James had suspected of following them. He composed himself quickly for Mrs. Thatcher's sake. "I can't think who it could have been, Mrs. Thatcher. If it was a matter of such urgency, he surely would have left a note."

"Could have been a bank manager from the way he was dressed. You are not over extended, are you?" asked Mrs. Thatcher with a smile.

"I don't think so," said Spindle, grinning back at her. "Perhaps this Mr. Atkins is, though."

He took his leave of Mrs. Thatcher and walked briskly along the deserted early morning paths. Occasionally he ducked into a shop doorway and looked to see if he was being followed. As an extra precaution, when he drew close to Chad House, he entered an underground station, bought a ticket and went down to the train platform. When the train arrived he waited for everyone to board, and then he exited the station from the other side. Still not content that he was not being followed, he crossed the road and went into a newspaper shop. He bought a newspaper and stood outside pretending to read it. The street became more crowded with people going to work and early morning shoppers.

After a while it dawned on him that there were hundreds of men dressed in bowler hats, pinstriped suits and overcoats walking in all directions. He realized that the get-up was the standard dress code for bankers, solicitors and stock exchange traders.

He tossed the newspaper into a waste bin and called out to an approaching hackney cab. The cab pulled up beside him, and the driver smiled down at him. "Good morning, Sir. Where to?"

Spindle glanced around, pulled an envelope and a half sovereign out of his coat pocket and handed them to the driver. "Please deliver this to the address on the envelope, my good man," instructed Spindle.

The driver put the sovereign between his teeth, bit down, grinned, and flicked the reins. Spindle watched for a bit as the hackney sped off down Cromwell Road. Then he turned and made his way swiftly to Chad House.

When he arrived in the map room, he noticed their sector of the Somme area had not changed since the day before. Hundreds of markers showed the British buildup of troops on the western side of No Man's Land and the German positions had not been altered. Spindle focused his field glasses on Hill Fifty-One. The Royal West Kents army marker was still there.

"I see Hill Fifty-One is still holding," said Spindle, looking at Roger with a knowing smile.

"Yes. GHQ received a message by carrier pigeon last night confirming our men are still holding the hill," said Roger.

"How's your grandmother's arthritis?" asked James. "The damp weather must be playing it up."

"Yes, indeed. I just sent her a parcel of wintergreen ointment," replied Spindle. "It's difficult for her to get out. It will save her a trip to the chemist."

"Hope she receives it soon and it does the trick," commented Roger with a straight face.

"Need to tell you about the visitor my mum had... ," began Spindle, but he quickly shut his mouth when he saw Sergeant Harvey enter the map room.

"Captain Adams, Sir. General Bottoms wants to see you right away," announced Harvey. "He wants to see your analysis on yesterday's casualties."

Spindle, Roger and James rolled their eyes as Harvey turned to leave, and Spindle silently marched down to General Bottoms's office.

"Sit down, Captain!" said the general in a gruff voice when Spindle entered his office. As soon as Spindle's bottom connected with the chair, the general lashed out at him. "It is not done, Captain! Your outburst about reinforcing Hill Fifty-One in front of my staff yesterday is not what is expected from an officer. I did not say anything to Five-O-One about your outburst, but he eventually found out. One of my staff used the back door, I'm afraid. Also, a member of your group has been to see me on several occasions, informing me of a disrespectful attitude amongst you."

The general paused and glared at Spindle. Then, he flung his hand toward the map pinned on the wall behind his desk. "Five-O-One knows it, I know it, and you captains know it. The whole damn offensive is a disaster, but we have to tolerate it, Captain. We all feel for our men over there, but now the push has begun, nothing can stop it. Too many egos, too many careers at stake, do you understand?"

Spindle sat rigidly in his chair, giving only a slight nod in answer to the general's question. Bottoms continued to glare at him.

"Now, then," he continued. "Five-O-One has given a great deal of thought as to what to do about the insubordination festering in your group. Believe me, Captain, I did my best for all of you, and under the circumstances, Five-O-One is, to say the least, a tolerant man." The general paused and looked intently at Spindle where he sat rigidly, a frozen expression on his face.

"I've been instructed by Five-O-One to reprimand you only. This will take the form of a letter to be placed in your file. What this means, Captain Adams, is that despite your genius and your valuable work for Section Z, you will not appear on any future list for promotion."

The general picked up the blue file that Spindle had seen on his desk earlier and placed a typewritten document inside. He laid the file down on his desk and looked back at Spindle with a slightly softer expression. "Well, what do you have to say? Much better than a court martial, what?"

"Yes, Sir," mumbled Spindle in a low voice. "Is that all, Sir?"

"No, there is more," said the general. He paused, and then smiled at Spindle's look of despair. "Despite all of this other matter, Captain Adams, Five-O-One is quite happy with your analysis. The unexploded shell situation is being taken care of. It's considered to be a matter of great importance. Woolwich Arsenal is at this moment correcting a fuse problem."

"Pleased to hear that, Sir," said Spindle, his face brightening a bit at the praise.

"Now, Captain, I have to tell you that Hill Fifty-One will not be reinforced. There will be no relief column sent in. The men there are on their own, I'm afraid. Either they fight their way back or surrender to the Germans. There are no other options. I overstepped my own authority, and Five-O-One went to bat for us, but to no avail. C in C in France has the final say, and that's the end of it."

"Yes, Sir, I understand. Pleased that you and Five-O-One at least tried," said Spindle, unable to keep the disappointed look from showing in his eyes. He started to get up from his chair, assuming the interview was over, but the general put up his hand.

"There is one more thing, Captain," said the general raising his eyebrows. "Sergeant Harvey is going to be promoted and transferred to the Orkneys. There his talents will be better appreciated, don't you agree?"

Spindle sat silently for a moment, and then the general's words sank in. "Yes, Sir!" he said unable to keep the gleeful grin from spreading across his face.

"Glad you agree, Captain. After all, we can't hold back a good man," said the general with a straight face.

"I know what you mean, Sir. Sergeant Harvey has very special talents, and he can do much better in the Orkneys," said Spindle through his grin.

The general grinned back at him and waved his hand in dismissal. "That is all, Captain!"

When Spindle walked into his office, he found Roger and James anxiously pacing the floor, waiting for him to return from the lion's den.

"See you are still in one piece," commented James in a hushed voice.

Spindle could not keep the grin off his face. "No scars or wounds," he said, rotating his arms to show them that they were still intact. "Some codswallop, that's all. Bottoms gave me a dressing down again because word got back to Five-O-One about my remarks in front of his staff. Bottoms said both he and Five-O-One tried, but there will be no attempt to rescue Bouncer. C in C France made the decision. Now it's up to us. Just hope grandmother got the ointment and her arthritis will not prevent her from going out tonight."

James put his finger to his lips and went over to the closed door. He listened at the door for a moment, and then quietly turned the key in the lock. "I've done my part," he said in a low voice. "I'll have the hackney waiting. Made a deal with the driver. Gave him a sovereign to rent it all night."

"We'll take Shoals to my place," said Roger in a hushed conspiratorial tone. "My landlady will be out tonight and it will be the safest place to take him without being seen. Once he's tucked away, Pete will send the telegram to Berlin."

"Good-o," said Spindle thoughtfully. "Must be careful. Must be on the lookout for someone following us. There should be many people about because of the theatres in the area. Need to tell you something. You remember that chap that James thought was following us the day we went to The Odeon?"

Roger and James listened with great concern as Spindle told them about the stranger confronting Mrs. Thatcher and inquiring about a Mr. Atkins. "Atkins? That's the name you're using with Shoals. What can it mean?" asked James with a worried expression.

"I know," said Spindle. "Can't think why someone would be following Mr. Atkins. We'll just have to be alert and on the lookout for anyone following us. So, everything is set for tonight?"

Roger and James nodded.

"Oh, I have some other news – nearly forgot," said Spindle. "Harvey is being promoted."

"That sorry sod promoted? What the hell for?" asked Roger angrily.

"Has very large ears, so Bottoms is reassigning him to the Orkneys where he can use them better!" laughed Spindle.

"Well, well. So Harvey is going to listen to the sea lions, eh?" said James.

"Who's he going to tell? The sea gulls?" quipped Roger.

They were laughing so hard they almost didn't hear the knock on the door. "Who is it?" yelled Spindle.

"Sergeant Harvey, Sir! I have some news for you!"

"I'll just bet you do, Sergeant!" said Spindle, as he went to open the door.

* * *

Just before eight o'clock that evening Spindle made his way up the passageway from Charring Cross Road to Nell Gwynne's pub. The pathway was narrow, and Spindle was grateful for the crowds of late theatre-goers headed in the same direction. He did his best to notice if anyone had been following him since he left his lodgings. He had changed underground trains several times and walked through the theatre district in the west end before doubling back to Charring Cross Road. He saw James dressed as a hackney driver waiting with the cab, but he did not say anything as he passed.

When he reached the pub he paused outside for a moment before entering. Finally he opened the door and went into the small dark room. There were a number of people sitting at the counter who turned to look at him. After his eyes adjusted to the dim gas light, he noticed a couple holding hands at a small table to his left. At another table a few feet away, two elderly men were deep in conversation. Shoals was nowhere to be seen.

"What will it be, Sir?" called out the barman from behind the counter.

"A half of Fremlin's Bitter," said Spindle, with a smile. He waited near the counter while the barman poured the bitter. Then he picked up the glass and carried it to a vacant table on the right-hand side of the door. He sipped the bitter, stared at the door each time another customer entered, and fidgeted. Before long, the pub was crowded with theatre employees – ticket clerks and ushers – who were in the habit of nipping around the corner to Nell Gwynne's for a quick pint before intermission.

He drained his glass and looked at his watch. Fifteen minutes had passed. He walked to the bar and ordered another half-pint. Just as the barman put the full glass in front of him, the door swung open, and Spindle saw Shoals walk in, nervously glancing around. He approached the bar, and still looking around, ordered a pint of Tetley's.

"A yank, are ye?" asked the barman upon hearing Shoals's accent.

"What? Oh, a yank, yes," said Shoals who had been distractedly glancing up and down the bar. Spindle walked back to his table. He saw Shoals pick up his drink and turn around looking for somewhere to sit.

Spindle stood up. "Is that you, Mr. Shoals? I'm by myself. You can sit here if you'd like," he said motioning to an empty chair at his table.

Shoals squinted at him in the dim gaslight, and hesitantly started to walk over to Spindle's table. "Remember me from the bookshop?" prompted Spindle when Shoals got closer. Shoals peered at him closely. "Bernard Atkins," Spindle reminded him. "Have you got the English language figured out yet?"

"Ah, yes, I remember now," said Shoals. "You're the one who wanted to know about American spelling." He put his glass down on the table, his eyes roving around the room.

"Are you busy at the embassy, Mr. Shoals? Have you determined if there are any sea gulls on the Great Salt Lake?" asked Spindle in a low voice.

Shoals started and looked back at him. "So it's you," he said in a near whisper. "You're the one who has been sending me information?"

"That's right," said Spindle, motioning for Shoals to sit down.

After they had both sat down, Shoals leaned across the table and said in a hushed voice, "You've been very helpful to the German cause, Mr. Atkins."

"Just been doing what I consider to be important - nothing much, really - but little bits now and again can sometimes add up and make a big impact," responded Spindle.

"We're very grateful, Mr. Atkins. But why have you chosen to reveal yourself and meet me here?" asked Shoals, glancing around over his shoulder to make sure they weren't being overheard.

Spindle leaned forward across the table, and said in a low voice. "A matter of extreme importance. I have information for you and thought I should tell you face to face."

"You could have sent it the normal way," said Shoals.

"This time I have something to show you and must take you there," said Spindle looking at his watch.

"Take me where? What have you got to show me?" asked Shoals, frowning.

"Maps, large maps, hanging on a wall. I must show you before... " Spindle stopped and stared meaningfully at Shoals.

"Is it far? How long will it take to get there?" queried Shoals.

"About fifteen minutes if we hurry," said Spindle, glancing at his watch again.

Shoals nodded his approval and looked around the bar. "All right, but I must go to the men's room first. This warm English beer goes right through me."

"I know what you mean," said Spindle with a laugh. He watched Shoals walk to the door of the men's toilet at the back of the pub. After several minutes, Shoals returned, this time with a more confident air.

Spindle stood up and opened the pub door. "Shall we be off?" he asked.

"After you," said Shoals, and followed him out of the pub.

Spindle turned around to Shoals in the dark passageway. "We can catch a hackney up on the Strand..." he began, and then he felt a crushing blow on the back of his head and everything went black.

When Spindle woke up he found himself in a very small windowless room. In the light of a single gas mantle he could see it was sparsely furnished with a chair, a bucket and the steel framed cot on which he was lying. His head was swimming, and he gingerly felt the painful lump on the back of his head. He slowly swung his legs over the side of the cot and sat for a moment, bracing himself on both arms, hands planted on either side of him. Then he heard the jangling of keys and the door swung open.

A policeman entered and said abruptly, "See you are awake. Get to your feet and come with me."

"Where am I?" asked Spindle, slowly getting to his feet and swaying unsteadily by the cot.

"Scotland Yard," replied the constable.

"Scotland Yard? But why?" asked Spindle in surprise.

The constable came over and roughly grabbed Spindle's hands, cuffing them together in front of him. "That's all I can say," he said, taking one of Spindle's arms and marching him out of the room. He led him to another windowless room where three men in pinstriped suits were waiting behind a plain wooden table with writing pads in front of them.

"Sit down," ordered the constable, pushing Spindle down into a chair at the table facing the three men. One of the men nodded at the constable, and he left the room, closing the door behind him.

"Why am I here? What's the meaning of this?" asked Spindle the moment the door closed.

"Name?" ordered the man in the middle. He and the other men stared expressionlessly at Spindle.

Spindle hesitated. "Bernard Atkins," he said.

"Nationality?"

"British," responded Spindle, raising his eyebrows in curiosity.

"Address?"

"15 Pearl Street, Hamstead."

The interviewer glanced down at his notepad and scowled. "You're lying, Mr. Atkins. We know where you live – 5 Greek Street just off Soho Square, isn't that correct?"

Spindle hung his throbbing head. "Yes, Sir," he mumbled.

"Why did your landlady deny that you live there?" he asked.

Spindle swallowed hard. His throat had gone dry. "She must have forgotten," he said. "She suffers from memory loss," he quickly added when he saw the men looking at him with disbelief.

"How do you know Mr. Shoals?" asked the man in the middle.

"Met him in a book shop about a year ago."

The man on the right suddenly cleared his throat and asked in a harsh voice, "What are these maps you want to show Mr. Shoals?"

Again Spindle hesitated. He could feel beads of perspiration popping out on his forehead.

"Answer the question!" shouted the man on the right.

"They are maps showing the salmon streams in Scotland," he blustered.

"What about Gommecourt and Armentiers?" yelled the man on the right, banging the table with his fist.

Spindle gritted his teeth and ducked his head, covering his face with his handcuffed hands.

The man on the right leaned aggressively across the table. "It's no good trying to lie, Mr. Atkins! We know all about you and how you have been passing military secrets to Mr. Shoals."

Spindle froze in his chair and tried to maintain a deadpan expression.

"Is there anyone else involved in your treason?" asked the man on the right.

Spindle did not open his mouth.

"How did you come up with these secrets, Mr. Atkins? Why did you give them to Mr. Shoals?"

Again Spindle did not answer.

The man on the right threw his pencil down angrily on the table.

"Very well, Mr. Atkins! If you won't cooperate, then sign this!" shouted the man in the middle. He shoved a typewritten document across the table, along with a pen.     Spindle    brought    down    his hands and looked at the document in front of him. "What is it?" he asked meekly, glancing up at the man in the middle.

"Your confession, Sir, that you have been passing on His Majesty's military secrets. Mr. Atkins, you are in violation of the Official Secrets Act."

Spindle looked down at the paper again. The name `Bernard Atkins' typed in capital letters below the signature line stared up at him.

"What are you going to do with Mr. Shoals – the receiver of this information?" asked Spindle, looking up at the men across the table again.

"None of your concern, Mr. Atkins. Just sign the confession," replied the middle man impatiently.

"I won't sign it without an answer to that question," declared Spindle. "Shoals is a bigger fish than me."

"Fish?" repeated the man on the left who up until now had said nothing. "Still maintaining your salmon ploy, are you?"

The three men laughed derisively at this comment. Spindle sat rigid, staring at them with a blank expression. After the laughter subsided, the man in the middle looked at Spindle with raised eyebrows. "Well, if you refuse to sign, Mr. Atkins, we will just have to lock you away until you do. We shall have to make your cell a little more uncomfortable, and perhaps in a day or two you will sign and we can dispense with this matter."

Spindle said nothing. After a moment, the man in the middle rapped loudly on the table with his fist to summon the constable. The policeman entered and roughly grabbed Spindle's arm, yanked him up from his chair and marched him back to his cell. He left the handcuffs on him, rudely shoved him into the cell and slammed the door behind him. Spindle stood, swaying weakly, in the pitch-black room as he listened to the constable turn the key in the lock. He paused to let his eyes adjust to the dark, but the unlit room was as black as the depths of a cave. Finally, he groped his way blindly around the room and discovered only two objects - a dented bucket and a straw mattress on the floor. No light, no chair, no cot this time. He relieved himself in the bucket and lay down cautiously on the mattress and tried to think.

The cold hard mattress did not help to relieve his aches and pains. His head continued to pound with a dull persistent throbbing. He went over the interrogation again and again in his mind. He needed to get the word to someone that he was not Bernard Atkins, but Brian Adams who worked in Section Z. But his work at Section Z was top secret, and he couldn't just go around telling anyone about it. He had to tell someone who had the position to know about Section Z and the pull to get him out of this predicament, but who? After he had lain there for more than an hour mulling over the situation, a name came into his mind. He decided it was a long shot, but he couldn't see how he had anything to lose by trying.

He got awkwardly to his feet, his hands still handcuffed in front of him, and crept along the wall until he found the door to the cell. He began to pound on the door. "Is anyone out there? I need to talk to someone!" he yelled.

After several minutes he heard the grate of a shutter being slid across the small barred window at the top of the door. A guard peered in at him. "Stop the bloody racket! What do you want?"

"I must speak to the Chief Constable," said Spindle with as much authority in his voice as he could muster.

"Oh, you do, do you?" sneered the guard. "And I'd like to speak with the King! The Chief Constable is too busy to deal with the likes of you."

"It's really important," said Spindle trying not to lose his temper. "The Chief Constable would be most upset if he doesn't hear what I have to say. When it comes out, he would blame you for not telling him."

The guard considered this for a moment and then sniffed. "Oh, all right, I'll tell him, but it bloody well better be important!" He slid the shutter back over the window, and Spindle waited by the door in the dark for what seemed to him to be an eternity.

At last he heard muffled voices on the other side of the door and the shutter slid open again. The Chief Constable looked in at him. "What is it, Atkins? Are you ready to sign the confession?"

"I have information that is of extreme importance, Sir. It is a matter of national security," said Spindle, as respectfully as he could.

"That's a matter for the Special Branch," said the Chief Constable. "I can't do anything for you. My responsibly is with the metropolitan police. You have been arrested under the Treason Act and the Special Branch is handling your case. If you sign the confession you will be handed over to us for internment."

"I really must see someone!" said Spindle, the tone of his voice conveying the urgency of the matter. "It has to do with Section Z."

"Section Z? Never heard of it." The Chief Constable put up his hand as if to close the shutter and end the conversation.

Spindle decided to risk it. "It's a secret Army operation located at Chad House," he said quickly before the man could close the shutter.

"Chad House! You mean Princess Alice's palace near Knightsbridge?" asked the Chief Constable in surprise. "The place where men are seen going in wearing uniforms and then they come out wearing civilian clothes?"

"Yes, Sir. I am one of those men. I am a captain in the Army."

"You a captain? So what does this so-called Section Z do?"

"I'm afraid I can't tell you that, Sir. That's why I need to speak with someone in high authority. I have information about a very urgent matter. It is top secret and it involves our national security."

"Who in high authority do you propose to share this information with, Mr. Atkins?"

Without hesitation, Spindle spoke the name that had come to him. "Mr. Churchill," he said quietly.

The Chief Constable snorted. "Mr. Churchill, indeed! Impossible. He's far too busy to waste time talking to a traitor!"

"Why don't you let Mr. Churchill be the judge of that? Get word to him that I have information about Mr. Zimmermann, the German foreign minister, and see if he wants to speak with me," persisted Spindle.

"What information do you have about this German?"

Spindle paused. "Tell Mr. Churchill just two words: Mexico and Zimmermann. That is all."

The Chief Constable shook his head. "I don't think I could inform Mr. Churchill without informing the Special Branch."

"Be that as it may. Please do whatever you have to do to get the message to Mr. Churchill. He is the one who needs to know what I have to say, and he is the only one I will talk to."

"Well, all right. I'll give it a go since you say it involves national security, but I wouldn't count on having an interview with Mr. Churchill if I were you." The Chief Constable slid the shutter closed, and Spindle was immersed in total darkness again. He made his way back to the straw mattress, lay down and tried to sleep.

Four hours later Spindle had finally fallen into a troubled sleep when the jangling of keys outside the cell door woke him. The door opened and the gas light went on, casting dim light and shadows all around the cell. Spindle shielded his eyes with his cuffed hands from the unaccustomed light. The same constable who had escorted him earlier strode over to Spindle, took his arm and helped him to his feet. Spindle shook his head groggily. "Where are we going?" he asked in a hoarse voice.

The constable did not reply. He just led Spindle down the hall to the room where he had been interrogated earlier. Spindle balked when he saw the door to the room that he remembered all too well. The constable tightened his grip on his arm and pulled him into the room. This time two men occupied the seats on the other side of the table. They were both well-dressed and distinguished looking. One man was fidgeting with a monocle, which he put up to his right eye when Spindle and the constable entered.

"I say, Constable. Do take the handcuffs off, would you?" he said.

The constable was quick to respond, and Spindle rubbed his chafed wrists in relief at being free of the heavy cuffs. The gentleman nodded at the chair across the table from him, indicating that Spindle should be seated.

"Now, then, Mr. Atkins," said the man with the monocle after Spindle was seated and the constable had left the room. "My name is Mr. Howard Fitzgerald and this is Mr. George Collingsworth. We understand you have something to tell us about the German foreign minister?"

"Who are you?" asked Spindle. "I wanted to see Mr. Churchill."

"Yes, we know that, Mr. Atkins. We are here to evaluate the information you have before a meeting with Mr. Churchill can be arranged," replied Collingsworth.

"Before I say anything, I need to know who you gentlemen are. The information I have is top secret, and I am only willing to give it to someone in a trusted high position. That is why I asked for Mr. Churchill," said Spindle cautiously.

The two men glanced at each other as if to decide which of them would respond to this question. Fitzgerald plucked the monocle from his eye and held it in his hand. He cleared his throat. "A fair question, Mr. Atkins, given the alleged nature of your information. Suffice it to say that both Mr. Collingsworth and I are in the security business, and we report to a government minister. It is our job to know what the Germans are thinking and doing."

"Do you report to Mr. Churchill?" asked Spindle. "Is he the minister?"

"Can't say, Mr. Atkins," said Fitzgerald, gesturing with his monocle at Spindle. He leaned forward slightly and continued in a lower voice. "You can think it, but you must never say."

Spindle started slightly at the familiar words. Then he grinned. "That's good enough for me," he said.

The two men smiled and leaned back in their chairs in a more relaxed posture. Fitzgerald put the monocle back in his eye and folded his hands together on the table in front of him. "Now, then, what is it you know about Zimmermann and Mexico?" he asked.

"I have evidence that Zimmermann is conspiring with Mexico to attack America," said Spindle in a hushed tone.

Both men sat straight up in their chairs again and stared at Spindle. Collingsworth's face had drained of color. "My word, Mr. Atkins! You have taken us aback. How do you know this? What evidence do you have? This will be of major significance to the foreign secretary!" exclaimed Fitzgerald.

"Do you work for the foreign secretary?" asked Spindle quickly.

Both men smiled slightly and shook their heads, still digesting Spindle's news.

"What evidence of this do you have, Mr. Atkins, and where is it?" asked Collingsworth.

"Telegrams. They are in a safe place, and I will show them only to your minister. For his eyes only," said Spindle somewhat cockily.

The men excused themselves and left the room. Spindle could hear them murmuring outside the door, but he couldn't make out what they were saying. Soon they returned with frowns on their faces.

Fitzgerald put the monocle in his eye and pulled out a pocket watch. "You're coming with us Mr. Atkins. We've decided you need to tell your intriguing story to someone else. Unfortunately, you will have to be handcuffed and blindfolded. You'll be escorted by one of our agents in plain clothes. I'm sure you won't mind."

Spindle nodded his agreement excitedly. "You won't regret this, Gentlemen. This is of vital importance to the war effort."

Collingsworth went to the door and motioned to someone in the hall. Shortly, a thin dark-haired man with a mustache entered. He was dressed in a tweed jacket and cap and wore wire-rimmed glasses. He came over to Spindle and produced a set of handcuffs. Spindle silently held out his hands. Without saying a word, the man handcuffed him and then pulled a black velvet bag from his pocket. This he placed over Spindle's head and took Spindle's arm.

"Right, then," said Fitzgerald. "Let's go. You will follow in the coach behind us."

"Yes, Sir," replied the man holding Spindle's arm.

Spindle could hear Fitzgerald and Collingsworth walking ahead as his escort led him along several corridors. Then he heard a door open and they came out into the brisk early morning air. Spindle estimated that it must be around four o'clock.

"Step up, Sir," said his escort. Spindle did as instructed and soon found himself sitting on a velvet seat. He heard the coach door close, and felt the presence of his escort in the seat across from him. Then he heard a coach driving off in front of them quickly followed by his own coach.

As the coach rumbled along in the darkness, Spindle remained silent. "You can think it, but you must not say it," he thought.

* * *

# Chapter 14
## *The Making of Heroes*

SPINDLE FELT THE coach stop. His escort said nothing, and they sat in silence for several minutes. He could hear the jangling of the horses' bridles as they tossed their heads. At last, he heard the coachman climb down from his box. He heard the coach door open, and felt a hand gripping his arm. "All right, then," said his escort. "We're getting out of the coach. Mind your step."

Spindle carefully felt his way out of the coach assisted by two hands, presumably those of the coachman and the escort. When he was outside, the escort gripped his left arm above the elbow and led him a short distance across what felt like cobblestone paving. They went up two stone steps and paused and went through a doorway onto what Spindle thought was a marble floor. They continued for about thirty steps and crossed another threshold. They stopped, and Spindle heard a door click shut behind him. Spindle took a deep breath and identified the pleasant odors of leather and cigar smoke. He heard the muffled rumble of men's voices coming from a distance, and then he heard a door open somewhere to his right.

"You can take off the blindfold and handcuffs now," said someone in a soft-spoken voice.

"Yes, Sir," said the escort who was still grasping Spindle's arm.

Spindle felt the handcuffs being released, and then the black velvet bag was quickly removed from his head. He opened his eyes and stared at his surroundings. He was in an elegantly furnished library. Leather-bound volumes lined the walls. A huge polished cherry wood desk occupied the far end of the room where heavy burgundy-colored velvet drapes were drawn over floor-to-ceiling windows. The room was gas lit by a huge crystal chandelier, and to the left was a massive Georgian fireplace with a grouping of leather furniture in front of it. An enormous oriental carpet covered the oak hardwood floor.

As he stared straight ahead at his surroundings, his eyes adjusting to the light, Spindle heard the door open and close behind his escort who had left the room. Then the same soft-spoken voice said, "Make yourself at home. Would you like a cup of tea and a biscuit? Does wonders for the nerves."

Spindle turned to his right and saw a round-faced man in a burgundy brocade smoking jacket gesturing with his cigar toward a sideboard that held a tea service and several plates of assorted biscuits. He looked just like the pictures he had seen when he had been appointed First Lord of the Admiralty in 1911, thought Spindle.

"Pleased to meet you, Mr. Churchill, Sir," said Spindle. "So good of you to take the time."

"And your name is Bernard Atkins, I've been told," said Churchill, motioning toward the open door behind him. Fitzgerald and Collingsworth entered, crossed the room and seated themselves on the leather couch near the fireplace. As they entered, Churchill motioned for Spindle to get himself some tea and biscuits, which he did somewhat nervously. Then he seated himself in the leather chair facing Fitzgerald and Collingsworth.

Churchill stood in front of the fireplace, leaning with one arm on the mantel and holding his cigar in the other hand. He took a long puff from the cigar, contemplatively blew the smoke up into the air making two perfect smoke rings, and then pointed the cigar at Spindle. "Now, then. Let's get on with it," he said with a twinkle in his eye. "Fitzgerald and Collingsworth here are in a tizzy. They said you know about Section Z and that you have evidence that the Germans and Mexicans are up to some mischief."

Spindle glanced at Collingsworth and Fitzgerald who were looking tentatively at him.

"Yes, Sir, that is correct," began Spindle. "The reason I know about Section Z is that I work there. My real name is Captain Brian Adams and I am a statistician there."

"A statistician," beamed Churchill. "Something to do with numbers, I believe."

"Yes, Sir. I work out factual conclusions based on what the numbers tell me."

"And your name is not Bernard Atkins?"

"No, Sir. It is a name I invented. You see, in the course of my duties at Section Z I discovered that the German foreign minister Zimmermann is sending telegrams to Mexico. The gist of these telegrams is that Germany is inciting Mexico to attack America, thus causing a diversion so that America will not enter the war on the side of the Allies. If that happens, we – Great Britain – will have great difficulty in defeating the Germans."

"I see," said Churchill slowly. "And who is your commanding officer at Section Z?"

"All of Section Z is under the command of a man known only as 'Five-O-One' to me, and my commanding officer under him is General Alfred Bottoms."

Churchill chortled and waved his cigar in the air. "Ah, yes... 'Stinky' Bottoms. I know him from my school days."

Spindle, Fitzgerald and Collingsworth laughed politely at Churchill's nickname for the general.

"Now then, Captain Adams, does 'Stinky'... er, General Bottoms know about these telegrams?" asked Churchill, watching another smoke ring rise toward the ceiling.

"No, Sir," replied Spindle, the color rising in his face.

"I see," said Churchill with a mischievous smile. He looked at his cigar, which had been smoked down to a stub and threw it into the fireplace. He sat down in the chair facing the fireplace and glanced over at Fitzgerald.

"Well, Mr. Fitzgerald, what do you know of these telegrams? Is it true?" he asked.

Fitzgerald plucked the monocle from his eye and rubbed it. This seemed to be response enough for Churchill because he nodded and turned his attention back to Spindle.

"Now, then, Captain Adams, what do you know about this Mr. Shoals?" he asked.

"Shoals works at the American Embassy and is a German spy," replied Spindle. "He has been sending our military secrets to Berlin by telegram, and I have evidence of that too. That is why I invented the name of Bernard Atkins. I gave him information under that name to test him and see if he would send it on to Berlin."

"How embarrassing for our American cousins to have a German spy working in their Embassy," said Churchill smiling gleefully.

Fitzgerald coughed and Churchill glanced at him and grinned merrily.

"May I have a word in private with you, Sir?" asked Fitzgerald.

"Yes, now is the appropriate time, I think," said Churchill still beaming. As he and Fitzgerald walked to the door to the adjoining room, he looked back over his shoulder. "Captain, help yourself to more tea and biscuits."

After the door closed behind them, Collingsworth smiled at Spindle. Spindle returned the smile somewhat nervously.

"Nice fire," he said, casting about for something to say. "It takes the chill out of the air."

"Yes, indeed," nodded Collingsworth. "The early morning weather is quite chilly for this time of year."

Spindle picked up the china teacup and took a sip. Collingsworth walked over to the sideboard and returned with a silver plate of biscuits, which he held out to Spindle. "Have another biscuit, Captain. These Scottish shortbreads are excellent."

Spindle finished drinking his tea and was munching on his second shortbread when Churchill and Fitzgerald returned.

"So far so good, Captain. Mr. Fitzgerald has confirmed your employment at Section Z," said Churchill sitting back down in his chair. His eyes still gleamed with merriment. "Now, what was the reason for your meeting with Shoals at Nell Gwynne's, and what about those maps?"

"The maps were a ploy to get Shoals to come with me so I could kidnap him, Sir," said Spindle.

"Kidnap?" chuckled Churchill. "For what reason, Captain? Surely, kidnapping is not the gentlemanly thing to do!" Churchill's smile broadened as he glanced at Fitzgerald and Collingsworth on the couch.

"Was going to trade him for a British platoon stranded behind German lines, Sir," explained Spindle with a puzzled look on his face, trying to fathom the reason for Churchill's humorous reaction.

Still looking at Spindle, Churchill took a cigar from a gold case, snipped the end of it with an expensive cigar clipper, put it in his mouth and lit it. He took a deep puff, all the while continuing to smile in amusement. Fitzgerald and Collingsworth cleared their throats.

Churchill looked at them. "Well, what do you think of that, Gentlemen? A fair trade, don't you think – a German spy for a British platoon?" He chuckled again and turned back to Spindle. "Where is this platoon, Captain?"

"On Hill Fifty-One, in the area of the Somme where our 34th Division is, Sir."

"Ah, Hill Fifty-One. I remember Davenville telling me about it. Seems to think the platoon leader would make a great hero to boost morale. Are those men still there?"

"Yes, Sir, and no attempt is being made to rescue them. I took it on myself to do something. I couldn't let them be overrun by Germans. They are occupying a position that is of vital strategic importance to our offensive, Sir."

"By Jove! Another Ladysmith!" exclaimed Churchill. "Get Morton in here," he added, addressing Collingsworth.

Collingsworth quickly got to his feet and went off to the adjacent room.

While waiting for Collingsworth to return, Churchill poured more tea and they each ate another biscuit.

"What is it Winston?" asked a tall distinguished-looking gentleman who strode into the room ahead of Collingsworth. Spindle's eyes lit up with recognition.

"What do you know about Hill Fifty-One, Charles? Captain Adams says we have men stranded there," said Churchill, waving his hand toward Spindle.

The gentleman looked closely at Spindle, then at Churchill, and smiled pleasantly. "The captain is correct, Winston. We do have men stranded there. A platoon of the Royal West Kents took that hill on the first day of the offensive."

"Well, what is being done about it?" asked Churchill in a rather querulous tone. "We can't treat our men that way. They should be relieved – reinforcements sent in – that type of thing."

"I agree, the Privy Council agrees, the King agrees, but C in C France does not. He says he has his hands full trying to break the German lines."

"I knew it!" shouted Churchill, slapping his hand on the arm of his chair. "That mother's boy does not want to be told what to do again. Acting like a spoiled baby. He should never have been made C in C! Leaving our boys to fend for themselves after such a heroic feat! What C in C needs is a steady kick up the Kyber Pass!"

The room went silent. Fitzgerald and Collingsworth looked down at their shoes obviously trying not to grin at Churchill's outburst. Churchill fumed in disgust, examined his cigar, discovered it had gone out, and lit it again. He took a long puff, looking at the ceiling. The gentleman Spindle had recognized took this opportunity to walk forward and extend his hand to Spindle. "I believe we have met before, Captain Adams. Charles Morton."

Spindle stood up and clasped his hand. "Yes, Sir. We met on the train from Bridgefield to London. Two friends and I were on our way to London to receive our Army assignments."

"Of course, I remember," said Morton, smiling warmly at Spindle. "Let me think, Captain. I believe you and your friends were assigned to Section Z. Am I correct?"

"Had our original assignments changed, Sir. We finished up at Chad House," said Spindle grinning.

"Pleased to hear that," said Morton, winking at him.

"Thank you, Sir," said Spindle.

"So you know this young chap, do you?" asked Churchill. Morton nodded, and Churchill smiled at him. Spindle sat back down in his chair, and Morton took the chair on his left. Churchill looked round the room, then his gaze settled on Fitzgerald. "What about trading the spy, like the captain had in mind?" he asked.

"Not possible, Sir. Shoals works for us," answered Fitzgerald.

352

"You mean he is a double agent!" gasped Spindle without thinking.

"Yes, Captain," said Collingsworth, smiling at Spindle's surprise. "He's been with us all along. Used him to send false information back to Berlin, you see. Saved many thousands of British and Empire lives. We've been on to you from the start. Read every letter Bernard Atkins sent to him. We didn't know who you were until... "

Fitzgerald held up his hand to prevent Collingsworth from saying anything further.

"Be that as it may, Gentlemen, but I want to know what we are going to do about those men on the hill. Every minute that goes by puts them in greater jeopardy," interrupted Churchill with an impatient wave of his cigar.

"The trade is out of the question. The only thing is for C in C France to get his finger out and rescue them," said Morton. "I will ask Davenville to get the King to send a dispatch insisting that he do so. Davenville has been following the situation closely. Seems to have a great interest in this particular platoon."

"Oh, I'm sure the King's the only one who can convince C in C to get his finger out!" quipped Churchill laughing. He took another puff from the cigar with an amused look on his face. "Where is the King now, Charles? I didn't see the flag yesterday evening when I came past Buckingham Palace."

"In Scotland, Winston. He went to Balmoral to get some fresh air while he decides on a British-sounding surname. He's thinking about taking the name Windsor."

"Good choice. A great name," grinned Churchill. "Glad he is not considering `Marlborough.'" The rest of the men in the room chuckled at Churchill's jest, except for Spindle, who did not understand what they were talking about. Why would King George want to change his surname, he wondered. Besides, he hadn't ever heard the King's last name; in fact, he hadn't thought he had one.

"Better get to it, Charles," said Churchill. "See Davenville and get this moving along. We have men that need help. Mustn't keep our heroes waiting."

When Morton left, Churchill sat back in his chair and puffed on his cigar thoughtfully, and then another mischievous grin spread across his face. "It appears this captain has more initiative and enterprise than Section Z can handle," he commented. "If Morton, who's not only the Earl of Camber but also the head of the War Department, is impressed with him, that's good enough for me. Mr. Fitzgerald and Mr. Collingsworth, I want you to put your heads together and come up with something where his talents can be fully utilized."

"What about my group, Sir?" asked Spindle. "I didn't do this alone. My partners are talented, too, and without them there would have been no telegrams."

"Hear that, Gentlemen? Section Z apparently has a whole bag full of endowed people. Let's put them to work where their skills will really make a difference," said Churchill, rising to his feet and putting out his hand to Spindle to indicate the session was over.

* * *

Later that morning Roger and James were sitting in their small office at Chad House worriedly speculating about Spindle.

"I saw him walking up the passageway to Nell Gwynne's just a little before eight o'clock," said James. "He passed right by the cab, and I'm sure he saw me. Later I saw Shoals walking toward the pub, but I waited and waited and I never saw either of them come out."

"I was a nervous wreck waiting for you to show up at my place," said Roger. "Finally, when it got to be around Midnight I thought you might have had a change of plans and taken Shoals somewhere else."

"Where are Pete and Ginger? Maybe they know something," said James anxiously.

"They've been at The Odeon all night waiting on the word to send the telegram to Berlin. We can't get in to see them until this afternoon when the theatre opens. If Spindle doesn't show up by then, we need to go over there and see if they know anything."

"Hope Pete didn't send the telegram to Berlin."

"No," said Roger reassuringly. "He knew not to send it unless he received definite word from us that we had Shoals."

"What are we going to say if someone wants to know where Spindle is?" asked James.

"Let's just tell them he went to Woolwich Arsenal to check on the new artillery ammunition," said Roger.

James nodded and they were both staring at each other with worried expressions when there was a loud knock on the door. They both jumped at the sound and after a moment, Roger asked, "Who is it?"

"Sergeant Jones, Sir, with a message from General Bottoms," came the reply.

Glancing with trepidation at James, Roger got up and went to the door. He opened it slowly and the sergeant handed him a folded piece of paper and saluted. "Thank you, Sergeant," said Roger, saluting. The sergeant left and Roger unfolded the paper and read it. "The general wants us in his office posthaste," he said. "It's odd. The message is just for the two of us - no mention of Spindle. Wonder what that could mean?"

"Guess we're about to find out," said James. He got up and straightened his uniform. His hands were shaking. "Once more into the lion's den..." he said with a quiver in his voice as he followed Roger out of the door.

General Bottoms was pacing up and down in front of his desk when they arrived at his open door. He motioned impatiently for them to enter. "Close the door behind you," he ordered.

"Yes, Sir!" said Roger, closing the door as he had been instructed.

Without preliminary, the general abruptly announced, "Captain Smith and Captain Taylor, as of this moment Section Z is off limits to you. I have just received orders from high authority that you are to be reassigned. You are to collect your things and report immediately to Winchester Barracks."

Roger's and James's mouths fell open in astonishment. Finally, Roger found his tongue. "May we ask why, Sir?"

"Not at liberty to say. Just obeying orders."

"What about Captain Adams? Is he being reassigned as well?" asked James.

The general simply shook his head. "That is all, Gentlemen," he said and turned toward his desk.

James and Roger looked at each other in shock. They hesitated, but the general did not turn around, so they left quietly and made their way back to their office to carry out their orders.

* * *

That afternoon The Odeon opened its doors at the usual time. People lined up to buy tickets for the film and ushers showed them to their seats in the auditorium. When the lights went down and the screen began to flicker, at various intervals several men made their way to the toilet and never returned.

When the men reached the listening operation center in the attic they were surprised to see several strangers in the room. All the newcomers wore pinstriped suits and bowler hats and seemed to be led by a man who wore a monocle in his right eye. The men wrote down the listeners' names as they appeared and told them to continue with their work. The listeners looked around for Mr. Court and Mr. Murphy, but they were not there. One of the men who had been on the previous shift told them that Pete and Ginger had been escorted away by two strangers about two hours before the theatre opened. He had overheard the man with the monocle telling them that they were being reassigned.

* * *

The hackney carrying Pete, Ginger and an escort wended its way through the mid-day traffic. "Where are we going?" asked Pete.

The escort, who was a burly fair-haired man, pursed his lips. "You'll find out soon enough," he said, and looked out the window as if to say "no more questions."

Pete looked at Ginger and raised an eyebrow. Ginger gave him a crooked grin and shrugged his shoulders. They remained silent for the rest of the journey.

Ten minutes later, the hackney pulled up outside a murky gray building on the Embankment. The three passengers got out and the escort led Pete and Ginger past naval sentries, through a pair of massive doors and into a large reception area.

"Here to see Admiral Tanner Smith," said the escort to a captain who was seated behind a desk in the reception hall.

The captain looked at the note the escort handed him and smiled up at them. "Yes, Sir, the Admiral is expecting you. Go to Room 207 down that corridor." He pointed to the corridor on his right.

The sign over the door of 207 said "Naval Intelligence." Pete and Ginger looked at each other in surprise. They followed the escort through the door and discovered a huge room divided up into many small cubicles. In each cubicle sat a man attired in naval uniform with earphones on his head.

A huge man with a weathered leathery face, a shock of thick white hair and closely trimmed white beard stepped forward to greet them. "Good day, Gentlemen. I am Admiral Tanner Smith. Welcome to Naval Intelligence," he said in a gravelly voice. "Mr. Court and Mr. Murphy?" he said, extending his hand to Pete.

"Yes, Sir. I am Peter Court and this is Patrick Murphy," said Pete, shaking the admiral's hand.

The escort bowed his head slightly to the admiral and left.

"Now, then, Gentlemen, what we do here is listen to the messages being sent by the German fleet and decode them," said the admiral, waving his hand at the men in the cubicles. "I'm told the two of you have excellent skills in decoding messages and that you will be a valuable asset to our mission."

The admiral looked from Pete to Ginger with a broad smile on his face. Neither of them could utter a word. They were astounded.

"Come. Let's put your talents to work," said the admiral. He turned to lead them to their own cubicles. Then, he added as an afterthought over his shoulder. "Oh, by the way, you're in the Navy now."

* * *

After Roger and James had departed for Winchester Barracks, a hackney pulled up to a service door at the back of Chad House where a sergeant in civilian clothes waited. The driver jumped down from his box and the sergeant handed him a tea chest and a gold sovereign. "Deliver this to 9 Greek Street in Soho. It's for Mr. Brian Adams. The name and address are on the envelope attached to the box," instructed the sergeant.

The cab driver nodded and hoisted the chest up into his box. When he arrived at Spindle's address, Mrs. Thatcher answered the door. Under her supervision, the hackney driver carried the chest to Spindle's room and placed it inside on the floor.

"Is there any message from Mr. Adams?" Mrs. Thatcher asked the driver as they walked back down the stairs to the entryway.

"Just told to deliver the box, Madam," replied the driver, tipping his hat to her.

"I do hope Mr. Adams is all right. He didn't come home last night," remarked Mrs. Thatcher.

"Not to worry, Madam. Lots of comings and goings these days, especially with the young gentlemen." The driver grinned and winked at her before he climbed up onto his box.

Mrs. Thatcher watched him drive away and then went back into the house shaking her head in puzzlement.

At approximately that same time, Spindle was knocking on a door at Number 147, Brompton Road. When they left Churchill's London residence (which Spindle discovered was on Baker Street), Collingsworth gave him the Brompton Road address and told him to report there without delay for his new assignment.

The door opened and Spindle was ushered in by a middle-aged man dressed in the ubiquitous pinstriped suit. Spindled followed the man down a winding staircase and then along a corridor. After passing a number of closed doors, the man showed him into a large room. A blast of hot, humid air assailed him as he entered the room causing beads of perspiration to pop out on his forehead.

Spindle's guide motioned to another man who was wearing a white surgeon's gown and was seated behind a desk. The man got up and came over to greet them.

"A new recruit for your section," said Spindle's escort. "This is Mr. Brian Adams, George. He comes with excellent credentials."

"Welcome, Mr. Adams. Pleased to have you in the sweatbox. My name is George Linwood," said the man. He smiled and shook Spindle's hand.

"Sweatbox is right. I'm perspiring already," said Spindle, taking out a handkerchief and wiping his forehead.

"Let me show you around, Brian. You should find it fascinating. What we do here is open letters and read them."

Spindle's escort held up his hand. "I'll leave you to it. The less I know the better," he said, turning and leaving the room.

"The steam room is back here," said George, motioning for Spindle to follow him to the far-left side of the room.

When they entered the steam room, George pointed to a contraption with small trap doors. "We place unopened envelopes inside here for two minutes," he said, pointing to the trap doors. "The steam unsticks the seal on the envelopes, and then these fellows open them and read the letters."

Spindle watched in amazement as several young men collected envelopes from the trap doors. They quickly opened them and began reading the contents.

"What are they looking for?" asked Spindle.

"Spies," said George, with a wave of his hand. "These particular letters are being mailed to America by people we suspect of spying. We read them to see if there are any secrets in them. Some letters are put under the microscope to examine small ink spots. Spies these days can be very creative, you know."

"Have you caught any?" asked Spindle.

"Don't know," said George, shrugging his shoulders. "Anything interesting is passed along, and that's the last we hear of it."

"What happens to the letters after you've read them?"

"Those that pass inspection are resealed and sent the normal way, through the post. You can't tell they've been opened."

"And those that don't?"

"Don't know. They go upstairs. That's all I know – not for me to ask," said George with a grin.

Spindle and George stood watching the process for a while. The steamed letters were opened and read in an orderly way, and then, each letter was attached to its envelope with a red, blue or green clip. After that, the letters were stacked neatly in color-coded boxes.

"What do the colors mean?" inquired Spindle.

"The red box contains suspicious letters, and they are taken upstairs. The blue box contains letters that are doubtful and are read by this section again. The greens are resealed and sent on their way. They go directly to the Post Office's overseas sorting depot in Paddington," explained George. "We can handle thousands of letters daily. Fortunately, we only get the cream here. We only check letters that are addressed to America, so we're at least dealing for the most part with the English language. Other countries each have a sweatbox located elsewhere. I, for one, wouldn't want to be in the Chinese box. They say they have eight hundred ways of writing!" George laughed at his little joke.

"What is my job George?" asked Spindle.

"We'll start you off in the steam room, Brian, and after a day or so you will become a reader. After that I can't be sure. All I know is the people at the top think you are a major asset and I am ordered to give you insights into spy catching."

* * *

That afternoon on Hill Fifty-One, Bouncer and his men were prepared. They had placed their hand-made bomb at the end of the west tunnel and blocked off the tunnel with sandbags to prevent blowback into the redoubt. They had finished digging the tunnel that led to the east and came up somewhere behind the second German trench line. Throughout the day they had been taking shifts at the gun slits, observing the battle and continuing to fire occasional bursts of ammunition.

Around three o'clock the loud buzzing of the telephonic device reverberated through the bunker startling Bouncer and his men.

Conway looked at Bouncer. "Wonder who that is? Fritz said he wouldn't call again until sunrise."

"Better answer it," directed Bouncer. He followed Conway to the telephonic and held his breath as Conway answered. Conway listened for a moment and then handed the receiver to Bouncer. "It's Fritz," he said.

Conway and the rest of the men watched with anxious eyes as Bouncer picked up the receiver.

"Fritz?" he inquired. Then there was a long silence as Bouncer listened. The men could hear the faint voice of the Saxon coming from the receiver, but they couldn't make out what he said. Finally, he said, "I understand, Fritz. Thanks for all you have done for us. You kept your word."

There was another pause as Bouncer listened again, and then he said, "If we both make it through this war, I'd be pleased to visit you. Goodbye, Fritz."

Bouncer put the receiver back slowly and turned to face his men who were staring at him in concerned silence.

"Well men, it's happened," Bouncer began. "The Germans are on to us. Fritz and his unit are being reassigned to a trench line further back right away. They are being replaced by a Prussian company."

The men groaned and looked fearfully at each other.

"Now, men, this is not good news, but it's what we expected. That is why we've been making our preparations. Now, it's time to put our plan into action," said Bouncer quickly before the men had too much time to think about the situation. He motioned for the men to gather round closer and he outlined the plan.

"We will break out just before sunset," he said. "As you know, there is generally a cease-fire at sunset for the armies to collect their dead and wounded. That will give us an advantage. Also, we are going to set off the bomb in the west tunnel to distract the Germans – make them think we're escaping that way, but we'll be going out the east tunnel behind the German trench line. Conway and I will lead the prisoners out first and you will follow. We'll all wear the German uniforms over our British ones so that if we are spotted, the Germans will think we're theirs. Once we're out, we'll send the prisoners on toward the German trenches and we'll make for the front line, shed the German uniforms and try to get back to our side while they're collecting the dead and wounded. Does everyone understand the plan? Any questions?"

The men were silent for a moment, and then a hand went up.

"Yes, Private?"

"What happens if we're discovered before we can get back across our line, Sir? Do we surrender?"

"If that happens, I'm leaving that decision up to each of you, but as for myself, I am going to fight – kill as many Germans as I can," said Bouncer. "That's why I volunteered – to fight, not to surrender."

Bouncer stood quietly looking at his men with a serious expression on his face. Again, there was complete silence as the men thought it over, and then Private Benson jumped to his feet. "I'm with you, Sir!" he cried. "I figure I can kill at least five Huns before they get me!"

One by one the other men jumped up and affirmed their decision to fight, until all of them stood together, united in their decision. Bouncer looked at his men with pride. A lump had formed in his throat, and he swallowed hard before he spoke.

"That's the spirit, lads! We have about two hours before sunset. Get your uniforms on and gather up as much ammunition as you can carry. For King and Empire!" he yelled, raising his fist in the air.

"For King and Empire!" shouted the men in unison.

* * *

Half an hour before sunset Lieutenant Colonel Hastings Jackson stood on his observation platform outside his battalion headquarters in Albert looking at Hill Fifty-One through his field glasses. The hill was bathed in the last of the sun's rays as it sank steadily behind him toward the western horizon. He heard footsteps climbing the ladder to the observation platform, and he turned just in time to see Captain Rupert Squires's head rising above the platform.

"Captain Squires reporting as ordered, Sir!" said Rupert, snapping to attention and saluting as soon as he had both feet on the platform.

The colonel returned the salute. "At ease, Captain. I have some good news for you. I have just received direct orders from C in C to rescue your platoon from Hill Fifty-One."

A wide smile spread across Rupert's face. "Ah, at last. That is good news, Sir. I have two platoons that have been standing by hoping for the go-ahead. I will lead them myself."

The colonel and Rupert walked to the edge of the platform and stood gazing at Hill Fifty-One as they talked. Hastings-Jackson waved a hand toward the hill. "Excellent, Captain. Wait until after dark. There will be the usual cease-fire at sunset, and you and your rescue party can sneak across while our men are out there collecting the casualties."

"Yes, Sir. Should be able to get across in about half an hour, and if all goes as planned, be back with Lieutenant Russell and his platoon well before Midnight."

"As soon as you return, bring Lieutenant Russell and report to me. I will see to it that he and his men are rewarded for this. They are heroes, and they should have been relieved long before this, but my hands were tied – had direct orders not to send in a relief column. Hope the men don't blame me."

"Oh, no, Sir. We know that you have to obey orders handed down through the chain of command. If the men blame anyone, it's..."

Suddenly, the flash of exploding shells lit up the sky around Hill Fifty-One. Rupert and the colonel stood watching in stunned silence as the hill became shrouded in the smoke and dust of an artillery barrage.

"Bloody Hell! The Huns are blowing the redoubt to smithereens!" exclaimed the colonel.

They watched helplessly as the shelling continued until the top of the hill became a blazing inferno. Then all went quiet. The shelling stopped, and only a black plume of smoke remained. A few seconds later, there was the bright orange flash of a large explosion, followed by a thunderous roar.

"Oh, my God!" cried Rupert as he stared in horror at the hill.

"Sir!" said a sergeant who appeared suddenly at the top of the ladder. "A message just arrived by carrier pigeon from Hill Fifty One.

"What does it say?" asked the colonel who did not take his eyes off the hill.

"Attempting breakout at sunset."

The colonel looked at Squires and shook his head. "Lieutenant Russell and his men were heroes. I will do my damnedest to get them medals. They could have been saved if we'd sent in a rescue team earlier as I wanted to, but unfortunately, military chess players and politicians are running this war. I'm sorry."

Rupert nodded in acknowledgement and looked down, tears standing in his eyes.

"Well Captain, we must get on with it," said Hastings-Jackson after a moment. "Go back and get your men ready to attack Hill Fifty-One, as we discussed."

Rupert looked up at him in disbelief. "Begging your pardon, Sir, but there is no point in it now. The platoon has surely been lost in that bombardment, and now there's no one to rescue."

"I know that, Captain, but we are obliged to carry out orders when they come down from C in C unless we get new orders. Do your duty, Captain Squires!" said the colonel with a painful expression in his eyes.

"Yes, Sir!" said Rupert, drawing himself up to attention. He saluted and turned to descend the ladder.

He paused for a moment when he heard the colonel say in a soft voice, "And Captain, do be careful and come back alive. That is an order from me."

\* \* \*

The next evening, Pete and Ginger found Spindle at his lodgings and they brought each other up to date on what had happened to each of them. They did not know what had become of Roger and James. On the following Saturday, Pete and Spindle took the train to Lunbury Hospital. The same lady was at the reception desk when they signed in, and she assured them that Freddie was still in Ward 26.

Pete tapped the bell inside Ward 26, and after a few minutes, a nurse appeared through the swinging doors. She looked at them questioningly. "We're here to see Freddie Simpson," said Pete.

"Wait here. I'll see if Freddie is awake, and if he is you can visit for a short while," said the nurse smiling. She disappeared back inside the swinging doors, and in a short while she was back. She motioned to Pete and Spindle to follow her. "This way, please. Freddie is awake and you can visit him."

"Is Nurse Davenville on duty?" asked Spindle. "We would like to see her too."

"Nurse Davenville has the day off, I'm afraid. The first day she's had off in the last three weeks," responded the nurse.

"What about Sam Baldwin? Is he here today?" asked Pete.

The nurse shook her head. "Sorry, but Mr. Baldwin also has the day off and won't be back until tomorrow."

Spindle and Pete followed the nurse between rows of beds equally spaced on either side of the ward. All of the beds were occupied by men, some sleeping, others awake with their heads propped up on pillows. V-shaped tents covered their bodies where their legs should have been. Those who were awake stared up at the ceiling, occasionally uttering small moans.

"We are full to the limit with leg amputees and the other wards are full as well," commented the nurse. "The hospital is adding temporary huts to cope with the new arrivals. Nobody expected so many casualties."

"Such a pity, Nurse," sympathized Spindle gazing sadly at the men lying in the beds.

"The newspapers say we are winning the war and that it will be over soon," said the nurse.

"If it's in the newspapers, it must be true," said Spindle with a touch of sarcasm in his voice. Pete nudged his arm and gave him a warning look.

"You have visitors Freddie. Two fine Gentlemen to see you," said the nurse softly as she stopped at a bed at the end of the ward.

Freddie slowly lifted his head from a white pillow and looked foggily up at Spindle and Pete. Then a weak smile lit up his face. "Spindle! Pete! So good to see you chaps," he exclaimed, struggling to prop himself up higher in the bed. The nurse placed a couple more pillows under his head, and then she went back down the ward to assist another patient.

Spindle and Pete came closer, each grasping one of Freddie's outstretched hands. "Tried to see you several days ago, but you were sedated," said Spindle.

"I know. Susan told me," said Freddie. Then a mischievous smile spread across his face. "What do you think of my luck – drawing Susan Davenville as my nurse, eh?"

"Couldn't be in better hands," remarked Pete, trying not to look at the tent that covered Freddie's legs.

"Not only that, but I had Sam as my field surgeon, and Susan's uncle as my doctor here. Imagine that – a Harley Street surgeon!"

"Susan told us that Sam performed the surgery," said Spindle cautiously.

"That he did. Saved my life and did a wonderful job," said Freddie. "I'm going to be measured for new wooden legs next week. Just think, I won't ever have to worry about blisters from tight-fitting shoes again. Also, you can smack me on the leg with your conker all you want and I won't feel a thing."

"What about wood worms?" asked Spindle, laughing at Freddie's good humor.

Freddie chuckled. "Oh, by the way, guess who came to see me earlier today? I've had a wealth of visitors today."

"Can't think," said Spindle.

"Rose, Martha and Elizabeth," said Freddie. "They came up from Bridgefield on the train.

"That's wonderful, Freddie!" exclaimed Pete. "I'd like to see them, too. Have they gone back to Bridgefield?"

"No. They're at Doctor Davenville's house. He and his wife and Susan are hosting a high tea this afternoon. Sam is there, too, with Rose, of course. It's the first day the doctor, Sam and Susan have had off in more than three weeks. I'm sure they'd love to have the two of you show up. Doctor Davenville lives at Number 10 Berkeley Square in Mayfair."

"We'll do that," said Spindle excitedly. "It will be good to see all of them, and we haven't had a chance to see Sam yet, either."

"When do they expect that you'll be out of hospital, Freddie?" asked Pete.

"As soon as they build my legs and make sure they fit. They'll move me to the recovery ward while I learn to use them. Then I'll be out and can go home to Bridgefield. They need the beds here. Ambulance loads of wounded coming in every day from the front," said Freddie. "Bloody generals don't care how many are killed or wounded," he added bitterly.

Spindle leaned closer to Freddie and asked in a low voice, "What happened over there, Freddie?"

"We were sent in to take a redoubt on a hill across from our trench line before the offensive began. Sam and I were in Bouncer's platoon. The generals had sent the word down that the artillery barrage that went on for a week before the battle had knocked out the barbed wire and driven the Germans back from their front trenches. It was a lie. We found the wire and the Germans still intact, but we couldn't send word back in time. We killed the Germans in the trench and put on their uniforms. Then, Bouncer told us to make grenades from bottles and lamp oil that we found in the trench. We sneaked up on the redoubt and took the Germans by surprise. Captured the redoubt, and I was the only casualty. My own damned fault, really," said Freddie, looking down at the tent that covered his legs. "Somehow, I dropped a flaming bottle of fuel oil and burnt my legs. Don't know how it happened - just slipped out of my hands, I guess."

"So sorry, Freddie," said Pete, shaking his head.

"I was lucky to have Bouncer and Sam there with me. Otherwise, I'd be dead. Bouncer ordered Sam to cut off my legs, and all the doctors that saw me later said he did a marvelous job of it. That's why he's Doctor Davenville's surgical assistant now."

"How did you and Sam get back here?" asked Spindle.

"It was Bouncer. He bargained an exchange with a German captain who agreed to get Sam and me back to our side in exchange for four wounded Huns. We captured about sixty Germans when we took the hill," said Freddie proudly. Then a shadow crossed his face. "Wish I knew what happened to the platoon. Bouncer had one carrier pigeon, and he sent a message back to HQ to let them know we had taken the hill. Hope he got reinforcements and is all right. He's a proper hero, you know. Have you heard anything?" asked Freddie anxiously.

Pete and Spindle glanced at each other over Freddie's head. "We don't know anything, Freddie," said Spindle regretfully. "But thankfully, you and Sam are out of harm's way and won't have to go back into that blood bath."

"That's right. Now you can concentrate on catching Jack the Ripper," said Pete, attempting to take Freddie's mind off Bouncer.

Freddie chuckled. "Oh, Jack the Ripper will have to wait. My father wants me to work in his law office in London. Just think, I'll be the only barrister around with wood for legs instead of brains!"

"Ha! If you had wood for brains you'd make an excellent general or a politician!" called out the patient in the next bed, who had overheard Freddie's remark.

Gales of laughter filled the ward.

"What's the joke?" called out the ward sister, poking her head out of a door at the end of the ward. "It's truly exciting to hear all you men laughing."

"Would like to tickle your fancy and make you laugh too!" called out a patient.

The sister blushed and her head disappeared just as quickly as it had appeared.

This provoked more laughter. The noise woke most of the sleeping patients who had to have the jokes repeated to them, and this in turn provoked more laughter.

When the laughter finally faded, Freddie tugged on Spindle's arm and looked up at him. "Susan said you are in some sort of sausage business. You're not in the black market, are you Spindle?"

Spindle laughed and grinned at Pete. "No, Freddie, it's not that type of thing. All I can tell you is that Pete and I work for the backroom boys in London. Can't talk about what we do. Do you know what I mean?"

Freddie looked puzzled for a moment, and then he grinned. "Oh, you mean you grind up German sausages?"

"Something like that," replied Pete. "You can think it, but you must not say."

"I understand. I won't ask any more questions," said Freddie with a knowing smile.

The nurse appeared at Freddie's bedside and smiled at all of them. "Time's up, I'm afraid, Gentlemen. Our patient needs to rest now. Must get his strength up for his new legs next week."

"Right," said Spindle. He squeezed Freddie's hand. "Awfully good to see you, Inky. We'll try to get back to see you again, or if not, we'll look you up at your dad's law office. Must go have a pint together. I know a good pub where you can really get whacked ... it's called Nell Gwynne's."

He grinned wickedly at Pete, who raised his eyebrows and rolled his eyes.

\* \* \*

Spindle and Pete took the train back into London and made their way to Berkeley Square. They found the address Freddie had given them, opened a large wrought iron gate, and walked up four stone steps to the ornately carved front door. Spindle rapped on the door with the bronze lion's head door knocker. In a few moments a butler opened the door. "Yes, Gentlemen?" he asked in a stiff, formal voice.

"We are here to see Miss Susan Davenville," said Spindle in his politest voice.

"Is Miss Davenville expecting you, Sirs?" inquired the butler.

"No, but I'm sure she will want to see us if you would be so kind as to tell her that Mr. Brian Adams and Mr. Peter Court are here."

"I will see if she wants to receive you," said the butler, stepping aside and holding the door for them. "Please come in and wait here in the foyer."

Spindle and Pete stepped inside and found themselves in a large hallway with black and white marble tiles on the floor. Directly ahead of them a double curved staircase rose to a second-floor balcony. The butler went off to their left and disappeared through a set of ornately carved oak doors.

Soon the doors burst open and Susan came rushing out to greet them, the butler following in her wake. "Spindle! Pete!" she cried. "So pleased you are here. You're just in time for tea."

Spindle and Pete each took one of her extended hands. "We went to visit Freddie and he told us that you were all here," said Spindle. He stepped back to admire her. She was looking resplendent in a green silk afternoon gown, her fiery red tresses cascading down to her shoulders. "My, but you look absolutely smashing," he said, giving her a warm smile.

"I'll double that," said Pete.

"Oh, still the charmers, I see," said Susan smiling gaily. "But do come in and see everyone – Martha and Elizabeth are here. They came up from Bridgefield with Rose. And, of course, Sam is here too, and I want you to meet my Uncle Tommy and Aunt Ann."

They handed their hats to the butler and followed Susan into the drawing room where a large selection of delicate sandwiches, assorted biscuits and teacakes had been laid out on a huge side table at the back of the room. Floor-to-ceiling French doors stood open near the table, and they could see that they gave access to a large stone veranda. They could hear female voices coming from beyond the French doors. As they entered the room, a tall handsome dark-haired gentleman rose from a blue damask-covered chair near the fireplace and walked toward them.

"Uncle Tommy, I would like to present two friends from Bridgefield – Mr. Brian Adams, whom we call Spindle, and Mr. Peter Court, Pete. This is my uncle Doctor Thomas Davenville. He is the chief surgeon at Lunbury Hospital," said Susan.

"Very pleased to meet you, Sir," said Pete, shaking Davenville's hand.

"And you, too, Mr. Court," said Davenville. "I've heard about all of you from Susan and Sam and Freddie," he added and held out his hand to Spindle.

"I'm honored to meet you as well, Sir," said Spindle. "Can certainly tell you're Lord Davenville's brother. You look just like him."

Doctor Davenville smiled. "Yes. Mother always said we could have been twins, except for the age difference, of course. Alfred and I take after father's side of the family, whereas Richard favors mother's side."

"You remember Uncle Dickie from my birthday party?" asked Susan.

"Certainly do," said Pete, and Spindle nodded.

"Come, meet Aunt Ann, and then we'll join the others on the veranda," said Susan. Doctor Davenville led the way over to the blue damask-covered sofa where a pretty blonde-haired lady sat with a book open on her lap. Next to her sat a little boy with a mop of curly dark hair dressed in a dark blue velvet suit.

"Darling, I'd like you to meet Susan's friends Brian Adams and Peter Court," said the doctor. He turned to Spindle and Pete. "This is my wife Ann."

The lady looked up at them and smiled. She had huge sapphire blue eyes. "So pleased to meet you," she said in a low musical voice.

"And now you must meet the love of my life," said Susan. She had sunk down on the sofa and was cuddling the child. "This is

Anthony," she said. The little boy was looking up at them shyly through thick curly eyelashes, a chubby finger stuck into his rosy mouth.

Spindle knelt down on one knee and took the child's hand in his. "Hello, Anthony. What a handsome lad you are. My name is Spindle and this is Pete."

Anthony beamed at him, and his bright blue eyes sparkled, but he didn't say anything. Then he giggled and hid his head under Susan's arm.

"He's quite shy, I'm afraid," said Ann, smiling at the child's antics.

"I was the same way when I was that age, or so I'm told," said Pete, smiling. "How old is he?"

"Just turned four in June," answered Doctor Davenville. "Talks up a storm when it's only us around, but becomes an absolute clam when we have visitors, don't you Anthony lad?" The doctor tickled the child's tummy and Anthony giggled and squirmed and burrowed his head further under Susan's arm.

"Well, I know what will make Anthony talk," said Ann, rising from the sofa. "I'll get him some of those cakes, and he can eat them in the nursery with Nanny who will read him a story. What do you say, Anthony? Then, these nice gentlemen and Aunt Susan can visit with their friends and have tea on the veranda."

At the sound of "cakes," Anthony's head popped out from under Susan's arm, and he gave a squeal of delight. Ann took his hand and led him over to the table while Doctor Davenville, Susan, Spindle and Pete all chuckled with amusement to see him hopping up and down on his sturdy little legs in anticipation.

"Look who came to see us!" cried Susan gaily to the group of four who were seated at a card table.

As she led Spindle and Pete onto the veranda, Sam jumped up from the table, dropping his cards. "Upon my word! If it isn't Spindle and Pete!" he exclaimed, rushing toward them. "It's so good to see you blokes!"

"Good to see you, too, Sam!" said Spindle, as he and Pete clapped Sam enthusiastically on the shoulders. The three young ladies who had been seated at the card table came over and waited with broad smiles on their faces until Spindle, Sam and Pete had had their little reunion.

"And who do we have here?" said Pete, looking up from Sam's grinning face. "Can it be Rose? And is that Martha and Elizabeth?"

"That's right, Pete," said Elizabeth, stepping forward to shake his hand. "Haven't seen you since Susan's birthday party, and it's been two years since we saw Spindle."

Spindle stepped forward and clasped Rose's hand. "How are you Rose? Your name serves you well. You're blooming like a rose!"

"Watch it! That's my girl!" said Sam, with a grin. He walked over and possessively put his arm around Rose's shoulder. She blushed and looked up at him adoringly.

"So, I see," laughed Spindle, turning to Martha. "And here is Martha. Haven't seen you since the dance at the Bridgefield Hotel."

Martha smiled up at him. "That's right, Spindle. I never did get my turn at dancing with you because you were preoccupied with that girl that worked in the chemist shop – Daisy something or other."

Susan looked at Spindle questioningly and he turned bright red. "Oh, that," he said waving his hand in dismissal. "That was a long time ago."

"Well, we almost have a reunion of The Bottom Five," said Sam. "At least we're all in England except... Bouncer." His face clouded over. "Susan said you had managed to get a message last week saying he was still on the hill. Have you heard any more?"

"Oh, I do hope they sent in a relief column and he's all right?" asked Susan, concern clouding her eyes. The rest of the group looked in anticipation and concern at Spindle and Pete.

Spindle shook his head sadly and looked down. "Haven't heard anymore," he said.

The group was silent for a moment, each person thinking of Bouncer somewhere on a hill behind German lines in France. Sam had told them the story of Bouncer's heroism and how he and Freddie had been sent back to England.

"Well, at least you haven't heard any news to the contrary, I take it. Perhaps our troops have broken through and rescued them. According to the newspapers, we're making progress," said Sam.

Pete and Spindle glanced at each other. "Yes, according to the newspapers, there is hope...," said Pete slowly.

As the group was contemplating this, Doctor Davenville suddenly appeared in the doorway and motioned to Susan. "Susan, come quickly. Your father is here and wishes to speak to you."

"Daddy is here?" asked Susan, a smile lighting up her face.

Doctor Davenville did not smile. "Yes, he just arrived and must talk to you right away." As Susan walked swiftly into the drawing room, he turned to the rest of the group. "Please, make yourselves at home. I'll have the maid serve tea out here, and we should be with you shortly."

The group went back to the card table and lounge chairs and tried to make small talk as they waited for Susan's return. A half hour passed and then Lord Davenville walked out onto the veranda and came towards them. He was not smiling and he looked haggard and much older than the last time they had seen him.

Spindle jumped up from his chair to greet him, but Lord Davenville motioned for him to sit down. "Ladies and Gentlemen, we must dispense with the formalities, I'm afraid. I am the bearer of some very bad news," he said, his voice cracking with emotion. He paused and covered his eyes with his hand as the tea party guests stared at him in awe. Finally, he looked up and they could see that his eyes were red-rimmed and watery. "I've just come from the War Office where I learned that my nephew Rupert Squires and your friend John Russell have both been killed..." His voice cracked and he could go no further.

"Oh, no! Bouncer and Rupert, dead?" cried Sam. The others were speechless with shock.

Spindle finally managed to find his tongue. "How did it happen? Do you know, Sir?"

Lord Davenville slumped down into a chair and looked up at them. "I blame myself really," he began in a tired voice. "You see, ever since the first day of the battle when it came out that Lieutenant Russell and his platoon had captured that hill, I've been trying to get General Haig to send in a relief column to rescue those men. Those men are heroes, and they deserved to be rescued!" he said in an angry tone and then stopped and tried to compose himself.

"For reasons I won't go into here, General Haig left it to the last minute before sending down the order to send in a rescue team. From what I have been able to learn, Rupert had just received the order to go in with two of his platoons when they saw the hill destroyed by a German artillery barrage. But they sent Rupert and his men in anyway – his commander claimed he was powerless to change the order that had come down through the chain of command. Rupert and his men didn't stand a chance – the hill had been destroyed and the Germans were just waiting for them. All of them, except one – a Private Harry Phillips – were shot to pieces. Private Phillips somehow managed to get back and tell the story." Lord Davenville paused again.

"Oh, my God," said Sam, tears flowing from his eyes. "Those bloody God-damned generals!" Rose squeezed his arm, tears running down her cheeks as well.

"If only I had tried harder to convince them to send in the relief column earlier, this would not have happened," said Lord Davenville in a low voice as he gazed unseeingly into the distance.

Spindle reached over and patted his hand. "Don't blame yourself, Sir. You tried everything you could. We know that, don't we Pete?"

Pete nodded and looked up at Lord Davenville through teary eyes. "That's right, Sir. You are not to blame."

Lord Davenville drew himself up in his chair and placed his hands on his knees. "Be that as it may. By God as my witness I intend to see that Rupert and John Russell are recognized as heroes, and no one is going to stand in my way this time!" he said fervently. Then he stood up and looked down at the group. "I am sorry that we all had to meet again under these circumstances. Deeply sorry that I am the bearer of this dreadful news. Now, I have another task. Must take the train down to Bridgefield and break the news to Daisy and Frederick about Rupert."

"We're so sorry, Lord Davenville," said Elizabeth who was sitting next to Pete. The others murmured their sentiments as well.

Lord Davenville nodded at them sadly, turned and strode back through the doors to the drawing room, and Doctor Davenville came out to them a few moments later.

"I'm very sorry that this has turned into a day of mourning for all of us," he said.

"Where is Susan? Does she know?" inquired Martha in a concerned voice.

"Yes. I have put her to bed and given her some laudanum to sedate her. My wife Ann is sitting with her. She nearly fainted and became quite hysterical when Alfred told her," he said. Then he turned to Sam. "We will have to tell Freddie, but I would like to let it be for another couple of days until he is stronger. Shall I tell him, or will you?"

"I'll tell him," said Sam quietly. "He's used to hearing bad news from me."

\* \* \*

# Chapter 15
## *The Backroom Boys*

IN THE MONTHS that followed since the announcement of Bouncer's death, Spindle distinguished himself in the eyes of his superiors by coming up with improved procedures for identifying and capturing German spies. In January 1917 he was promoted to head up the letter-opening operation.

Pete had also risen to a position of authority in Naval Intelligence, and Ginger's inventiveness with cameras and lenses had earned him several commendations.

In their spare time, Spindle and Pete were frequent guests at Doctor Davenville's home in Mayfair, which, at Susan's instigation, had become a sort of hub for her Bridgefield friends.

Rose often came up on the train to stay with Susan so that she could be with Sam, who continued to work as a surgical assistant to Doctor Davenville.

Occasionally, Elizabeth would be there as well, especially if it was known that Pete would be present. Martha had her wish granted and had gone off to America to live with relatives on their ranch in an unheard-of place called Montana.

Freddie became a near permanent fixture at the Davenville's after he had moved back to London in January to join his father in his law offices. Following a two-week setback caused by grief over Bouncer's death, Freddie had snapped to and quickly learned to use his new legs. At the Davenville's he was constantly entertaining little Anthony with silly antics with his legs and beleaguering the adults with his never-ending supply of "wooden leg" jokes.

Sometimes Lord Davenville would appear, looking tired and worn, and he would bring them up to date on what news he was at liberty to share about the war effort. Often on such occasions, he and Susan would closet themselves in the library for a private chat and when Susan returned, despite her forced smiles, they could tell she had been crying. The first time this happened, Spindle walked over to her and quietly patted her hand and said nothing. She looked up into his eyes and he held her gaze for a short time. Thereafter, Susan always turned to Spindle for silent comfort after these chats with her father.

Meanwhile, in France, the Battle of the Somme continued to rage. Finally, in March 1917 – nearly nine months after the battle began – the British broke the German lines and took Baupaume. The cost was enormous: as Spindle had predicted, the British had lost nearly half a million men.

One morning in April, Spindle was in his office on Brompton Road perusing the latest red-coded letters when there was a knock on the door. "Enter," said Spindle absent-mindedly. The door opened and he looked up to see the man in the pinstriped suit and bowler hat who had escorted him to Mr. Churchill's on that fateful day last July. He had since learned that his name was Jack Ross.

"Hello, Mr. Adams," said Ross. "I have a message for you from Mr. Churchill."

"Hello, Mr. Ross. A message from Mr. Churchill? Hope it doesn't involve being handcuffed and blindfolded again," said Spindle with a grin.

Ross grinned back at him. "No, Sir, not this time. Mr. Churchill wants you to join him for dinner at his club on Pall Mall at one o'clock today."

"His club? Never been to one of those gentlemen's clubs before. Am I dressed properly?" asked Spindle, pointing to his own

377

black pinstriped suit, which he had discovered, was the uniform of those working in the secret services.

Ross laughed. "Oh, yes, Mr. Adams. You'll fit right in. At any rate, you are to be there precisely at one o'clock. Mr. Churchill is quite punctual and can't abide tardiness in others. It's the Duke of Wellington Club, Number 23 Pall Mall. Just go in and give your name to the gentleman who greets you. You will be expected."

"I'll be there," said Spindle. "Thanks for bringing the message, Mr. Ross."

Ross tipped his hat to Spindle. "Quite all right, Mr. Adams. My pleasure," he said as he left and closed the door behind him.

Not wanting to be late, Spindle arrived on Pall Mall forty-five minutes ahead of time. He found Number 23, which had a small bronze plaque below the number upon which was engraved simply "Duke of Wellington." He walked nervously up and down Pall Mall a couple of times checking his watch frequently. Finally, at five minutes till one o'clock, he decided to enter the club.

A valet wearing a white powdered wig, green and gold livery and silver buckled shoes opened the door for him. When he entered the small reception area, another gentleman in the same attire came forward to greet him. Observing the colors in the Persian carpet that covered the dark hardwood floor, Spindle decided that green and gold must be the colors of the club.

"Yes, Sir?" asked the bewigged gentleman.

"Mr. Brian Adams," said Spindle in his most formal voice.

"Yes, Sir. Mr. Churchill is expecting you. May I take your hat, Sir?"

Spindle handed him his hat and waited while he disappeared briefly into a cloakroom to the right of the door. He looked about him at the dark polished wood paneling and noted an excellent painting of the Duke of Wellington, sword drawn, astride a white charger, presumably at the Battle of Waterloo. The greeter returned, smiled and bowed slightly. "Please be so good as to follow me, Sir."

Spindle nodded and followed him up two flights of stairs to a huge dark paneled room that reminded him of the lobby at the Bridgefield Hotel. Green leather wingback chairs were grouped here and there around the room with their own lamps and side tables. Several finely dressed gentlemen sat about, reading newspapers, brandy snifters within easy reach. The room was redolent of pipe and cigar smoke.

Spindle's guide led him to a set of closed double doors at the far-left side of the room. He tapped on the door. Spindle could hear footsteps, and then the door swung wide open and there stood Mr. Winston Churchill, cigar in hand. "Mr. Brian Adams, Sir," said Spindle's guide, bowing slightly and stepping aside for Spindle to pass.

Churchill beamed from ear to ear. "Ah, Brian! Right on time. Come in, come in, my boy. Think you already know my other guest."

"Pleased to see you again, Sir," said Spindle, shaking Churchill's hand and stepping into the private dining room that was complete with fireplace, a sitting area with bookshelves lining the walls, and a large Queen Anne style dining table and chairs. Lord Davenville was sitting in one of the green leather chairs by the fireplace, sipping a brandy. "Hello, Brian," he said with a pleasant smile.

"Lord Davenville!" said Spindle. "What a pleasant surprise!"

"Come, sit down," said Churchill steering Spindle towards a chair with one hand on his shoulder. "What will you have to drink? I highly recommend the brandy – it's a vintage Napoleon. Rather fitting, wouldn't you say, for the Duke of Wellington club?" Churchill chuckled gleefully at his little joke.

Spindle accepted the brandy and had just taken another sip when there was a tap on the door. "Ah, my other guest," said Churchill going to answer the door. "Phillip, do come in," he said.

"Hello Winston," said a crusty voice that had a ring of familiarity to Spindle. "Late, I'm afraid."

"You are forgiven," said Churchill. "After all, you have an excuse, with those legs. Come on over and say hello to Lord Alfred and Brian Adams. I'll get you a brandy."

Spindle looked around from his chair and saw a man he guessed to be in his mid-sixties hobbling toward them on a cane.

"Hello, Phillip," said Lord Davenville.

"Lord Alfred," said the man, pausing near Spindle's chair. He looked down at Spindle. "Hello, Mr. Adams. Do you remember me?"

Spindle looked up into his face and then bolted up from his chair. "Of course I remember you, Sir! Didn't recognize you at first without your hat and your overcoat. Very pleased to meet you again, Major General Wallis."

Churchill returned with the major general's brandy and helped ease him down into a chair. "Cigar, Phillip?" he asked, offering his gold cigar case.

"Yes, I don't mind if I do," said Wallis, selecting a cigar from the case. He held it up and looked at it, and then moistened it with his mouth. Churchill cupped a match in his hands and lit it for him.

"Anyone else for a cigar?" asked Churchill. Lord Davenville declined and Spindle followed his lead. "All right, then, Gentlemen. Enjoy the brandy for a bit. They have an excellent roast dinner today and will be serving it in about ten minutes. We can talk business. Let Mr. Adams know why he's here." He smiled mysteriously at Spindle and raised his brandy snifter in a toast. The others raised their glasses in acknowledgement.

Churchill swirled the brandy in his glass and continued. "Well, Gentlemen, finally we have a breakthrough. It's just a question of time before the Germans surrender."

"But at what a great cost, Winston. The Somme alone has cost us nearly half a million casualties," interjected Major General Wallis. He pointed his cigar at Spindle. "Brian here made that prediction way back in 1915."

Churchill nodded and took a puff on his cigar. "Unfortunately, what was done was done, regardless of the predictions. At least the offensive was a political success. If we hadn't attacked, the French would have lost at Verdun and our forces would have been surrounded. Then the Germans would have held all the aces and we would have peace only on their terms." Churchill looked at Spindle with a smile and waved his cigar at him. "Young Brian seems to have caused quite a rumble with his endeavors," he commented.

"Yes, indeed, Winston," responded Wallis, grinning at Spindle knowingly. "He received a reprimand in his file for stating his feelings about how the war is being managed." Wallis snorted disdainfully. "But his contributions to Section Z far outweigh his verbal criticism of those who are managing the war."

Spindle looked at Wallis in surprise, as Churchill continued. "Yes, I read his file, and I understand his motives. Would have done the same if I'd been in his position: speak up, make people responsible for their actions. We need more of that. I've done that many times myself, and you know what happened to me."

"Yes, Winston, your Gallipoli campaign did cause some difficulties," chuckled Lord Davenville, raising his brandy snifter in salute to Churchill.

"What I needed were young men like Brian here to speak up and tell me the fallacy of it all. Instead, I relied on advice from people who said the Turks were untrained and ill-equipped to fight such a large landing force as ours," said Churchill.

"But if your campaign had succeeded, it would have shortened the war, Winston," said Wallis. "And now Lawrence is making inroads with the Arabs and they are attacking the Turks from the southeast."

"Lawrence proves my point," said Churchill. "He's the perfect example of how a single Englishman who dares to defy convention can make a great impact – just like Brian here. Remember the Zimmermann telegrams, Brian?" Churchill asked suddenly, turning his gaze back on Spindle.

"Yes, Sir," answered Spindle.

"Turned out to be a hot potato, that!" Churchill laughed heartily. "You see, we didn't know what to do with those telegrams. Needed to tell the Americans, but didn't dare because it would have caused a diplomatic incident if they thought we'd been listening into messages through their embassy here. Caused many headaches for Collingsworth and Fitzgerald until they devised a way of getting the information to Washington."

"Washington, Sir?" asked Spindle.

Churchill's eyes twinkled with merriment. "Yes. The Zimmermann telegrams inciting Mexico to attack America proved the final straw that convinced our cousins to come into the war with us. That, along with the U-boat attacks on their merchant ships, finally convinced them they had no choice but to declare war on Germany. As I'm sure you've read in the papers, the United States declared war two days ago on April 6."

"Yes, Sir, but how did the Americans find out about the telegrams?" asked Spindle curiously.

Churchill's eyes sparkled and he smiled mischievously. "As far as the Americans are concerned, our agents in Mexico City recovered them – with the help, I might add, of American agents. Collingsworth and Fitzgerald concocted the perfect scheme. And, we have you to thank, Brian, for unearthing those telegrams in the first place."

"Yes, Brian. If it wasn't for your listeners at The Odeon, we would never have thought that the Germans would have the audacity to come up with such a scheme," added Major General Wallis. "Collingsworth and Fitzgerald maintained the operation at The Odeon until last November, and then they moved it to a nonpublic facility."

Spindle looked curiously again at Major General Wallis. "Excuse me, Sir, but I am at a loss to understand how you know all these things about my work with Section Z," he said.

Major General Wallis laughed and looked at Churchill before answering.

"Oh, go ahead and tell him, Phillip. He's proved he can keep a secret," said Churchill with a chuckle.

"General Bottoms reports to me," said Major General Wallis, looking at Spindle with a smile on his face.

"You mean... ?" asked Spindle, his face registering shock at this revelation.

"That's right, Brian. I am Five-O-One – head of Section Z. I've been following your exploits ever since you applied to gain entry into the Army as an officer."

"You know about the letter?" asked Spindle, sitting bolt upright, his face reddening.

"Even that," said Wallis with a grin. "Most enterprising, I must say."

"What letter, Phillip?" asked Churchill, looking from one to the other.

"Oh, nothing really," said Wallis, noticing Spindle's nervousness. "Just Brian's letter of application – showed his talent for coming up with quick answers even then."

Churchill looked questioningly at him and began to ask more but was interrupted by a gentle knocking on the service door. He put down his brandy snifter and rose energetically to his feet. "Our roast beef dinner has arrived, Gentlemen," he said, motioning for them to move to the dining table.

After they were seated, Churchill rang a small bell that had been placed near his napkin on the table. The door opened and a serving man wheeled in a trolley on which were several silver platters covered with silver dome-shaped lids. The diners looked at him expectantly, and he bowed slightly and announced, "Today we have a roast dinner of the finest Black Angus beef with Brussels sprouts, potatoes and Yorkshire pudding. For dessert there is a bread and butter pudding."

A wine steward came into the room and poured claret into their glasses while the serving man dished up generous helpings of the dinner onto monogrammed gold-rimmed Spode plates. He gave the first plate to Churchill, and then served the others.

"Will that be all, Sir?" he asked.

"I believe we have everything we could wish for," said Churchill, admiring the food on his plate.

"Enjoy your dinner, Gentlemen. If you need anything, just ring the bell, Sir," he added to Churchill as he left the room.

"My word, I daren't tell Clementine what I had for dinner. She would be furious with envy. Food such as this is quite difficult to find during times of war," remarked Churchill.

"I know what you mean, Winston. Mrs. Wallis is constantly complaining about the lack of decent food in the markets," said Wallis.

"The German U-boats are close to bringing us to our knees. From what I hear, we only have about six weeks of food left," said Lord Davenville, spearing a Brussels sprout with his fork.

"Despite the efforts of the Navy and our intelligence," said Wallis, shaking his head as he carved a bite of the roast beef.

"What do you think of that, Brian? Why are the U-boats so successful in finding out where our convoys are?" asked Churchill.

"We haven't found evidence of German spies in our ports, Sir," said Spindle slowly. "The Germans must be getting their information by some other means."

"American and Canadian ports?" questioned Churchill.

"We believe that is covered, Winston. We work closely with both the American and the Canadian secret services," interjected Wallis.

"Any ideas, Brian, on how the Germans could be getting hold of this information?" queried Churchill again as he pressed a small roast potato and a Brussels sprout onto his fork.

Spindle laid down his knife and fork and thought for a moment, frowning slightly. Then his eyes lit up with an idea. "I seem to remember, Sir, that when we were listening to telegram messages from America, there were many being sent to Lloyds of London regarding shipping insurance. Many queries about insurance costs for goods the Americans were shipping to us across the Atlantic. Perhaps this information got into the wrong hands?"

Churchill, Wallis and Davenville abruptly stopped eating, and the sprout fell off Churchill's fork. "Of course! Must get Fitzgerald and Collingsworth on that right away!" exclaimed Churchill. "In Heaven's name, why haven't they thought of that? Well done, Brian. You do have a brilliant mind."

"Yes, indeed, he does," said Major General Wallis. "Do you remember me telling you about the dud shells, Winston? It was Brian here who figured that out without even going to the front. Figured it out from casualty statistics. Woolwich Arsenal got chewed on and thankfully the problem was fixed immediately. Had something to do with faulty fuses."

After they had finished their bread and butter pudding, Churchill placed his napkin on the table, leaned back in his chair and lit up another cigar. "I have another meeting I must get to soon, so we'd best get down to the business of why you're here, Brian," he said.

"Yes, Sir," said Spindle, placing his knife and fork neatly on the sides of his plate and giving Churchill his full attention.

"You have once again demonstrated to Phillip and to me your enterprise and ingenuity. Young men possessing these gifts are few, and I have something in mind for you. Major General Wallis agrees with me," he said, pausing to take a puff of his cigar.

Wallis nodded his head in agreement.

"You see, Brian, it's not an easy task for me to keep abreast on the intelligence front – too much going on. I have a need for someone to act as my liaison to the various secret service groups and tell me what they're up to. And Major General Wallis and I have decided that someone is you," Churchill pronounced with a grin, flicking his cigar ash into a cut glass ashtray.

Spindle was dumbfounded for a moment. Everyone was looking at him waiting for a response. Then he drew himself up confidently in his chair. "Yes, Sir. I'm willing to serve in any way I can, and I believe the job would suit me well," he said.

"Done then. Glad you agree," said Churchill, putting out his cigar and rising from the table. "Report to my house on Baker Street tomorrow morning at eight o'clock and we'll get started. Phillip and I must be off now, but you and Lord Davenville can stay as long as you want. Have more bread and butter pudding, a glass of port."

"Thank you, Winston. I will see you at the meeting on Friday," said Lord Davenville as Churchill went around the table to assist Major General Wallis to his feet.

"Thank you, Sir," said Spindle as Churchill and Wallis reached the door.

"That's quite all right," said Churchill, waving his hand. "You've earned it, and you're about to earn it even more."

After Churchill and Major General Wallis had departed, Lord Davenville rose from the dining table. "Come over by the fireplace and join me in a glass of port. I have a private matter I wish to discuss with you, Brian."

"Yes, Sir," said Spindle curiously, following Lord Davenville over to the chairs by the fireplace. Lord Davenville poured two glasses of port from a decanter and handed one to Spindle.

After they were ensconced in their chairs and had taken a sip of their port, Lord Davenville looked intensely at Spindle. Spindle met his gaze nervously, wondering if he had done something wrong.

Lord Davenville took another sip of port, cleared his throat, and began. "Now, then, Brian, I wish to say that I am quite impressed with your ingenuity and the manner in which you have gained Mr. Churchill's trust. If he can trust you with secrets, surely I can. Am I right?"

Spindle swallowed nervously. "Oh, yes, Sir. I would never betray your trust."

"Good, because what I am about to tell you involves a delicate family matter, and I want it to be our secret."

Spindle looked at him in surprise. "Of course, Lord Alfred, Sir. You can count on me."

"Now, then, Brian, I have been observing that you seem to be quite fond of my Susan. Am I correct?" asked Lord Davenville with a faint smile.

Spindle's heart beat faster. "Oh, yes, Sir. I have always been fond of Susan from the first moment I met her at the birthday party. May I say, Sir, that I admire her greatly – not just because she is a beautiful lady, but also because of her vibrant spirit and intelligence," he added hastily.

Lord Davenville smiled. "I thought as much. I also know Susan is quite fond of you. My question is: Brian, do you love her?"

Spindle was taken aback for a moment at the straightforwardness of the question. Then he blurted out the words he had never dared to speak. "Oh, yes, Sir! I do love her, have always loved her from the start!"

"Enough to marry her?"

Spindle gulped – his heart felt as if it had leapt into his throat. Lord Davenville smiled encouragingly at him. "Yes, Sir, I would like to marry Susan provided she is willing and I have your consent."

"That is very good to hear, Brian, because I happen to know that Susan is willing and you have my consent," said Lord Davenville, leaning back in his chair to observe Spindle's reaction.

After a few seconds, a smile of joy spread across Spindle's face, lighting up his eyes. "Ah, Lord Davenville, this is extremely happy news. I had not dared to hope... that is, I promise you neither Susan nor you will regret it. I will pledge to be the best of husbands to her as well as a good son-in-law to you."

"I am happy to hear it, Brian, because I would not tell you the rest of what I have to say were it otherwise," said Lord Davenville, leaning forward in his chair and speaking in a confidential tone. "It involves Anthony."

"Anthony?" asked Spindle in a hushed voice.

"Yes. I'm sure you've noticed how Susan dotes on that little lad?" asked Davenville.

Spindle smiled fondly. "Yes, Sir."

"That is because he is her child," announced Davenville. He sat back in his chair, looking intently at Spindle.

Spindle's mouth dropped open. He was speechless. Finally, he managed to ask, "You mean... Anthony's not Doctor Davenville's...?"

"That's correct. Anthony is Susan's son and therefore my grandchild."

Spindle could only stare at him in wide-eyed silence as he tried to comprehend the meaning of this information.

"You see, Brian, these things happen, even in the best of families - perhaps especially in the best of families," he said. "When my late wife learned of Susan's condition, she insisted on booting her out, disowning her. The social disgrace would have been too much for Mary to bear, God rest her soul. I, on the other hand, could not bear to disown my favorite daughter. Thus, I arranged for Susan to live with my brother Thomas - she had always wanted to become a nurse - and we put it about that Anthony was Thomas's son."

Spindle's mind was whirling. Lord Davenville paused and took a sip of port. Spindle took a huge gulp of his, nearly choking on it.

"You see, Brian, I have another problem. I have no male heirs. When I die, the title would go to my next eldest brother - Richard. Richard, however, has no intentions of marrying, nor does he want the title because it would die out with him. Both my brothers are in agreement with me that the title should continue through my line. The only hope of that at this point is that it must go to my grandson - Anthony - but he must have the Davenville surname in order to inherit. Do you understand?"

"Yes, I think so... ," said Spindle, quite befuddled.

"I have given this a great deal of thought over the past several months and have decided on a procedure. I am going to adopt Anthony as my own son so that he will have my name and be my legal heir. My solicitor is working up the necessary documents as we speak."

Lord Davenville paused again and looked at Spindle to see if this information was sinking in. "Do I make myself clear? Do you understand that what this means is that the child will be known as Anthony Davenville – that he will not carry your surname when you marry Susan?"

Spindle was speechless. He could only nod his agreement.

Lord Davenville read the question in his eyes. "Just in case you have been wondering, you should know that Anthony was born on June 10, 1912... nine months after Susan's sixteenth birthday party," he said quietly.

Spindle reddened and cast his eyes down, remembering Susan's party and the game they had played.

"But you see, Brian, Susan refused from the beginning to tell anyone which of you five lads was responsible. So, along with Major General Wallis who had his own interest in protecting you, we did all that we possibly could to keep the five of you out of harm's way."

Spindle's head jerked up. "You mean the two of you were behind my reassignment to Section Z, Sir?"

Davenville nodded. "And Mr. Court's subsequent reassignment as well. It was more difficult with the others. On two occasions – once before the Battle of Ypres and then again before the offensive at the Somme – John Russell was given the option of having himself and his men transferred to a quieter sector, but being the dedicated heroic type, he refused."

Lord Davenville sipped his port and sat in silence for a while to allow Spindle to mull over these revelations. After a while, he began again, somewhat hesitantly. "There is another matter I wish to discuss with you." Spindle looked up at him again with a sober expression.

"What I am about to tell you is something I have kept a secret for many years and it has been a great burden on my shoulders. Because you were a close friend of John Russell and because you are to be part of my family, I am compelled to tell you."

Spindle looked at him in surprise at this mention of Bouncer's name. Lord Davenville reached inside his suit coat and withdrew a photograph. "I have something I wish to show you. This picture was taken when our troops broke through the German lines and marched up the main road to Baupaume."

He handed the photograph to Spindle. Spindle looked closely at it and saw that it was a picture of a grave marked by a crude handmade cross. He saw that the photograph had been enlarged so that the words on the marker were visible. "What does it say, Sir? The words are in German."

"The translation is written on the back of the photograph." Davenville twirled a finger indicating that Spindle should turn the photograph over. "Read it aloud."

Spindle turned the photograph over and read, "Here is buried English Bouncer – a brave and honorable lieutenant of the British Army. The Saxons will remember that he kept his word. July 6, 1916."

Spindle looked up at Lord Davenville who was staring morosely into the fireplace. "Bouncer's grave?" he asked.

Lord Davenville slowly returned his gaze. "That is the nickname you had for John Russell, is it not?"

"Yes," said Spindle, tears stinging his eyes. He handed the photograph back to Lord Davenville. "I guess that confirms that there is no longer any hope that he somehow managed to survive."

"Yes, I'm afraid so," said Lord Davenville, replacing the photograph inside his suit coat. "And there is something else," he added, reaching into his pocket and extracting something. He held up a gold coin. "You remember this?" he asked.

Spindle leaned forward to look more closely at it. "It's one of Major General Wallis's half-sovereigns!" he exclaimed.

Lord Davenville nodded. "As I recall Wallis gave each of you lads one of these for rescuing him from Squires's Bristol Bomber."

"That's right," said Spindle. "I always carry mine with me." He pulled a leather wallet out of his inside coat pocket and produced the coin from one of its compartments. He held it up for Lord Davenville's inspection.

"Yes, I see," said Davenville. "John Russell carried his with him also, and this is his."

"Bouncer's half-sovereign? But how did you...?" asked Spindle.

Lord Davenville paused, and then looked at Spindle with determination as he laid the gold coin on the table next to his glass of port. "Brian, I have done for John in death what I should have done for him in life. I have had his body brought back and properly buried on the Davenville estate under his rightful name. You see, Brian, it is true that he came from a long line of military men, but they were Davenvilles not Russells. He was my son."

"Bouncer is... was... your son?!!" exclaimed Spindle, a shiver running down his spine.

Tears were streaming down Davenville's cheeks. He took a handkerchief from his pocket and held it to his face for a moment. "Yes, he was my son, and I cannot forgive myself for not acknowledging him before he... " He paused again, swallowing hard. "You see, Brian, I tried to keep him out of harm's way... tried everything I knew to get him rescued from that hill. After Mary died last year I intended to acknowledge him - make him my heir. Unfortunately, I did not have the courage to do so while she was still living."

He paused again and took a sip of port. Spindle fumbled for words. He had had too many surprises for one day. Finally, he managed to ask, "Do you mean Lady Mary was not Bouncer's...?"

Lord Davenville looked up at him with a sad smile. "No, Brian, Mary was not his mother. John's mother was a lady with whom I fell in love even though I was married. I could not help myself. I loved her so very much. It nearly destroyed me when she died having our child - John. I placed him with Mrs. Barclay to raise until the time came when I could acknowledge him. He thought Mrs. Barclay was his aunt - his mother's sister, you see. I chose the name of a dead war hero to be his father so that he could have some pride in his heritage. At least I was able to give him that."

"So, Bouncer was Susan's half-brother... " Spindle said, musing aloud.

Lord Davenville nodded, his eyes boring into Spindle's.

"Does she know?"

"She does now." Lord Davenville covered his eyes with his hand and massaged his temples. "I shall never forgive myself for not having the courage to acknowledge John long ago..." he murmured.

Spindle remained silent, waiting. Finally, Lord Davenville looked up again. He slowly picked up the half-sovereign and held it between thumb and forefinger. The light from the lamp played upon its surface. The two of them gazed at it for a while as if mesmerized.

At last Davenville spoke. "I will save this for Anthony. It is his heritage from his father, and he will know he comes from a long line of military heroes."

* * *

# Epilogue

THE GREAT WAR ended with the signing of the Armistice at the eleventh hour on the eleventh day of November 1918.

Shortly after the war ended, Lord Davenville and Major General Wallis called for an inquiry into Field Marshall Haig's military decisions as Commander in Chief of the Western Front. Despite the high number of casualties suffered under his command, Haig was exonerated and in 1919 was given an earldom and one hundred thousand pounds. Regardless of his new title, the populace persisted in referring to him as "The Butcher of the Somme."

William Shoals, the German spy turned double agent, was given a new identity and five thousand pounds. He emigrated to Australia and was never heard from again.

The surviving veterans received no compensation for their part in the victory or for loss of limbs or other injuries.

Lord Davenville installed a bust of Bouncer in the family niche at Westminster Abbey, along with a plaque that extolled his heroic feat at the Battle of the Somme.

Spindle married Susan in a quiet ceremony at St. James Cathedral on June 10, 1919. Following the ceremony, they returned to Doctor Davenville's where two cakes were cut to celebrate their wedding and Anthony's seventh birthday.

Spindle and Pete rose to high positions in the secret services, and in 1935 were knighted for "Service to King and Country." They believed, but were not entirely sure, that Mr. Churchill had recommended them for the honor.

Freddie Simpson became a Queen's Counselor and in 1934 published a book revealing the identity of Jack the Ripper.

Sam married Rose in 1920 and returned to Bridgefield to carry on in the family butcher business as he had promised his father.

Ginger resigned from Naval Intelligence in 1933 and went to America where he found backing from the movie industry to develop his latest invention, a process for making colored film.

Roger Smith and James Taylor continued to work for a British undercover secret service operation on one of His Majesty's islands in the Caribbean until their retirement in the 1940s.

Lord Davenville died in October 1935, and Anthony became Lord Davenville at the age of twenty-three. He had recently graduated from Sandhurst and was fond of taking his friends to the cloisters at Westminster Abbey. There he would show them the busts of his great-great-grandfather who had fought with Wellington, his great-grandfather who had distinguished himself in the Crimea, and best of all, his father who had taken Hill Fifty-One on the first day of the Battle of the Somme. His friends would always exclaim upon the resemblance he bore to his father as he stood there looking quite handsome in his captain's uniform. And Anthony would always say with pride, "As you can see, I come from a long line of military heroes." Then he would show the half-sovereign he always carried with him.

* * *

# Acknowledgements

THE AUTHOR WISHES to acknowledge the following: The late Marjorie Kirrie, former professor of English and former Director of Composition at Portland State University, Portland, Oregon, who provided valuable critique and deemed this novel "a good yarn" woven from accurate historical events.

The late Glenn and Della Forbes, who, through their enthusiasm and support encouraged the author to complete this novel.

The author further acknowledges insight gained from two historical works: *The First Day on the Somme* by Martin Middlebrook, and *Churchill and the Secret Service* by David Stafford.

# About the Author

BENSON S. FORBES is the pen name for co-authors and married couple John Benson and Shari S. Forbes.

Benson grew up in Tunbridge Wells, England and worked for the British Ministry of Defense before immigrating to the United States. For 25 years he headed up design engineering for several high tech companies including several that he started.

Forbes grew up in Rush County, Kansas. She is an award-winning writer and editor, a former English and journalism teacher, and a former editor of a nationally-distributed magazine aimed at the education community.

The couple currently divides their time between their home in the country near Portland, Oregon and their second home in Redlands, California where they continue to draw on their combined experiences and expertise to collaborate on works of fiction.

*The Bottom Five* is their first novel, first published in 2002. Other novels include *Mad Cows Come Back To Bite*, published in 2004, and *Cracking Heads*, published in 2007.